The
Wind in the
Willows

This is the delightful, the utterly enchanting story of life on the river bank—the community of little animals whose problems and joys and escapades are not far different from our own. You will meet Water Rat, a friendly, home-loving fellow who only once is tempted to wander; Toad of Toad Hall, vain, boastful, impetuous, but lovable at that; Mole, a sensitive youngster eager for adventure; and Badger, who with his strength and kindly wisdom more than once comes to his little friends' rescue. This is one of the best loved children's classics of all time, and one which enriches the reader of any age.

A feeble voice said, "Ratty, is that really you?"

The

Wind in the

Willows

By
KENNETH GRAHAME

Illustrations by
ROBERTA CARTER CLARK

Companion Library

Grosset & Dunlap

PUBLISHERS   NEW YORK

Contents

1 THE RIVER BANK 9
2 THE OPEN ROAD 27
3 THE WILD WOOD 46
4 MR. BADGER 64
5 DULCE DOMUM 84
6 MR. TOAD 106
7 THE PIPER AT THE GATES OF DAWN 126
8 TOAD'S ADVENTURES 141
9 WAYFARERS ALL 161
10 THE FURTHER ADVENTURES OF TOAD 185
11 "LIKE SUMMER TEMPESTS CAME HIS
     TEARS" 209
12 THE RETURN OF ULYSSES 234

The
Wind in the
Willows

1

The River Bank

THE MOLE had been working very hard all the morning, spring-cleaning his little home. First with brooms, then with dusters; then on ladders and steps and chairs, with a brush and a pail of whitewash; till he had dust in his throat and eyes and splashes of whitewash all over his black fur, and an aching back and weary arms. Spring was moving in the air above and in the earth below and around him, penetrating even his dark and lowly little house with its spirit of divine discontent and longing. It was small wonder, then, that he suddenly flung down his brush on the floor, said, "Bother!" and "Oh Blow!" and also "Hang spring cleaning!" and bolted out of the house without even waiting to put on his coat. Something up above was calling him

imperiously, and he made for the steep little tunnel
which answered in his case to the graveled carriage
drive owned by animals whose residences are nearer
to the sun and air. So he scraped and scratched and
scrabbled and scrooged, and then he scrooged again
and scrabbled and scratched and scraped, working
busily with his little paws and muttering to himself, "Up we go! Up we go!" till at last, pop! his
snout came out into the sunlight, and he found himself rolling in the warm grass of a great meadow.

"This is fine!" he said to himself. "This is better
than whitewashing!" The sunshine struck hot on
his fur, soft breezes caressed his heated brow, and
after the seclusion of the cellarage he had lived in
so long the carol of happy birds fell on his dulled
hearing almost like a shout. Jumping off all his four
legs at once, in the joy of living and the delight of
spring without its cleaning, he pursued his way
across the meadow till he reached the hedge on the
farther side.

"Hold up!" said an elderly rabbit at the gap.
"Sixpence for the privilege of passing by the private
road!" He was bowled over in an instant by the
impatient and contemptuous Mole, who trotted
along the side of the hedge chaffing the other rabbits as they peeped hurriedly from their holes to see
what the row was about. "Onion sauce! Onion
sauce!" he remarked jeeringly, and was gone before they could think of a thoroughly satisfactory
reply. Then they all started grumbling at each other.
"How *stupid* you are! Why didn't you tell him——"

"Well, why didn't *you* say——" "You might have reminded him——" and so on, in the usual way; but, of course, it was then much too late, as is always the case.

It all seemed too good to be true. Hither and thither through the meadows he rambled busily, along the hedgerows, across the copses, finding everywhere birds building, flowers budding, leaves thrusting—everything happy, and progressive, and occupied. And instead of having an uneasy conscience pricking him and whispering, "Whitewash!" he somehow could only feel how jolly it was to be the only idle dog among all these busy citizens. After all, the best part of a holiday is perhaps not so much to be resting yourself, as to see all the other fellows busy working.

He thought his happiness was complete when, as he meandered aimlessly along, suddenly he stood by the edge of a full-fed river. Never in his life had he seen a river before—this sleek, sinuous, full-bodied animal, chasing and chuckling, gripping things with a gurgle and leaving them with a laugh, to fling on fresh playmates that shook themselves free, and were caught and held again. All was a-shake and a-shiver—glints and gleams and sparkles, rustle and swirl, chatter and bubble. The Mole was bewitched, entranced, fascinated. By the side of the river he trotted as one trots, when very small, by the side of a man who holds one spellbound by exciting stories; and when tired at last, he sat on the bank, while the river still chattered on to him, a babbling procession of the best stories in the world, sent from the heart of the earth to be told at last to the insatiable sea.

As he sat on the grass and looked across the river, a dark hole in the bank opposite, just above the water's edge, caught his eye, and dreamily he fell to considering what a nice snug dwelling place it would make for an animal with few wants and fond of a bijou riverside residence, above flood level and remote from noise and dust. As he gazed, something bright and small seemed to twinkle down in the heart of it, vanished, then twinkled once more like a tiny star. But it could hardly be a star in such an unlikely situation; and it was too glittering and small for a glowworm. Then, as he looked, it winked at him, and so declared itself to be an eye; and a small face began gradually to grow up round it, like a frame round a picture.

A brown little face, with whiskers.

A grave round face, with the same twinkle in its eye that had first attracted his notice.

Small neat ears and thick silky hair.

It was the Water Rat!

Then the two animals stood and regarded each other cautiously.

"Hullo, Mole!" said the Water Rat.

"Hullo, Rat!" said the Mole.

"Would you like to come over?" inquired the Rat presently.

"Oh, it's all very well to *talk*," said the Mole

rather pettishly, he being new to a river and riverside life and its ways.

The Rat said nothing, but stooped and unfastened a rope and hauled on it; then lightly stepped
into a little boat which the Mole had not observed.
It was painted blue outside and white within, and
was just the size for two animals; and the Mole's
whole heart went out to it at once, even though he
did not yet fully understand its uses.

The Rat sculled smartly across and made fast.
Then he held up his forepaw as the Mole stepped
gingerly down. "Lean on that!" he said. "Now then,
step lively!" and the Mole to his surprise and rapture found himself actually seated in the stern of
a real boat.

"This has been a wonderful day!" said he, as the
Rat shoved off and took to the sculls again. "Do
you know, I've never been in a boat in all my life."

"What?" cried the Rat, open-mouthed: "Never
been in a—you never—well, I—what have you
been doing, then?"

"Is it so nice as all that?" asked the Mole shyly,
though he was quite prepared to believe it as he
leaned back in his seat and surveyed the cushions,
the oars, the rowlocks, and all the fascinating fit-
tings, and felt the boat sway lightly under him.

"Nice? It's the *only* thing," said the Water Rat
solemnly, as he leaned forward for his stroke. "Believe me, my young friend, there is *nothing*—
absolutely nothing—half so much worth doing as

simply messing about in boats. Simply messing," he went on dreamily, "messing—about—in—boats; messing—"

"Look ahead, Rat!" cried the Mole suddenly.

It was too late. The boat struck the bank full tilt. The dreamer, the joyous oarsman, lay on his back at the bottom of the boat, his heels in the air.

"—about in boats—or *with* boats," the Rat went on composedly, picking himself up with a pleasant laugh. "In or out of 'em, it doesn't matter. Nothing seems really to matter, that's the charm of it. Whether you get away, or whether you don't; whether you arrive at your destination or whether you reach somewhere else, or whether you never get anywhere at all, you're always busy, and you never do anything in particular; and when you've done it there's always something else to do, and you can do it if you like, but you'd much better not. Look here! If you've really nothing else on hand this morning, supposing we drop down the river together, and have a long day of it?"

The Mole waggled his toes from sheer happiness, spread his chest with a sigh of full contentment, and leaned back blissfully into the soft cushions. "*What* a day I'm having!" he said. "Let us start at once!"

"Hold hard a minute, then!" said the Rat. He looped the painter through a ring in his landing stage, climbed up into his hole above, and after a short interval reappeared staggering under a fat, wicker luncheon basket.

"Shove that under your feet," he observed to the Mole, as he passed it down into the boat. Then he untied the painter and took the sculls again.

"What's inside it?" asked the Mole, wiggling with curiosity.

"There's cold chicken inside it," replied the Rat briefly; "coldtonguecoldhamcoldbeefpickledgherkins salad french rolls cress sandwiches potted meat ginger beerlemonadesodawater—"

"Oh stop, stop," cried the Mole in ecstasies. "This is too much!"

"Do you really think so?" inquired the Rat seriously. "It's only what I always take on these little excursions; and the other animals are always telling me that I'm a mean beast and cut it *very* fine!"

The Mole never heard a word he was saying. Absorbed in the new life he was entering upon, intoxicated with the sparkle, the ripple, the scents and the sounds and the sunlight, he trailed a paw in the water and dreamed long waking dreams. The Water Rat, like the good little fellow he was, sculled steadily on and forbore to disturb him.

"I like your clothes awfully, old chap," he remarked after some half an hour or so had passed. "I'm going to get a black velvet smoking suit myself some day, as soon as I can afford it."

"I beg your pardon," said the Mole, pulling himself together with an effort. "You must think me very rude; but all this is so new to me. So—this—is —a—River!"

"*The* River," corrected the Rat.

"And you really live by the river? What a jolly life!"

"By it and with it and on it and in it," said the Rat. "It's brother and sister to me, and aunts, and company, and food and drink, and (naturally) washing. It's my world, and I don't want any other. What it hasn't got is not worth having, and what it doesn't know is not worth knowing. Lord! the times we've had together! Whether in winter or summer, spring or autumn, it's always got its fun and its excitements. When the floods are on in February, and my cellars and basement are brimming with drink that's no good to me, and the brown water runs by my best bedroom window; or again when it all drops away and shows patches of mud that smells like plum cake, and the rushes and weed clog the channels, and I can potter about dry-shod over most of the bed of it and find fresh food to eat, and things careless people have dropped out of boats!"

"But isn't it a bit dull at times?" the Mole ventured to ask. "Just you and the river, and no one else to pass a word with?"

"No one else to—well, I mustn't be hard on you," said the Rat with forbearance. "You're new to it, and of course you don't know. The bank is so crowded nowadays that many people are moving away altogether. Oh no, it isn't what it used to be, at all. Otters, kingfishers, dabchicks, moorhens, all of them about all day long and always wanting you to *do* something—as if a fellow had no business of his own to attend to!"

"What lies over *there*?" asked the Mole, waving a paw towards a background of woodland that darkly framed the water-meadows on one side of the river.

"That? Oh, that's just the Wild Wood," said the Rat shortly. "We don't go there very much, we river-bankers."

"Aren't they—aren't they very *nice* people in there?" said the Mole a trifle nervously.

"W-e-ll," replied the Rat, "let me see. The squirrels are all right. *And* the rabbits—some of 'em, but rabbits are a mixed lot. And then there's Badger, of course. He lives right in the heart of it; wouldn't live anywhere else, either, if you paid him to do it. Dear old Badger! Nobody interferes with *him*. They'd better not," he added significantly.

"Why, who *should* interfere with him?" asked the Mole.

"Well, of course—there are others," explained the Rat in a hesitating sort of way. "Weasels—and stoats—and foxes—and so on. They're all right in a way—I'm very good friends with them—pass the time of day when we meet, and all that—but they break out sometimes, there's no denying it, and then —well, you can't really trust them, and that's the fact."

The Mole knew well that it is quite against animal etiquette to dwell on possible trouble ahead, or even to allude to it, so he dropped the subject.

"And beyond the Wild Wood again?" he asked. "Where it's all blue and dim, and one sees what may be hills or perhaps they mayn't, and something like the smoke of towns, or is it only cloud-drift?"

"Beyond the Wild Wood comes the Wide World," said the Rat. "And that's something that doesn't matter, either to you or me. I've never been there, and I'm never going, nor you either, if you've got any sense at all. Don't ever refer to it again, please. Now then! Here's our backwater at last, where we're going to lunch."

Leaving the main stream, they now passed into what seemed at first sight like a little landlocked lake. Green turf sloped down to either edge, brown snaky tree roots gleamed below the surface of the quiet water, while ahead of them the silvery shoulder and foamy tumble of a weir, arm-in-arm with a restless dripping mill wheel, that held up in its turn a gray-gabled millhouse, filled the air with a soothing murmur of sound, dull and smothery, yet with little clear voices speaking up cheerfully out of it at intervals. It was so very beautiful that the Mole could only hold up both forepaws and gasp, "Oh my! Oh my! Oh my!"

The Rat brought the boat alongside the bank, made her fast, helped the still awkward Mole safely ashore, and swung out the luncheon basket.

The Mole begged as a favor to be allowed to unpack it all by himself; and the Rat was very pleased to indulge him, and to sprawl at full length on the grass and rest, while his excited friend shook out the tablecloth and spread it, took out all the mysterious packets one by one and arranged their contents in due order, still gasping, "Oh my! Oh my!" at each fresh revelation. When all was ready, the Rat said, "Now, pitch in, old fellow!" and the Mole was indeed very glad to obey, for he had started his spring cleaning at a very early hour that morning, as people *will* do, and had not paused for bite or sup; and he had been through a very great deal since that distant time which now seemed so many days ago.

"What are you looking at?" said the Rat presently, when the edge of their hunger was somewhat dulled, and the Mole's eyes were able to wander off the tablecloth a little.

"I am looking," said the Mole, "at a streak of bubbles that I see traveling along the surface of the water. That is a thing that strikes me as funny."

"Bubbles? Oho!" said the Rat, and chirruped cheerily in an inviting sort of way.

A broad glistening muzzle showed itself above the edge of the bank, and the Otter hauled himself out and shook the water from his coat.

"Greedy beggars!" he observed, making for the provender. "Why didn't you invite me, Ratty?"

"This was an impromptu affair," explained the Rat. "By the way—my friend Mr. Mole."

"Proud, I'm sure," said the Otter, and the two animals were friends forthwith.

"Such a rumpus everywhere!" continued the Otter. "All the world seems out on the river today. I came up this backwater to try and get a moment's peace, and then stumble upon you fellows!—At least—I beg pardon—I don't exactly mean that, you know."

There was a rustle behind them, proceeding from a hedge wherein last year's leaves still clung thick, and a stripy head, with high shoulders behind it, peered forth on them.

"Come on, old Badger," shouted the Rat.

The Badger trotted forward a pace or two; then grunted, "H'm! Company," and turned his back and disappeared from view.

"That's *just* the sort of fellow he is!" observed the disappointed Rat. "Simply hates Society! Now we shan't see any more of him today. Well, tell us *who's* out on the river?"

"Toad's out, for one," replied the Otter. "In his brand-new wager-boat; new togs, new everything!"

The two animals looked at each other and laughed.

"Once, it was nothing but sailing," said the Rat. "Then he tired of that and took to punting. Nothing would please him but to punt all day and every day, and a nice mess he made of it. Last year it was houseboating, and we all had to go and stay with him in his houseboat, and pretend we liked it. He was going to spend the rest of his life in a houseboat. It's all the same whatever he takes up; he gets tired of it, and starts on something fresh."

"Such a good fellow, too," remarked the Otter reflectively: "But no stability—especially in a boat!"

From where they sat they could get a glimpse of the main stream across the island that separated them; and just then a wager-boat flashed into view, the rower—a short, stout figure—splashing badly and rolling a good deal, but working his hardest. The Rat stood up and hailed him, but Toad—for it was he—shook his head and settled sternly to his work.

"He'll be out of the boat in a minute if he rolls like that," said the Rat, sitting down again.

"Of course he will," chuckled the Otter. "Did I ever tell you that good story about Toad and the lock-keeper? It happened this way. Toad . . ."

An errant May fly swerved unsteadily athwart the current in the intoxicated fashion affected by young bloods of May flies seeing life. A swirl of water and a "cloop!" and the May fly was visible no more.

Neither was the Otter.

The Mole looked down. The voice was still in his ears, but the turf whereon he had sprawled was clearly vacant. Not an Otter to be seen, as far as the distant horizon.

But again there was a streak of bubbles on the surface of the river.

The Rat hummed a tune, and the Mole recollected that animal etiquette forbade any sort of comment on the sudden disappearance of one's

friends at any moment, for any reason or no reason whatever.

"Well, well," said the Rat, "I suppose we ought
to be moving. I wonder which of us had better pack
the luncheon basket?" He did not speak as if he
was frightfully eager for the treat.

"Oh, please let me," said the Mole. So, of course,
the Rat let him.

Packing the basket was not quite such pleasant
work as unpacking the basket. It never is. But the
Mole was bent on enjoying everything, and although just when he had got the basket packed and
strapped up tightly he saw a plate staring up at him
from the grass, and when the job had been done
again the Rat pointed out a fork which anybody
ought to have seen, and last of all, behold! the
mustard pot, which he had been sitting on without
knowing it—still, somehow, the thing got finished
at last, without much loss of temper.

The afternoon sun was getting low as the Rat
sculled gently homewards in a dreamy mood,
murmuring poetry-things over to himself, and not
paying much attention to Mole. But the Mole was
very full of lunch, and self-satisfaction, and pride,
and already quite at home in a boat (so he thought)
and was getting a bit restless besides: and presently
he said, "Ratty! Please, *I* want to row now!"

The Rat shook his head with a smile. "Not yet,
my young friend," he said. "Wait till you've had a
few lessons. It's not so easy as it looks."

The Mole was quiet for a minute or two. But he

began to feel more and more jealous of Rat, scul-
ling so strongly and so easily along, and his pride
began to whisper that he could do it every bit as
well. He jumped up and seized the sculls so suddenly that the Rat, who was gazing out over the
water and saying more poetry-things to himself, was
taken by surprise and fell backwards off his seat
with his legs in the air for the second time, while
the triumphant Mole took his place and grabbed
the sculls with entire confidence.

"Stop it, you *silly* ass!" cried the Rat, from the
bottom of the boat. "You can't do it! You'll have
us over!"

The Mole flung his sculls with a flourish, and
made a great dig at the water. He missed the surface altogether, his legs flew up above his head, and
he found himself lying on top of the prostrate
Rat. Greatly alarmed, he made a grab at the side
of the boat, and the next moment—Sploosh!

Over went the boat, and he found himself struggling in the river.

Oh my, how cold the water was, and oh, how
very wet it felt! How it sang in his ears as he went
down, down, down! How bright and welcome the
sun looked as he rose to the surface coughing and
spluttering! How black was his despair when he
felt himself sinking again! Then a firm paw gripped
him by the back of his neck. It was the Rat, and
he was evidently laughing—the Mole could *feel*
him laughing, right down his arm and through his
paw, and so into his—the Mole's—neck.

The Rat got hold of a scull and shoved it under the Mole's arm; then he did the same by the other side of him and, swimming behind, propelled the helpless animal to shore, hauled him out, and set him down on the bank, a squashy, pulpy lump of misery.

When the Rat had rubbed him down a bit, and wrung some of the wet out of him, he said, "Now, then, old fellow! Trot up and down the towing path as hard as you can, till you're warm and dry again, while I dive for the luncheon basket."

So the dismal Mole, wet without and ashamed within, trotted about till he was fairly dry, while the Rat plunged into the water again, recovered the boat, righted her and made her fast, fetched his floating property to shore by degrees, and finally dived successfully for the luncheon basket and struggled to land with it.

When all was ready for a start once more, the Mole, limp and dejected, took his seat in the stern of the boat; and as they set off, he said in a low voice, broken with emotion, "Ratty, my generous friend! I am very sorry indeed for my foolish and ungrateful conduct. My heart quite fails me when I think how I might have lost that beautiful luncheon basket. Indeed, I have been a complete ass, and I know it. Will you overlook it this once and forgive me, and let things go on as before?"

"That's all right, bless you!" responded the Rat cheerily. "What's a little wet to a Water Rat? I'm more in the water than out of it most days. Don't you think any more about it; and, look here! I really think you had better come and stop with me for a little time. It's very plain and rough, you know —not like Toad's house at all—but you haven't seen that yet; still, I can make you comfortable. And I'll teach you to row, and to swim, and you'll soon be as handy on the water as any of us."

The Mole was so touched by his kind manner of speaking that he could find no voice to answer him; and he had to brush away a tear or two with the back of his paw. But the Rat kindly looked in another direction, and presently the Mole's spirits revived again, and he was even able to give some straight backtalk to a couple of moorhens who were sniggering to each other about his bedraggled appearance.

When they got home, the Rat made a bright fire in the parlor, and planted the Mole in an armchair in front of it, having fetched down a dressing gown and slippers for him, and told him river stories till suppertime. Very thrilling stories they were, too, to an earth-dwelling animal like Mole. Stories about weirs, and sudden floods, and leaping pike, and steamers that flung hard bottles—at least bottles were certainly flung, and *from* steamers, so presumably *by* them; and about herons, and how particular they were whom they spoke to; and about adventures down drains, and night-fishings with Otter, or excursions far afield with Badger. Supper was a most cheerful meal; but very shortly afterwards a terribly sleepy Mole had to be escorted upstairs by his considerate host, to the best bedroom, where he soon laid his head on his pillow in great peace and contentment, knowing that his new-found friend the River was lapping the sill of his window.

This day was only the first of many similar ones for the emancipated Mole, each of them longer and fuller of interest as the ripening summer moved onward. He learned to swim and to row, and entered into the joy of running water; and with his ear to the reed stems he caught, at intervals, something of what the wind went whispering so constantly among them.

2

The Open Road

"RATTY," SAID the Mole suddenly, one bright summer morning, "if you please, I want to ask you a favor."

The Rat was sitting on the river bank, singing a little song. He had just composed it himself, so he was very taken up with it, and would not pay proper attention to Mole or anything else. Since early morning he had been swimming in the river in company with his friends the ducks. And when the ducks stood on their heads suddenly, as ducks will, he would dive down and tickle their necks just under where their chins would be if ducks had chins, till they were forced to come to the surface again in a hurry, spluttering and angry and shaking their feathers at him, for it is impossible to say quite

all you feel when your head is under water. At last
they implored him to go away and attend to his own
affairs and leave them to mind theirs. So the Rat
went away, and sat on the river bank in the sun,
and made up a song about them, which he called:

DUCKS' DITTY

> All along the backwater,
> Through the rushes tall,
> Ducks are a-dabbling,
> Up tails all!
>
> Ducks' tails, drakes' tails,
> Yellow feet a-quiver,
> Yellow bills all out of sight
> Busy in the river!
>
> Slushy green undergrowth
> Where the roach swim—
> Here we keep our larder,
> Cool and full and dim.
>
> Everyone for what he likes!
> *We* like to be
> Heads down, tails up,
> Dabbling free!
>
> High in the blue above
> Swifts whirl and call—
> *We* are down a-dabbling,
> Up tails all!

"I don't know that I think so *very* much of that little song, Rat," observed the Mole cautiously. He was no poet himself and didn't care who knew it; and he had a candid nature.

"Nor don't the ducks neither," replied the Rat cheerfully. "They say, '*Why* can't fellows be allowed to do what they like *when* they like and *as* they like, instead of other fellows sitting on banks and watching them all the time and making remarks and poetry and things about them? What *nonsense* it all is!' That's what the ducks say."

"So it is, so it is," said the Mole, with great heartiness.

"No, it isn't," cried the Rat indignantly.

"Well then, it isn't, it isn't," replied the Mole soothingly. "But what I wanted to ask you was, won't you take me to call on Mr. Toad? I've heard so much about him, and I do so want to make his acquaintance."

"Why, certainly," said the good-natured Rat, jumping to his feet and dismissing poetry from his mind for the day. "Get the boat out, and we'll paddle up there at once. It's never the wrong time to call on Toad. Early or late he's always the same fellow. Always good-tempered, always glad to see you, always sorry when you go!"

"He must be a very nice animal," observed the Mole, as he got in the boat and took the sculls, while the Rat settled himself comfortably in the stern.

"He is indeed the best of animals," replied Rat.

"So simple, so good-natured, and so affectionate. Perhaps he's not very clever—we can't all be geniuses; and it may be that he is both boastful and conceited. But he has got some great qualities, has Toady."

Rounding a bend in the river, they came in sight of a handsome, dignified old house of mellowed red brick, with well-kept lawns reaching down to the water's edge.

"There's Toad Hall," said the Rat, "and that creek on the left, where the notice board says, 'Private. No landing allowed,' leads to his boat-house, where we'll leave the boat. The stables are over there to the right. That's the banqueting hall you're looking at now—very old, that is. Toad is

rather rich, you know, and this is really one of the nicest houses in these parts, though we never admit as much to Toad."

They glided up the creek, and the Mole shipped his sculls as they passed into the shadow of a large boathouse. Here they saw many handsome boats, slung from the crossbeams or hauled up on a slip, but none in the water; and the place had an unused and a deserted air.

The Rat looked around him. "I understand," said he. "Boating is played out. He's tired of it, and done with it. I wonder what new fad he has taken up now? Come along and let's look him up. We shall hear all about it quite soon enough."

They disembarked and strolled across the gay

flower-decked lawns in search of Toad, whom they presently happened upon resting in a wicker garden chair, with a preoccupied expression of face, and a large map spread out on his knees.

"Hooray!" he cried, jumping up on seeing them, "this is splendid!" He shook the paws of both of them warmly, never waiting for an introduction to the Mole. "How *kind* of you!" he went on, dancing round them. "I was just going to send a boat down the river for you, Ratty, with strict orders that you were to be fetched up here at once, whatever you were doing. I want you badly—both of you. Now what will you take? Come inside and have something! You don't know how lucky it is, your turning up just now!"

"Let's sit quiet a bit, Toady!" said the Rat, throwing himself into an easy chair, while the Mole took another by the side of him and made some civil remark about Toad's "delightful residence."

"Finest house on the whole river," cried Toad boisterously. "Or anywhere else, for that matter," he could not help adding.

Here the Rat nudged the Mole. Unfortunately the Toad saw him do it, and turned very red. There was a moment's painful silence. Then Toad burst out laughing. "All right, Ratty," he said. "It's only my way, you know. And it's not such a very bad house, is it? You know you rather like it yourself. Now, look here. Let's be sensible. You are the very animals I wanted. You've got to help me. It's most important!"

"It's about your rowing, I suppose," said the Rat, with an innocent air. "You're getting on fairly well, though you splash a good bit still. With a great deal of patience, and any quantity of coaching, you may—"

"Oh, pooh! Boating!" interrupted the Toad, in great disgust. "Silly boyish amusement. I've given that up *long* ago. Sheer waste of time, that's what it is. It makes me downright sorry to see you fellows, who ought to know better, spending all your energies in that aimless manner. No, I've discovered the real thing, the only genuine occupation for a lifetime. I propose to devote the remainder of mine to it, and can only regret the wasted years, that lie behind me, squandered in trivialities. Come with me, dear Ratty, and your amiable friend also, if he will be so good, just as far as the stableyard, and you shall see what you shall see!"

He led the way to the stableyard accordingly, the Rat following with a most mistrustful expression; and there, drawn out of the coachhouse into the open, they saw a gypsy caravan, shining with newness, painted a canary yellow picked out with green, and red wheels.

"There you are!" cried the Toad, straddling and expanding himself. "There's real life for you, embodied in that little cart. The open road, the dusty highway, the heath, the common, the hedgerows, the rolling downs! Camps, villages, towns, cities! Here today, up and off to somewhere else tomorrow! Travel, change, interest, excitement! The whole world before you, and a horizon that's always changing! And mind, this is the very finest cart of its sort that was ever built, without any exception. Come inside and look at the arrangements. Planned 'em all myself, I did!"

The Mole was tremendously interested and excited, and followed him eagerly up the steps and into the interior of the caravan. The Rat only snorted and thrust his hands deep into his pockets, remaining where he was.

It was indeed very compact and comfortable. Little sleeping bunks—a little table that folded up against the wall—a cooking-stove, lockers, bookshelves, a birdcage with a bird in it; and pots, pans, jugs, and kettles of every size and variety.

"All complete!" said the Toad triumphantly, pulling open a locker. "You see—biscuits, potted lobster, sardines—everything you can possibly want. Soda water here—baccy there—letter paper, bacon, jam, cards and dominoes. You'll find," he continued, as they descended the steps again, "you'll find that nothing whatever has been forgotten, when we make our start this afternoon."

"I beg your pardon," said the Rat slowly, as he chewed a straw, "but did I overhear you say something about '*we*' and '*start*' and '*this afternoon*'?"

"Now, you dear good old Ratty," said Toad imploringly, "don't begin talking in that stiff and sniffy sort of way, because you know you've *got* to come. I can't possibly manage without you, so please consider it settled, and don't argue—it's the one thing I can't stand. You surely don't mean to stick to your dull fusty old river all your life, and just live in a hole in a bank, and *boat?* I want to show you the world! I'm going to make an *animal* of you, my boy!"

"I don't care," said the Rat doggedly. "I'm not coming, and that's flat. And I *am* going to stick to my old river, *and* live in a hole, *and* boat, as I've always done. And what's more, Mole's going to stick to me and do as I do, aren't you, Mole?"

"Of course I am," said the Mole loyally. "I'll always stick to you, Rat, and what you say is to be—has got to be. All the same, it sounds as if it might have been—well, rather fun, you know!" he added wistfully. Poor Mole! The Life Adventurous was so new a thing to him, and so thrilling; and this fresh aspect of it was so tempting; and he had fallen in love at first sight with the canary-colored cart and all its little fitments.

The Rat saw what was passing in his mind, and wavered. He hated disappointing people, and he was fond of the Mole, and would do almost anything to oblige him. Toad was watching both of them closely.

"Come along in and have some lunch," he said diplomatically, "and we'll talk it over. We needn't decide anything in a hurry. Of course, I don't really care. I only want to give pleasure to you fellows. 'Live for others!' That's my motto in life."

During luncheon — which was excellent, of

course, as everything at Toad Hall always was—the Toad simply let himself go. Disregarding the Rat, he proceeded to play upon the inexperienced Mole as on a harp. Naturally a voluble animal, and always mastered by his imagination, he painted the prospects of the trip and the joys of the open life and the roadside in such glowing colors that the Mole could hardly sit in his chair for excitement. Somehow, it soon seemed taken for granted by all three of them that the trip was a settled thing; and the Rat, though still unconvinced in his mind, allowed his good nature to override his personal objections. He could not bear to disappoint his two friends, who were already deep in schemes and anticipations, planning out each day's separate occupation for several weeks ahead.

When they were quite ready, the now triumphant Toad led his companions to the paddock and set them to capture the old gray horse, who, without having been consulted, and to his own extreme annoyance, had been told off by Toad for the dustiest job in this dusty expedition. He frankly preferred the paddock, and took a deal of catching. Meantime Toad packed the lockers still tighter with necessaries, and hung nosebags, nets of onions, bundles of hay, and baskets from the bottom of the cart. At last the horse was caught and harnessed, and they set off, all talking at once, each animal either trudging by the side of the cart or sitting on the shaft, as the humor took him. It was a golden afternoon. The smell of the dust they kicked up was rich and satisfying; out of thick orchards on either side the road, birds called and whistled to them cheerily; good-natured wayfarers passing them gave them "Good day," or stopped to say nice things about their beautiful cart; and rabbits, sitting at their front doors in the hedgerows, held up their forepaws, and said, "Oh my! Oh my! Oh my!"

Late in the evening, tired and happy and miles from home, they drew up on a remote common far from habitations, turned the horse loose to graze, and ate their simple supper sitting on the grass by the side of the cart. Toad talked big about all he was going to do in the days to come, while stars grew fuller and larger all around them, and a yellow moon, appearing suddenly and silently from nowhere in particular, came to keep them company and listen to their talk. At last they turned into their little bunks in the cart; and Toad, kicking out his legs, sleepily said, "Well, good night, you fellows! This is the real life for a gentleman! Talk about your old river!"

"I *don't* talk about my river," replied the patient Rat. "You *know* I don't, Toad. But I *think* about it," he added pathetically, in a lower tone. "I think about it—all the time!"

The Mole reached out from under his blanket, felt for the Rat's paw in the darkness, and gave it a squeeze. "I'll do whatever you like, Ratty," he whispered. "Shall we run away tomorrow morning, quite early—*very* early—and go back to our dear old hole on the river?"

"No, no, we'll see it out," whispered back the Rat. "Thanks awfully, but I ought to stick by Toad till this trip is ended. It wouldn't be safe for him to be left to himself. It won't take very long. His fads never do. Good night!"

The end was indeed nearer than even the Rat suspected.

After so much open air and excitement the Toad slept very soundly, and no amount of shaking could rouse him out of bed next morning. So the Mole and Rat turned to, quietly and manfully, and while the Rat saw to the horse, and lit a fire, and cleaned last night's cups and platters, and got things ready for breakfast, the Mole trudged off to the nearest village, a long way off, for milk and eggs and various necessaries the Toad had, of course, forgotten to provide. The hard work had all been done, and the two animals were resting, thoroughly exhausted, by the time Toad appeared on the scene, fresh and gay, remarking what a pleasant easy life it was they were all leading now, after the cares and worries and fatigues of housekeeping at home.

They had a pleasant ramble that day over grassy downs and along narrow by-lanes, and camped, as before, on a common, only this time the two guests took care that Toad should do his fair share of work. In consequence, when the time came for starting next morning, Toad was by no means so rapturous about the simplicity of the primitive life, and indeed attempted to resume his place in his bunk, whence he was hauled by force. Their way lay, as before, across country by narrow lanes, and it was not till the afternoon that they came out on the highroad, their first highroad; and there disaster, fleet and unforeseen, sprang out on them—disaster momentous indeed to their expedition, but simply overwhelming in its effect on the after-career of Toad.

They were strolling along the highroad easily, the Mole by the horse's head, talking to him, since the horse had complained that he was being frightfully left out of it, and nobody considered him in the least; the Toad and the Water Rat walking behind the cart talking together—at least Toad was talking, and Rat was saying at intervals, "Yes, precisely; and what did *you* say to *him?*"—and thinking all the time of something very different, when far behind them they heard a faint warning hum, like the drone of a distant bee. Glancing back, they saw a small cloud of dust, with a dark center of energy, advancing on them at incredible speed, while from out the dust a faint "Poop-poop!" wailed like an uneasy animal in pain. Hardly regarding it, they turned to resume their conversation, when in an instant (as it seemed) the peaceful scene was changed, and with a blast of wind and a whirl of sound that made them jump for the nearest ditch, it was on them! The "poop-poop" rang with a brazen shout in their ears, they had a moment's glimpse of an interior of glittering plate glass and rich morocco, and the magnificent motorcar, immense, breath-snatching, passionate, with its pilot tense and

hugging his wheel, possessed all earth and air for
the fraction of a second, flung an enveloping cloud
of dust that blinded and enwrapped them utterly,
and then dwindled to a speck in the far distance,
changed back into a droning bee once more.

The old gray horse, dreaming, as he plodded
along, of his quiet paddock, in a new raw situation
such as this simply abandoned himself to his natural
emotions. Rearing, plunging, backing steadily, in
spite of all the Mole's efforts at his head, and all
the Mole's lively language directed at his better
feelings, he drove the cart backwards towards the
deep ditch at the side of the road. It wavered an
instant—then there was a heart-rending crash—and
the canary-colored cart, their pride and their joy,
lay on its side in the ditch, an irredeemable wreck.

The Rat danced up and down in the road, simply
transported with passion. "You villains!" he shouted,
shaking both fists. "You scoundrels, you highway-
men, you—you—roadhogs!—I'll have the law on
you! I'll report you! I'll take you through all the
Courts!" His homesickness had quite slipped away
from him, and for the moment he was the skipper
of the canary-colored vessel driven on a shoal by
the reckless jockeying of rival mariners, and he was
trying to recollect all the fine and biting things he
used to say to masters of steam launches when their
wash, as they drove too near the bank, used to flood
his parlor carpet at home.

Toad sat straight down in the middle of the dusty

road, his legs stretched out before him, and stared fixedly in the direction of the disappearing motor-car. He breathed short, his face wore a placid, satisfied expression, and at intervals he faintly murmured, "Poop-poop!"

The Mole was busy trying to quiet the horse, which he succeeded in doing after a time. Then he went to look at the cart, on its side in the ditch. It was indeed a sorry sight. Panels and windows smashed, axles hopelessly bent, one wheel off, sardine tins scattered over the wide world, and the bird in the birdcage sobbing pitifully and calling to be let out.

The Rat came to help him, but their united efforts were not sufficient to right the cart. "Hi! Toad!" they cried. "Come and bear a hand, can't you?"

The Toad never answered a word, or budged from his seat in the road; so they went to see what was the matter with him. They found him in a sort of trance, a happy smile on his face, his eyes still fixed on the dusty wake of their destroyer. At intervals he was still heard to murmur, "Poop-poop!"

The Rat shook him by the shoulder. "Are you coming to help us, Toad?" he demanded sternly.

"Glorious, stirring sight!" murmured Toad, never offering to move. "The poetry of motion! The *real* way to travel! The *only* way to travel! Here today —in next week tomorrow! Villages skipped, towns and cities jumped—always somebody else's horizon! Oh bliss! Oh poop-poop! Oh my! Oh my!"

"Oh, *stop* being an ass, Toad!" cried the Mole despairingly.

"And to think I never *knew!*" went on the Toad in a dreamy monotone. "All those wasted years that lie behind me, I never knew, never *dreamt!* But *now*—but now that I know, now that I fully realize! Oh, what a flowery track lies spread before me, henceforth! What dust-clouds shall spring up behind me as I speed on my reckless way! What carts I shall fling carelessly into the ditch in the wake of my magnificent onset! Horrid little carts—common carts—canary-colored carts!"

"What are we to do with him?" asked the Mole of the Water Rat.

"Nothing at all," replied the Rat firmly. "Because there is really nothing to be done. You see, I know him from old. He is now possessed. He has got a new craze, and it always takes him that way, in its first stage. He'll continue like that for days now, like an animal walking in a happy dream, quite useless for all practical purposes. Never mind him. Let's go and see what there is to be done about the cart."

A careful inspection showed them that, even if they succeeded in righting it by themselves, the cart would travel no longer. The axles were in a hopeless state, and the missing wheel was shattered into pieces.

The Rat knotted the horse's reins over his back and took him by the head, carrying the birdcage and its hysterical occupant in the other hand. "Come on!" he said grimly to the Mole. "It's five or six miles to the nearest town, and we shall just have to walk it. The sooner we make a start the better."

"But what about Toad?" asked the Mole anxiously, as they set off together. "We can't leave him here, sitting in the middle of the road by himself, in the distracted state he's in! It's not safe. Supposing another Thing were to come along?"

"Oh, *bother* Toad," said the Rat savagely; "I've done with him!"

They had not proceeded very far on their way, however, when there was a pattering of feet behind them, and Toad caught them up and thrust a paw inside the elbow of each of them; still breathing short and staring into vacancy.

"Now, look here, Toad!" said the Rat sharply: "as soon as we get to the town, you'll have to go straight to the police station, and see if they know anything about that motorcar and who it belongs to, and lodge a complaint against it. And then you'll have to go to a blacksmith's or a wheelwright's and arrange for the cart to be fetched and mended and put to rights. It'll take time, but it's not quite a hopeless smash. Meanwhile, the Mole and I will go to an inn and find comfortable rooms where we can stay till the cart's ready, and till your nerves have recovered their shock."

"Police station! Complaint!" murmured Toad dreamily. "Me *complain* of that beautiful, that

heavenly vision that has been vouchsafed me! *Mend
the cart!* I've done with carts forever. I never want
to see the cart, or to hear of it, again. Oh, Ratty!
You can't think how obliged I am to you for con-
senting to come on this trip! I wouldn't have gone
without you, and then I might never have seen that
—that swan, that sunbeam, that thunderbolt! I
might never have heard that entrancing sound, or
smelled that bewitching smell! I owe it all to you,
my best of friends!"

The Rat turned from him in despair."You see
what it is?" he said to the Mole, addressing him
across Toad's head: "He's quite hopeless. I give it
up—when we get to the town we'll go to the railway station, and with luck we may pick up a train
there that'll get us back to River Bank tonight. And
if ever you catch me going a-pleasuring with this
provoking animal again!"——He snorted, and during the rest of that weary trudge addressed his remarks exclusively to Mole.

On reaching the town they went straight to the
station and deposited Toad in the second-class waiting room, giving a porter twopence to keep a strict
eye on him. They then left the horse at an inn
stable, and gave what directions they could about
the cart and its contents. Eventually, a slow train
having landed them at a station not very far from
Toad Hall, they escorted the spellbound, sleep-
walking Toad to his door, put him inside it, and
instructed his housekeeper to feed him, undress
him, and put him to bed. Then they got out their

boat from the boathouse, sculled down the river home, and at a very late hour sat down to supper in their own cozy riverside parlor, to the Rat's great joy and contentment.

The following evening the Mole, who had risen late and taken things very easy all day, was sitting on the bank fishing, when the Rat, who had been looking up his friends and gossiping, came strolling along to find him. "Heard the news?" he said. "There's nothing else being talked about, all along the river bank. Toad went up to town by an early train this morning. And he has ordered a large and very expensive motorcar."

3

The Wild Wood

THE MOLE had long wanted to make the acquaintance of the Badger. He seemed, by all accounts, to be such an important personage and, though rarely visible, to make his unseen influence felt by everybody about the place. But whenever the Mole mentioned his wish to the Water Rat he always found himself put off. "It's all right," the Rat would say, "Badger'll turn up some day or other—he's always turning up—and then I'll introduce you. The best of fellows! But you must not only take him *as* you find him, but *when* you find him."

"Couldn't you ask him here—dinner or something?" said the Mole.

"He wouldn't come," replied the Rat simply.

46

"Badger hates Society, and invitations, and dinner, and all that sort of thing."

"Well, then, supposing we go and call on *him?*" suggested the Mole.

"Oh, I'm sure he wouldn't like that at *all,*" said the Rat, quite alarmed. "He's so very shy, he'd be sure to be offended. I've never even ventured to call on him at his home myself, though I know him so well. Besides, we can't. It's quite out of the question, because he lives in the very middle of the Wild Wood."

"Well, supposing he does," said the Mole. "You told me the Wild Wood was all right, you know."

"Oh, I know, I know, so it is," replied the Rat evasively. "But I think we won't go there just now. Not *just* yet. It's a long way, and he wouldn't be at home at this time of year anyhow, and he'll be coming along some day, if you'll wait quietly."

The Mole had to be content with this. But the Badger never came along, and every day brought its amusements, and it was not till summer was long over, and cold and frost and miry ways kept them much indoors, and the swollen river raced past outside their windows with a speed that mocked at boating of any sort or kind, that he found his thoughts dwelling again with much persistence on the solitary gray Badger, who lived his own life by himself, in his hole in the middle of the Wild Wood.

In the wintertime the Rat slept a great deal, retiring early and rising late. During his short day he

sometimes scribbled poetry or did other small domestic jobs about the house; and, of course, there
were always animals dropping in for a chat, and
consequently there was a good deal of storytelling
and comparing notes on the past summer and all
its doings.

Such a rich chapter it had been, when one came
to look back on it all! With illustrations so numerous and so very highly colored! The pageant of the
river bank had marched steadily along, unfolding
itself in scene-pictures that succeeded each other in
stately procession. Purple loosestrife arrived early,
shaking luxuriant tangled locks along the edge of
the mirror whence its own face laughed back at it.
Willow-herb, tender and wistful, like a pink sunset
cloud, was not slow to follow. Comfrey, the purple
hand-in-hand with the white, crept forth to take its
place in the line; and at last one morning the
diffident and delaying dog-rose stepped delicately
on the stage, and one knew, as if string music had
announced it in stately chords that strayed into a
gavotte, that June at last was here. One member
of the company was still awaited; the shepherd boy
for the nymphs to woo, the knight for whom the
ladies waited at the window, the prince that was to
kiss the sleeping summer back to life and love. But
when meadow-sweet, debonair and odorous in amber jerkin, moved graciously to his place in the
group, then the play was ready to begin.

And what a play it had been! Drowsy animals,
snug in their holes while wind and rain were batter-

ing at their doors, recalled still keen mornings, an hour before sunrise, when the white mist, as yet undispersed, clung closely along the surface of the water; then the shock of the early plunge, the scamper along the bank, and the radiant transformation of earth, air, and water, when suddenly the sun was with them again, and gray was gold and color was born and sprang out of the earth once more. They recalled the languorous siesta of hot midday, deep in green undergrowth, the sun striking through in tiny golden shafts and spots; the boating and bathing of the afternoon, the rambles along dusty lanes and through yellow cornfields; and the long, cool evening at last, when so many threads were gathered up, so many friendships rounded, and so many adventures planned for the morrow. There was plenty to talk about on those short winter days when the animals found themselves round the fire; still, the Mole had a good deal of spare time on his hands, and so one afternoon, when the Rat in his armchair before the blaze was alternately dozing and trying over rhymes that wouldn't fit, he formed the resolution to go out by himself and explore the Wild Wood, and perhaps strike up an acquaintance with Mr. Badger.

It was a cold still afternoon with a hard steely sky overhead, when he slipped out of the warm parlor into the open air. The country lay bare and entirely leafless around him, and he thought that he had never seen so far and so intimately into the insides of things as on that winter day when Nature was deep in her annual slumber and seemed to have kicked the clothes off. Copses, dells, quarries and all hidden places, which had been mysterious mines for exploration in leafy summer, now exposed themselves and their secrets pathetically, and seemed to ask him to overlook their shabby poverty for a while, till they could riot in rich masquerade as before, and trick and entice him with the old deceptions. It was pitiful in a way, and yet cheering—even exhilarating. He was glad that he liked the country undecorated, hard, and stripped of its finery. He had got down to the bare bones of it, and they were fine and strong and simple. He did not want the warm clover and the play of seeding grasses; the screens of quickset, the billowy drapery of beech and elm seemed best away; and with great cheerfulness of spirit he pushed on towards the Wild Wood, which lay before him low and threatening, like a black reef in some still southern sea.

There was nothing to alarm him at first entry. Twigs crackled under his feet, logs tripped him, funguses on stumps resembled caricatures, and startled him for the moment by their likeness to something familiar and far away; but that was all fun, and exciting. It led him on, and he penetrated to where the light was less, and trees crouched nearer and nearer, and holes made ugly mouths at him on either side.

Everything was still now. The dusk advanced on him steadily, rapidly, gathering in behind and before; and the light seemed to be draining away like floodwater.

Then the faces began.

It was over his shoulder, and indistinctly, that he first thought he saw a face: a little evil wedge-shaped face, looking out at him from a hole. When he turned and confronted it, the thing had vanished.

He quickened his pace, telling himself cheerfully not to begin imagining things, or there would be simply no end to it. He passed another hole, and another, and another; and then—yes!—no!—yes! certainly a little narrow face, with hard eyes, had flashed up for an instant from a hole, and was gone. He hesitated—braced himself up for an effort and strode on. Then suddenly, as if it had been so all the time, every hole, far and near, and there were hundreds of them, seemed to possess its face, coming and going rapidly, all fixing on him glances of malice and hatred: all hard-eyed and evil and sharp.

If he could only get away from the holes in the banks, he thought, there would be no more faces. He swung off the path and plunged into the untrodden places of the wood.

Then the whistling began.

Very faint and shrill it was, and far behind him, when first he heard it; but somehow it made him hurry forward. Then, still very faint and shrill, it sounded far ahead of him, and made him hesitate and want to go back. As he halted in indecision it broke out on either side, and seemed to be caught up and passed on throughout the whole length of the wood to its farthest limit. They were up and alert and ready, evidently, whoever they were! And he—he was alone, and unarmed, and far from any help; and the night was closing in.

Then the pattering began.

He thought it was only falling leaves at first, so slight and delicate was the sound of it. Then as it grew it took a regular rhythm, and he knew it for nothing else but the pat-pat-pat of little feet, still a very long way off. Was it in front or behind? It seemed to be first one, then the other, then both. It grew and it multiplied, till from every quarter as he listened anxiously, leaning this way and that, it seemed to be closing in on him. As he stood still to hearken, a rabbit came running hard towards him through the trees. He waited, expecting it to slacken pace, or to swerve from him into a different course. Instead, the animal almost brushed him as it dashed past, his face set and hard, his eyes staring. "Get out of this, you fool, get out!" the Mole heard him mutter as he swung round a stump and disappeared down a friendly burrow.

The pattering increased till it sounded like sudden hail on the dry-leaf carpet spread around him. The whole wood seemed running now, running hard, hunting, chasing, closing in round something or—somebody? In panic, he began to run too, aimlessly, he knew not whither. He ran up against things, he fell over things and into things, he darted under things and dodged round things. At last he took refuge in the deep dark hollow of an old beech tree, which offered shelter, concealment—perhaps even safety, but who could tell? Anyhow, he was too tired to run any farther and could only snuggle down into the dry leaves which had drifted into the hollow and hope he was safe for the time. And as he lay there panting and trembling, and listened to the whistlings and the patterings outside, he knew it at last, in all its fullness, that dread thing which other little dwellers in field and hedgerow had encountered here, and known as their darkest moment—that thing which the Rat had vainly tried to shield him from—the Terror of the Wild Wood!

Meantime the Rat, warm and comfortable, dozed by his fireside. His paper of half-finished verses slipped from his knee, his head fell back, his mouth opened, and he wandered by the verdant banks of dream rivers. Then a coal slipped, the fire crackled and sent up a spurt of flame, and he woke with a start. Remembering what he had been engaged upon, he reached down to the floor for his verses, pored over them for a minute, and then looked round for the Mole to ask him if he knew a good rhyme for something or other.

But the Mole was not there.

He listened for a time. The house seemed very quiet.

Then he called "Moly!" several times, and, receiving no answer, got up and went out into the hall.

The Mole's cap was missing from its accustomed peg. His galoshes, which always lay by the umbrella stand, were also gone.

The Rat left the house and carefully examined the muddy surface of the ground outside, hoping to find the Mole's tracks. There they were, sure enough. The galoshes were new, just bought for the winter, and the pimples on their soles were fresh and sharp. He could see the imprints of them in the mud, running along straight and purposeful, leading direct to the Wild Wood.

The Rat looked very grave, and stood in deep thought for a minute or two. Then he re-entered the house, strapped a belt around his waist, shoved a brace of pistols into it, took up a stout cudgel that stood in a corner of the hall, and set off for the Wild Wood at a smart pace.

It was already getting towards dusk when he reached the first fringe of trees and plunged without hesitation into the wood, looking anxiously on either side for any sign of his friend. Here and there wicked little faces popped out of holes, but vanished immediately at sight of the valorous animal, his pistols, and the great ugly cudgel in his grasp; and the whistling and pattering, which he had heard quite plainly on his first entry, died away and ceased, and all was very still. He made his way manfully through the length of the wood, to its farthest edge; then, forsaking all paths, he set himself to traverse it, laboriously working over the whole ground, and all the time calling out cheerfully, "Moly, Moly, Moly! Where are you? It's me—it's old Rat!"

He had patiently hunted through the wood for an hour or more, when at last to his joy he heard a little answering cry. Guiding himself by the sound, he made his way through the gathering darkness to the foot of an old beech tree, with a hole in it, and from out of the hole came a feeble voice, saying, "Ratty! Is that really you?"

The Rat crept into the hollow, and there he found the Mole, exhausted and still trembling. "Oh, Rat!" he cried, "I've been so frightened, you can't think!"

"Oh, I quite understand," said the Rat soothingly. "You shouldn't really have gone and done it, Mole. I did my best to keep you from it. We river-bankers, we hardly ever come here by ourselves. If we have to come, we come in couples, at least; then we're generally all right. Besides, there are a hundred things one has to know, which we understand all about and you don't, as yet. I mean passwords, and signs, and sayings which have power and effect, and plants you carry in your pocket, and verses you repeat, and dodges and tricks you practice; all simple enough when you know them, but they've got to be known if you're small, or you'll find yourself in trouble. Of course if you were Badger or Otter, it would be quite another matter."

"Surely the brave Mr. Toad wouldn't mind coming here by himself, would he?" inquired the Mole.

"Old Toad?" said the Rat, laughing heartily. "He wouldn't show his face here alone, not for a whole hatful of golden guineas, Toad wouldn't."

The Mole was greatly cheered by the sound of the Rat's careless laughter, as well as by the sight of his stick and his gleaming pistols, and he stopped shivering and began to feel bolder and more himself again.

"Now then," said the Rat presently, "we really must pull ourselves together and make a start for home while there's still a little light left. It will never do to spend the night here, you understand. Too cold, for one thing."

"Dear Ratty," said the poor Mole, "I'm dreadfully sorry, but I'm simply dead beat and that's a solid fact. You *must* let me rest here awhile longer, and get my strength back, if I'm to get home at all."

"Oh, all right," said the good-natured Rat, "rest away. It's pretty nearly pitch dark now, anyhow, and there ought to be a bit of a moon later."

So the Mole got well into the dry leaves and stretched himself out, and presently dropped off into sleep, though of a broken and troubled sort; while the Rat covered himself up, too, as best he might, for warmth, and lay patiently waiting, with a pistol in his paw.

When at last the Mole woke up, much refreshed and in his usual spirits, the Rat said, "Now then! I'll just take a look outside and see if everything's quiet, and then we really must be off."

He went to the entrance of their retreat and put his head out. Then the Mole heard him saying quietly to himself, "Hullo! hullo! Here—*is*—a—go!"

"What's up, Ratty?" asked the Mole.

"*Snow* is up," replied the Rat briefly, "or rather, *down*. It's snowing hard."

The Mole came and crouched beside him, and, looking out, saw the wood that had been so dreadful to him in quite a changed aspect. Holes, hollows, pools, pitfalls, and other black menaces to the wayfarer were vanishing fast, and a gleaming carpet of faery was springing up everywhere, that looked too delicate to be trodden upon by rough feet. A fine powder filled the air and caressed the cheek with a tingle in its touch, and the black boles of the trees showed up in a light that seemed to come from below.

"Well, well, it can't be helped," said the Rat, after pondering. "We must make a start, and take our chance, I suppose. The worst of it is, I don't exactly know where we are. And now this snow makes everything look so very different."

It did indeed. The Mole would not have known that it was the same wood. However, they set out bravely, and took the line that seemed most promising, holding on to each other and pretending with invincible cheerfulness that they recognized an old friend in every fresh tree that grimly and silently greeted them, or saw openings, gaps, or paths with a familiar turn in them, in the monotony of white space and black tree trunks that refused to vary.

An hour or two later—they had lost all count of time—they pulled up, dispirited, weary, and hopelessly at sea, and sat down on a fallen tree trunk to recover their breath and consider what was to be done. They were aching with fatigue and bruised with tumbles; they had fallen into several holes and got wet through; the snow was getting so deep that they could hardly drag their little legs through it, and the trees were thicker and more like each other than ever. There seemed to be no end to this wood, and no beginning, and no difference in it, and, worst of all, no way out.

"We can't sit here very long," said the Rat. "We shall have to make another push for it, and do something or other. The cold is too awful for anything, and the snow will soon be too deep for us to wade through." He peered about him and considered. "Look here," he went on, "this is what occurs to me. There's a sort of dell down there in front of us, where the ground seems all hilly and humpy and hummocky. We'll make our way down into that, and try and find some sort of shelter, a cave or hole with a dry floor to it, out of the snow and the wind, and there we'll have a good rest before we try again, for we're both of us pretty dead beat. Besides, the snow may leave off, or something may turn up."

So once more they got on their feet, and struggled down into the dell, where they hunted about for a cave or some corner that was dry and a protection from the keen wind and the whirling snow. They were investigating one of the hummocky bits the Rat had spoken of, when suddenly the Mole tripped up and fell forward on his face with a squeal.

"Oh, my leg!" he cried. "Oh, my poor shin!" and he sat up on the snow and nursed his leg in both his front paws.

"Poor old Mole!" said the Rat kindly. "You don't seem to be having much luck today, do you? Let's have a look at the leg. Yes," he went on, going down on his knees to look, "you've cut your shin, sure enough. Wait till I get at my handkerchief, and I'll tie it up for you."

"I must have tripped over a hidden branch or a stump," said the Mole miserably. "Oh my! Oh my!"

"It's a very clean cut," said the Rat, examining it again attentively. "That was never done by a branch or a stump. Looks as it was made by a sharp edge of something in metal. Funny!" He pondered awhile, and examined the humps and slopes that surrounded them.

"Well, never mind what done it," said the Mole, forgetting his grammar in his pain. "It hurts just the same, whatever done it."

But the Rat, after carefully tying up the leg with his handkerchief, had left him and was busy scraping in the snow. He scratched and shoveled and explored, all four legs working busily, while the Mole waited impatiently, remarking at intervals, "Oh, *come* on, Rat!"

Suddenly the Rat cried, "Hooray!" and then "Hooray-oo-ray-oo-ray-oo-ray!" and fell to executing a feeble jig in the snow.

"What *have* you found, Ratty?" asked the Mole, still nursing his leg.

"Come and see!" said the delighted Rat as he jigged on.

The Mole hobbled up to the spot and had a good look.

"Well," he said at last, slowly, "I *see* it right enough. Seen the same sort of thing before, lots of times. Familiar object, I call it. A door scraper! Well, what of it? Why dance jigs round a door scraper?"

"But don't you see what it *means,* you—you dull-witted animal?" cried the Rat impatiently.

"Of course I see what it means," replied the Mole. "It simply means that some *very* careless and forgetful person has left his door scraper lying about in the middle of the Wild Wood, *just* where it's *sure* to trip *everybody* up. Very thoughtless of him, I call it. When I get home I shall go and complain about it to—to somebody or other, see if I don't!"

"Oh dear! Oh dear!" cried the Rat, in despair at his obtuseness. "Here, stop arguing and come and scrape!" And he set to work again and made the snow fly in all directions around him.

After some further toil his efforts were rewarded, and a very shabby doormat lay exposed to view.

"There, what did I tell you?" exclaimed the Rat, in great triumph.

"Absolutely nothing whatever," replied the Mole, with perfect truthfulness. "Well now," he went on, "you seem to have found another piece of domestic litter, done for and thrown away, and I suppose you're perfectly happy. Better go ahead and dance your jig round that if you've got to, and get it over, and then perhaps we can go on and not waste any more time over rubbish heaps. Can we *eat* a doormat? Or sleep under the doormat? Or sit on a doormat and sledge home over the snow on it, you exasperating rodent?"

"Do—you—mean—to—say," cried the excited Rat, "that this doormat doesn't *tell* you anything?"

"Really, Rat," said the Mole quite pettishly, "I think we've had enough of this folly. Who ever heard of a doormat *telling* anyone anything? They simply don't go do it. They are not that sort at all. Doormats know their place."

"Now look here, you—you thick-headed beast," replied the Rat, really angry, "this must stop. Not another word, but scrape—scrape and scratch and dig and hunt around, especially on the sides of the hummocks, if you want to sleep dry and warm tonight, for it's our last chance!"

The Rat attacked a snowbank beside them with ardor, probing with his cudgel everywhere and then digging with fury; and the Mole scraped busily too, more to oblige the Rat than for any other reason, for his opinion was that his friend was getting lightheaded.

Some ten minutes' hard work, and the point of the Rat's cudgel struck something that sounded hollow. He worked till he could get a paw through and feel; then called to Mole to come and help him. Hard at it went the two animals, till at last the result of their labors stood full in view of the astonished and hitherto incredulous Mole.

In the side of what had seemed to be a snow-bank stood a solid-looking little door, painted a dark green. An iron bellpull hung by the side, and below it, on a small brass plate, neatly engraved in square capital letters, they could read by the aid of moonlight:

MR. BADGER.

The Mole fell backwards on the snow from sheer surprise and delight. "Rat!" he cried in penitence, "you're a wonder! A real wonder, that's what you are. I see it all now! You argued it out, step by step, in that wise head of yours, from the very moment that I fell and cut my shin, and you looked at the cut, and at once your majestic mind said to itself, 'Door scraper!' And then you turned to and found the very door scraper that done it! Did you stop there? No. Some people would have been quite satisfied; but not you. Your intellect went on working. 'Let me only just find a doormat,' says you to yourself, 'and my theory is proved!' And of course you found your doormat. You're so clever, I believe you could find anything you liked. 'Now,' says you, 'that door exists, as plain as if I saw it. There's nothing else remains to be done but to find it!' Well, I've read about that sort of thing in books, but I've never come across it before in real life. You ought to go where you'll be properly appreciated. You're simply wasted here, among us fellows. If I only had your head, Ratty——"

"But as you haven't," interrupted the Rat rather unkindly, "I suppose you're going to sit on the snow all night and *talk?* Get up at once and hang onto that bellpull you see there, and ring hard, as hard as you can, while I hammer!"

While the Rat attacked the door with his stick, the Mole sprang up at the bellpull, clutched it and swung there, both feet well off the ground, and from quite a long way off they could faintly hear a deep-toned bell respond.

4

Mr. Badger

THEY WAITED patiently for what seemed a very long time, stamping in the snow to keep their feet warm. At last they heard the sound of slow shuffling footsteps approaching the door from the inside. It seemed, as the Mole remarked to the Rat, like someone walking in carpet slippers that were too large for him and down-at-heel; which was intelligent of Mole, because that was exactly what it was.

There was the noise of a bolt shot back, and the door opened a few inches, enough to show a long snout and a pair of sleepy blinking eyes.

"Now, the *very* next time this happens," said a gruff and suspicious voice, "I shall be exceedingly angry. Who is it *this* time, disturbing people on such a night? Speak up!"

"Oh, Badger," cried the Rat, "let us in, please. It's me, Rat, and my friend Mole, and we've lost our way in the snow."

"What, Ratty, my dear little man!" exclaimed the Badger, in quite a different voice. "Come along in, both of you, at once. Why, you must be perished. Well I never! Lost in the snow! And in the Wild Wood, too, and at this time of night! But come in with you."

The two animals tumbled over each other in their eagerness to get inside, and heard the door shut behind them with great joy and relief.

The Badger, who wore a long dressing gown, and whose slippers were indeed very down-at-heel, carried a flat candlestick in his paw and had probably been on his way to bed when their summons sounded. He looked kindly down on them and patted both their heads. "This is not the sort of night for small animals to be out," he said paternally. "I'm afraid you've been up to some of your pranks again, Ratty. But come along; come into the kitchen. There's a first-rate fire there, and supper and everything."

He shuffled on in front of them, carrying the light, and they followed him, nudging each other in an anticipating sort of way, down a long, gloomy, and, to tell the truth, decidedly shabby passage, into a sort of a central hall, out of which they could dimly see other long tunnel-like passages branching, passages mysterious and without apparent end. But there were doors in the hall as well—stout oaken comfortable-looking doors. One of these the Badger flung open, and at once they found themselves in all the glow and warmth of a large fire-lit kitchen.

The floor was well-worn red brick, and on the wide hearth burned a fire of logs, between two attractive chimney corners tucked away in the wall, well out of any suspicion of draft. A couple of high-backed settles, facing each other on either side of the fire, gave further sitting accommodation for the sociably disposed. In the middle of the room stood a long table of plain boards placed on trestles, with benches down each side. At one end of it, where an armchair stood pushed back, were spread the remains of the Badger's plain but ample supper. Rows of spotless plates winked from the shelves of the dresser at the far end of the room, and from the rafters overhead hung hams, bundles of dried herbs, nets of onions, and baskets of eggs. It seemed a place where heroes could fitly feast after victory, where weary harvesters could line up in scores along the table and keep their Harvest Home with mirth and song, or where two or three friends of simple tastes could sit about as they pleased and eat and smoke and talk in comfort and contentment. The ruddy brick floor smiled up at the smoky ceiling; the oaken settles, shiny with long wear, exchanged cheerful glances with each other; plates on the dresser grinned at pots on the shelf, and the merry firelight flickered and played over everything without distinction.

The kindly Badger thrust them down on a settle to toast themselves at the fire, and bade them remove their wet coats and boots. Then he fetched them dressing gowns and slippers, and himself bathed the Mole's shin with warm water and mended the cut with sticking plaster till the whole thing was just as good as new, if not better. In the embracing light and warmth, warm and dry at last, with weary legs propped up in front of them, and a suggestive clink of plates being arranged on the table behind, it seemed to the storm-driven animals, now in safe anchorage, that the cold and trackless Wild Wood just left outside was miles and miles away, and all that they had suffered in it a half-forgotten dream.

When at last they were thoroughly toasted, the Badger summoned them to the table, where he had been busy laying a repast. They had felt pretty hungry before, but when they actually saw at last the supper that was spread for them, really it seemed only a question of what they should attack first where all was so attractive, and whether the other things would obligingly wait for them till they had time to give them attention. Conversation was impossible for a long time; and when it was slowly resumed, it was that regrettable sort of conversation that results from talking with your mouth full. The Badger did not mind that sort of thing at all, nor did he take any notice of elbows on the table, or everybody speaking at once. As he did not go into Society himself, he had got an idea that these things belonged to the things that didn't really matter. (We know of course that he was wrong, and took too narrow a view; because they do matter very much, though it would take too long to explain why.) He sat in his armchair at the head of the table, and nodded gravely at intervals as the animals told their story; and he did not seem surprised or shocked at anything, and he never said, "I told you so," or, "Just what I always said," or remarked that they ought to have done so-and-so, or ought not to have done something else. The Mole began to feel very friendly towards him.

When supper was really finished at last, and each animal felt that his skin was now as tight as was decently safe, and that by this time he didn't care a hang for anybody or anything, they gathered round the glowing embers of the great wood fire, and thought how jolly it was to be sitting up so late, and *so* independent, and *so* full; and after they had chatted for a time about things in general, the Badger said heartily, "Now then! tell us the news from your part of the world. How's old Toad going on?"

"Oh, from bad to worse," said the Rat gravely, while the Mole, cocked up on a settle and basking in the firelight, his heels higher than his head, tried to look properly mournful. "Another smashup only last week, a bad one. You see, he will insist on driving himself, and he's hopelessly incapable. If he'd only employ a decent, steady, well-trained animal, pay him good wages, and leave everything to him, he'd get on all right. But no; he's convinced he's a heaven-born driver, and nobody can teach him anything; and all the rest follows."

"How many has he had?" inquired the Badger gloomily.

"Smashes, or machines?" asked the Rat. "Oh, well, after all, it's the same thing—with Toad. This is the seventh. As for the others—you know that coach house of his? Well, it's piled up—literally piled up to the roof—with fragments of motorcars none of them bigger than your hat! That accounts for the other six—so far as they can be accounted for."

"He's been in hospital three times," put in the Mole, "and as for the fines he's had to pay, it's simply awful to think of."

"Yes, and that's part of the trouble," continued the Rat. "Toad's rich, we all know; but he's not a millionaire. And he's a hopelessly bad driver, and quite regardless of law and order. Killed or ruined —it's got to be one of the two things, sooner or later. Badger! we're his friends—oughtn't we to do something?"

The Badger went through a bit of hard thinking. "Now look here!" he said at last, rather severely, "of course you know I can't do anything *now*?"

His two friends assented, quite understanding his point. No animal, according to the rules of animal etiquette, is ever expected to do anything strenuous, or heroic, or even moderately active during the off-season of winter. All are sleepy—some actually asleep. All are weather-bound, more or less; and all are resting from arduous days and nights, during which every muscle in them has been severely tested, and every energy kept at full stretch.

"Very well then!" continued the Badger. "*But,* when once the year has really turned, and the nights are shorter, and halfway through them one rouses and feels fidgety and wanting to be up and doing by sunrise, if not before—*you* know!—"

Both animals nodded gravely. *They* knew!

"Well, *then,*" went on the Badger, "we—that is, you and me and our friend the Mole here—we'll take Toad seriously in hand. We'll stand no nonsense whatever. We'll bring him back to reason, by force if need be. We'll *make* him be a sensible Toad. We'll—you're asleep, Rat!"

"Not me!" said the Rat, waking up with a jerk.

"He's been asleep two or three times since supper," said the Mole, laughing. He himself was feeling quite wakeful and even lively, though he didn't know why. The reason was, of course, that he being naturally an underground animal by birth and breeding, the situation of Badger's house exactly suited him and made him feel at home; while the Rat, who slept every night in a bedroom the windows of which opened on a breezy river, naturally felt the atmosphere still and oppressive.

"Well, it's time we were all in bed," said the Badger, getting up and fetching flat candlesticks. "Come along, you two, and I'll show you your quarters. And take your time tomorrow morning—breakfast at any hour you please!"

He conducted the two animals to a long room that seemed half bedchamber and half loft. The Badger's winter stores, which indeed were visible everywhere, took up half the room—piles of apples, turnips, and potatoes, baskets full of nuts, and jars of honey; but the two little white beds on the remainder of the floor looked soft and inviting, and the linen on them, though coarse, was clean and smelled beautifully of lavender; and the Mole and the Water Rat, shaking off their garments in some thirty seconds, tumbled in between the sheets in great joy and contentment.

In accordance with the kindly Badger's injunctions, the two tired animals came down to breakfast very late next morning, and found a bright fire burning in the kitchen, and two young hedgehogs sitting on a bench at the table, eating oatmeal porridge out of wooden bowls. The hedgehogs dropped their spoons, rose to their feet, and ducked their heads respectfully as the two entered.

"There, sit down, sit down," said the Rat pleasantly, "and go on with your porridge. Where have you youngsters come from? Lost your way in the snow, I suppose?"

"Yes, please, sir," said the elder of the two hedgehogs respectfully. "Me and little Billy here, we was trying to find our way to school—mother *would* have us go, was the weather ever so—and of course we lost ourselves, sir, and Billy he got frightened. And at last we happened up against Mr. Badger's back door, and made so bold as to knock, sir, for Mr. Badger he's a kindhearted gentleman, as everyone knows—"

"I understand," said the Rat, cutting himself some rashers from a side of bacon, while the Mole dropped some eggs into a saucepan. "And what's the weather like outside? You needn't 'sir' me quite so much," he added.

"Oh, terrible bad, sir, terrible deep the snow is," said the hedgehog. "No getting out for the likes of you gentlemen today."

"Where's Mr. Badger?" inquired the Mole, as he warmed the coffeepot before the fire.

"The master's gone into his study, sir," replied the hedgehog, "and he said as how he was going to be particular busy this morning, and on no account was he to be disturbed."

This explanation, of course, was thoroughly understood by everyone present. The fact is, as already set forth, when you live a life of intense activity for six months in the year, and of comparative or actual somnolence for the other six, during the latter period you cannot be continually pleading sleepiness when there are people about or things to be done. The excuse gets monotonous. The animals well knew that Badger, having eaten a hearty breakfast, had retired to his study and settled himself in an armchair with his legs up on another and a red cotton handkerchief over his face, and was being "busy" in the usual way at this time of the year.

The front doorbell clanged loudly, and the Rat,

who was very greasy with buttered toast, sent Billy, the smaller hedgehog, to see who it might be. There was a sound of much stamping in the hall, and presently Billy returned in front of the Otter, who threw himself on the Rat with an embrace and a shout of affectionate greeting.

"Get off!" spluttered the Rat, with his mouth full.

"Thought I should find you here all right," said the Otter cheerfully. "They were all in a great state of alarm along River Bank when I arrived this morning. Rat never been home all night—nor Mole either—something dreadful must have happened, they said; and the snow had covered up all your tracks, of course. But I knew that when people were in any fix they mostly went to Badger, or else Badger got to know of it somehow, so I came straight off here, through the Wild Wood and the snow! My! it was fine, coming through the snow as the red sun was rising and showing against the black tree trunks! As you went along in the stillness, every now and then masses of snow slid off the branches suddenly with a flop! making you jump and run for cover. Snow castles and snow caverns had sprung up out of nowhere in the night —and snow bridges, terraces, ramparts—I could have stayed and played with them for hours. Here and there great branches had been torn away by the sheer weight of the snow, and robins perched and hopped on them in their perky conceited way, just as if they had done it themselves. A ragged string of wild geese passed overhead, high on the gray sky, and a few rooks whirled over the trees, inspected, and flapped off homewards with a disgusted expression; but I met no sensible being to ask the news of. About halfway across I came on a rabbit sitting on a stump, cleaning his silly face with his paws. He was a pretty scared animal when I crept up behind him and placed a heavy forepaw on his shoulder. I had to cuff his head once or twice to get any sense out of it at all. At last I managed to extract from him that Mole had been seen in the Wild Wood last night by one of them. It was the talk of the burrows, he said, how Mole, Mr. Rat's particular friend, was in a bad fix; how he had lost his way, and 'They' were up and out hunting, and were chivvying him round and round. 'Then why didn't any of you do something?' I asked. 'You mayn't be blessed with brains, but there are hundreds and hundreds of you big stout fellows, as fat as butter, and your burrows running in all directions, and you could have taken him in and made him safe and comfortable, or tried to, at all events.' 'What, *us?*' he merely said, '*do* something? Us rabbits?' So I cuffed him again and left him. There was nothing else to be done. At any rate, I had learned something; and if I had had the luck to meet any of 'Them' I'd have learned something more—or *they* would."

"Weren't you at all—er—nervous?" asked the Mole, some of yesterday's terror coming back to him at the mention of the Wild Wood.

"Nervous?" The Otter showed a gleaming set of

strong white teeth as he laughed. "I'd give 'em nerves if any of them tried anything on me. Here, Mole, fry me some slices of ham, like the good little chap you are. I'm frightfully hungry, and I've got any amount to say to Ratty here. Haven't seen him for an age."

So the good-natured Mole, having cut some slices of ham, set the hedgehogs to fry it, and returned to his own breakfast, while the Otter and the Rat, their heads together, eagerly talked river-shop, which is long shop and talk that is endless, running on like the babbling river itself.

A plate of fried ham had just been cleared and sent back for more, when the Badger entered, yawning and rubbing his eyes, and greeted them all in his quiet, simple way, with kind inquiries for everyone. "It must be getting on for luncheon time," he remarked to the Otter. "Better stop and have it with us. You must be hungry, this cold morning."

"Rather!" replied the Otter, winking at the Mole. "The sight of these greedy young hedgehogs stuffing themselves with fried ham makes me feel positively famished."

The hedgehogs, who were just beginning to feel hungry again after their porridge, and after working so hard at their frying, looked timidly up at Mr. Badger, but were too shy to say anything.

"Here, you two youngsters be off home to your mother," said the Badger kindly. "I'll send someone with you to show you the way. You won't want any dinner today, I'll be bound."

He gave them sixpence apiece and a pat on the head, and they went off with much respectful swinging of caps and touching of forelocks.

Presently they all sat down to luncheon together. The Mole found himself placed next to Mr. Badger, and, as the other two were still deep in river-gossip from which nothing could divert them, he took the opportunity to tell Badger how comfortable and homelike it all felt to him. "Once well underground," he said, "you know exactly where you are. Nothing can happen to you, and nothing can get at you. You're entirely your own master, and you don't have to consult anybody or

mind what they say. Things go on all the same overhead, and you let 'em, and don't bother about 'em. When you want to, up you go, and there the things are, waiting for you."

The Badger simply beamed on him. "That's exactly what I say," he replied. "There's no security, or peace and tranquillity, except underground. And then, if your ideas get larger and you want to expand—why, a dig and a scrape, and there you are! If you feel your house is a bit too big, you stop up a hole or two, and there you are again! No builders, no tradesmen, no remarks passed on you by fellows looking over your wall, and, above all, no *weather*. Look at Rat, now. A couple of feet of floodwater, and he's got to move into hired lodgings; uncomfortable, inconveniently situated, and horribly expensive. Take Toad. I say nothing against Toad Hall; quite the best house in these parts, *as* a house. But supposing a fire breaks out —where's Toad? Supposing tiles are blown off, or walls sink or crack, or windows get broken— where's Toad? Supposing the rooms are drafty—I *hate* a draft myself—where's Toad? No, up and out of doors is good enough to roam about and get one's living in; but underground to come back to at last—that's my idea of *home!*"

The Mole assented heartily; and the Badger in consequence got very friendly with him. "When lunch is over," he said, "I'll take you all around this little place of mine. I can see you'll appreciate it. You understand what domestic architecture ought to be, you do."

After luncheon, accordingly, when the other two had settled themselves into the chimney corner and had started a heated argument on the subject of eels, the Badger lighted a lantern and bade the Mole follow him. Crossing the hall, they passed down one of the principal tunnels, and the wavering light of the lantern gave glimpses on either side of rooms both large and small, some mere cupboards, others nearly as broad and imposing as Toad's dining hall. A narrow passage at right angles led them into another corridor, and here the same thing was repeated. The Mole was stag-

gered at the size, the extent, the ramifications of it
all; at the length of the dim passages, the solid
vaultings of the crammed storechambers, the
masonry everywhere, the pillars, the arches, the
pavements. "How on earth, Badger," he said at last,
"did you ever find time and strength to do all this?
It's astonishing!"

"It *would* be astonishing indeed," said the Badger
simply, "if I *had* done it. But as a matter of fact I
did none of it—only cleaned out the passages and
chambers, as far as I had need of them. There's lots
more of it, all round about. I see you don't understand, and I must explain it to you. Well, very
long ago, on the spot where the Wild Wood waves
now, before ever it had planted itself and grown up
to what is now is, there was a city—a city of people, you know. Here, where we are standing, they
lived, and walked, and talked, and slept, and carried on their business. Here they stabled their
horses and feasted, from here they rode out to fight
or drove out to trade. They were a powerful people,
and rich, and great builders. They built to last, for
they thought their city would last forever."

"But what has become of them all?" asked the
Mole.

"Who can tell?" said the Badger. "People come
—they stay for a while, they flourish, they build—
and they go. It is their way. But we remain. There
were badgers here, I've been told, long before that
same city ever came to be. And now there are
badgers here again. We are an enduring lot, and

we may move out for a time, but we wait, and are patient, and back we come. And so it will ever be."

"Well, and when they went at last, those people?" said the Mole.

"When they went," continued the Badger, "the strong winds and persistent rains took the matter in hand, patiently, ceaselessly, year after year. Perhaps we badgers too, in our small way, helped a little—who knows? It was all down, down, down, gradually—ruin and leveling and disappearance. Then it was all up, up, up, gradually, as seeds grew to saplings, and saplings to forest trees, and bramble and fern came creeping in to help. Leaf mold rose and obliterated, streams in their winter freshets brought sand and soil to clog and to cover, and in course of time our home was ready for us again, and we moved in. Up above us, on the surface, the same thing happened. Animals arrived, liked the look of the place, took up their quarters, settled down, spread, and flourished. They didn't bother themselves about the past—they never do; they're too busy. The place was a bit humpy and hillocky, naturally, and full of holes; but that was rather an advantage. And they don't bother about the future, either—the future when perhaps the people will move in again—for a time—as may very well be. The Wild Wood is pretty well populated by now; with all the usual lot, good, bad, and indifferent— I name no names. It takes all sorts to make a world. But I fancy you know something about them yourself by this time."

"I do indeed," said the Mole, with a slight shiver.

"Well, well," said the Badger, patting him on the shoulder, "it was your first experience of them, you see. They're not so bad really; and we must all live and let live. But I'll pass the word round tomorrow, and I think you'll have no further trouble. Any friend of *mine* walks where he likes in this country, or I'll know the reason why!"

When they got back to the kitchen again, they found the Rat walking up and down, very restless. The underground atmosphere was oppressing him and getting on his nerves, and he seemed really to be afraid that the river would run away if he wasn't there to look after it. So he had his overcoat on, and his pistols thrust into his belt again. "Come along, Mole," he said anxiously, as soon as he caught sight of them. "We must get off while it's daylight. Don't want to spend another night in the Wild Wood again."

"It'll be all right, my fine fellow," said the Otter. "I'm coming along with you, and I know every path blindfold; and if there's a head that needs to be punched, you can confidently rely upon me to punch it."

"You really needn't fret, Ratty," added the Badger placidly. "My passages run farther than you think, and I've bolt-holes to the edge of the wood in several directions, though I don't care for everybody to know about them. When you really have to go, you shall leave by one of my short cuts. Meantime, make yourself easy, and sit down again."

The Rat was nevertheless still anxious to be off and attend to his river, so the Badger, taking up his lantern again, led the way along a damp and airless tunnel that wound and dipped, part vaulted, part hewn through solid rock, for a weary distance that seemed to be miles. At last daylight began to show itself confusedly through tangled growth over-hanging the mouth of the passage; and the Badger, bidding them a hasty good-bye, pushed them hur-riedly through the opening, made everything look as natural as possible again, with creepers, brushwood, and dead leaves, and retreated.

They found themselves standing on the very edge of the Wild Wood. Rocks and brambles and tree roots behind them, confusedly heaped and tangled; in front, a great space of quiet fields, hemmed by lines of hedges black on the snow, and, far ahead, a glint of the familiar old river, while the wintry sun hung red and low on the horizon. The Otter, as knowing all the paths, took charge of the party, and they trailed out on a beeline for a distant stile. Pausing there a moment and look-ing back, they saw the whole mass of the Wild Wood, dense, menacing, compact, grimly set in vast white surroundings; simultaneously they turned and made swiftly for home, for firelight and the familiar things it played on, for the voice, sounding cheerily outside their window, of the river that they knew and trusted in all its moods, that never made them afraid with any amazement.

As he hurried along, eagerly anticipating the

moment when he would be at home again among the things he knew and liked, the Mole saw clearly that he was an animal of tilled field and hedgerow, linked to the plowed furrow, the frequented pasture, the lane of evening lingerings, the cultivated garden plot. For others the asperities, the stubborn endurance, or the clash of actual conflict, that went with Nature in the rough; he must be wise, must keep to the pleasant places in which his lines were laid and which held adventure enough, in their way, to last for a lifetime.

5

Dulce Domum

THE SHEEP ran huddling together against the hurdles, blowing out thin nostrils and stamping with delicate forefeet, their heads thrown back and a light steam rising from the crowded sheep pen into the frosty air, as the two animals hastened by in high spirits, with much chatter and laughter. They were returning across country after a long day's outing with Otter, hunting and exploring on the wide uplands where certain streams tributary to their own river had their first small beginnings; and the shades of the short winter day were closing in on them, and they had still some distance to go. Plodding at random across the plow, they had heard the sheep and had made for them; and now, leading from the sheep pen, they found a beaten track that made walking a lighter business, and responded, moreover, to that small inquiring something which all animals carry inside them, saying unmistakably, "Yes, quite right; *this* leads home!"

"It looks as if we were coming to a village," said the Mole somewhat dubiously, slackening his pace, as the track, that had in time become a path and then had developed into a lane, now handed them over to the charge of a well-metaled road. The animals did not hold with villages, and their own highways, thickly frequented as they were, took an independent course, regardless of church, post office, or public house.

"Oh, never mind," said the Rat. "At this season of the year they're all safe indoors by this time, sitting round the fire; men, women, and children, dogs and cats and all. We shall slip through all right, without any bother or unpleasantness, and we can have a look at them through their windows if you like, and see what they're doing."

The rapid nightfall of mid-December had quite beset the little village as they approached it on soft feet over a thin fall of powdery snow. Little was visible but squares of a dusky orange-red on either side of the street, where the firelight or lamplight of each cottage overflowed through the casements into the dark world without. Most of the low latticed windows were innocent of blinds, and to the lookers-in from outside, the inmates, gathered round the tea table, absorbed in handiwork, or talking with laughter and gesture, had each that happy

grace which is the last thing the skilled actor shall
capture—the natural grace which goes with perfect
unconsciousness of observation. Moving at will
from one theater to another, the two spectators, so
far from home themselves, had something of wist-
fulness in their eyes as they watched a cat being
stroked, a sleepy child picked up and huddled off
to bed, or a tired man stretch and knock out his
pipe on the end of a smoldering log.

But it was from one little window, with its blind
drawn down, a mere blank transparency on the
night, that the sense of home and the little curtained
world within walls—the larger stressful world of
outside Nature shut out and forgotten—most pul-
sated. Close against the white blind hung a birdcage, clearly silhouetted, every wire, perch, and
appurtenance distinct and recognizable, even to yesterday's dull-edged lump of sugar. On the middle
perch the fluffy occupant, head tucked well into
feathers, seemed so near to them as to be easily
stroked, had they tried; even the delicate tips of
his plumped-out plumage penciled plainly on the
illuminated screen. As they looked, the sleepy little
fellow stirred uneasily, woke, shook himself, and
raised his head. They could see the gape of his
tiny beak as he yawned in a bored sort of way,
looked round, and then settled his head into his
back again, while the ruffled feathers gradually subsided into perfect stillness. Then a gust of bitter
wind took them in the back of the neck, a small
sting of frozen sleet on the skin woke them as from

a dream, and they knew their toes to be cold and
their legs tired, and their own home distant a weary
way.

Once beyond the village, where the cottages
ceased abruptly, on either side of the road they
could smell through the darkness the friendly fields
again; and they braced themselves for the last long
stretch, the home stretch, the stretch that we know
is bound to end, some time, in the rattle of the
door latch, the sudden firelight, and the sight of
familiar things greeting us as long-absent travelers
from far oversea. They plodded along steadily and
silently, each of them thinking his own thoughts.
The Mole's ran a good deal on supper, as it was
pitch-dark, and it was all a strange country to him
as far as he knew, and he was following obediently
in the wake of the Rat, leaving the guidance entirely
to him. As for the Rat, he was walking a little way
ahead, as his habit was, his shoulders humped, his
eyes fixed on the straight gray road in front of him;
so he did not notice poor Mole when suddenly
the summons reached him, and took him like an
electric shock.

We others, who have long lost the more subtle of
the physical senses, have not even proper terms to
express an animal's intercommunications with his
surroundings, living or otherwise, and have only the
word "smell," for instance, to include the whole
range of delicate thrills which murmur in the nose
of the animal night and day, summoning, warning,
inciting, repelling. It was one of these mysterious

fairy calls from out the void that suddenly reached
Mole in the darkness, making him tingle through
and through with its very familiar appeal, even
while as yet he could not clearly remember what it
was. He stopped dead in his tracks, his nose searching hither and thither in its efforts to recapture the
fine filament, the telegraphic current, that had so
strongly moved him. A moment, and he had
caught it again; and with it this time came recollection in fullest flood.

Home! That was what they meant, those caress-
ing appeals, those soft touches wafted through the
air, those invisible little hands pulling and tugging,
all one way! Why, it must be quite close by him at
that moment, his old home that he had hurriedly
forsaken and never sought again, that day when he
first found the river! And now it was sending out
its scouts and its messengers to capture him and
bring him in. Since his escape on that bright morning he had hardly given it a thought, so absorbed
had he been in his new life, in all its pleasures, its
surprises, its fresh and captivating experiences.
Now, with a rush of old memories, how clearly it
stood up before him, in the darkness! Shabby indeed, and small and poorly furnished, and yet his,
the home he had made for himself, the home he had
been so happy to get back to after his day's work.
And the home had been happy with him, too, evidently, and was missing him, and wanted him back,
and was telling him so, through his nose, sorrowfully, reproachfully, but with no bitterness or anger;

only with plaintive reminder that it was there, and wanted him.

The call was clear, the summons was plain. He must obey it instantly, and go. "Ratty!" he called, full of joyful excitement, "hold on! Come back! I want you, quick!"

"Oh, *come* along, Mole, do!" replied the Rat cheerfully, still plodding along.

"*Please* stop, Ratty!" pleaded the poor Mole, in anguish of heart. "You don't understand! It's my home, my old home! I've just come across the smell of it, and it's close by here, really quite close. And I *must* go to it, I must, I must! Oh, come back, Ratty! Please, please come back!"

The Rat was by this time very far ahead, too far to catch the sharp note of painful appeal in his voice. And he was much taken up with the weather, for he too could smell something—something suspiciously like approaching snow.

"Mole, we mustn't stop now, really!" he called back. "We'll come for it tomorrow, whatever it is you've found. But I daren't stop now—it's late, and the snow's coming on again, and I'm not sure of the way! And I want your nose, Mole, so come on quick, there's a good fellow!" And the Rat pressed forward on his way without waiting for an answer.

Poor Mole stood alone in the road, his heart torn asunder, and a big sob gathering, gathering, somewhere low down inside him, to leap up to the surface presently, he knew, in passionate escape. But even under such a test as this his loyalty to his

friend stood firm. Never for a moment did he dream
of abandoning him. Meanwhile, the wafts from his
old home pleaded, whispered, conjured, and finally
claimed him imperiously. He dared not tarry longer
within their magic circle. With a wrench that tore
his very heartstrings he set his face down the road
and followed submissively in the track of the Rat,
while faint, thin little smells, still dogging his retreating nose, reproached him for his new friendship
and his callous forgetfulness.

With an effort he caught up the unsuspecting
Rat, who began chattering cheerfully about what
they would do when they got back, and how jolly
a fire of logs in the parlor would be, and what a
supper he meant to eat; never noticing his companion's silence and distressful state of mind. At
last, however, when they had gone some considerable way farther, and were passing some tree stumps
at the edge of a copse that bordered the road, he
stopped and said kindly, "Look here, Mole, old
chap, you seem dead tired. No talk left in you,
and your feet dragging like lead. We'll sit down
here for a minute and rest. The snow has held off
so far, and the best part of our journey is over."

The Mole subsided forlornly on a tree stump and
tried to control himself, for he felt it surely coming.
The sob he had fought with so long refused to be
beaten. Up and up, it forced its way to the air, and
then another, and another, and others thick and
fast; till poor Mole at last gave up the struggle, and
cried freely and helplessly and openly, now that he

knew it was all over and he had lost what he could hardly be said to have found.

The Rat, astonished and dismayed at the violence of Mole's paroxysm of grief, did not dare to speak for a while. At last he said, very quietly and sympathetically, "What is it, old fellow? Whatever can be the matter? Tell us your trouble, and let me see what I can do."

Poor Mole found it difficult to get any words out between the upheavals of his chest that followed one upon another so quickly and held back speech and choked it as it came. "I know it's a—shabby, dingy little place," he sobbed forth at last, brokenly: "not like—your cozy quarters—or Toad's beautiful hall—or Badger's great house—but it was my own little home—and I was fond of it—and I went away and forgot all about it—and then I smelled it suddenly—on the road, when I called and you wouldn't listen, Rat—and everything came back to me with a rush—and I *wanted* it!—Oh dear! Oh dear!—and when you *wouldn't* turn back, Ratty—and I had to leave it, though I was smelling it all the time—I thought my heart would break. We might have just gone and had one look at it, Ratty—only one look—it was close by—but you wouldn't turn back, Ratty, you wouldn't turn back! Oh dear! Oh dear!"

Recollection brought fresh waves of sorrow, and sobs again took full charge of him, preventing further speech.

The Rat stared straight in front of him, saying

nothing, only patting Mole gently on the shoulder. After a time he muttered gloomily, "I see it all now! What a *pig* I have been! A pig—that's me! Just a pig—a plain pig!"

He waited till Mole's sobs became gradually less stormy and more rhythmical; he waited till at last sniffs were frequent and sobs only intermittent. Then he rose from his seat, and, remarking carelessly, "Well, now we'd really better be getting on, old chap!" set off up the road again, over the toilsome way they had come.

"Wherever are you (hic) going to (hic), Ratty?" cried the tearful Mole, looking up in alarm.

"We're going to find that home of yours, old fellow," replied the Rat pleasantly, "so you had better come along, for it will take some finding, and we shall want your nose."

"Oh, come back, Ratty, do!" cried the Mole, getting up and hurrying after him. "It's no good, I tell you! It's too late, and too dark, and the place is too far off, and the snow's coming! And—and I never meant to let you know I was feeling that way about it—it was all an accident and a mistake! And think of River Bank, and your supper!"

"Hang River Bank, and supper too!" said the Rat heartily. "I tell you, I'm going to find this place now, if I stay out all night. So cheer up, old chap, and take my arm, and we'll very soon be back there again."

Still snuffling, pleading, and reluctant, Mole suffered himself to be dragged back along the road by his imperious companion, who by a flow of cheerful talk and anecdote endeavored to beguile his spirits back and make the weary way seem shorter. When at last it seemed to the Rat that they must be nearing that part of the road where the Mole had been "held up," he said, "Now, no more talking. Business! Use your nose, and give your mind to it."

They moved on in silence for some little way, when suddenly the Rat was conscious, through his arm that was linked in Mole's, of a faint sort of electric thrill that was passing down the animal's body. Instantly he disengaged himself, fell back a pace, and waited, all attention,

The signals were coming through!

Mole stood a moment rigid, while his uplifted nose, quivering slightly, felt the air.

Then a short, quick run forward—a fault—a check—a try back; and then a slow, steady, confident advance.

The Rat, much excited, kept close to his heels as the Mole, with something of the air of a sleepwalker, crossed a dry ditch, scrambled through a hedge, and nosed his way over a field open and trackless and bare in the faint starlight.

Suddenly, without giving warning, he dived; but the Rat was on the alert, and promptly followed him down the tunnel to which his unerring nose had faithfully led him.

It was close and airless, and the earthy smell was strong, and it seemed a long time to Rat ere the passage ended and he could stand erect and stretch and shake himself. The Mole struck a match, and by its light the Rat saw that they were standing in an open space neatly swept and sanded underfoot, and directly facing them was Mole's little front door, with "Mole End" painted, in Gothic lettering, over the bellpull at the side.

Mole reached down a lantern from a nail on the wall and lit it, and the Rat, looking round him, saw that they were in a sort of forecourt. A garden seat stood on one side of the door, and on the other, a roller; for the Mole, who was a tidy animal when at home, could not stand having his ground kicked up by other animals into little runs that ended in earth heaps. On the walls hung wire baskets with ferns in them, alternating with brackets carrying plaster statuary—Garibaldi, and the infant Samuel, and Queen Victoria, and other heroes of modern Italy. Down one side of the forecourt ran a skittle alley, with benches along it and little wooden tables marked with rings that hinted at beer mugs. In the middle was a small round pond containing goldfish, and surrounded by a cockleshell border. Out of the center of the pond rose a fanciful erection clothed in more cockleshells and topped by a large silvered glass ball that reflected everything all wrong and had a very pleasing effect.

Mole's face beamed at the sight of all these objects so dear to him, and he hurried Rat through the door, lit a lamp in the hall, and took one glance around his old home. He saw the dust lying thick on everything, saw the cheerless, deserted look of the long-neglected house, and its narrow, meager dimensions, its worn and shabby contents—and collapsed again on a hall chair, his nose in his paws. "Oh, Ratty!" he cried dismally, "why ever did I do it? Why did I bring you to this poor, cold little place, on a night like this, when you might have been at River Bank by this time, toasting your toes before a blazing fire, with all your own nice things about you!"

The Rat paid no heed to his doleful self-re-proaches. He was running here and there, opening doors, inspecting rooms and cupboards, and light-ing lamps and candles and sticking them up every-where. "What a capital little house this is!" he called out cheerily. "So compact! So well planned! Everything here and everything in its place! We'll make a jolly night of it. The first thing we want is a good fire; I'll see to that—I always know where to find things. So this is the parlor? Splendid! Your own idea, those little sleeping bunks in the wall? Capital! Now, I'll fetch the wood and the coals, and you get a duster, Mole—you'll find one in the drawer of the kitchen table—and try and smarten things up a bit. Bustle about, old chap!"

Encouraged by his inspiriting companion, the Mole roused himself and dusted and polished with energy and heartiness, while the Rat, running to and fro with armfuls of fuel, soon had a cheerful blaze roaring up the chimney. He hailed the Mole to come and warm himself; but Mole promptly had another fit of the blues, dropping down on a couch in dark despair and burying his face in his duster.

"Rat," he moaned, "how about your supper, you poor, cold, hungry, weary animal? I've nothing to give you—nothing—not a crumb!"

"What a fellow you are for giving in!" said the Rat reproachfully. "Why, only just now I saw a sardine opener on the kitchen dresser, quite distinctly; and everybody knows that means there are sardines about somewhere in the neighborhood. Rouse yourself! Pull yourself together, and come with me and forage."

They went and foraged accordingly, hunting through every cupboard and turning out every drawer. The result was not so very depressing after all, though of course it might have been better; a tin of sardines—a box of captain's biscuits, nearly full —and a German sausage encased in silver paper.

"There's a banquet for you!" observed the Rat, as he arranged the table. "I know some animals who would give their ears to be sitting down to supper with us tonight!"

"No bread!" groaned the Mole dolorously; "no butter, no—"

"No *pâté de foie gras,* no champagne!" continued the Rat, grinning. "And that reminds me—what's that little door at the end of the passage? Your cellar, of course! Every luxury in this house! Just you wait a minute."

He made for the cellar door, and presently reappeared, somewhat dusty, with a bottle of beer in each paw and another under each arm. "Self-indulgent beggar you seem to be, Mole," he observed. "Deny yourself nothing. This is really the jolliest little place I ever was in. Now, wherever did you pick up those prints? Make the place look so homelike, they do. No wonder you're so fond of it, Mole. Tell us all about it, and how you came to make it what it is."

Then, while the Rat busied himself fetching plates, and knives and forks, and mustard which he mixed in an eggcup, the Mole, his bosom still heaving with the stress of his recent emotion, related—somewhat shyly at first, but with more freedom as he warmed to his subject—how this was planned, and how that was thought out, and how this was got through a windfall from his aunt, and that was a wonderful find and a bargain, and this other thing was bought out of laborious savings and a certain amount of "going without." His spirits finally quite restored, he must needs go and caress his possessions, and take a lamp and show off their points to his visitor and expatiate on them, quite forgetful of the supper they both so much needed; Rat, who was desperately hungry but strove to conceal it, nodding seriously, examining with a puckered brow, and saying, "Wonderful," and "Most remarkable," at intervals, when the chance for an observation was given him.

At last the Rat succeeded in decoying him to the table, and had just got seriously to work with the sardine opener when sounds were heard from the

forecourt without—sounds like the scuffling of small
feet in the gravel and a confused murmur of tiny
voices, while broken sentences reached them—
"Now, all in a line—hold the lantern up a bit,
Tommy—clear your throats first—no coughing
after I say one, two, three—Where's young Bill?—
Here, come on, do, we're all a-waiting—"

"What's up?" inquired the Rat, pausing in his
labors.

"I think it must be the field mice," replied the
Mole, with a touch of pride in his manner. "They
go round carol-singing regularly at this time of the
year. They're quite an institution in these parts.
And they never pass me over—they come to Mole

End last of all; and I used to give them hot drinks, and supper too sometimes, when I could afford it. It will be like old times to hear them again."

"Let's have a look at them!" cried the Rat, jumping up and running to the door.

It was a pretty sight, and a seasonable one, that met their eyes when they flung the door open. In the forecourt, lit by the dim rays of a horn lantern, some eight or ten little field mice stood in a semicircle, red worsted comforters round their throats, their forepaws thrust deep into their pockets, their feet jiggling for warmth. With bright beady eyes they glanced shyly at each other sniggering a little, sniffing and applying coat sleeves a good deal. As the door opened, one of the elder ones that carried the lantern was just saying, "Now then, one, two, three!" and forthwith their shrill little voices uprose on the air, singing one of the old-time carols that their forefathers composed in fields that were fallow and held by frost, or when snowbound in chimney corners, and handed down to be sung in the miry streets to lamplit windows at Yuletime.

CAROL

Villagers all, this frosty tide,
Let your door swing open wide,
Though wind may follow, and snow beside,
Yet draw us in by your fire to bide;
    Joy shall be yours in the morning!

Here we stand in the cold and the sleet,
Blowing fingers and stamping feet,
Come from far away you to greet—
You by the fire and we in the street—
  Bidding you joy in the morning!

For ere one half of the night was gone,
Sudden a star has led us on,
Raining bliss and benison—
Bliss tomorrow and more anon,
  Joy for every morning!

Goodman Joseph toiled through the snow—
Saw the star o'er a stable low;
Mary she might no farther go—
Welcome thatch, and litter below!
  Joy was hers in the morning!

And then they heard the angels tell
"Who were the first to cry Nowell?
Animals all, as it befell,
In the stable where they did dwell!
  Joy shall be theirs in the morning!"

The voices ceased, the singers, bashful but smiling, exchanged sidelong glances, and silence succeeded—but for a moment only. Then, from up above and far away, down the tunnel they had so lately traveled was born to their ears in a faint musical hum the sound of distant bells ringing a joyful and clangorous peal.

"Very well sung, boys!" cried the Rat heartily. "And now come along in, all of you, and warm yourselves by the fire, and have something hot!"

"Yes, come along, field mice," cried the Mole eagerly. "This is quite like old times! Shut the door after you. Pull up that settle to the fire. Now, you just wait a minute, while we— Oh, Ratty!" he cried in despair, plumping down on a seat, with tears impending. "Whatever are we doing? We've nothing to give them!"

"You leave all that to me," said the masterful Rat. "Here, you with the lantern! Come over this way. I want to talk to you. Now, tell me, are there any shops open at this hour of the night?"

"Why, certainly, sir," replied the field mouse respectfully. "At this time of the year our shops keep open to all sorts of hours."

"Then look here!" said the Rat. "You go off at once, you and your lantern, and you get me—"

Here much muttered conversation ensued, and the Mole only heard bits of it, such as—"Fresh, mind! —no, a pound of that will do—see you get Buggins's, for I won't have any other—no, only the best—if you can't get it there, try somewhere else— yes, of course, homemade, no tinned stuff—well then, do the best you can!" Finally, there was a chink of coin passing from paw to paw, the field mouse was provided with an ample basket for his purchases, and off he hurried, he and his lantern.

The rest of the field mice, perched in a row on the settle, their small legs swinging, gave themselves up to enjoyment of the fire, and toasted their chilblains till they tingled; while the Mole, failing to draw them into easy conversation, plunged into family history and made each of them recite the names of his numerous brothers, who were too young, it appeared, to be allowed to go out a-caroling this year, but looked forward very shortly to winning the parental consent.

The Rat, meanwhile, was busy examining the label on one of the beer bottles. "I perceive this to be Old Burton," he remarked approvingly. "*Sensible* Mole! The very thing! Now we shall be able to mull some ale! Get the things ready, Mole, while I draw the corks."

It did not take long to prepare the brew and thrust the tin heater well into the red heart of the fire; and soon every field mouse was sipping and coughing and choking (for a little mulled ale goes a long way) and wiping his eyes and laughing and forgetting he had ever been cold in all his life.

"They act plays too, these fellows," the Mole explained to the Rat. "Make them up all by themselves, and act them afterwards. And very well they do it, too! They gave us a capital one last year, about a field mouse who was captured at sea by a Barbary corsair, and made to row in a galley; and when he escaped and got home again, his ladylove had gone into a convent. Here, *you!* You were in it, I remember. Get up and recite a bit."

The field mouse addressed got up on his legs, giggled shyly, looked round the room, and remained absolutely tongue-tied. His comrades cheered him on, Mole coaxed and encouraged him, and the Rat went so far as to take him by the shoulders and shake him; but nothing could overcome his stage fright. They were all busily engaged on him like water men applying the Royal Humane Society's regulations to a case of long submersion, when the latch clicked, the door opened, and the field mouse with the lantern reappeared, staggering under the weight of his basket.

There was no more talk of play-acting once the very real and solid contents of the basket had been tumbled out on the table. Under the generalship of Rat, everybody was set to do something or to fetch something. In a very few minutes supper was ready, and Mole, as he took the head of the table in a sort of dream, saw a lately barren board set thick with savory comforts; saw his little friends' faces brighten and beam as they fell to without delay; and then let himself loose—for he was famished indeed—on the provender so magically provided, thinking what a happy homecoming this had turned out, after all. As they ate, they talked of old times, and the field mice gave him the local gossip up to date, and answered as well as they could the hundred questions he had to ask them. The Rat said little or nothing, only taking care that each guest had what he wanted, and plenty of it, and that Mole had no trouble or anxiety about anything.

They clattered off at last, very grateful and showering wishes of the season, with their jacket pockets stuffed with remembrances for the small brothers and sisters at home. When the door had closed on the last of them and the chink of the lanterns had died away, Mole and Rat kicked the fire up, drew their chairs in, brewed themselves a last nightcap of mulled ale, and discussed the events of the long day. At last the Rat, with a tremendous yawn, said, "Mole, old chap, I'm ready to drop. Sleepy is simply not the word. That your own bunk over on that side? Very well, then, I'll take this. What a ripping little house this is! Everything so handy!"

He clambered into his bunk and rolled himself well up in the blankets, and slumber gathered him forthwith, as a swath of barley is folded into the arms of the reaping machine.

The weary Mole also was glad to turn in without delay, and soon had his head on his pillow, in great joy and contentment. But ere he closed his eyes he let them wander round his old room, mellow in the glow of the firelight that played or rested on familiar and friendly things which had long been unconsciously a part of him, and now smilingly received him back, without rancor. He was now in just the frame of mind that the tactful Rat had quietly worked to bring about in him. He saw clearly how plain and simple—how narrow, even —it all was; but clearly, too, how much it all meant to him, and the special value of some such anchorage in one's existence. He did not at all want to abandon the new life and its splendid spaces, to turn his back on sun and air and all they offered him and creep home and stay there; the upper world was all too strong, it called to him still, even down there, and he knew he must return to the larger stage. But it was good to think he had this to come back to, this place which was all his own, these things which were so glad to see him again and could always be counted upon for the same simple welcome.

6

Mr. Toad

IT WAS a bright morning in the early part of summer; the river had resumed its wonted banks and its accustomed pace, and a hot sun seemed to be pulling everything green and bushy and spiky up out of the earth towards him, as if by strings. The Mole and the Water Rat had been up since dawn very busy on matters connected with boats and the opening of the boating season; painting and varnishing, mending paddles, repairing cushions, hunting for missing boathooks, and so on; and were finishing breakfast in their little parlor and eagerly discussing their plans for the day, when a heavy knock sounded at the door.

"Bother!" said the Rat, all over egg. "See who it is, Mole, like a good chap, since you've finished."

The Mole went to attend the summons, and the Rat heard him utter a cry of surprise. Then he flung the parlor door open, and announced with much importance, "Mr. Badger!"

This was a wonderful thing, indeed, that the Badger should pay a formal call on them, or indeed on anybody. He generally had to be caught, if you wanted him badly, as he slipped quietly along a hedgerow of an early morning or a late evening, or else hunted up in his own house in the middle of the wood, which was a serious undertaking.

The Badger strode heavily into the room, and stood looking at the two animals with an expression full of seriousness. The Rat let his egg spoon fall on the tablecloth, and sat openmouthed.

"The hour has come!" said the Badger at last with great solemnity.

"What hour?" asked the Rat uneasily, glancing at the clock on the mantelpiece.

"*Whose* hour, you should rather say," replied the Badger. "Why, Toad's hour! The hour of Toad! I said I would take him in hand as soon as the winter was well over, and I'm going to take him in hand today!"

"Toad's hour, of course!" cried the Mole delightedly. "Hooray! I remember now! *We'll* teach him to be a sensible Toad!"

"This very morning," continued the Badger, taking an armchair, "as I learned last night from a trustworthy source, another new and exceptionally powerful motorcar will arrive at Toad Hall on approval or return. At this very moment, perhaps, Toad is busy arraying himself in those singularly hideous habiliments so dear to him, which transform him from a (comparatively) good-looking Toad into an Object which throws any decent-minded animal that comes across it into a violent fit. We must be up and doing, ere it is too late. You two animals will accompany me instantly to Toad Hall, and the work of rescue shall be accomplished."

"Right you are!" cried the Rat, starting up. "We'll rescue the poor unhappy animal! We'll convert him! He'll be the most converted Toad that ever was before we've done with him!"

They set off up the road on their mission of mercy, Badger leading the way. Animals when in company walk in a proper and sensible manner, in single file, instead of sprawling all across the road and being of no use or support to each other in case of sudden trouble or danger.

They reached the carriage drive of Toad Hall to find, as the Badger had anticipated, a shiny new motorcar, of great size, painted a bright red (Toad's favorite color), standing in front of the house. As they neared the door it was flung open, and Mr. Toad, arrayed in goggles, cap, gaiters, and enormous overcoat, came swaggering down the steps, drawing on his gauntleted gloves.

"Hullo! come on, you fellows!" he cried cheerfully on catching sight of them. "You're just in time to come with me for a jolly—to come for a jolly—for a—er—jolly—"

His hearty accents faltered and fell away as he noticed the stern unbending look on the countenances of his silent friends, and his invitation remained unfinished.

The Badger strode up the steps. "Take him inside," he said sternly to his companions. Then, as Toad was hustled through the door struggling and protesting, he turned to the chauffeur in charge of the new motorcar.

"I'm afraid you won't be wanted today," he said. "Mr. Toad has changed his mind. He will not require the car. Please understand that this is final. You needn't wait." Then he followed the others inside and shut the door.

"Now, then!" he said to the Toad, when the four of them stood together in the hall, "first of all, take those ridiculous things off!"

"Shan't!" replied Toad, with great spirit. "What is the meaning of this gross outrage? I demand an instant explanation."

"Take them off him, then, you two," ordered the Badger briefly.

They had to lay Toad out on the floor, kicking and calling all sort of names, before they could get to work properly. Then the Rat sat on him, and the Mole got his motor clothes off him bit by bit, and they stood him up on his legs again. A good deal of his blustering spirit seemed to have evaporated with the removal of his fine panoply. Now that he was merely Toad, and no longer the Terror of the Highway, he giggled feebly and look-

ed from one to the other appealingly, seeming quite
to understand the situation.

"You knew it must come to this, sooner or later,
Toad," the Badger explained severely. "You've dis-
regarded all the warnings we've given you, you've
gone on squandering the money your father left
you, and you're getting us animals a bad name in
the district by your furious driving and your
smashes and your rows with the police. Independ-
ence is all very well, but we animals never allow our
friends to make fools of themselves beyond a certain limit; and that limit you've reached. Now,
you're a good fellow in many respects, and I don't
want to be too hard on you. I'll make one more
effort to bring you to reason. You will come with
me into the smoking room, and there you will hear
some facts about yourself; and we'll see whether
you come out of that room the same Toad that you
went in."

He took Toad firmly by the arm, led him into the
smoking room, and closed the door behind them.

"*That's* no good!" said the Rat contemptuously.
"*Talking* to Toad'll never cure him. He'll *say* anything."

They made themselves comfortable in armchairs
and waited patiently. Through the closed doors they
could just hear the long continuous drone of the
Badger's voice, rising and falling in waves of ora-
tory; and presently they noticed that the sermon began to be punctuated at intervals by long-drawn
sobs, evidently proceeding from the bosom of Toad,

who was a soft-hearted and affectionate fellow, very easily converted—for the time being—to any point of view.

After some three-quarters of an hour the door opened, and the Badger reappeared, solemnly leading by the paw a very limp and dejected Toad. His skin hung baggily about him; his legs wobbled, and his cheeks were furrowed by the tears so plentifully called forth by the Badger's moving discourse.

"Sit down there, Toad," said the Badger kindly, pointing to a chair. "My friends," he went on, "I am pleased to inform you that Toad has at last seen the error of his ways. He is truly sorry for his misguided conduct in the past, and he has undertaken to give up motorcars entirely and forever. I have his solemn promise to that effect."

"That is very good news," said the Mole gravely.

"Very good news indeed," observed the Rat dubiously, "if only—*if* only—"

He was looking very hard at Toad as he said this, and could not help thinking he perceived something vaguely resembling a twinkle in that animal's still sorrowful eye.

"There's only one thing more to be done," continued the gratified Badger. "Toad, I want you solemnly to repeat, before your friends here, what you fully admitted to me in the smoking room just now. First, you are sorry for what you've done, and you see the folly of it all?"

There was a long, long pause. Toad looked desperately this way and that, while the other animals waited in grave silence. At last he spoke.

"No!" he said a little sullenly, but stoutly, "I'm *not* sorry. And it wasn't folly at all! It was simply glorious!"

"What?" cried the Badger, greatly scandalized. "You backsliding animal, didn't you tell me just now, in there—"

"Oh, yes, yes, in *there*," said Toad impatiently. "I'd have said anything in *there*. You're so eloquent, dear Badger, and so moving, and so convincing, and put all your points so frightfully well—you can do what you like with me in *there,* and you know it. But I've been searching my mind since, and going over things in it, and I find that I'm not a bit sorry or repentant really, so it's no earthly good saying I am; now, is it?"

"Then you don't promise," said the Badger, "never to touch a motorcar again?"

"Certainly not!" replied Toad emphatically. "On the contrary, I faithfully promise that the very first motorcar I see, poop-poop! Off I go in it!"

"Told you so, didn't I?" observed the Rat to the Mole.

"Very well, then," said the Badger firmly, rising to his feet. "Since you won't yield to persuasion, we'll try what force can do. I feared it would come to this all along. You've often asked us three to come and stay with you, Toad, in this handsome house of yours; well, now we're going to. When we've converted you to a proper point of view we may quit, but not before. Take him upstairs, you two, and lock him in his bedroom, while we arrange matters between ourselves."

"It's for your own good, Toady, you know," said the Rat kindly, as Toad, kicking and struggling, was hauled up the stairs by his two faithful friends. "Think what fun we shall have together, just as we used to, when you've quite got over this—this painful attack of yours!"

"We'll take great care of everything for you till you're well, Toad," said the Mole; "and we'll see your money isn't wasted, as it has been."

"No more of those regrettable incidents with the police, Toad," said the Rat, as they thrust him into his bedroom.

"And no more weeks in hospital, being ordered about by female nurses, Toad," added the Mole, turning the key on him.

They descended the stair, Toad shouting abuse at them through the keyhole, and the three friends then met in conference on the situation.

"It's going to be a tedious business," said the Badger, sighing. "I've never seen Toad so determined. However, we will see it out. He must never be left an instant unguarded. We shall have to take turns to be with him, till the poison has worked itself out of his system."

They arranged watches accordingly. Each animal took it in turns to sleep in Toad's room at night, and they divided the day up between them. At first Toad was undoubtedly very trying to his careful guardians. When his violent paroxysms possessed him he would arrange his bedroom chairs in rude resemblance of a motorcar and would crouch on the foremost of them, bent forward and staring fixedly ahead, making uncouth and ghastly noises, till the climax was reached, when, turning a complete somersault, he would lie prostrate amidst the ruins of the chairs, apparently completely satisfied for the moment. As time passed, however, these painful seizures grew gradually less frequent, and his friends strove to divert his mind into fresh channels. But his interest in other matters did not seem to revive, and he grew apparently languid and depressed.

One fine morning the Rat, whose turn it was to go on duty, went upstairs to relieve Badger, whom he found fidgeting to be off and stretch his legs in a long ramble round his wood and down his earths and burrows. "Toad's still in bed," he told the Rat, outside the door. "Can't get much out of him, except, 'Oh, leave him alone, he wants nothing, perhaps he'll be better presently, it may pass off in time, don't be unduly anxious,' and so on. Now, you look out, Rat! When Toad's quiet and submissive, and playing at being the hero of a Sunday school prize, then he's at his artfullest. There's sure to be something up. I know him. Well, now I must be off."

"How are you today, old chap?" inquired the Rat cheerfully, as he approached Toad's bedside.

He had to wait some minutes for an answer. At last a feeble voice replied, "Thank you so much, dear Ratty! So good of you to inquire! But first tell me how you are yourself, and the excellent Mole?"

"Oh, *we're* all right," replied the Rat. "Mole," he added incautiously, "is going out for a run round with Badger. They be out till luncheontime, so you and I will spend a pleasant morning together, and I'll do my best to amuse you. Now jump up, there's a good fellow, and don't lie moping there on a fine morning like this!"

"Dear, kind Rat," murmured Toad, "how little you realize my condition, and how ˜ery far I am from 'jumping up' now—if ever! But do not trouble about me. I hate being a burden to my friends, and I do not expect to be one much longer. Indeed, I almost hope not."

"Well, I hope not, too," said the Rat heartily. "You've been a fine bother to us all this time, and I'm glad to hear it's going to stop. And in weather like this, and the boating season just beginning! It's too bad of you, Toad! It isn't the trouble we mind, but you're making us miss such an awful lot."

"I'm afraid it *is* the trouble you mind, though," replied the Toad languidly. "I can quite understand it. It's natural enough. You're tired of bothering about me. I mustn't ask you to do anything further. I'm a nuisance, I know."

"You are, indeed," said the Rat. "But I tell you, I'd take any trouble on earth for you, if only you'd be a sensible animal."

"If I thought that, Ratty," murmured Toad, more

feebly than ever, "then I would beg you—for the last time, probably—to step round to the village as quickly as possible—even now it may be too late —and fetch the doctor. But don't you bother. It's only a trouble, and perhaps we may as well let things take their course."

"Why, what do you want a doctor for?" inquired the Rat, coming closer and examining him. He certainly lay very still and flat, and his voice was weaker and his manner much changed.

"Surely you have noticed of late—" murmured Toad. "But no—why should you? Noticing things is only a trouble. Tomorrow, indeed, you may be saying to yourself, 'Oh, if only I had noticed sooner! If only I had done something!' But no; it's a trouble. Never mind—forget that I asked."

"Look here, old man," said the Rat, beginning to get rather alarmed, "of course I'll fetch a doctor to you, if you really think you want him. But you can hardly be bad enough for that yet. Let's talk about something else."

"I fear, dear friend," said Toad, with a sad smile, "that 'talk' can do little in a case like this—or doctors either, for that matter; still, one must grasp at the slightest straw. And, by the way—while you are about it—I *hate* to give you additional trouble, but I happen to remember that you will pass the door— would you mind at the same time asking the lawyer to step up? It would be a convenience to me, and there are moments—perhaps I should say there is *a* moment—when one must face disagreeable tasks, at whatever cost to exhausted nature!"

"A lawyer! Oh, he must be really bad!" the affrighted Rat said to himself, as he hurried from the room, not forgetting, however, to lock the door carefully behind him.

Outside, he stopped to consider. The other two were far away, and he had no one to consult.

"It's best to be on the safe side," he said, on reflection. "I've known Toad fancy himself frightfully bad before, without the slightest reason; but I've never heard him ask for a lawyer! If there's nothing really the matter, the doctor will tell him he's an old ass, and cheer him up; and that will be something gained. I'd better humor him and go; it won't take very long." So he ran off to the village on his errand of mercy.

The Toad, who had hopped lightly out of bed as soon as he heard the key turned in the lock, watched him eagerly from the window till he disappeared down the carriage drive. Then, laughing heartily, he dressed as quickly as possible in the smartest suit he could lay hands on at the moment, filled his pockets with cash which he took from a small drawer in the dressing table, and next, knotting the sheets from his bed together and tying one end of the improvised rope round the central mullion of the handsome Tudor window which formed such a feature of his bedroom, he scrambled out, slid lightly to the ground, and, taking the opposite direction to the Rat, marched off lightheartedly, whistling a merry tune.

It was a gloomy luncheon for Rat when the Badger and the Mole at length returned, and he had to face them at table with his pitiful and unconvincing story. The Badger's caustic, not to say brutal, remarks may be imagined, and therefore passed over; but it was painful to the Rat that even the Mole, though he took his friend's side as far as possible, could not help saying, "You've been a bit of a duffer this time, Ratty! Toad, too, of all animals!"

"He did it awfully well," said the crestfallen Rat.

"He did *you* awfully well!" rejoined the Badger hotly. "However, talking won't mend matters. He's got clear away for the time, that's certain; and the worst of it is, he'll be so conceited with what he'll think is his cleverness that he may commit any folly. One comfort is, we're free now, and needn't waste any more of our precious time doing sentry-go. But we'd better continue to sleep at Toad Hall for a while longer. Toad may be brought back at any moment—on a stretcher, or between two policemen."

So spoke the Badger, not knowing what the future held in store, or how much water, and of how turbid a character, was to run under bridges before Toad should sit at ease again in his ancestral Hall.

Meanwhile, Toad, gay and irresponsible, was walking briskly along the highroad, some miles from home. At first he had taken bypaths, and crossed many fields, and changed his course several times, in case of pursuit; but now, feeling by this time safe from recapture, and the sun smiling brightly on him, and all Nature joining in a chorus of approval to the song of self-praise that his own heart was singing to him, he almost danced along the road in his satisfaction and conceit.

"Smart piece of work that!" he remarked to himself, chuckling. "Brain against brute force—and brain came out on the top—as it's bound to do. Poor old Ratty! My! won't he catch it when the Badger gets back! A worthy fellow, Ratty, with many good qualities, but very little intelligence and absolutely no education. I must take him in hand some day, and see if I can make something of him."

Filled full of conceited thoughts such as these, he strode along, his head in the air, till he reached a little town, where the sign of "The Red Lion," swinging across the road halfway down the main street, reminded him that he had not breakfasted that day, and that he was exceedingly hungry after his long walk. He marched into the inn, ordered the best luncheon that could be provided at so short a notice, and sat down to eat it in the coffee room.

He was about halfway through his meal when an only too familiar sound, approaching down the street, made him start and fall a-trembling all over. The poop-poop! drew nearer and nearer, the car could be heard to turn into the inn yard and come to a stop, and Toad had to hold on to the leg of the table to conceal his overmastering emotion. Presently the party entered the coffee room, hungry, talkative, and gay, voluble on their experiences of the morning and the merits of the chariot that had brought them along so well. Toad listened eagerly, all ears, for a time; at last he could stand it no longer. He slipped out of the room quietly, paid his bill at the bar. and as soon as he got outside sauntered round quietly to the inn yard. "There cannot be any harm," he said to himself, "in my only *looking* at it!"

The car stood in the middle of the yard, quite unattended, the stable-helps and other hangers-on being all at their dinner. Toad walked slowly round it, inspecting, criticizing, musing deeply.

"I wonder," he said to himself presently, "I wonder if this sort of car *starts* easily?"

Next moment, hardly knowing how it came about, he found he had hold of the crank and was turning it. As the familiar sound broke forth, the old passion seized on Toad and completely mastered him, body and soul. As if in a dream he found himself, somehow, seated in the driver's seat, as if in a dream, he pulled the lever and swung the car round the yard and out through the archway and, as if in a dream, all sense of right and wrong, all fear of obvious consequences, seemed temporarily suspended. He increased his pace, and as the car devoured the street and leapt forth on the highroad through the open country, he was only conscious that he was Toad once more, Toad at his best and highest, Toad the terror, the traffic-queller, the Lord of the lone trail, before whom all must give way or be smitten into nothingness and everlasting night. He chanted as he flew, and the car responded with sonorous drone; the miles were eaten up under him as he sped he knew not whither, fulfilling his instincts, living his hours, reckless of what might come to him.

* * * * *

"To my mind," observed the Chairman of the Bench of Magistrates cheerfully, "the *only* difficulty that presents itself in this otherwise very clear case is, how we can possibly make it sufficiently hot for the incorrigible rogue and hardened ruffian whom we see cowering in the dock before us. Let me see: he has been found guilty, on the clearest evidence, first, of stealing a valuable motorcar; secondly, of driving to the public danger; and, thirdly, of gross impertinence to the rural police. Mr. Clerk, will you tell us, please, what is the very stiffest penalty we can impose for each of these offenses? Without, of course, giving the prisoner the benefit of any doubt, because there isn't any."

The Clerk scratched his nose with his pen. "Some people would consider," he observed, "that stealing the motorcar was the worst offense; and so it is. But cheeking the police undoubtedly carries the severest penalty; and so it ought. Supposing you were to say twelve months for the theft, which is mild; and three years for the furious driving, which is lenient; and fifteen years for the cheek, which was pretty bad sort of cheek, judging by what we've heard from the witness box, even if you only believe one-tenth part of what you heard, and I never believe more myself—those figures, if added together correctly, tot up to nineteen years—"

"First-rate!" said the Chairman.

At last they paused where an ancient jailer

sat fingering a bunch of mighty keys

"—So you had better make it a round twenty years and be on the safe side," concluded the Clerk.

"An excellent suggestion!" said the Chairman approvingly. "Prisoner! Pull yourself together and try and stand up straight. It's going to be twenty years for you this time. And mind, if you appear before us again, upon any charge whatever, we shall have to deal with you very seriously!"

Then the brutal minions of the law fell upon the hapless Toad; loaded him with chains, and dragged him from the Courthouse, shrieking, praying, protesting; across the marketplace, where the playful populace, always as severe upon detected crime as they are sympathetic and helpful when one is merely "wanted," assailed him with jeers, carrots, and popular catchwords; past hooting school children, their innocent faces lit up with the pleasure they ever derive from the sight of a gentleman in difficulties; across the hollow-sounding drawbridge, below the spiky portcullis, under the frowning archway of the grim old castle, whose ancient towers soared high overhead; past guardrooms full of grinning soldiery off duty, past sentries who coughed in a horrid sarcastic way, because that is as much as a sentry on his post dare do to show his contempt and abhorrence of crime; up timeworn winding stairs, past men-at-arms in casquet and corselet of steel, darting threatening looks through the vizards; across courtyards, where mastiffs strained at their leash and pawed the air to get at him; past ancient warders, their halberds leaned against the wall, doz-

ing over a pasty and a flagon of brown ale; on and
on, past the rack-chamber and the thumbscrew-
room, past the turning that led to the private scaf-
fold, till they reached the door of the grimmest
dungeon that lay in the heart of the innermost
keep. There at last they paused, where an ancient
jailer sat fingering a bunch of mighty keys.

"Oddsbodikins!" said the sergeant of police, taking off his helmet and wiping his forehead. "Rouse
thee, old loon, and take over from us this vile Toad,
a criminal of deepest guilt and matchless artfulness
and resource. Watch and ward him with all thy
skill; and mark thee well, graybeard, should aught
untoward befall, thy old head shall answer for his
—and a murrain on both of them!"

The jailer nodded grimly, laying his withered
hand on the shoulder of the miserable Toad. The
rusty key creaked in the lock, the great door clanged
behind them; and Toad was a helpless prisoner in
the remotest dungeon of the best-guarded keep of
the stoutest castle in all the length and breadth of
Merry England.

7

The Piper at the
Gates of Dawn

THE WILLOW Wren was twittering his thin little
song, having hidden himself in the dark selvedge
of the river bank. Though it was past ten o'clock at
night, the sky still clung to and retained some lingering skirts of light from the departed day; and the
sullen heat of the torrid afternoon broke up and
rolled away at the dispersing touch of the cool
fingers of the short midsummer night. Mole lay
stretched on the bank, still panting from the stress
of the fierce day that had been cloudless from dawn
to late sunset, and waited for his friend to return.
He had been on the river with some companions,
leaving the Water Rat free to keep an engagement
of long standing with Otter; and he had come back
to find the house dark and deserted, and no sign

of Rat, who was doubtless keeping it up late with his old comrade. It was still too hot to think of staying indoors, so he lay on some cool dock leaves, and thought over the past day and its doings, and how very good they all had been.

The Rat's light footfall was presently heard approaching over the parched grass. "Oh, the blessed coolness!" he said, and sat down, gazing thoughtfully into the river, silent and preoccupied.

"You stayed to supper, of course?" said the Mole presently.

"Simply had to," said the Rat. "They wouldn't hear of my going before. You know how kind they always are. And they made things as jolly for me as ever they could, right up to the moment I left. But I felt a brute all the time, as it was clear to me they were very unhappy, though they tried to hide it. Mole, I'm afraid they're in trouble. Little Portly is missing again, and you know what a lot his father thinks of him, though he never says much about it."

"What, that child?" said the Mole lightly. "Well, suppose he is; why worry about it? He's always straying off and getting lost, and turning up again; he's so adventurous. But no harm ever happens to him. Everybody hereabouts knows him and likes him, just as they do old Otter, and you may be sure some animal or other will come across him and bring him back again, all right. Why, we've found him ourselves, miles from home and quite self-possessed and cheerful!"

"Yes; but this time it's more serious," said the

Rat gravely. "He's been missing for some days now, and the Otters have hunted everywhere, high and low, without finding the slightest trace. And they've asked every animal, too, for miles around, and no one knows anything about him. Otter's evidently more anxious than he'll admit. I got out of him that young Portly hasn't learned to swim very well yet, and I can see he's thinking of the weir. There's a lot of water coming down still, considering the time of year, and the place always has a fascination for the child. And then there are—well, traps, and things —*you* know. Otter's not the fellow to be nervous about any son of his before it's time. And now he *is* nervous. When I left, he came out with me—said he wanted some air, and talked about stretching his legs. But I could see it wasn't that, so I drew him out and pumped him, and got it all from him at last. He was going to spend the night watching by the ford. You know the place where the old ford used to be, in bygone days before they built the bridge?"

"I know it well," said the Mole. "But why should Otter choose to watch there?"

"Well, it seems that it was there he gave Portly his first swimming lesson," continued the Rat. "From that shallow, gravelly spit near the bank. And it was there he used to teach him fishing, and there young Portly caught his first fish, of which he was so very proud. The child loved the spot, and Otter thinks that if he came wandering back from wherever he is—if he *is* anywhere by this time, poor little chap—he might make for the ford he was so fond of; or if he came across it he'd remember it well, and stop there and play, perhaps. So Otter goes there every night and watches—on the chance, you know, just on the chance!"

They were silent for a time, both thinking of the same thing—the lonely, heartsore animal, crouched by the ford, watching and waiting, the long night through—on the chance.

"Well, well," said the Rat presently, "I suppose we ought to be thinking about turning in." But he never offered to move.

"Rat," said the Mole, "I simply can't go and turn in, and go to sleep, and *do* nothing, even though there doesn't seem to be anything to be done. We'll get the boat out, and paddle upstream. The moon will be up in an hour or so, and then we will search as well as we can—anyhow, it will be better than going to bed and doing *nothing*."

"Just what I was thinking myself," said the Rat. "It's not the sort of night for bed anyhow; and daybreak is not so very far off, and then we may pick up some news of him from early risers as we go along."

They got the boat out, and the Rat took the sculls, paddling with caution. Out in midstream there was a clear, narrow track that faintly reflected the sky; but wherever shadow fell on the water from bank, bush, or tree, they were as solid to all appearance as the banks themselves, and the Mole had to steer with judgment accordingly. Dark and deserted as it was, the night was full of small

noises, song and chatter and rustling, telling of the
busy little population who were up and about, ply-
ing their trades and vocations through the night till
sunshine should fall on them at last and send them
off to their well-earned repose. The water's own
noises, too, were more apparent than by day, its
gurglings and "cloops" more unexpected and near
at hand; and constantly they started at what seemed
a sudden clear call from an actual articulate voice.

The line of the horizon was clear and hard
against the sky, and in one particular quarter it
showed black against a silvery climbing phosphores-
cence that grew and grew. At last, over the rim of
the waiting earth the moon lifted with slow majesty
till it swung clear of the horizon and rode off, free
of moorings; and once more they began to see sur-
faces—meadows widespread, and quiet gardens,
and the river itself from bank to bank, all softly
disclosed, all washed clean of mystery and terror,
all radiant again as by day, but with a difference
that was tremendous. Their old haunts greeted them
again in other raiment, as if they had slipped away
and put on this pure new apparel and come quietly
back, smiling as they shyly waited to see if they
would be recognized again under it.

Fastening their boat to a willow, the friends landed
in this silent, silver kingdom, and patiently explored the hedges, the hollow trees, the tunnels and
their little culverts, the ditches and dry waterways.
Embarking again and crossing over, they worked
their way up the stream in this manner, while the
moon, serene and detached in a cloudless sky, did

what she could, though so far off, to help them in their quest; till her hour came and she sank earthward reluctantly, and left them, and mystery once more held field and river.

Then a change began slowly to declare itself. The horizon became clearer, field and tree came more into sight, and somehow with a different look; the mystery began to drop away from them. A bird piped suddenly, and was still; and a light breeze sprang up and set the reeds and bulrushes rustling. Rat, who was in the stern of the boat, while Mole sculled, sat up suddenly and listened with a passionate intentness. Mole, who with gentle strokes was just keeping the boat moving while he scanned the banks with care, looked at him with curiosity.

"It's gone!" sighed the Rat, sinking back in his seat again. "So beautiful and strange and new! Since it was to end so soon, I almost wish I had never heard it. For it has roused a longing in me that is pain, and nothing seems worth while but just to hear that sound once more and go on listening to it forever. No! There it is again!" he cried, alert once more. Entranced, he was silent for a long space, spellbound.

"Now it passes on and I begin to lose it," he said presently. "Oh, Mole! the beauty of it! The merry bubble and joy, the thin, clear, happy call of the distant piping! Such music I never dreamed of, and the call in it is stronger even than the music is sweet! Row on, Mole, row! For the music and the call must be for us."

The Mole, greatly wondering, obeyed. "I hear

nothing myself," he said, "but the wind playing in the reeds and rushes and osiers."

The Rat never answered, if indeed he heard. Rapt, transported, trembling, he was possessed in all his senses by this new divine thing that caught up his helpless soul and swung and dandled it, a powerless but happy infant, in a strong sustaining grasp.

In silence Mole rowed steadily, and soon they came to a point where the river divided, a long backwater branching off to one side. With a slight movement of his head Rat, who had long dropped the rudder lines, directed the rower to take the backwater. The creeping tide of light gained and gained, and now they could see the color of the flowers that gemmed the water's edge.

"Clearer and nearer still," cried the Rat joyously. "Now you must surely hear it! Ah—at last—I see you do!"

Breathless and transfixed, the Mole stopped rowing as the liquid run of that glad piping broke on him like a wave, caught him up, and possessed him utterly. He saw the tears on his comrade's cheeks, and bowed his head and understood. For a space they hung there, brushed by the purple loosestrife that fringed the bank; then the clear imperious summons that marched hand-in-hand with the intoxicating melody imposed its will on Mole, and mechanically he bent to his oars again. And the light grew steadily stronger, but no birds sang as they were wont to do at the approach of dawn; and but for the heavenly music all was marvelously still.

On either side of them, as they glided onwards, the rich meadow grass seemed that morning of a freshness and a greenness unsurpassable. Never had they noticed the roses so vivid, the willow-herb so riotous, the meadowsweet so odorous and pervading. Then the murmur of the approaching weir began to hold the air, and they felt a consciousness that they were nearing the end, whatever it might be, that surely awaited their expedition.

A wide half-circle of foam and glinting lights and shining shoulders of green water, the great weir closed the backwater from bank to bank, troubled all the quiet surface with twirling eddies and floating foam streaks, and deadened all other sounds with its solemn and soothing rumble. In midmost of the stream, embraced in the weir's shimmering armspread, a small island lay anchored, fringed close with willow and silver birch and alder. Reserved, shy, but full of significance, it hid whatever it might hold behind a veil, keeping it till the hour should come, and, with the hour, those who were called and chosen.

Slowly, but with no doubt or hesitation whatever, and in something of a solemn expectancy, the two animals passed through the broken, tumultuous water and moored their boat at the flowery margin of the island. In silence they landed, and pushed through the blossom and scented herbage and undergrowth that led up to the level ground, till they stood on a little lawn of a marvelous green, set round with Nature's own orchard trees—crab apple, wild cherry, and sloe.

"This is the place of my song-dream, the place the music played to me," whispered the Rat, as if in a trance. "Here, in this holy place, here if anywhere, surely we shall find Him!"

Then suddenly the Mole felt a great Awe fall upon him, an awe that turned his muscles to water, bowed his head, and rooted his feet to the ground. It was no panic terror—indeed he felt wonderfully at peace and happy—but it was an awe that smote and held him and, without seeing, he knew it could only mean that some august Presence was very, very near. With difficulty he turned to look for his friend, and saw him at his side cowed, stricken, and trembling violently. And still there was utter silence in the populous bird-haunted branches around them; and still the light grew and grew.

Perhaps he would never have dared to raise his eyes, but that, though the piping was now hushed, the call and the summons seemed still dominant and imperious. He might not refuse, were Death himself waiting to strike him instantly, once he had looked with mortal eye on things rightly kept hidden. Trembling, he obeyed, and raised his humble head; and then, in that utter clearness of the imminent dawn, while Nature, flushed with fullness of incredible color, seemed to hold her breath for the event, he looked in the very eyes of the Friend and Helper; saw the backward sweep of the curved horns, gleaming in the growing daylight; saw the stern, hooked nose between the kindly eyes that were looking down on them humorously, while the bearded mouth broke into a half-smile at the corners; saw the rippling muscles on the arm that lay across the broad chest, the long supple hand still holding the pan-pipes only just fallen away from the parted lips; saw the splendid curves of the shaggy limbs disposed in majestic ease on the sward; saw, last of all, nestling between his very hooves, sleeping soundly in entire peace and contentment, the little round podgy, childish form of the baby otter. All this he saw, for one moment breathless and intense, vivid on the morning sky; and still, as he looked, he lived; and still, as he lived, he wondered.

"Rat!" he found breath to whisper, shaking. "Are you afraid?"

"Afraid?" murmured the Rat, his eyes shining with unutterable love. "Afraid! Of *Him?* Oh, never, never! And yet—and yet—Oh, Mole, I am afraid!"

Then the two animals, crouching to the earth, bowed their heads and did worship.

Sudden and magnificent, the sun's broad golden disc showed itself over the horizon facing them; and the first rays, shooting across the level water meadows, took the animals full in the eyes and dazzled them. When they were able to look once more, the Vision had vanished, and the air was full of the carol of birds that hailed the dawn.

As they stared blankly, in dumb misery deepening as they slowly realized all they had seen and all they had lost, a capricious little breeze, dancing up from the surface of the water, tossed the aspens, shook the dewy roses, and blew lightly and caressingly in their faces, and with its soft touch came instant oblivion. For this is the last best gift that the kindly demigod is careful to bestow on those to whom he has revealed himself in their helping: the gift of forgetfulness. Lest the awful remembrance should remain and grow, and overshadow mirth and pleasure, and the great haunting memory should spoil all the afterlives of little animals helped out of difficulties, in order that they should be happy and lighthearted as before.

Mole rubbed his eyes and stared at Rat, who was looking about him in a puzzled sort of way. "I beg your pardon; what did you say, Rat?" he asked.

"I think I was only remarking," said Rat slowly, "that this was the right sort of place, and that here, if anywhere, we should find him. And look! Why, there he is, the little fellow!" And with a cry of delight he ran towards the slumbering Portly.

But Mole stood still a moment, held in thought. As one wakened suddenly from a beautiful dream, who struggles to recall it, and can recapture nothing but a dim sense of the beauty of it, the beauty! Till that, too, fades away in its turn, and the dreamer bitterly accepts the hard, cold waking and all its penalties; so Mole, after struggling with his memory for a brief space, shook his head sadly and followed the Rat.

Portly woke up with a joyous squeak, and wriggled with pleasure at the sight of his father's friends, who had played with him so often in past

days. In a moment, however, his face grew blank,
and he fell to hunting round in a circle with pleading whine. As a child that has fallen happily asleep
in its nurse's arms, and wakes to find itself alone
and laid in a strange place, and searches corners
and cupboards, and runs from room to room, despair growing silently in its heart, even so Portly
searched the island and searched, dogged and un-
wearying, till at last the black moment came for giving it up, and sitting down and crying bitterly.

The Mole ran quickly to comfort the little animal; but Rat, lingering, looked long and doubtfully
at certain hoofmarks deep in the sward.

"Some—great—animal—has been here," he murmured slowly and thoughtfully; and stood musing, musing; his mind strangely stirred.

"Come along, Rat!" called the Mole. "Think of poor Otter, waiting up there by the ford!"

Portly had soon been comforted by the promise of a treat—a jaunt on the river in Mr. Rat's real boat; and the two animals conducted him to the water's side, placed him securely between them in the bottom of the boat, and paddled off down the backwater. The sun was fully up by now, and hot on them, birds sang lustily and without restraint, and flowers smiled and nodded from either bank, but somehow—so thought the animals—with less of richness and blaze of color than they seemed to remember seeing quite recently somewhere—they wondered where.

The main river reached again, they turned the boat's head upstream, toward the point where they knew their friend was keeping his lonely vigil. As they drew near the familiar ford, the Mole took the boat in to the bank, and they lifted Portly out and set him on his legs on the towpath, gave him his marching orders and a friendly farewell pat on the back, and shoved out into midstream. They watched the little animal as he waddled along the path contentedly and with importance; watched him till they saw his muzzle suddenly lift and his waddle break into a clumsy amble as he quickened his pace with shrill whines and wriggles of recognition. Looking up the river, they could see Otter start up, tense and rigid, from out of the shallows where he crouched in dumb patience, and could hear his amazed and joyous bark as he bounded up through the osiers onto the path. Then the Mole, with a strong pull on one oar, swung the boat round and let the full stream bear them down again whither it would, their quest now happily ended.

"I feel strangely tired, Rat," said the Mole, leaning wearily over his oars as the boat drifted. "It's being up all night, you'll say, perhaps; but that's nothing. We do as much half the nights of the week, at this time of the year. No; I feel as if I had been through something very exciting and rather terrible, and it was just over; and yet nothing particular has happened."

"Or something very surprising and splendid and beautiful," murmured the Rat, leaning back and closing his eyes. "I feel just as you do, Mole; simply dead tired, though not body-tired. It's lucky we've got the stream with us, to take us home. Isn't it jolly to feel the sun again, soaking into one's bones! And hark to the wind playing in the reeds!"

"It's like music—faraway music," said the Mole, nodding drowsily.

"So I was thinking," murmured the Rat, dreamful and languid. "Dance music—the lilting sort that runs on without a stop—but with words in it, too—it passes into words and out of them again—I catch them at intervals—then it is dance music once more, and then nothing but the reeds' soft thin whispering."

"You hear better than I," said the Mole sadly. "I cannot catch the words."

"Let me try and give you them," said the Rat

softly, his eyes still closed. "Now it is turning into words again—faint but clear—*Lest the awe should dwell—And turn your frolic to fret—You shall look on my power at the helping hour—But then you shall forget*. Now the reeds take it up—*forget, forget*, they sigh, and it dies away in a rustle and a whisper. Then the voice returns—

"*Lest limbs be reddened and rent—I spring the trap that is set—As I loose the snare you may glimpse me there—For surely you shall forget!* Row nearer, Mole, nearer to the reeds! It is hard to catch and grows each minute fainter.

"*Helper and healer, I cheer—Small waifs in the woodland wet—Strays I find in it, wounds I bind in it—Bidding them all forget!* Nearer, Mole nearer! No, it is no good; the song has died away into reed-talk."

"But what do the words mean?" asked the wondering Mole.

"That I do not know," said the Rat simply. "I passed them on to you as they reached me. Ah! now they return again, and this time full and clear! This time, at last, it is the real, the unmistakable thing, simple—passionate—perfect—"

"Well, let's have it, then," said the Mole, after he had waited patiently for a few minutes, half dozing in the hot sun.

But no answer came. He looked, and understood the silence. With a smile of much happiness on his face, and something of a listening look still lingering there, the weary Rat was fast asleep.

8

Toad's Adventures

WHEN TOAD found himself immured in a dank and noisome dungeon, and knew that all the grim darkness of a medieval fortress lay between him and the outer world of sunshine and well-metaled highroads where he had lately been so happy, disporting himself as if he had bought up every road in England, he flung himself at full length on the floor, and shed bitter tears, and abandoned himself to dark despair. "This is the end of everything" (he said), "at least it is the end of the career of Toad, which is the same thing; the popular and handsome Toad, the rich and hospitable Toad, the Toad so free and careless and debonair! How can I hope to be ever set at large again" (he said), "who have been imprisoned so justly for stealing so handsome a motorcar in such an audacious manner, and for such lurid and imaginative cheek, bestowed upon such a number of fat, red-faced policemen!" (Here his sobs choked him.) "Stupid animal that I was" (he said), "now I must languish in this dungeon, till people who were proud to say they knew me, have forgotten the very name of Toad! Oh, wise old Badger!" (he said), "Oh, clever, intelligent Rat and sensible Mole! What sound judgments, what a knowledge of men and matters you possess! Oh, unhappy and forsaken Toad!" With lamentations such as these he passed his days and nights for several weeks, refusing his meals or intermediate light refreshments, though the grim and ancient jailer, knowing that Toad's pockets were well lined, frequently pointed out that many comforts, and indeed luxuries, could by arrangement be sent in—at a price—from outside.

Now the jailer had a daughter, a pleasant wench and goodhearted, who assisted her father in the lighter duties of his post. She was particularly fond of animals, and, beside her canary, whose cage hung on a nail in the massive wall of the keep by day, to the great annoyance of prisoners who relished an after-dinner nap, and was shrouded in an antimacassar on the parlor table at night, she kept several piebald mice and a restless revolving squirrel. This kindhearted girl, pitying the misery of Toad, said to her father one day, "Father! I can't bear to see that poor beast so unhappy, and getting so thin! You let me have the managing of him. You know how fond of animals I am. I'll make him eat from my hand, and sit up, and do all sorts of things."

Her father replied that she could do what she liked with him. He was tired of Toad, and his sulks and his airs and his meanness. So that day she went on her errand of mercy, and knocked at the door of Toad's cell.

"Now, cheer up, Toad," she said coaxingly, on entering, "and sit up and dry your eyes and be a sensible animal. And do try and eat a bit of dinner. See, I've brought you some of mine, hot from the oven!"

It was bubble-and-squeak, between two plates, and its fragance filled the narrow cell. The penetrating smell of cabbage reached the nose of Toad as he lay prostrate in his misery on the floor, and gave him the idea for a moment that perhaps life was not such a blank and desperate thing as he had imagined. But still he wailed, and kicked with his legs, and refused to be comforted. So the wise girl retired for the time, but, of course, a good deal of the smell of hot cabbage remained behind, as it will do, and Toad, between his sobs, sniffed and reflected, and gradually began to think new and inspiring thoughts: of chivalry, and poetry, and deeds still to be done; of broad meadows, and cattle browsing in them, raked by sun and wind; of kitchen gardens, and straight herb borders, and warm snapdragon beset by bees; and of the comforting clink of dishes set down on the table at Toad

Hall, and the scrape of chair legs on the floor as everyone pulled himself close up to his work. The air of the narrow cell took on a rosy tinge; he began to think of his friends, and how they would surely be able to do something; of lawyers, and how they would have enjoyed his case, and what an ass he had been not to get in a few; and lastly, he thought of his own great cleverness and resource, and all that he was capable of if he only gave his great mind to it; and the cure was almost complete.

When the girl returned, some hours later, she carried a tray, with a cup of fragrant tea steaming on it; and a plate piled up with very hot buttered toast, cut thick, very brown on both sides, with the butter running through the holes in it in great golden drops, like honey from the honeycomb. The smell of that buttered toast simply talked to Toad, and with no uncertain voice; talked of warm kitchens, of breakfast on bright frosty mornings, of cozy parlor firesides on winter evenings, when one's ramble was over and slippered feet were propped on the fender; of the purring of contented cats, and the twitter of sleepy canaries. Toad sat up on end once more, dried his eyes, sipped his tea and munched his toast, and soon began talking freely about himself, and the house he lived in, and his doings there, and how important he was, and what a lot his friends thought of him.

The jailer's daughter saw that the topic was doing him as much good as the tea, as indeed it was, and encouraged him to go on.

"Tell me about Toad Hall," said she. "It sounds beautiful."

"Toad Hall," said the Toad proudly, "is an eligible self-contained gentleman's residence, very unique; dating in part from the fourteenth century, but replete with every modern convenience. Up-to-date sanitation. Five minutes from church, post office, and golf links. Suitable for—"

"Bless the animal," said the girl, laughing, "I don't want to *take* it. Tell me something *real* about it. But first wait till I fetch you some more tea and toast."

She tripped away, and presently returned with a fresh trayful; and Toad, pitching into the toast with avidity, his spirits quite restored to their usual level, told her about the boathouse, and the fishpond, and the old walled kitchen garden; and about the pigsties, and the stables, and the pigeonhouse, and the henhouse; and about the dairy, and the washhouse, and the china cupboards, and the linen presses (she liked that bit especially); and about the banqueting hall, and the fun they had there when the other animals were gathered round the table and Toad was at his best, singing songs, telling stories, carrying on generally. Then she wanted to know about his animal friends, and was very interested in all he had to tell her about them and how they lived, and what they did to pass their time. Of course, she did not say she was fond of animals as *pets,* because she had the sense to see that Toad would be extremely offended. When she said good night, having filled his water jug and shaken up his straw for him, Toad was very much the same sanguine, self-satisfied animal that he had been of old. He sang a little song or two, of the sort he used to sing at his dinner parties, curled himself up in the straw, and had an excellent night's rest and the pleasantest of dreams.

They had many interesting talks together, after that, as the dreary days went on; and the jailer's daughter grew very sorry for Toad, and thought it a great shame that a poor little animal should be locked up in prison for what seemed to her a very trivial offence. Toad, of course, in his vanity, thought that her interest in him proceeded from a growing tenderness; and he could not help half regretting that the social gulf between them was so very wide, for she was a comely lass, and evidently admired him very much.

One morning the girl was very thoughtful, and answered at random, and did not seem to Toad to be paying proper attention to his witty sayings and sparkling comments.

"Toad," she said presently, "just listen, please. I have an aunt who is a washerwoman."

"There, there," said Toad graciously and affably, "never mind; think no more about it. *I* have several aunts who *ought* to be washerwomen."

"Do be quiet a minute, Toad," said the girl. "You talk too much, that's your chief fault, and I'm trying to think, and you hurt my head. As I said, I have an aunt who is a washerwoman; she does the washing for all the prisoners in this castle—we try to keep any paying business of that sort in the family, you understand. She takes out the washing on Monday morning, and brings it in on Friday evening. This is a Thursday. Now, this is what occurs to me: you're very rich—at least you're always telling me so—and she's very poor. A few pounds wouldn't make any difference to you, and it would mean a lot to her. Now, I think if she were properly approached—squared, I believe is the word you animals use—you could come to some arrangement by which she would let you have her dress and bonnet and so on, and you could escape from the castle as the official washerwoman. You're very alike in many respects—particularly about the figure."

"We're *not*," said the Toad in a huff. "I have a very elegant figure—for what I am."

"So has my aunt," replied the girl, "for what *she* is. But have it your own way. You horrid, proud, ungrateful animal, when I'm sorry for you, and trying to help you!"

"Yes, yes, that's all right; thank you very much indeed," said the Toad hurriedly. "But look here! You wouldn't surely have Mr. Toad, of Toad Hall, going about the country disguised as a washer-woman!"

"Then you can stop here as a Toad," replied the girl with much spirit. "I suppose you want to go off in a coach-and-four!"

Honest Toad was always ready to admit himself

in the wrong. "You are a good, kind, clever girl," he said, "and I am indeed a proud and a stupid toad. Introduce me to your worthy aunt, if you will be so kind, and I have no doubt that the excellent lady and I will be able to arrange terms satisfactory to both parties."

Next evening the girl ushered her aunt into Toad's cell, bearing his week's washing pinned up in a towel. The old lady had been prepared beforehand for the interview, and the sight of certain golden sovereigns that Toad had thoughtfully placed on the table in full view practically completed the matter and left little further to discuss. In return for his cash, Toad received a cotton print gown, an apron, a shawl, and a rusty black bonnet; the only stipulation the old lady made being that she should be gagged and bound and dumped in a corner. By this not very convincing artifice, she explained, aided by picturesque fiction which she could supply herself, she hoped to retain her situation, in spite of the suspicious appearance of things.

Toad was delighted with the suggestion. It would enable him to leave the prison in some style, and with his reputation for being a desperate and dangerous fellow untarnished; and he readily helped the jailer's daughter to make her aunt appear as much as possible the victim of circumstances over which she had no control.

"Now it's your turn, Toad," said the girl. "Take off that coat and waistcoat of yours; you're fat enough as it is."

Shaking with laughter, she proceeded to "hook-and-eye" him into the cotton print gown, arranged the shawl with a professional fold, and tied the strings of the rusty bonnet under his chin.

"You're the very image of her," she giggled, "only I'm sure you never looked half so respectable in all your life before. Now, good-bye, Toad, and good luck. Go straight down the way you came up; and if anyone says anything to you, as they probably will, being but men, you can chaff back a bit, of course, but remember you're a widow woman, quite alone in the world, with a character to lose."

With a quaking heart, but as firm a footstep as he could command, Toad set forth cautiously on what seemed to be a most harebrained and hazardous undertaking; but he was soon agreeably surprised to find how easy everything was made for him, and a little humbled at the thought that both his popularity, and the sex that seemed to inspire it, were really another's. The washerwoman's squat figure in its familiar cotton print seemed a passport for every barred door and grim gateway; even when he hesitated, uncertain as to the right turning to take, he found himself helped out of his difficulty by the warder at the next gate, anxious to be off to his tea, summoning him to come along sharp and not keep him waiting there all night. The chaff and the humorous sallies to which he was subjected, and to which, of course, he had to provide prompt and effective reply, formed, indeed, his chief danger; for Toad was an animal with a strong sense of his own dignity, and the chaff was mostly (he thought) poor and clumsy, and the humor of the sallies entirely lacking. However, he kept his temper, though with great difficulty, suited his retorts to his company and his supposed character, and did his best not to overstep the limits of good taste.

It seemed hours before he crossed the last courtyard, rejected the pressing invitations from the last guardroom, and dodged the outspread arms of the last warder, pleading with simulated passion for just one farewell embrace. But at last he heard the wicket gate in the great outer door click behind him, felt the fresh air of the outer world upon his anxious brow, and knew that he was free!

Dizzy with the easy success of his daring exploit, he walked quickly towards the lights of the town, not knowing in the least what he should do next, only quite certain of one thing, that he must remove himself as quickly as possible from a neighborhood where the lady he was forced to represent was so well known and so popular a character.

As he walked along, considering, his attention was caught by some red and green lights a little way off, to one side of the town, and the sound of the puffing and snorting of engines and the banging of shunted trucks fell on his ear. "Aha!" he thought, "this is a piece of luck! A railway station is the thing I want most in the whole world at this moment; and what's more, I needn't go through the town to get it, and shan't have to support this humiliating character by repartees which, though thoroughly effective, do not assist one's sense of self-respect."

He made his way to the station accordingly, consulted a timetable, and found that a train, bound more or less in the direction of his home, was due to start in half an hour. "More luck!" said Toad, his spirits rising rapidly, and went off to the booking office to buy his ticket.

He gave the name of the station that he knew to be nearest to the village of which Toad Hall was the principal feature, and mechanically put his fingers, in search of the necessary money, where his waistcoat pocket should have been. But here the cotton gown, which had nobly stood by him so far, and which he had basely forgotten, intervened, and frustrated his efforts. In a sort of nightmare he struggled with the strange uncanny thing that seemed to hold his hands, turn all muscular strivings to water, and laugh at him all the time; while other travelers, forming up in a line behind, waited with impatience, making suggestions of more or less value and comments of more or less stringency and point. At last—somehow—he never rightly understood how—he burst the barriers, attained the goal, arrived at where all waistcoat pockets are eternally situated, and found—not only no money, but no pocket to hold it, and no waistcoat to hold the pocket!

To his horror he recollected that he had left both coat and waistcoat behind him in his cell, and with them his pocketbook, money, keys, watch, matches, pencil case—all that makes life worth living, all that distinguishes the many-pocketed animal, the lord of creation, from the inferior one-pocketed or no-pocketed productions that hop or trip about permissively, unequipped for the real contest.

In his misery he made one desperate effort to carry the thing off, and, with a return to his fine old manner—a blend of the Squire and the College Don—he said, "Look here! I find I've left my purse behind. Just give me that ticket, will you, and I'll send the money on tomorrow. I'm well known in these parts."

The clerk stared at him and the rusty black bonnet a moment, and then laughed. "I should think you were pretty well known in these parts," he said, "if you've tried this game on often. Here, stand away from the window, please, madam; you're obstructing the other passengers!"

An old gentleman who had been prodding him in the back for some moments here thrust him away, and, what was worse, addressed him as his good woman, which angered Toad more than anything that had occurred that evening.

Baffled and full of despair, he wandered blindly down the platform where the train was standing, and tears trickled down each side of his nose. It was hard, he thought, to be within sight of safety and almost home, and to be balked by the want of a few wretched shillings and by the pettifogging mistrustfulness of paid officials. Very soon his escape would be discovered, the hunt would be up, he would be caught, reviled, loaded with chains, dragged back again to prison and bread-and-water and straw; his guards and penalties would be doubled; and oh, what sarcastic remarks the girl would make! What was to be done? He was not swift of foot; his figure was unfortunately recognizable. Could he not squeeze under the seat of a carriage? He had seen this method adopted by schoolboys, when the journey money provided by thoughtful parents had been diverted to other and better ends. As he pondered, he found himself opposite the engine, which was being oiled, a burly man with an oilcan in one hand and a lump of cotton waste in the other.

"Hullo, mother!" said the engine driver, "what's

the trouble? You don't look particularly cheerful."

"Oh, sir!" said Toad, crying afresh, "I am a poor unhappy washerwoman, and I've lost all my money, and can't pay for a ticket, and I *must* get home tonight somehow, and whatever I am to do I don't know. Oh dear! Oh dear!"

"That's a bad business, indeed," said the engine driver reflectively. "Lost your money—and can't get home—and got some kids, too, waiting for you, I dare say?"

"Any amount of 'em," sobbed Toad. "And they'll be hungry—and playing with matches—and upsetting lamps, the little innocents!—and quarreling, and going on generally. Oh dear! Oh dear!"

"Well, I'll tell you what I'll do," said the good engine driver. "You're a washerwoman to your trade, says you. Very well, that's that. And I'm an engine driver, as you may well see, and there's no denying it's terribly dirty work. Uses up a power of shirts, it does, till my missus is fair tired of washing 'em. If you'll wash a few shirts for me when you get home, and send 'em along, I'll give you a ride on my engine. It's against the Company's regulations, but we're not so very particular in these out-of-the-way parts."

The Toad's misery turned into rapture as he eagerly scrambled up into the cab of the engine. Of course, he had never washed a shirt in his life, and couldn't if he tried and, anyhow, he wasn't going to begin; but he thought: "When I get safely home to Toad Hall, and have money again, and pockets to put it in, I will send the engine driver enough to pay for quite a quantity of washing, and that will be the same thing, or better."

The guard waved his welcome flag, the engine driver whistled in cheerful response, and the train moved out of the station. As the speed increased, and the Toad could see on either side of him real fields and trees, and hedges, and cows, and horses, all flying past him, and as he thought how every minute was bringing him nearer to Toad Hall, and sympathetic friends, and money to chink in his pocket, and a soft bed to sleep in, and good things to eat, and praise and admiration at the recital of his adventures and his surpassing cleverness, he began to skip up and down and shout and sing snatches of song, to the great astonishment of the engine driver, who had come across washerwomen before, at long intervals, but never one at all like this.

They had covered many and many a mile, and Toad was already considering what he would have for supper as soon as he got home, when he noticed that the engine driver, with a puzzled expression on his face was leaning over the side of the engine and listening hard. Then he saw him climb on to the coals and gaze out over the top of the train; then he returned and said to Toad: "It's very strange; we're the last train running in this direction tonight, yet I could be sworn that I heard another following us!"

Toad ceased his frivolous antics at once. He

became grave and depressed, and a dull pain in the lower part of his spine, communicating itself to his legs, made him want to sit down and try desperately not to think of all the possibilities.

By this time the moon was shining brightly, and the engine driver, steadying himself on the coal, could command a view of the line behind them for a long distance.

Presently he called out, "I can see it clearly now! It is an engine, on our rails, coming along at a great pace! It looks as if we were being pursued!"

The miserable Toad, crouching in the coal dust, tried hard to think of something to do, with dismal want of success.

"They are gaining on us fast!" cried the engine driver. "And the engine is crowded with the queerest lot of people! Men like ancient warders, waving halberds; policemen in their helmets, waving truncheons; and shabbily dressed men in pot-hats, obvious and unmistakable plainclothes detectives even at this distance, waving revolvers and walking sticks; all waving, and all shouting the same thing —'Stop, stop, stop!' "

Then Toad fell on his knees among the coals and, raising his clasped paws in supplication, cried, "Save me, only save me, dear kind Mr. Engine driver, and I will confess everything! I am not the simple washerwoman I seem to be! I have no children waiting for me, innocent or otherwise! I am a toad—the well-known and popular Mr. Toad, a landed proprietor; I have just escaped, by my great daring and cleverness, from a loathsome dungeon into which my enemies had flung me; and if those fellows on that engine recapture me, it will be chains and bread and water and straw and *misery* once more for poor, unhappy, innocent Toad!"

The engine driver looked down upon him very sternly, and said, "Now tell the truth, what were you put in prison for?"

"It was nothing very much," said poor Toad, coloring deeply. "I only borrowed a motorcar while the owners were at lunch; they had no need of it at the time. I didn't mean to steal it, really; but people —especially magistrates—take such harsh views of thoughtless and high-spirited actions."

The engine driver looked very grave and said, "I fear that you have been indeed a wicked toad, and by rights I ought to give you up to offended justice. But you are evidently in sore trouble and distress, so I will not desert you. I don't hold with motorcars, for one thing; and I don't hold with being ordered about by policemen when I'm on my own engine, for another. And the sight of an animal in tears always makes me feel queer and soft-hearted. So cheer up, Toad! I'll do my best, and we may beat them yet!"

They piled on more coals, shoveling furiously; the furnace roared, the sparks flew, the engine leapt and swung, but still their pursuers slowly gained. The engine driver, with a sigh, wiped his brow with a handful of cotton waste, and said, "I'm afraid it's no good, Toad. You see, they are running light,

and they have the better engine. There's just one
thing left for us to do, and it's your only chance,
so attend very carefully to what I tell you. A short
way ahead of us is a long tunnel, and on the other
side of that the line passes through a thick wood.
Now, I will put on all the speed I can while we are
running through the tunnel, but the other fellows
will slow down a bit, naturally, for fear of an
accident. When we are through, I will shut off
steam and put on brakes as hard as I can, and the
moment it's safe to do so you must jump and hide
in the wood, before they get through the tunnel and
see you. Then I will go full speed ahead again, and
they can chase *me* if they like, for as long as they
like and as far as they like. Now mind and be
ready to jump when I tell you!"

They piled on more coals, and the train shot into
the tunnel, and the engine rushed and roared and
rattled, till at last they shot out at the other end
into fresh air and the peaceful moonlight, and saw
the wood lying dark and helpful upon either side of
the line. The driver shut off steam and put on
brakes, the Toad got down on the step, and as the
train slowed down to almost a walking pace he
heard the driver call out, "Now, jump!"

Toad jumped, rolled down a short embankment,
picked himself up unhurt, scrambled into the wood
and hid.

Peeping out, he saw his train get up speed again
and disappear at a great pace. Then out of the
tunnel burst the pursuing engine, roaring and

whistling, her motley crew waving their various weapons and shouting, "Stop! stop! stop!" When they were past, the Toad had a hearty laugh—for the first time since he was thrown into prison.

But he soon stopped laughing when he came to consider that it was now very late and dark and cold, and he was in an unknown wood, with no money and no chance of supper, and still far from friends and home; and the dead silence of everything, after the roar and rattle of the train, was something of a shock. He dared not leave the shelter of the trees, so he struck into the wood, with the idea of leaving the railway as far as possible behind him.

After so many weeks within walls, he found the wood strange and unfriendly and inclined, he thought, to make fun of him. Nightjars, sounding their mechanical rattle, made him think that the wood was full of searching warders, closing in on him. An owl, swooping noiselessly towards him, brushed his shoulder with its wing, making him jump with the horrid certainty that it was a hand; then flitted off, mothlike, laughing its low ho! ho! ho! which Toad thought in very poor taste. Once he met a fox, who stopped, looked him up and down in a sarcastic sort of way, and said, "Hullo, washerwoman! Half a pair of socks and a pillowcase short this week! Mind it doesn't occur again!" and swaggered off, sniggering. Toad looked about for a stone to throw at him, but could not succeed in finding one, which vexed him more than anything. At last, cold, hungry, and tired out, he sought the shelter of a hollow tree, where with branches and dead leaves he made himself as comfortable a bed as he could, and slept soundly till the morning.

9

Wayfarers All

THE WATER Rat was restless, and he did not exactly know why. To all appearance the summer's pomp was still at fullest height, and although in the tilled acres green had given way to gold, though rowans were reddening, and the woods were dashed here and there with a tawny fierceness, yet light and warmth and color were still present in undiminished measure, clean of any chilly premonitions of the passing year. But the constant chorus of the orchards and hedges had shrunk to a casual evensong from a few yet unwearied performers; the robin was beginning to assert himself once more; and there was a feeling in the air of change and departure. The cuckoo, of course, had long been silent; but many another feathered friend, for

months a part of the familiar landscape and its
small society, was missing too, and it seemed that
the ranks thinned steadily day by day. Rat, ever
observant of all winged movement, saw that it was
taking daily a southing tendency; and even as he
lay in bed at night he thought he could make out,
passing in the darkness overhead, the beat and
quiver of impatient pinions, obedient to the per-
emptory call.

Nature's Grand Hotel has its Season, like the
others. As the guests one by one pack, pay, and
depart, and the seats at the *table-d'hôte* shrink
pitifully at each succeeding meal; as suites of rooms
are closed, carpets taken up, and waiters sent away;
those boarders who are staying on, *en pension*, until
the next year's full reopening, cannot help being
somewhat affected by all these flittings and fare-
wells, this eager discussion of plans, routes, and
fresh quarters, this daily shrinkage in the stream of
comradeship. One gets unsettled, depressed, and
inclined to be querulous. Why this craving for
change? Why not stay on quietly here, like us, and
be jolly? You don't know this hotel out of the
season, and what fun we have among ourselves, we
fellows who remain and see the whole interesting
year out. All very true, no doubt, the others always
reply; we quite envy you—and some other year
perhaps—but just now we have engagements—and
there's the bus at the door—our time is up! So
they depart, with a smile and a nod, and we miss
them, and feel resentful. The Rat was a self-sufficing

sort of animal, rooted to the land, and whoever
went, he stayed; still, he could not help noticing
what was in the air, and feeling some of its influence in his bones.

It was difficult to settle down to anything seriously, with all this flitting going on. Leaving the
waterside, where rushes stood thick and tall in a
stream that was becoming sluggish and low, he
wandered countrywards, crossed a field or two of
pasturage already looking dusty and parched, and
thrust into the great realm of wheat, yellow, wavy,
and murmurous, full of quiet motion and small
whisperings. Here he often loved to wander,
through the forest of stiff strong stalks that carried
their own golden sky away over his head—a sky
that was always dancing, shimmering, softly talking; or swaying strongly to the passing wind and
recovering itself with a toss and a merry laugh.
Here, too, he had many small friends, a society
complete in itself, leading full and busy lives, but
always with a spare moment to gossip and exchange
news with a visitor. Today, however, though they
were civil enough, the field mice and harvest mice
seemed preoccupied. Many were digging and tun-
neling busily; others, gathered together in small
groups, examined plans and drawings of small flats,
stated to be desirable and compact, and situated
conveniently near the stores. Some were hauling
out dusty trunks and dress baskets, others were
already elbow-deep packing their belongings; while
everywhere piles and bundles of wheat, oats, barley,

beechmast and nuts, lay about ready for transport.

"Here's old Ratty!" they cried as soon as they saw him. "Come and bear a hand, Rat, and don't stand about idle!"

"What sort of games are you up to?" said the Water Rat severely. "You know it isn't time to be thinking of winter quarters yet, by a long way!"

"Oh yes, we know that," explained a field mouse rather shamefacedly, "but it's always as well to be in good time, isn't it? We really *must* get all the furniture and baggage and stores moved out of this before those horrid machines begin clicking round the fields; and then, you know, the best flats get picked up so quickly nowadays, and if you're late you have to put up with *anything;* and they want such a lot of doing up, too, before they're fit to move into. Of course, we're early, we know that; but we're only just making a start."

"Oh bother *starts,*" said the Rat. "It's a splendid day. Come for a row, or a stroll along the hedges, or a picnic in the woods, or something."

"Well, I *think* not *today,* thank you," replied the field mouse hurriedly. "Perhaps some *other* day—when we've more *time*—"

The Rat, with a snort of contempt, swung round to go, tripped over a hatbox, and fell, with undignified remarks.

"If people would be more careful," said a field mouse rather stiffly, "and look where they're going, people wouldn't hurt themselves—and forget themselves. Mind that hold-all, Rat! You'd better sit down somewhere. In an hour or two we may be more free to attend to you."

"You won't be 'free,' as you call it, much this side of Christmas, I can see that," retorted the Rat grumpily, as he picked his way out of the field.

He returned somewhat despondently to his river again—his faithful, steadygoing old river, which never packed up, flitted, or went into winter quarters.

In the osiers which fringed the bank he spied a swallow sitting. Presently it was joined by another, and then by a third; and the birds, fidgeting restlessly on their bough, talked together earnestly and low.

"What, *already?*" said the Rat, strolling up to them. "What's the hurry? I call it simply ridiculous."

"Oh, we're not off yet, if that's what you mean," replied the first swallow. "We're only making plans and arranging things. Talking it over, you know—what route we're taking this year, and where we'll stop, and so on. That's half the fun!"

"Fun?" said the Rat. "Now that's just what I don't understand. If you've *got* to leave this pleasant place, and your friends who will miss you, and your snug homes that you've just settled into, why, when the hour strikes I've no doubt you'll go bravely, and face all the trouble and discomfort and change and newness, and make believe that you're not very unhappy. But to want to talk about it, or even think about it, till you really need—"

"No, you don't understand, naturally," said the second swallow. "First, we feel it stirring within us, a sweet unrest; then back come the recollections one by one, like homing pigeons. They flutter through our dreams at night, they fly with us in our wheelings and circlings by day. We hunger to inquire of each other, to compare notes and assure ourselves that it was all really true, as one by one the scents and sounds and names of long-forgotten places come gradually back and beckon to us."

"Couldn't you stop on for just this year?" suggested the Water Rat wistfully. "We'll all do our best to make you feel at home. You've no idea what good times we have here, while you are far away."

"I tried 'stopping on' one year," said the third swallow. "I had grown so fond of the place that when the time came I hung back and let the others go on without me. For a few weeks it was all well enough, but afterwards, oh, the weary length of the nights! The shivering, sunless days! The air so clammy and chill, and not an insect in an acre of it! No, it was no good; my courage broke down, and one cold, stormy night I took wing, flying well inland on account of the strong easterly gales. It was snowing hard as I beat through the passes of the great mountains, and I had a stiff fight to win through; but never shall I forget the blissful feeling of the hot sun again on my back as I sped down to the lakes that lay so blue and placid below me, and the taste of my first fat insect! The past was like a bad dream; the future was all happy holiday as I moved southwards week by week, easily, lazily, lingering as long as I dared, but always heeding the call! No, I had had my warning; never again did I think of disobedience."

"Ah, yes, the call of the South, of the South!" twittered the other two dreamily. "Its songs, its hues, its radiant air! Oh, do you remember—" and, forgetting the Rat, they slid into passionate reminiscence, while he listened fascinated, and his heart burned within him. In himself, too, he knew that it was vibrating at last, that chord hitherto dormant and unsuspecting. The mere chatter of these southern-bound birds, their pale and second-hand reports, had yet power to awaken this wild new sensation and thrill him through and through with it; what would one moment of the real thing work in him—one passionate touch of the real southern sun, one waft of the authentic odor? With closed eyes he dared to dream a moment in full abandonment, and when he looked again the river seemed steely and chill, the green fields gray and lightless. Then his loyal heart seemed to cry out on his weaker self for its treachery.

"Why do you ever come back, then, at all?" he demanded of the swallows jealously. "What do you find to attract you in this poor drab little country?"

"And do you think," said the first swallow, "that the other call is not for us too, in its due season? The call of lush meadow grass, wet orchards, warm, insect-haunted ponds, of browsing cattle, of hay-making, and all the farm buildings clustering round the House of the perfect Eaves?"

"Do you suppose," asked the second one, "that

you are the only living thing that craves with a hungry longing to hear the cuckoo's note again?"

"In due time," said the third, "we shall be homesick once more for quiet water lilies swaying on the surface of an English stream. But today all that seems pale and thin and very far away. Just now our blood dances to other music."

They fell a-twittering among themselves once more, and this time their intoxicating babble was of violet seas, tawny sands, and lizard-haunted walls.

Restlessly the Rat wandered off once more, climbed the slope that rose gently from the north bank of the river, and lay looking out towards the great ring of Downs that barred his vision farther southwards—his simple horizon hitherto, his Mountains of the Moon, his limit behind which lay nothing he had cared to see or to know. Today, to him gazing south with newborn need stirring in his heart, the clear sky over their long low outline seemed to pulsate with promise; today, the unseen was everything, the unknown the only real fact of life. On this side of the hills was now the real blank, on the other lay the crowded and colored panorama that his inner eye was seeing so clearly. What seas lay beyond, green, leaping, and crested! What sun-bathed coasts, along which the white villas glittered against the olive woods! What quiet harbors, thronged with gallant shipping bound for purple islands of wine and spice, islands set low in languorous waters!

He rose and descended riverwards once more;
then changed his mind and sought the side of the
dusty lane. There, lying half-buried in the thick,
cool under-hedge tangle that bordered it, he could
muse on the metaled road and all the wondrous
world that it led to; on all the wayfarers, too, that
might have trodden it, and the fortunes and adventures they had gone to seek or found unseeking
—out there, beyond—beyond!

Footsteps fell on his ear, and the figure of one
that walked somewhat wearily came into view; and
he saw that it was a rat, and a very dusty one. The
wayfarer, as he reached him, saluted with a gesture
of courtesy that had something foreign about it—
hesitated a moment—then with a pleasant smile
turned from the track and sat down by his side in
the cool herbage. He seemed tired, and the Rat let
him rest unquestioned, understanding something of
what was in his thoughts; knowing too, the value
all animals attach at times to mere silent companionship, when the weary muscles slacken and the
mind marks time.

The wayfarer was lean and keen-featured, and
somewhat bowed at the shoulders; his paws were
thin and long, his eyes much wrinkled at the
corners, and he wore small gold earrings in his
neatly set, well-shaped ears. His knitted jersey was
of a faded blue, his breeches, patched and stained,
were based on a blue foundation, and his small
belongings that he carried were tied up in a blue
cotton handkerchief.

When he had rested awhile the stranger sighed, snuffed the air, and looked about him.

"That was clover, that warm whiff on the breeze," he remarked, "and those are cows we hear cropping the grass behind us and blowing softly between mouthfuls. There is a sound of distant reapers, and yonder rises a blue line of cottage smoke against the woodland. The river runs somewhere close by, for I hear the call of a moorhen, and I see by your build that you're a fresh-water mariner. Everything seems asleep, and yet going on all the time. It is a goodly life that you lead, friend; no doubt the best in the world, if only you are strong enough to lead it!"

"Yes, it's *the* life, the only life, to live," responded the Water Rat dreamily, and without his usual wholehearted conviction.

"I did not say exactly that," replied the stranger cautiously, "but no doubt it's the best. I've tried it, and I know. And because I've just tried it— six months of it—and know it's the best, here am I, footsore and hungry, tramping away from it, tramping southward, following the old call, back to the old life, *the* life which is mine and which will not let me go."

"Is this, then, yet another of them?" mused the Rat. "And where have you just come from?" he asked. He hardly dared to ask where he was bound for; he seemed to know the answer only too well.

"Nice little farm," replied the wayfarer briefly. "Up along in that direction"—he nodded northwards. "Never mind about it. I had everything I could want—everything I had any right to expect of life, and more; and here I am! Glad to be here all the same, though, glad to be here! So many miles farther on the road, so many hours nearer to my heart's desire!"

His shining eyes held fast to the horizon, and he seemed to be listening for some sound that was wanting from that inland acreage, vocal as it was with the cheerful music of pasturage and farmyard.

"You are not one of *us*," said the Water Rat, "nor yet a farmer; nor even, I should judge, of this country."

"Right," replied the stranger. "I'm a seafaring rat, I am, and the port I originally hail from is Constantinople, though I'm a sort of a foreigner there too, in a manner of speaking. You will have heard of Constantinople, friend? A fair city, and an ancient and glorious one. And you may have heard, too, of Sigurd, King of Norway, and how he sailed thither with sixty ships, and how he and his men rode up through streets all canopied in their honor with purple and gold; and how the Emperor and Empress came down and banqueted with him on board his ship. When Sigurd returned home, many of his Northmen remained behind and entered the Emperor's bodyguard, and my ancestor, a Norwegian born, stayed behind too, with the ships that Sigurd gave the Emperor. Seafarers we have ever been, and no wonder; as for me, the city of my birth is no more my home than any pleasant port between there and the London River. I know them all, and they know me. Set me down on any of their quays or foreshores, and I am home again."

"I suppose you go on great voyages," said the Water Rat with growing interest. "Months and months out of sight of land, and provisions running short, and allowanced as to water, and your mind communing with the mighty ocean, and all that sort of thing?"

"By no means," said the Sea Rat frankly. "Such a life as you describe would not suit me at all. I'm in the coasting trade, and rarely out of sight of land. It's the jolly times on shore that appeal to me, as much as any seafaring. Oh, those southern seaports! The smell of them, the riding lights at night, the glamor!"

"Well, perhaps you have chosen the better way," said the Water Rat, but rather doubtfully. "Tell me something of your coasting, then, if you have a mind to, and what sort of harvest an animal of spirit might hope to bring home from it to warm his latter days with gallant memories by the fireside; for my life, I confess to you, feels to me today somewhat narrow and circumscribed."

"My last voyage," began the Sea Rat, "that landed me eventually in this country, bound with high hopes for my inland farm, will serve as a good example of any of them, and, indeed, as an epitome of my highly colored life. Family troubles, as usual, began it. The domestic storm-cone was hoisted, and I shipped myself on board a small

trading vessel bound from Constantinople, by classic seas whose every wave throbs with a deathless memory, to the Grecian Islands and the Levant. Those were golden days and balmy nights! In and out of harbor all the time—old friends everywhere—sleeping in some cool temple or ruined cistern during the heat of the day—feasting and song after sundown, under great stars set in a velvet sky! Thence we turned and coasted up the Adriatic, its shores swimming in an atmosphere of amber, rose, and aquamarine; we lay in wide landlocked harbors, we roamed through ancient and noble cities, until at last one morning, as the sun rose royally behind us, we rode into Venice down a path of gold. Oh, Venice is a fine city, wherein a rat can wander at his ease and take his pleasure! Or, when weary of wandering, can sit at the edge of the Grand Canal at night, feasting with his friends, when the air is full of music and the sky full of stars, and the lights flash and shimmer on the polished steel prows of the swaying gondolas, packed so that you could walk across the canal on them from side to side! And then the food—do you like the shellfish? Well, well, we won't linger over that now."

He was silent for a time; and the Water Rat, silent too and enthralled, floated on dream canals and heard a phantom song pealing high between vaporous gray wave-lapped walls.

"Southwards we sailed again at last," continued the Sea Rat, "coasting down the Italian shore, till finally we made Palermo, and there I quitted for a long, happy spell on shore. I never stick too long to one ship; one gets narrow-minded and prejudiced. Besides, Sicily is one of my happy hunting grounds. I know everybody there, and their ways just suit me. I spent many jolly weeks in the island, staying with friends upcountry. When I grew restless again I took advantage of a ship that was trading to Sardinia and Corsica; and very glad I was to feel the fresh breeze and the sea spray in my face once more."

"But isn't it very hot and stuffy, down in the—hold, I think you call it?" asked the Water Rat.

The seafarer looked at him with the suspicion

of a wink. "I'm an old hand," he remarked with much simplicity. "The captain's cabin's good enough for me."

"It's a hard life, by all accounts," murmured the Rat, sunk in deep thought.

"For the crew it is," replied the seafarer gravely, again with the ghost of a wink.

"From Corsica," he went on, "I made use of a ship that was taking wine to the mainland. We made Alassio in the evening, lay to, hauled up our wine casks, and hove them overboard, tied one to the other by a long line. Then the crew took to the boats and rowed shorewards, singing as they went, and drawing after them the long bobbing procession of casks, like a mile of porpoises. On the sands they had horses waiting, which dragged the casks upon the steep street of the little town with a fine rush and clatter and scramble. When the last cask was in, we went and refreshed and rested, and sat late into the night, drinking with our friends; and next morning I was off to the great olive woods for a spell and a rest. For now I had done with islands for the time, and ports and shipping were plentiful; so I led a lazy life among the peasants, lying and watching them work, or stretched high on the hillside with the blue Mediterranean far below me. And so at length, by easy stages, and partly on foot, partly by sea, to Marseilles, and the meeting of old shipmates, and the visiting of great oceanbound vessels, and feasting once more. Talk of shellfish! Why, sometimes

I dream of the shellfish of Marseilles, and wake up crying!"

"That reminds me," said the polite Water Rat; "you happened to mention that you were hungry, and I ought to have spoken earlier. Of course you will stop and take your midday meal with me? My hole is close by; it is some time past noon, and you are very welcome to whatever there is."

"Now I call that kind and brotherly of you," said the Sea Rat. "I was indeed hungry when I sat down, and ever since I inadvertently happened to mention shellfish, my pangs have been extreme. But couldn't you fetch it along out here? I am none too fond of going under hatches, unless I'm obliged to; and then, while we eat, I could tell you more concerning my voyages and the pleasant life I lead—at least, it is very pleasant to me, and by your attention I judge it commends itself to you; whereas if we go indoors it is a hundred to one that I shall presently fall asleep."

"That is indeed an excellent suggestion," said the Water Rat, and hurried off home. There he got out the luncheon basket and packed a simple meal, in which, remembering the stranger's origin and preferences, he took care to include a yard of long French bread, a sausage out of which the garlic sang, some cheese which lay down and cried, and a long-necked straw-covered flask containing bottle sunshine shed and garnered on far Southern slopes. Thus laden, he returned with all speed, and blushed for pleasure at the old seaman's commendations of his taste and judgment, as together they unpacked the basket and laid out the contents on the grass by the roadside.

The Sea Rat, as soon as his hunger was somewhat assuaged, continued the history of his latest voyage, conducting his simple hearer from port to port of Spain, landing him at Lisbon, Oporto, and Bordeaux, introducing him to the pleasant harbors of Cornwall and Devon, and so up the Channel to that final quayside, where, landing after winds long contrary, storm-driven and weather-beaten, he had caught the first magical hints and heraldings of another Spring, and, fired by these, had sped on a long tramp inland, hungry for the experiment of life on some quiet farmstead, very far from the weary beating of any sea.

Spellbound and quivering with excitement, the Water Rat followed the Adventurer league by league, over stormy bays, through crowded road-steads, across harbor bars on a racing tide, up winding rivers that hid their busy little towns round a sudden turn; and left him with a regretful sigh planted at his dull inland farm, about which he desired to hear nothing.

By this time their meal was over, and the Sea-farer, refreshed and strengthened, his voice more vibrant, his eye lit with a brightness that seemed caught from some faraway sea beacon, filled his glass with the red and glowing vintage of the South, and, leaning towards the Water Rat, compelled his gaze and held him, body and soul, while

he talked. Those eyes were of the changing foam-
streaked gray-green of leaping Northern seas; in the
glass shone a hot ruby that seemed the very heart of
the South, beating for him who had courage to
respond to its pulsation. The twin lights, the shifting gray and the steadfast red, mastered the Water
Rat and held him bound, fascinated, powerless.
The quiet world outside their rays receded far
away and ceased to be. And the talk, the wonderful
talk flowed on—or was it speech entirely, or did
it pass at times into song—chanty of the sailors
weighing the dripping anchor, sonorous hum of
the shrouds in a tearing northeaster, ballad of the
fisherman hauling his nets at sundown against an
apricot sky, chords of guitar and mandolin from
gondola or caique? Did it change into the cry of
the wind, plaintive at first, angrily shrill as it
freshened, rising to a tearing whistle, sinking to a
musical trickle of air from the leech of the bellying
sail? All these sounds the spellbound listener seemed
to hear, and with them the hungry complaint of the
gulls and the sea mews, the soft thunder of the
breaking wave, the cry of the protesting shingle.
Back into speech again it passed, and with beating
heart he was following the adventures of a dozen
seaports, the fights, the escapes, the rallies, the
comradeships, the gallant undertakings; or he
searched islands for treasure, fished in still lagoons
and dozed daylong on warm white sand. Of deep-
sea fishings he heard tell, and mighty silver gather-
ings, of the mile-long net; of sudden perils, noise of

breakers on a moonless night, or the tall bows of the great liner taking shape overhead through the fog; of the merry homecoming, the headland rounded, the harbor lights opened out; the groups seen dimly on the quay, the cheery hail, the splash of the hawser; the trudge up the steep little street towards the comforting glow of red-curtained windows.

Lastly, in his waking dream it seemed to him that the Adventurer had risen to his feet, but was still speaking, still holding him fast with his sea-gray eyes.

"And now," he was softly saying, "I take to the road again, holding on southwestwards for many a long and dusty day; till at last I reach the little gray sea town I know so well, that clings along one steep side of the harbor. There through dark doorways you look down flights of stone steps, overhung by great pink tufts of valerian and ending in a patch of sparkling blue water. The little boats that lie tethered to the rings and stanchions of the old sea wall are gaily painted as those I clambered in and out of in my childhood; the salmon leap on the flood tide, schools of mackerel flash and play past quaysides and foreshores, and by the windows the great vessels glide, night and day, up to their moorings or forth to the open sea. There, sooner or later, the ships of all seafaring nations arrive; and there, at its destined hour, the ship of my choice will let go its anchor. I shall take my time, I shall tarry and bide, till at last the right one lies waiting for me, warped out into midstream, loaded low, her bow-sprit pointing down harbor. I shall slip on board, by boat or along hawser; and then one morning I shall wake to the song and tramp of the sailors, the clink of the capstan, and the rattle of the anchor chain coming merrily in. We shall break out the jib and the foresail, the white houses on the harbor side will glide slowly past us as she gathers steering-way, and the voyage will have begun! As she forges towards the headland she will clothe herself with canvas; and then, once outside, the sounding slap of great green seas as she heels to the wind, point-ing South!

"And you, you will come too, young brother; for the days pass, and never return, and the South still waits for you. Take the Adventure, heed the call, now ere the irrevocable moment passes! 'Tis but a banging of the door behind you, a blithesome step forward, and you are out of the old life and into the new! Then some day, some day long hence, jog home here if you will, when the cup has been drained and the play has been played, and sit down by your quiet river with a store of goodly memories for company. You can easily overtake me on the road, for you are young, and I am ageing and go softly. I will linger, and look back; and at last I will surely see you coming, eager and lighthearted, with all the South in your face!"

The voice died away and ceased, as an insect's tiny trumpet dwindles swiftly into silence; and the Water Rat, paralyzed and staring, saw at last but a distant speck on the white surface of the road.

Mechanically he rose and proceeded to repack the luncheon basket, carefully and without haste. Mechanically he returned home, gathered together a few small necessaries and special treasures he was fond of, and put them in a satchel; acting with slow deliberation, moving about the room like a sleepwalker; listening ever with parted lips. He swung the satchel over his shoulder, carefully selected a stout stick for his wayfaring and with no haste, but with no hesitation at all, he stepped across the threshold just as the Mole appeared at the door.

"Why, where are you off to, Ratty?" asked the Mole in great surprise, grasping him by the arm.

"Going South, with the rest of them," murmured the Rat in a dreamy monotone, never looking at him. "Seawards first and then on shipboard, and so to the shores that are calling me!"

He pressed resolutely forward, still without haste, but with dogged fixity of purpose; but the Mole, now thoroughly alarmed, placed himself in front of him, and looking into his eyes saw that they were glazed and set and turned a streaked and shifting gray—not his friend's eyes, but the eyes of some other animal. Grappling with him strongly, he dragged him inside, threw him down, and held him.

The Rat struggled desperately for a few moments, and then his strength seemed suddenly to leave him, and he lay still and exhausted, with closed eyes,

trembling. Presently the Mole assisted him to rise
and placed him in a chair, where he sat collapsed
and shrunken into himself, his body shaken by a
violent shivering, passing in time into an hysterical
fit of dry sobbing. Mole made the door fast, threw
the satchel into a drawer and locked it, and sat
down quietly on the table by his friend, waiting for
the strange seizure to pass. Gradually the Rat sank
into a troubled doze, broken by starts and confused
murmurings of things strange and wild and foreign
to the unenlightened Mole; and from that he passed
into a deep slumber.

Very anxious in mind, the Mole left him for a
time and busied himself with household matters;
and it was getting dark when he returned to the
parlor and found the Rat where he had left him,
wide awake indeed, but listless, silent, and dejected.
He took one hasty glance at his eyes; found them,
to his great gratification, clear and dark and brown
again as before; and then sat down and tried to
cheer him up and help him to relate what had happened to him.

Poor Ratty did his best, by degrees, to explain
things; but how could he put into cold words what
had mostly been suggestion? How recall, for another's benefit, the haunting sea voices that had
sung to him, how reproduce at second hand the
magic of the Seafarer's hundred reminiscences?
Even to himself, now the spell was broken and
the glamor gone, he found it difficult to account
for what had seemed, some hours ago, the inevi-

table and only thing. It is not surprising, then, that he failed to convey to the Mole any clear idea of what he had been through that day.

To the Mole this much was plain: the fit, or attack, had passed away, and had left him sane again, though shaken and cast down by the reaction. But he seemed to have lost all interest for the time in the things that went to make up his daily life, as well as in all pleasant forecastings of the altered days and doings that the changing season was surely bringing.

Casually, then, and with seeming indifference, the Mole turned his talk to the harvest that was being gathered in, the towering wagons and their straining teams, the growing ricks, and the large moon rising over bare acres dotted with sheaves. He talked of the reddening apples around, of the browning nuts, of jams and preserves and the distilling of cordials; till by easy stages such as these he reached midwinter, its hearty joys and its snug home life, and then he became simply lyrical.

By degrees the Rat began to sit up and to join in. His dull eyes brightened, and he lost some of his listless air.

Presently the tactful Mole slipped away and returned with a pencil and a few half-sheets of paper, which he placed on the table at his friend's elbow.

"It's quite a long time since you did any poetry," he remarked. "You might have a try at it this evening, instead of—well, brooding over things so

much. I've an idea that you'll feel a lot better when
you've got something jotted down—if it's only just
the rhymes."

The Rat pushed the paper away from him
wearily, but the discreet Mole took occasion to leave
the room, and when he peeped in again some time
later, the Rat was absorbed and deaf to the world;
alternately scribbling and sucking the top of his
pencil. It is true that he sucked a good deal more
than he scribbled; but it was joy to the Mole to
know that the cure had at least begun.

10

The Further
Adventures of Toad

THE FRONT door of the hollow tree faced east-
wards, so Toad was called at an early hour; partly
by the bright sunlight streaming in on him, partly
by the exceeding coldness of his toes, which made
him dream that he was at home in bed in his own
handsome room with the Tudor window, on a cold
winter's night, and his bedclothes had got up,
grumbling and protesting they couldn't stand the
cold any longer, and had run downstairs to the
kitchen fire to warm themselves; and he had followed, on bare feet, along miles and miles of icy
stone-paved passages, arguing and beseeching them
to be reasonable. He would probably have been
aroused much earlier, had he not slept for some
weeks on straw over stone flags, and almost for-

gotten the friendly feeling of thick blankets pulled well up round the chin.

Sitting up, he rubbed his eyes first and his complaining toes next, wondered for a moment where he was, looking round for familiar stone wall and little barred window; then, with a leap of the heart, remembered everything—his escape, his flight, his pursuit; remembered, first and best thing of all, that he was free!

Free! The word and the thought alone were worth fifty blankets. He was warm from end to end as he thought of the jolly world outside, waiting eagerly for him to make his triumphal entrance, ready to serve him and play up to him, anxious to help him and to keep him company, as it always had been in days of old before misfortune fell upon him. He shook himself and combed the dry leaves out of his hair with his fingers; and, his toilet complete, marched forth into the comfortable morning sun, cold but confident, hungry but hopeful, all nervous terrors of yesterday dispelled by rest and sleep and frank and heartening sunshine.

He had the world all to himself, that early summer morning. The dewy woodland, as he threaded it, was solitary and still; the green fields that succeeded the trees were his own to do as he liked with; the road itself, when he reached it, in that loneliness that was everywhere, seemed, like a stray dog, to be looking anxiously for company. Toad, however, was looking for something that could talk, and tell him clearly which way he ought to go. It is all very well, when you have a light heart, and a clear conscience, and money in your pocket, and nobody scouring the country for you to drag you off to prison again, to follow where the road beckons and points, not caring whither. The practical Toad cared very much indeed, and he could have kicked the road for its helpless silence when every minute was of importance to him.

The reserved rustic road was presently joined by a shy little brother in the shape of a canal, which took its hand and ambled along by its side in perfect confidence, but with the same tongue-tied, uncommunicative attitude towards strangers. "Bother them!" said Toad to himself. "But, anyhow, one thing's clear. They must both be coming *from* somewhere, and going to somewhere. You can't get over that, Toad, my boy!" So he marched on patiently by the water's edge.

Round a bend in the canal came plodding a solitary horse, stooping forward as if in anxious thought. From rope traces attached to his collar stretched a long line, taut, but dipping with his stride, the further part of it dripping pearly drops. Toad let the horse pass, and stood waiting for what the fates were sending him.

With a pleasant swirl of quiet water at its blunt bow the barge slid up alongside of him, its gaily painted gunwale level with the towing path, its sole occupant a big stout woman wearing a linen sunbonnet, one brawny arm laid along the tiller.

"A nice morning, ma'am!" she remarked to Toad, as she drew up level with him.

"I dare say it is, ma'am!" responded Toad

politely, as he walked along the towpath abreast of
her. "I dare say it *is* a nice morning to them that's
not in sore trouble, like what I am. Here's my married daughter, she sends off to me posthaste to
come to her at once; so off I comes, not knowing
what may be happening or going to happen, but
fearing the worst, as you will understand, ma'am,
if you're a mother, too. And I've left my business
to look after itself—I'm in the washing and launder-
ing line, you must know, ma'am—and I've left my
young children to look after themselves, and a more
mischievous and troublesome set of young imps
doesn't exist, ma'am, and I've lost all my money,
and lost my way, and as for what may be happening
to my married daughter, why, I don't like to think
of it, ma'am!"

"Where might your married daughter be living,
ma'am?" asked the bargewoman.

"She lives near to the river, ma'am," replied
Toad. "Close to a fine house called Toad Hall,
that's somewheres hereabouts in these parts. Perhaps you may have heard of it."

"Toad Hall? Why, I'm going that way myself,"
replied the bargewoman. "This canal joins the river
some miles farther on, a little above Toad Hall, and
then it's an easy walk. You come along in the barge
with me, and I'll give you a lift."

She steered the barge close to the bank, and
Toad, with many humble and grateful acknowledg-
ments, stepped lightly on board and sat down with
great satisfaction. "Toad's luck again!" thought
he. "I always come out on top."

"So you're in the washing business, ma'am?" said the bargewoman politely, as they glided along. "And a very good business you've got too, I dare say, if I'm not making too free in saying so."

"Finest business in the whole county," said Toad airily. "All the gentry come to me—wouldn't go to anyone else if they were paid, they know me so well. You see, I understand my work thoroughly, and attend to it all myself. Washing, ironing, clear-starching; making up gents' fine shirts for evening wear—everything's done under my own eye!"

"But surely you don't *do* all that work yourself, ma'am?" asked the bargewoman respectfully.

"Oh, I have girls," said Toad lightly: "twenty girls or thereabouts, always at work. But you know what *girls* are, ma'am! Nasty little hussies, that's what *I* call 'em!"

"So do I, too," said the bargewoman with great heartiness. "But I dare say you set yours to rights, the idle trollops! And are you *very* fond of washing?"

"I love it," said Toad. "I simply dote on it. Never so happy as when I've got both arms in the washtub. But, then, it comes so easy to me! No trouble at all! A real pleasure, I assure you, ma'am!"

"What a bit of luck, meeting you!" observed the bargewoman thoughtfully. "A regular piece of good fortune for both of us!"

"Why, what do you mean?" asked Toad nervously.

"Well, look at me, now," replied the bargewoman. "*I* like washing, too, just the same as you do; and for that matter, whether I like it or not I have got to do all my own, naturally, moving about as I do. Now my husband, he's such a fellow for shirking his work and leaving the barge to me, that never a moment do I get for seeing to my own affairs. By rights he ought to be here now, either steering or attending to the horse, though luckily the horse has sense enough to attend to himself. Instead of which, he's off with the dog, to see if they can't pick up a rabbit for dinner somewhere. Says he'll catch me up at the next lock. Well, that's as may be—I don't trust him, once he gets off with that dog, who's worse than he is. But meantime, how am to get on with my washing?"

"Oh, never mind about the washing," said Toad, not liking the subject. "Try and fix your mind on that rabbit. A nice fat young rabbit, I'll be bound. Got any onions?"

"I can't fix my mind on anything but my washing," said the bargewoman, "and I wonder you can be talking of rabbits, with such a joyful prospect before you. There's a heap of things of mine that you'll find in a corner of the cabin. If you'll just take one or two of the most necessary sort—I won't venture to describe them to a lady like you, but you'll recognize 'em at a glance—and put them through the washtub as we go along, why, it'll be a pleasure to you, as you rightly say, and a real help to me. You'll find a tub handy, and soap, and a kettle on the stove, and a bucket to haul up water from the canal with. Then I shall know you're enjoying yourself, instead of sitting here idle, looking at the scenery and yawning your head off."

"Here, you let me steer!" said Toad, now thoroughly frightened, "and then you can get on with your washing your own way. I might spoil your things, or not do 'em as you like. I'm more used to gentlemen's things myself. It's my special line."

"Let you steer?" replied the bargewoman, laughing. "It takes some practice to steer a barge properly. Besides, it's dull work, and I want you to be happy. No, you shall do the washing you are so fond of, and I'll stick to the steering that I understand. Don't try and deprive me of the pleasure of giving you a treat!"

Toad was fairly cornered. He looked for escape this way and that, saw that he was too far from the bank for a flying leap, and sullenly resigned himself to his fate. "If it comes to that," he thought in desperation, "I suppose any fool can *wash!*"

He fetched tub, soap, and other necessaries from the cabin, selected a few garments at random, tried to recollect what he had seen in casual glances through laundry windows, and set to.

A long half-hour passed, and every minute of it saw Toad getting crosser and crosser. Nothing that he could do to the things seemed to please them or do them good. He tried coaxing, he tried slapping, he tried punching; they smiled back at him out of the tub unconverted, happy in their original sin. Once or twice he looked nervously over his shoulder at the bargewoman, but she appeared to be gazing out in front of her, absorbed in her steering. His back ached badly, and he noticed with dismay that his paws were beginning to get all crinkly. Now Toad was very proud of his paws. He muttered under his breath words that should never pass the lips of either washerwomen or Toads; and lost the soap, for the fiftieth time.

A burst of laughter made him straighten himself and look around. The bargewoman was leaning back and laughing unrestrainedly, till the tears ran down her cheeks.

"I've been watching you all the time," she gasped. "I thought you must be a humbug all along, from the conceited way you talked. Pretty washerwoman you are! Never washed so much as a dish-clout in your life, I'll lay!"

Toad's temper, which had been simmering viciously for some time, now fairly boiled over, and he lost all control of himself.

"You common, low, *fat* bargewoman!" he shouted. "Don't you dare to talk to your betters like that! Washerwoman indeed! I would have you know that I am a Toad, a very well-known, respected, distinguished Toad! I may be under a bit of a cloud at present, but I will *not* be laughed at by a bargewoman!"

The woman moved nearer to him and peered under his bonnet keenly and closely. "Why, so you are!" she cried. "Well, I never! A horrid, nasty, crawly Toad! And in my nice clean barge, too! Now that is a thing that I will *not* have."

She relinquished the tiller for a moment. One big mottled arm shot out and caught Toad by a foreleg, while the other gripped him fast by a hind leg. Then the world turned suddenly upside down, the barge seemed to flit lightly across the sky, the wind whistled in his ears, and Toad found himself flying through the air, revolving rapidly as he went.

The water, when he eventually reached it with a loud splash, proved quite cold enough for his taste, though its chill was not sufficient to quell his proud spirit, or shake the heat of his furious temper. He rose to the surface spluttering, and when he had wiped the duckweed out of his eyes the first thing he saw was the fat bargewoman looking back at him over the stern of the retreating barge and laughing; and he vowed, as he coughed and choked, to be even with her.

He struck out for the shore, but the cotton gown greatly impeded his efforts, and when at length he touched land he found it hard to climb up the steep bank unassisted. He had to take a minute or two's rest to recover his breath; then gathering his wet skirts well over his arms, he started to run after the barge as fast as his legs would carry him, wild with indignation, thirsting for revenge.

The bargewoman was still laughing when he drew up level with her. "Put yourself through your mangle, washerwoman," she called out, "and iron your face and crimp it, and you'll pass for quite a decent-looking Toad!"

Toad never paused to reply. Solid revenge was what he wanted, not cheap, windy, verbal triumphs,

though he had a thing or two in his mind that he
would have liked to say. He saw what he wanted
ahead of him. Running swiftly on, he overtook the
horse, unfastened the towrope and cast off, jumped
lightly on the horse's back, and urged it to a gallop
by kicking it vigorously in the sides. He steered for
the open country, abandoning the towpath, and
swinging his steed down a rutty lane. Once he
looked back, and saw that the barge had run
aground on the other side of the canal, and the
bargewoman was gesticulating wildly and shouting,
"Stop, stop, stop!" "I've heard that song before,"
said Toad, laughing, as he continued to spur his
steed onward in its wild career.

The barge horse was not capable of any very sustained effort, and its gallop soon subsided into a trot, and its trot into an easy walk; but Toad was quite contented with this, knowing that he, at any rate, was moving, and the barge was not. He had quite recovered his temper, now that he had done something he thought really clever; and he was satisfied to jog along quietly in the sun, taking advantage of any byways and bridlepaths, and trying to forget how very long it was since he had had a square meal, till the canal had been left very far behind him.

He had traveled some miles, his horse and he, and he was feeling drowsy in the hot sunshine, when the horse stopped, lowered his head, and began to nibble the grass; and Toad, waking up, just saved himself from falling off by an effort. He looked about him and found he was on a wide common, dotted with patches of gorse and bramble as far as he could see. Near him stood a dingy gypsy caravan, and beside it a man was sitting on a bucket turned upside down, very busy smoking and staring into the wide world. A fire of sticks was burning near by, and over the fire hung an iron pot, and out of that pot came forth bubblings and gurglings, and a vague suggestive steaminess. Also smells—warm, rich, and varied smells—that twined and twisted and wreathed themselves at last into one complete, voluptuous, perfect smell that seemed like the very soul of Nature taking form and appearing to her children, a true Goddess, a mother of solace and comfort. Toad now knew well that he had not been really hungry before. What he had felt earlier in the day had been a mere trifling qualm. This was the real thing at last, and no mistake; and it would have to be dealt with speedily, too, or there would be trouble for somebody or something. He looked the gypsy over carefully, wondering vaguely whether it would be easier to fight him or cajole him. So there he sat, and sniffed and sniffed, and looked at the gypsy; and the gypsy sat and smoked, and looked at him.

Presently the gypsy took his pipe out of his mouth and remarked in a careless way, "Want to sell that there horse of yours?"

Toad was completely taken aback. He did not know that gypsies were very fond of horse-dealing, and never missed an opportunity, and he had not reflected that caravans were always on the move and took a deal of drawing. It had not occurred to him to turn the horse into cash, but the gypsy's suggestion seemed to smooth the way towards the two things he wanted so badly—ready money and a solid breakfast.

"What?" he said, "me sell this beautiful young horse of mine? Oh no; it's out of the question. Who's going to take the washing home to my customers every week? Besides, I'm too fond of him, and he simply dotes on me."

"Try and love a donkey," suggested the gypsy. "Some people do."

"You don't seem to see," continued Toad, "that this fine horse of mine is a cut above you altogether. He's a blood horse, he is, partly; not the part you see, of course—another part. And he's been a Prize Hackney, too, in his time—that was the time before you knew him, but you can still tell it on him at a glance, if you understand anything about horses. No, it's not to be thought of for a moment. All the same, how much might you be disposed to offer me for this beautiful young horse of mine?"

The gypsy looked the horse over, and then he looked Toad over with equal care, and looked at the horse again. "Shillin' a leg," he said briefly, and turned away, continuing to smoke and try to stare the wide world out of countenance.

"A shilling a leg?" cried Toad. "If you please, I must take a little time to work that out, and see just what it comes to."

He climbed down off his horse, and left it to graze, and sat down by the gypsy, and did sums on his fingers, and at last he said, "A shilling a leg? Why, that comes to exactly four shillings, and no more. Oh, no; I could not think of accepting four shillings for this beautiful young horse of mine."

"Well," said the gypsy, "I'll tell you what I will do. I'll make it five shillings, and that's three-and-sixpence more than the animal's worth. And that's my last word."

Then Toad sat and pondered long and deeply. For he was hungry and quite penniless, and still some way—he knew not how far—from home, and enemies might still be looking for him. To one in such a situation, five shillings may very well appear a large sum of money. On the other hand, it did not seem very much to get for a horse. But then, again, the horse hadn't cost him anything; so whatever he got was all clear profit. At last he said firmly, "Look here, gypsy! I tell you what we will do; and this is *my* last word. You shall hand me over six shillings and sixpence, cash down; and further, in addition thereto, you shall give me as much breakfast as I can possibly eat, at one sitting of course, out of that iron pot of yours that keeps sending forth such delicious and exciting smells. In return, I will make over to you my spirited young horse, with all the beautiful harness and trappings that are on him, freely thrown in.

If that's not good enough for you, say so, and I'll be getting on. I know a man near here who's wanted this horse of mine for years."

The gypsy grumbled frightfully, and declared if he did a few more deals of that sort he'd be ruined. But in the end he lugged a dirty canvas bag out of the depths of his trouser pocket, and counted out six shillings and sixpence into Toad's paw. Then he disappeared into the caravan for an instant, and returned with a large iron plate and a knife, fork, and spoon. He tilted up the pot, and a glorious stream of hot rich stew gurgled into the plate. It was, indeed, the most beautiful stew in the world, being made of partridges, and pheasants, and chickens, and hares, and rabbits, and peahens, and guinea fowls, and one or two other things. Toad took the plate on his lap, almost crying, and stuffed, and stuffed, and stuffed, and kept asking for more, and the gypsy never grudged it him. He thought that he had never eaten so good a breakfast in all his life.

When Toad had taken as much stew on board as he thought he could possibly hold, he got up and said good-bye to the gypsy, and took an affectionate farewell of the horse; and the gypsy, who knew the riverside well, gave him directions which way to go, and he set forth on his travels again in the best possible spirits. He was, indeed, a very different Toad from the animal of an hour ago. The sun was shining brightly, his wet clothes were quite dry again, he had money in his pocket once more, he was nearing home and friends and safety, and, most and best of all, he had had a substantial meal, hot and nourishing, and felt big, and strong, and careless, and self-confident.

As he tramped along gaily, he thought of his adventures and escapes, and how when things seemed at their worst he had always managed to find a way out; and his pride and conceit began to swell within him. "Ho, ho!" he said to himself as he marched along with his chin in the air, "what a clever Toad I am! There is surely no animal equal to me for cleverness in the whole world! My enemies shut me up in prison, encircled by sentries, watched night and day by warders; I walk out through them all, by sheer ability coupled with courage. They pursue me with engines, and policemen, and revolvers; I snap my fingers at them, and vanish, laughing, into space. I am, unfortunately, thrown into a canal by a woman fat of body and very evil-minded. What of it? I swim ashore, I seize her horse, I ride off in triumph, and I sell the horse for a whole pocketful of money and an excellent breakfast! Ho, ho! I am The Toad, the handsome, the popular, the successful Toad!" He got so puffed up with conceit that he made up a song as he walked in praise of himself, and sang it at the top of his voice, though there was no one to hear it but him. It was perhaps the most conceited song that any animal ever composed.

"The world has held great Heroes,
    As history books have showed;

But never a name to go down to fame
 Compared with that of Toad!

"The clever men at Oxford
 Know all that there is to be knowed.
But they none of them know one half as much
 As intelligent Mr. Toad!

"The animals sat in the Ark and cried,
 Their tears in torrents flowed.
Who was it said, 'There's land ahead?'
 Encouraging Mr. Toad!

"The Army all saluted
 As they marched along the road.
Was it the King? Or Kitchener?
 No. It was Mr. Toad!

"The Queen and her Ladies-in-waiting
 Sat at the window and sewed.
She cried, 'Look! who's that *handsome* man?'
 They answered, 'Mr. Toad.' "

There was a great deal more of the same sort,
but too dreadfully conceited to be written down.
These are some of the milder verses.

He sang as he walked, and he walked as he sang,
and got more inflated every minute. But his pride
was shortly to have a severe fall.

After some miles of country lanes he reached
the highroad, and as he turned into it and glanced

along its white length, he saw approaching him a speck that turned into a dot and then into a blob, and then into something very familiar; and a double note of warning, only too well known, fell on his delighted ear.

"This is something like!" said the excited Toad. "This is real life again, this is once more the great world from which I have been missed so long! I will hail them, my brothers of the wheel, and pitch them a yarn, of the sort that has been so successful hitherto; and they will give me a lift, of course, and then I will talk to them some more; and, perhaps, with luck, it may even end in my driving up to Toad Hall in a motorcar! That will be one in the eye for Badger!"

He stepped confidently out into the road to hail the motorcar, which came along at an easy pace, slowing down as it neared the lane; when suddenly he became very pale, his heart turned to water, his knees shook and yielded under him, and he doubled up and collapsed with a sickening pain in his interior. And well he might, the unhappy animal; for the approaching car was the very one he had stolen out of the yard of the Red Lion Hotel on that fatal day when all his troubles began! And the people in it were the very same people he had sat and watched at luncheon in the coffee room!

He sank down in a shabby, miserable heap in the road, murmuring to himself in his despair, "It's all up! It's all over now! Chains and policemen again! Prison again! Dry bread and water again! Oh, what a fool I have been! What did I want to go strutting about the country for, singing conceited songs, and hailing people in broad day on the high-road, instead of hiding till nightfall and slipping home quietly by back ways! Oh hapless Toad! Oh ill-fated animal!"

The terrible motorcar drew slowly nearer and nearer, till at last he heard it stop just short of him. Two gentlemen got out and walked round the trembling heap of crumpled misery lying in the road, and one of them said, "Oh dear! this is very sad! Here is a poor old thing—a washerwoman apparently—who has fainted in the road! Perhaps she is overcome by the heat, poor creature, or possibly she has not had any food today. Let us lift her into the car and take her to the nearest village, where doubtless she has friends."

They tenderly lifted Toad into the motorcar and propped him up with soft cushions, and proceeded on their way.

When Toad heard them talk in so kind and sympathetic a manner, and knew that he was not recognized, his courage began to revive, and he cautiously opened first one eye and then the other.

"Look!" said one of the gentlemen, "she is better already. The fresh air is doing her good. How do you feel now, ma'am?"

"Thank you kindly, sir," said Toad in a feeble voice, "I'm feeling a great deal better!"

"That's right," said the gentleman. "Now keep quite still, and, above all, don't try to talk."

"I won't," said Toad. "I was only thinking, if I might sit on the front seat there, beside the driver, where I could get the fresh air full in my face, I should soon be all right again."

"What a very sensible woman!" said the gentleman. "Of course you shall." So they carefully helped Toad into the front seat beside the driver, and on they went once more.

Toad was almost himself again by now. He sat up, looked about him, and tried to beat down the tremors, the yearnings, the old cravings that rose up and beset him and took possession of him entirely.

"It is fate!" he said to himself. "Why strive? Why struggle?" and he turned to the driver at his side.

"Please, sir," he said, "I wish you would kindly let me try and drive the car for a little. I've been watching you carefully, and it looks so easy and so interesting, and I should like to be able to tell my friends that once I had driven a motorcar!"

The driver laughed at the proposal, so heartily that the gentleman inquired what the matter was. When he heard, he said, to Toad's delight, "Bravo, ma'am! I like your spirit. Let her have a try, and look after her. She won't do any harm." Toad eagerly scrambled into the seat vacated by the driver, took the steering wheel in his hands, listened with affected humility to the instructions given him, and set the car in motion, but very slowly and carefully at first, for he was determined to be prudent.

The gentlemen behind clapped their hands and applauded, and Toad heard them saying, "How well she does it! Fancy a washerwoman driving a car as well as that, the first time!"

Toad went a little faster; then faster still, and faster. He heard the gentlemen call out warningly, "Be careful, washerwoman!" And this annoyed him, and he began to lose his head.

The driver tried to interfere, but he pinned him down in his seat with one elbow and put on full speed. The rush of air in his face, the hum of the engine, and the light jump of the car beneath him intoxicated his weak brain. "Washerwoman, indeed!" he shouted recklessly. "Ho! ho! I am the Toad, the motorcar snatcher, the prison-breaker, the Toad who always escapes! Sit still, and you shall know what driving really is, for you are in the hands of the famous, the skillful, the entirely fearless Toad!"

With a cry of horror the whole party rose and flung themselves on him. "Seize him!" they cried, "seize the Toad, the wicked animal who stole our motorcar! Bind him, chain him, drag him to the nearest police station! Down with the desperate and dangerous Toad!"

Alas! they should have thought, they ought to have been more prudent, they should have remembered to stop the motorcar somehow before playing any pranks of that sort. With a half-turn of the wheel the Toad sent the car crashing through the low hedge that ran along the roadside. One mighty bound, a violent shock, and the wheels of the car were churning up the thick mud of a horsepond.

Toad found himself flying through the air with the strong upward rush and delicate curve of a swallow. He liked the motion, and was just beginning to wonder whether it would go on until he developed wings and turned into a Toad-bird, when he landed on his back with a thump, in the soft rich grass of a meadow. Sitting up, he could just see the motorcar in the pond, nearly submerged; the gentlemen and the driver, encumbered by their long coats, were floundering helplessly in the water.

He picked himself up rapidly, and set off running across country as hard as he could, scrambling through hedges, jumping ditches, pounding across fields, till he was breathless and weary, and had to settle down into an easy walk. When he had recovered his breath somewhat, and was able to think calmly, he began to giggle, and from giggling he took to laughing, and he laughed till he had to sit down under a hedge. "Ho, ho!" he cried, in ecstasies of self-admiration, "Toad again! Toad, as usual, comes out on top! Who was it got them to give him a lift? Who managed to get on the front seat for the sake of fresh air? Who persuaded them into letting him see if he could drive? Who landed them all in a horsepond? Who escaped, flying gaily and unscathed through the air, leaving the narrow-minded, grudging, timid excursionists in the mud where they should rightly be? Why, Toad, of course; clever Toad, great Toad, *good* Toad!"

Then he burst into song again, and chanted with uplifted voice—

"The motorcar went Poop-poop-poop,
    As it raced along the road.
Who was it steered it into a pond?
Ingenious Mr. Toad!

Oh, how clever I am! How clever, how clever, how very, very clev—"

A slight noise at a distance behind him made him turn his head and look. Oh horror! Oh misery! Oh despair!

About two fields off, a chauffeur in his leather gaiters and two large rural policemen were visible, running towards him as hard as they could go!

Poor Toad sprang to his feet and pelted away again, his heart in his mouth. "Oh my!" he gasped, as he panted along, "what an *ass* I am! What a *conceited* and heedless ass! Swaggering again! Shouting and singing songs again! Sitting still and gassing again! Oh my! Oh my! Oh my!"

He glanced back, and saw to his dismay that they were gaining on him. On he ran desperately, but kept looking back, and saw that they still gained steadily. He did his best, but he was a fat animal, and his legs were short, and still they gained. He could hear them close behind him now. Ceasing to heed where he was going, he struggled on blindly and wildly, looking back over his shoulder at the now triumphant enemy, when suddenly the earth failed under his feet, he grasped at

the air, and splash! he found himself head over
ears in deep water, rapid water, water that bore
him along with a force he could not contend with;
and he knew that in his blind panic he had run
straight into the river!

He rose to the surface and tried to grasp the
reeds and the rushes that grew along the water's
edge close under the bank, but the stream was so
strong that it tore them out of his hands. "Oh my!"
gasped poor Toad, "if ever I steal a motorcar again!
If ever I sing another conceited song"—then down
he went, and came up breathless and spluttering.
Presently he saw that he was approaching a big
dark hole in the bank, just above his head, and
as the stream bore him past, he reached up with
a paw and caught hold of the edge and held on.
Then slowly and with difficulty he drew himself
up out of the water, till at last he was able to rest
his elbows on the edge of the hole. There he remained for some minutes, puffing and panting, for
he was quite exhausted.

As he sighed and blew and stared before him
into the dark hole, some bright small thing shone
and twinkled in its depths, moving towards him.
As it approached, a face grew up gradually around
it, and it was a familiar face!

Brown and small with whiskers.

Grave and round, with neat ears and silky hair.

It was the Water Rat!

11

"Like Summer Tempests Came His Tears"

THE RAT put out a neat little brown paw, gripped Toad firmly by the scruff of the neck, and gave a great hoist and a pull; and the waterlogged Toad came up slowly but surely over the edge of the hole, till at last he stood safe and sound in the hall, streaked with mud and weed to be sure, and with the water streaming off him, but happy and high-spirited as of old, now that he found himself once more in the house of a friend, and dodgings and evasions were over, and he could lay aside a disguise that was unworthy of his position and wanted such a lot of living up to.

"Oh, Ratty!" he cried. "I've been through such times since I saw you last, you can't think! Such trials, such sufferings, and all so nobly borne!

209

Then such escapes, such disguises, such subterfuges, and all so cleverly planned and carried out! Been in prison—got out of it, of course! Been thrown into a canal—swam ashore! Stole a horse—sold him for a large sum of money! Humbugged everybody—made 'em all do exactly what I wanted! Oh, I *am* a smart Toad, and no mistake! What do you think my last exploit was? Just hold on till I tell you—"

"Toad," said the Water Rat, gravely and firmly, "you go off upstairs at once, and take off that old cotton rag that looks as if it might formerly have belonged to some washerwoman, and clean yourself thoroughly, and put on some of my clothes and try and come down looking like a gentleman if you *can;* for a more shabby, bedraggled, disreputable-looking object than you are I never set eyes on in my whole life! Now, stop swaggering and arguing, and be off! I'll have something to say to you later!"

Toad was at first inclined to stop and do some talking back at him. He had had enough of being ordered about when he was in prison, and here was the thing being begun all over again, apparently; and by a Rat, too! However, he caught sight of himself in the looking glass over the hatstand, with the rusty black bonnet perched rakishly over one eye, and he changed his mind and went very quickly and humbly upstairs to the Rat's dressing room. There he had a thorough wash and brush-up, changed his clothes, and stood for a long time before the glass, contemplating himself with pride and pleasure, and thinking what utter idiots all the people must have been to have ever mistaken him for one moment for a washerwoman.

By the time he came down again luncheon was on the table, and very glad Toad was to see it, for he had been through some trying experiences and had taken much hard exercise since the excellent breakfast provided for him by the gypsy. While they ate Toad told the Rat all his adventures, dwelling chiefly on his own cleverness, and presence of mind in emergencies, and cunning in tight places; and rather making out that he had been having a gay and highly colored experience. But the more he talked and boasted, the more grave and silent the Rat became.

When at last Toad had talked himself to a standstill, there was silence for a while; and then the Rat said, "Now, Toady, I don't want to give you pain, after all you've been through already; but seriously, don't you see what an awful ass you've been making of yourself? On your own admission you have been handcuffed, imprisoned, starved, chased, terrified out of your life, insulted, jeered at, and ignominiously flung into the water—by a woman, too. Where's the amusement in that? Where does the fun come in? And all because you must needs go and steal a motorcar. You know that you've never had anything but trouble from motorcars from the moment you first set eyes on one. But if you *will* be mixed up with them—as you generally are, five minutes after you've started—why *steal* them? Be a cripple, if you think it's exciting; be a bankrupt, for a change, if you've set your mind on it; but why choose to be a convict? When are you going to be sensible, and think of your friends, and try and be a credit to them? Do you suppose it's any pleasure for me, for instance, to hear animals saying, as I go about, that I'm the chap that keeps company with jailbirds?"

Now, it was a very comforting point in Toad's character that he was a thoroughly goodhearted animal, and never minded being jawed by those who were his real friends. And even when most set upon a thing, he was always able to see the other side of the question. So although, while the Rat was talking so seriously, he kept saying to himself mutinously, "But it *was* fun, though! Awful fun!" and making strange suppressed noises inside him, k-i-ck-ck-ck, and poop-p-p, and other sounds resembling stifled snorts, or the opening of sodawater bottles, yet when the Rat had quite finished, he heaved a deep sigh and said, very nicely and humbly, "Quite right, Ratty! How *sound* you always are! Yes, I've been a conceited old ass, I can quite see that; but now I'm going to be a good Toad, and not do it any more. As for motorcars, I've not been at all so keen about them since my last ducking in that river of yours. The fact is, while I was hanging on to the edge of your hole and getting my breath, I had a sudden idea—a really brilliant idea—connected with motorboats—there, there! don't take on so, old chap, and stamp, and upset things; it was only an idea, and we won't talk any more about it now.

We'll have our coffee, *and* a smoke, and a quiet chat, and then I'm going to stroll gently down to Toad Hall, and get into clothes of my own, and set things going again on the old lines. I've had enough of adventures. I shall lead a quiet, steady, respectable life, pottering about my property, and improving it, and doing a little landscape gardening at times. There will always be a bit of dinner for my friends when they come to see me; and I shall keep a pony-chaise to jog about the country in, just as I used to in the good old days, before I got restless, and wanted to *do* things."

"Stroll gently down to Toad Hall?" cried the Rat, greatly excited. "What are you talking about? Do you mean to say you haven't *heard?*"

"Heard what?" said Toad, turning rather pale. "Go on, Ratty! Quick! Don't spare me! What haven't I heard?"

"Do you mean to tell me," shouted the Rat, thumping with his little fist upon the table, "that you've heard nothing about the Stoats and Weasels?"

"What, the Wild Wooders?" cried Toad, trembling in every limb. "No, not a word! What have they been doing?'

"—And how they've been and taken Toad Hall?" continued the Rat.

Toad leaned his elbows on the table, and his chin on his paws; and a large tear welled up in each of his eyes, overflowed and splashed on the table, plop! plop!

"Go on, Ratty," he murmured presently, "tell

me all. The worst is over. I am an animal again. I can bear it."

"When you—got—into that—that—trouble of yours," said the Rat slowly and impressively, "I mean, when you—disappeared from society for a time, over that misunderstanding about a—a machine, you know—"

Toad merely nodded.

"Well, it was a good deal talked about down here naturally," continued the Rat, "not only along the riverside, but even in the Wild Wood. Animals took sides, as always happens. The River-bankers stuck up for you, and said you had been infamously treated, and there was no justice to be had in the land nowadays. But the Wild Wood animals said hard things, and served you right, and it was time this sort of thing was stopped. And they got very cocky, and went about saying you were done for this time! You would never come back again, never, never!"

Toad nodded once more, keeping silence.

"That's the sort of little beasts they are," the Rat went on. "But Mole and Badger, they stuck out, through thick and thin, that you would come back again soon, somehow. They didn't know exactly how, but somehow!"

Toad began to sit up in his chair again, and to smirk a little.

"They argued from history," continued the Rat. "They said that no criminal laws had ever been known to prevail against cheek and plausibility such as yours, combined with the power of a long purse. So they arranged to move their things into Toad Hall, and sleep there, and keep it aired, and have it all ready for you when you turned up. They didn't guess what was going to happen, of course; still, they had their suspicions of the Wild Wood animals. Now I come to the most painful and tragic part of my story. One dark night—it was a *very* dark night, and blowing hard, too, and raining simply cats and dogs—a band of weasels, armed to the teeth, crept silently up the carriage drive to the front entrance. Simultaneously, a body of desperate ferrets, advancing through the kitchen garden, possessed themselves of the backyard and offices; while a company of skirmishing stoats who stuck at nothing occupied the conservatory and the billiard room, and held the French windows opening onto the lawn.

"The Mole and the Badger were sitting by the fire in the smoking room, telling stories and suspecting nothing, for it wasn't a night for any animals to be out in, when those bloodthirsty villains broke down the doors and rushed in upon them from every side. They made the best fight they could, but what was the good? They were unarmed, and taken by surprise, and what can two animals do against hundreds? They took and beat them severely with sticks, those two poor faithful creatures, and turned them out into the cold and wet, with many insulting and uncalled-for remarks!"

Here the unfeeling Toad broke into a snigger, and

then pulled himself together and tried to look particularly solemn.

"And the Wild Wooders have been living in Toad Hall ever since," continued the Rat; "and going on simply anyhow! Lying in bed half the day, and breakfast at all hours, and the place in such a mess (I'm told) it's not fit to be seen! Eating your grub, and drinking your drink, and making bad jokes about you, and singing vulgar songs, about—well, about prisons, and magistrates, and policemen; horrid personal songs, with no humor in them. And they're telling the tradespeople and everybody that they've come to stay for good."

"Oh, have they!" said Toad, getting up and seizing a stick. "I'll jolly soon see about that!"

"It's no good, Toad!" called the Rat after him. "You'd better come back and sit down; you'll only get into trouble."

But the Toad was off, and there was no holding him. He marched rapidly down the road, his stick over his shoulder, fuming and muttering to himself in his anger, till he got near his front gate, when suddenly there popped up from behind the palings a long yellow ferret with a gun.

"Who comes there?" said the ferret sharply.

"Stuff and nonsense!" said Toad very angrily. "What do you mean by talking like that to me? Come out of it at once, or I'll—"

The ferret said never a word, but he brought his gun up to his shoulder. Toad prudently dropped flat in the road, and *Bang!* a bullet whistled over his head.

The startled Toad scrambled to his feet and scampered off down the road as hard as he could; and as he ran he heard the ferret laughing, and other horrid thin little laughs taking it up and carrying on the sound.

He went back, very crestfallen, and told the Water Rat.

"What did I tell you?" said the Rat. "It's no good. They've got sentries posted, and they are all armed. You must just wait."

Still, Toad was not inclined to give in all at once. So he got out the boat, and set off rowing up the river to where the garden front of Toad Hall came down to the waterside.

Arriving within sight of his old home, he rested on his oars and surveyed the land cautiously. All seemed very peaceful and deserted and quiet. He could see the whole front of Toad Hall, glowing in the evening sunshine, the pigeons settling by twos and threes along the straight line of the roof; the garden, a blaze of flowers; the creek that led up to the boathouse, the little wooden bridge that crossed it; all tranquil, uninhabited, apparently waiting for his return. He would try the boathouse first, he thought. Very warily he paddled up to the mouth of the creek, and was just passing under the bridge, when . . . *Crash!*

A giant stone, dropped from above, smashed through the bottom of the boat. It filled and sank, and Toad found himself struggling in deep water. Looking up, he saw two stoats leaning over the parapet of the bridge and watching him with great glee. "It will be your head next time, Toady!" they called out to him. The indignant Toad swam to shore, while the stoats laughed and laughed, supporting each other, and laughed again, till they nearly had two fits—that is, one fit each, of course.

The Toad retraced his weary way on foot, and related his disappointing experiences to the Water Rat once more.

"Well, *what* did I tell you?" said the Rat very crossly. "And, now, look here! See what you've been and done! Lost me my boat that I was so fond of, that's what you've done! And simply ruined that nice suit of clothes that I lent you! Really, Toad, of all the trying animals—I wonder you manage to keep any friends at all!"

The Toad saw at once how wrongly and foolishly he had acted. He admitted his errors and wrong-headedness and made a full apology to Rat for losing his boat and spoiling his clothes. And he wound up by saying, with that frank self-surrender which always disarmed his friends' criticism and won them back to his side, "Ratty! I see that I have been a headstrong and a willful Toad! Henceforth, believe me, I will be humble and submissive, and will take no action without your kind advice and full approval!"

"If that is really so," said the good-natured Rat, already appeased, "then my advice to you is, considering the lateness of the hour, to sit down and have your supper, which will be on the table in a minute, and be very patient. For I am convinced

Toad was just passing under the bridge when . . .Crash!

that we can do nothing until we have seen the Mole and the Badger, and heard their latest news, and held conference and taken their advice in this difficult matter."

"Oh, ah, yes, of course, the Mole and the Badger," said Toad lightly. "What's become of them, the dear fellows? I had forgotten all about them."

"Well may you ask!" said the Rat reproachfully. "While you were riding about the country in expensive motorcars, and galloping proudly on blood horses, and breakfasting on the fat of the land, those two poor devoted animals have been camping out in the open, in every sort of weather, living very rough by day and lying very hard by night; watching over your house, patrolling your boundaries, keeping a constant eye on the stoats and the weasels, scheming and planning and contriving how to get your property back for you. You don't deserve to have such true and loyal friends, Toad, you don't, really. Some day, when it's too late, you'll be sorry you didn't value them more while you had them!"

"I'm an ungrateful beast, I know," sobbed Toad, shedding bitter tears. "Let me go out and find them, out into the cold, dark night, and share their hardships, and try and prove by— Hold on a bit! Surely I heard the chink of dishes on a tray! Supper's here at last, hooray! Come on, Ratty!"

The Rat remembered that poor Toad had been on prison fare for a considerable time, and that large allowances had therefore to be made. He followed him to the table accordingly, and hospitably encouraged him in his gallant efforts to make up for past privations.

They had just finished their meal and resumed their armchairs, when there came a heavy knock at the door.

Toad was nervous, but the Rat, nodding mysteriously at him, went straight up to the door and opened it, and in walked Mr. Badger.

He had all the appearance of one who for some nights had been kept away from home and all its little comforts and conveniences. His shoes were covered with mud, and he was looking very rough and tousled; but then he had never been a very smart man, the Badger, at the best of times. He came solemnly up to Toad, shook him by the paw, and said, "Welcome home, Toad! Alas! what am I saying? Home, indeed! This is a poor homecoming. Unhappy Toad!" Then he turned his back on him, sat down to the table, drew his chair up, and helped himself to a large slice of cold pie.

Toad was quite alarmed at this very serious and portentous style of greeting; but the Rat whispered to him, "Never mind; don't take any notice; and don't say anything to him just yet. He's always rather low and despondent when he's wanting his victuals. In half an hour's time he'll be quite a different animal."

So they waited in silence, and presently there came another and a lighter knock. The Rat, with a nod to Toad, went to the door and ushered in the Mole, very shabby and unwashed, with bits of hay and straw sticking in his fur.

"Hooray! Here's old Toad!" cried the Mole, his face beaming. "Fancy having you back again!" And he began to dance round him. "We never dreamed you would turn up so soon! Why, you must have managed to escape, you clever, ingenious, intelligent Toad!"

The Rat, alarmed, pulled him by the elbow; but it was too late. Toad was puffing and swelling already.

"Clever? Oh, no!" he said. "I'm not really clever, according to my friends. I've only broken out of the strongest prison in England, that's all! And captured a railway train and escaped on it, that's all! And disguised myself and gone about the country humbugging everybody, that's all! Oh, no! I'm a stupid ass, I am! I'll tell you one or two of my little adventures, Mole, and you shall judge for yourself!"

"Well, well," said the Mole, moving towards the supper table; "supposing you talk while I eat. Not a bite since breakfast! Oh my! Oh my!" And he sat down and helped himself liberally to cold beef and pickles.

Toad straddled on the hearthrug, thrust his paw into his trouser pocket and pulled out a handful of silver. "Look at that!" he cried, displaying it. "That's not so bad, is it, for a few minutes' work? And how do you think I done it, Mole? Horse dealing! That's how I done it!"

"Go on, Toad," said the Mole, immensely interested.

"Toad, do be quiet, please!" said the Rat. "And don't you egg him on, Mole, when you know what he is; but please tell us as soon as possible what the position is, and what's best to be done, now that Toad is back at last."

"The position's about as bad as it can be," replied Mole grumpily, "and as for what's to be done, why, blest if I know! The Badger and I have been round and round the place, by night and by day; always the same thing. Sentries posted everywhere, guns poked out at us, stones thrown at us; always an animal on the lookout, and when they see us, my! how they do laugh! That's what annoys me most!"

"It's a very difficult situation," said the Rat, reflecting deeply. "But I think I see now, in the depths of my mind, what Toad really ought to do. I will tell you. He ought to—"

"No, he oughtn't!" shouted the Mole, with his mouth full. "Nothing of the sort! You don't understand. What he ought to do is, he ought to—"

"Well, I shan't do it, anyway!" cried the Toad, getting excited. "I'm not going to be ordered about by you fellows! It's my house we're talking about, and I know exactly what to do, and I'll tell you. I'm going to—"

By this time they were all three talking at once, at the top of their voices, and the noise was simply deafening, when a thin, dry voice made itself heard, saying, "Be quiet at once, all of you!" and instantly everyone was silent.

It was the Badger, who, having finished his pie, had turned round in his chair and was looking at them severely. When he saw that he had secured their attention, and that they were evidently waiting for him to address them, he turned back to the table again and reached out for the cheese. And so great was the respect commanded by the solid qualities of that admirable animal, that not another word was uttered until he had quite finished his repast and brushed the crumbs from his knees. The Toad fidgeted a good deal, but the Rat held him firmly down.

When the Badger had quite done, he got up from his seat and stood before the fireplace, reflecting deeply. At last he spoke.

"Toad!" he said severely. "You bad, troublesome little animal! Aren't you ashamed of yourself? What do you think your father, my old friend, would have said if he had been here tonight, and had known of all your goings on?"

Toad, who was on the sofa by this time, with his legs up, rolled over on his face, shaken by sobs of contrition.

"There, there!" went on the Badger more kindly. "Never mind. Stop crying. We're going to let bygones be bygones, and try and turn over a new leaf. But what the Mole says is quite true. The stoats are on guard, at every point, and they make the best sentinels in the world. It's quite useless to think of attacking the place. They're too strong for us."

"Then it's all over," sobbed the Toad, crying into the sofa cushion. "I shall go and enlist for a soldier, and never see my dear Toad Hall any more!"

"Come, cheer up, Toady!" said the Badger. "There are more ways of getting back a place than taking it by storm. I haven't said my last word yet. Now I'm going to tell you a great secret."

Toad sat up slowly and dried his eyes. Secrets had an immense attraction for him, because he never could keep one, and he enjoyed the sort of unhallowed thrill he experienced when he went and told another animal, after having faithfully promised not to.

"There—is—an—underground—passage," said the Badger impressively, "that leads from the river bank, quite near here, up into the middle of Toad Hall."

"Oh, nonsense, Badger!" said Toad rather airily. "You've been listening to some of the yarns they spin in the public houses about here. I know every inch of Toad Hall, inside and out. Nothing of the sort, I do assure you!"

"My young friend," said the Badger with great severity, "your father, who was a worthy animal—a lot worthier than some others I know—was a particular friend of mine, and told me a great deal he wouldn't have dreamed of telling you. He discovered that passage— he didn't make it, of course; that was hundreds of years before he ever came to live there—and he repaired it and cleaned it out, because he thought it might come in useful some day, in case of trouble or danger; and he showed it to me. 'Don't let my son know about it,' he said. 'He's a good boy, but very light and volatile in character, and simply cannot hold his tongue. If he's ever in a real fix, and it would be of use to him, you may tell him about the secret passage; but not before.' "

The other animals looked hard at Toad to see how he would take it. Toad was inclined to be sulky at first; but he brightened up immediately, like the good fellow he was.

"Well, well," he said, "perhaps I am a bit of a talker. A popular fellow such as I am—my friends get round me—we chaff, we sparkle, we tell witty stories—and somehow my tongue gets wagging. I have the gift of conversation. I've been told I ought to have a *salon,* whatever that may be. Never mind. Go on, Badger. How's this passage of yours going to help us?"

"I've found out a thing or two lately," continued the Badger. "I got Otter to disguise himself as a sweep and call at the back door with brushes over his shoulder, asking for a job. There's going to be a big banquet tomorrow night. It's somebody's birthday—the Chief Weasel's, I believe—and all the weasels will be gathered together in the dining hall, eating and drinking and laughing and carrying on, suspecting nothing. No guns, no swords, no sticks, no arms of any sort whatever!"

"But the sentinels will be posted as usual," remarked the Rat.

"Exactly," said the Badger; "that is my point. The weasels will trust entirely to the excellent sentinels. And that is where the passage comes in. That very useful tunnel leads right up under the butler's pantry, next to the dining hall!"

"Aha! that squeaky board in the butler's pantry!" said Toad. "Now I understand it!"

"We shall creep out quietly into the butler's pantry—" cried the Mole.

"—with our pistols and swords and sticks—" shouted the Rat.

"—and rush in upon them," said the Badger.

"—and whack 'em, and whack 'em, and whack 'em!" cried the Toad in ecstasy, running round and round the room, and jumping over the chairs.

"Very well, then," said the Badger, resuming his usual dry manner, "our plan is settled, and there's nothing more for you to argue and squabble about. So, as it's getting very late, all of you go right off to bed at once. We will make all the necessary arrangements in the course of the morning tomorrow."

Toad, of course, went off to bed dutifully with the rest—he knew better than to refuse—though he was feeling much too excited to sleep. But he had had a long day, with many events crowded into it; and sheets and blankets were very friendly and comforting things, after plain straw, and not too much of it, spread on the stone floor of a drafty cell; and his head had not been many seconds on his pillow before he was snoring happily. Naturally, he dreamed a good deal; about roads than ran away from him just when he wanted them, and canals that chased him and caught him, and a barge that sailed into the banqueting hall with his week's washing, just as he was giving a dinner party; and he was alone in the secret passage, pushing onwards, but it twisted and turned round and shook itself, and sat up on its end; yet somehow, at the last, he found himself back in Toad Hall, safe and triumphant, with all his friends gathered round about him, earnestly assuring him that he really was a clever Toad.

He slept till a late hour next morning, and by the time he got down he found that the other animals had finished their breakfast some time before. The Mole had slipped off somewhere by himself, without telling anyone where he was going. The Badger sat in the armchair, reading the paper, and not concerning himself in the slightest about what was going to happen that very evening. The Rat, on the other hand, was running round the room busily, with his arms full of weapons of every kind, distributing them in four little heaps on the floor and saying excitedly under his breath, as he ran, "Here's-a-sword-for-the-Rat, here's-a-sword-for-the-Mole, here's-a-sword-for-the-Toad, here's-a-sword-for-the-Badger! Here's-a-pistol-for-the-Rat, here's-a-pistol-for-the-Mole, here's-a-pistol-for-the-Toad, here's-a-pistol-for-the-Badger!" And so on, in a regular, rhythmical way, while the four little heaps gradually grew and grew.

"That's all very well, Rat," said the Badger

presently, looking at the busy little animal over the edge of his newspaper; "I'm not blaming you. But just let us once get past the stoats, with those detestable guns of theirs, and I assure you we shan't want any swords or pistols. We four, with our sticks, once we're inside the dining hall, why, we shall clear the floor of all the lot of them in five minutes. I'd have done the whole thing by myself, only I didn't want to deprive you fellows of the fun!"

"It's as well to be on the safe side," said the Rat reflectively, polishing a pistol-barrel on his sleeve and looking along it.

The Toad, having finished his breakfast, picked up a stout stick and swung it vigorously, belaboring imaginary animals. "I'll learn 'em to steal my house!" he cried. "I'll learn 'em, I'll learn 'em!"

"Don't say 'learn 'em,' Toad," said the Rat, greatly shocked. "It's not good English."

"What are you always nagging at Toad for?" inquired the Badger rather peevishly. "What's the matter with his English? It's the same what I use myself, and if it's good enough for me, it ought to be good enough for you!"

"I'm very sorry," said the Rat humbly. "Only I *think* it ought to be 'teach 'em,' not 'learn 'em.' "

"But we don't *want* to teach 'em," replied the Badger. "We want to *learn* 'em—learn 'em, learn 'em! And what's more, we're going to *do* it, too!"

"Oh, very well, have it your own way," said the Rat. He was getting rather muddled about it himself, and presently he retired into a corner, where

he could be heard muttering, "Learn 'em, teach
'em, teach 'em, learn 'em!" till the Badger told
him rather sharply to leave off.

Presently the Mole came tumbling into the room,
evidently very pleased with himself. "I've been having such fun!" he began at once; "I've been getting
a rise out of the stoats!"

"I hope you've been very careful, Mole?" said
the Rat anxiously.

"I should hope so, too," said the Mole confidently. "I got the idea when I went into the kitchen,
to see about Toad's breakfast being kept hot for
him. I found that old washerwoman dress that he
came home in yesterday hanging on a towel-horse
before the fire. So I put it on, and the bonnet as
well, and the shawl, and off I went to Toad Hall,
as bold as you please. The sentries were on the
lookout, of course, with their guns and their 'Who
comes there?' and all the rest of their nonsense.
'Good morning, gentlemen!' says I, very respectful.
'Want any washing done today?'

"They looked at me very proud and stiff and
haughty, and said, 'Go away, washerwoman! We
don't do any washing on duty.' 'Or any other time?'
says I. Ho, ho, ho! Wasn't I *funny*, Toad?"

"Poor, frivolous animal!" said Toad very loftily.
The fact is, he felt exceeding jealous of Mole for
what he had just done. It was exactly what he
would have liked to have done himself, if only he
had thought of it first, and hadn't gone and overslept himself.

"Some of the stoats turned quite pink," continued the Mole, "and the sergeant in charge, he said to me, very short, he said, 'Now run away, my good woman, run away! Don't keep my men idling and talking on their posts.' 'Run away?' says I; 'it won't be me that'll be running away, in a very short time from now!' "

"Oh, *Moly,* how could you?" said the Rat, dismayed.

The Badger laid down his paper.

"I could see them pricking up their ears and looking at each other," went on the Mole, "and the sergeant said to them, 'Never mind *her,* she doesn't know what she's talking about.'

" 'Oh, don't I?' said I. 'Well, let me tell you this. My daughter, she washes for Mr. Badger, and that'll show you whether I know what I'm talking about; and *you'll* know pretty soon, too! A hundred bloodthirsty Badgers, armed with rifles, are going to attack Toad Hall this very night, by way of the paddock. Six boatloads of Rats, with pistols and cutlasses, will come up the river and effect a landing in the garden, while a picked body of Toads, known as the Die-hards, or the Death-or-Glory Toads, will storm the orchard and carry everything before them, yelling for vengeance. There won't be much left of you to wash, by the time they've done with you, unless you clear out while you have the chance!' Then I ran away, and when I was out of sight I hid; and presently I came creeping back along the ditch and took a peep at them through the hedge. They were all as nervous and flustered as could be, running all ways at once, and falling over each other, and everyone giving orders to everybody else and not listening; and the sergeant kept sending off parties of stoats to distant parts of the grounds, and then sending other fellows to fetch 'em back again; and I heard them saying to each other, 'That's *just* like the weasels; they're to stop comfortably in the banqueting hall, and have feasting and toasts and songs and all sorts of fun, while we must stay on guard in the cold and the dark, and in the end be cut to pieces by bloodthirsty Badgers!' "

"Oh, you silly ass, Mole!" cried the Toad. "You've been and spoiled everything!"

"Mole," said the Badger, in his dry, quiet way, "I perceive you have more sense in your little finger than some other animals have in the whole of their fat bodies. You have managed excellently, and I begin to have great hopes of you. Good Mole! Clever Mole!"

The Toad was simply wild with jealousy, more especially as he couldn't make out for the life of him what the Mole had done that was so particularly clever, but fortunately for him, before he could show temper or expose himself to the Badger's sarcasm, the bell rang for luncheon.

It was a simple but sustaining meal—bacon and broad beans, and a macaroni pudding; and when they had quite done, the Badger settled himself into an armchair, and said, "Well, we've got our work cut out for us tonight, and it will probably be pretty late before we're quite through with it; so I'm just going to take forty winks, while I can." And he drew a handkerchief over his face and was soon snoring.

The anxious and laborious Rat at once resumed his preparations, and started running between his four little heaps, muttering, "Here's-a-belt-for-the-Rat, here's-a-belt-for-the-Mole, here's-a-belt-for-the-Toad, here's-a-belt-for-the-Badger!" and so on, with every fresh accouterment he produced, to which there seemed really no end; so the Mole drew his arm through Toad's, led him out into the open air, shoved him into a wicker chair, and made him tell him all his adventures from beginning to end, which Toad was only too willing to do. The Mole was a good listener, and Toad, with no one to check his statements or to criticize in an unfriendly spirit, rather let himself go. Indeed, much that he related belonged more properly to the category of what-might-have-happened-had-I-only thought-of-it-in-time-instead-of-ten-minutes-afterwards. Those are always the best and the raciest adventures; and why should they not be truly ours, as much as the somewhat inadequate things that really come off?

12
The Return of Ulysses

When it began to grow dark, the Rat, with an air of excitement and mystery, summoned them back into the parlor, stood each of them up alongside of his little heap, and proceeded to dress them up for the coming expedition. He was very earnest and thoroughgoing about it, and the affair took quite a long time. First, there was a belt to go round each animal, and then a sword to be stuck into each belt, and then a cutlass on the other side to balance it. Then a pair of pistols, a policeman's truncheon, several sets of handcuffs, some bandages and sticking plaster, and a flash and a sandwich case. The Badger laughed good-humoredly and said, "All right, Ratty! It amuses you and it doesn't hurt me. I'm going to do all I've got to do with this here stick." But the Rat only said, *"Please,* Badger! You know I shouldn't like you to blame me afterwards and say I had forgotten *anything!"*

When all was quite ready, the Badger took a dark lantern in one paw; grasped his great stick with the other, and said, "Now then, follow me! Mole first, 'cos I'm very pleased with him; Rat next; Toad last. And look here, Toady! Don't you chatter so much as usual, or you'll be sent back, as sure as fate!"

The Toad was so anxious not to be left out that he took up the inferior position assigned to him without a murmur, and the animals set off. The Badger led them along by the river for a little way, and then suddenly swung himself over the edge into a hole in the river bank, a little above the water. The Mole and the Rat followed silently, swinging themselves successfully into the hole as they had seen the Badger do; but when it came to Toad's turn, of course he managed to slip and fall into the water with a loud splash and a squeal of alarm. He was hauled out by his friends, rubbed down and wrung out hastily, comforted, and set on his legs; but the Badger was seriously angry, and told him that the very next time he made a fool of himself he would most certainly be left behind.

So at last they were in the secret passage, and the cutting-out expedition had really begun!

It was cold, and dark, and damp, and low, and narrow, and poor Toad began to shiver, partly from dread of what might be before him, partly because he was wet through. The lantern was far ahead, and he could not help lagging behind a little in the darkness. Then he heard the Rat call out warningly, "*Come* on, Toad!" and a terror seized him of being left behind, alone in the darkness, and he "came on" with such a rush that he upset the Rat into the Mole and the Mole into the Badger, and for a moment all was confusion. The Badger thought they were being attacked from behind, and, as there was no room to use a stick or a cutlass, drew a pistol, and was on the point of putting a bullet into Toad. When he found out what had really happened he was very angry indeed, and said, "Now this time that tiresome Toad *shall* be left behind!"

But Toad whimpered, and the other two promised that they would be answerable for his good conduct, and at last the Badger was pacified, and the procession moved on; only this time the Rat brought up the rear, with a firm grip on the shoulder of Toad.

So they groped and shuffled along, with their ears pricked up and their paws on their pistols, till at last the Badger said, "We ought by now to be pretty nearly under the Hall."

Then suddenly they heard, far away as it might be, and yet apparently nearly over their heads, a confused murmur of sound, as if people were shouting and cheering and stamping on the floor and hammering on tables. The Toad's nervous terrors all returned, but the Badger only remarked placidly, "They *are* going it, the weasels!"

The passage now began to slope upward; they groped onward a little farther, and then noise broke out again, quite distinct this time, and very close above them. "Ooo-ray-oo-ray-oo-ray-ooray!" they heard, and the stamping of little feet on the floor, and the clinking of glasses as little fists pounded on the table. "*What* a time they're having!" said the Badger. "Come on!" They hurried along the passage till it came to a full stop, and they found themselves standing under the trap door that led up into the butler's pantry.

Such a tremendous noise was going on in the banqueting hall that there was little danger of their being overheard. The Badger said, "Now, boys, all together!" and the four of them put their shoulders to the trap door and heaved it back. Hoisting each other up, they found themselves standing in the pantry, with only a door between them and the banqueting hall, where the unconscious enemies were carousing.

The noise, as they emerged from the passage, was simply deafening. At last, as the cheering and hammering slowly subsided, a voice could be made out saying, "Well, I do not propose to detain you much longer"—(great applause)—"but before I resume my seat"—(renewed cheering)—"I should like to say one word about our kind host, Mr. Toad. We all know Toad"—(great laughter)—"*Good* Toad, *modest* Toad, *honest* Toad!" (shrieks of merriment).

"Only just let me get at him!" muttered Toad, grinding his teeth.

"Hold hard a minute!" said the Badger, restraining him with difficulty. "Get ready, all of you!"

"—Let me sing you a little song," went on the voice, "which I have composed on the subject of Toad"—(prolonged applause).

Then the Chief Weasel—for it was he—began in a high squeaky voice—

> *"Toad he went a-pleasuring*
> *Gaily down the street—"*

The Badger drew himself up, took a firm grip of his stick with both paws, glanced round at his comrades, and cried—

"The hour is come! Follow me!"

And flung the door open wide.

My!

What a squealing and a squeaking and a screeching filled the air!

Well might the terrified weasels dive under the tables and spring madly up at the windows! Well might the ferrets rush wildly for the fireplace and get hopelessly jammed in the chimney! Well might tables and chairs be upset, and glass and china be sent crashing on the floor, in the panic of that terrible moment when the four Heroes strode wrathfully into the room! The mighty Badger, his whiskers bristling, his great cudgel whistling through the air; Mole, black and grim, brandishing his stick and shouting his awful war cry, "A Mole! A Mole!" Rat, desperate and determined, his belt bulging with weapons of every age and every variety; Toad, frenzied with excitement and injured pride, swollen to twice his ordinary size, leaping into the air and emitting Toad-whoops that chilled them to the marrow! "Toad he went a-pleasuring!" he yelled. "*I'll* pleasure 'em!" And he went straight for the Chief Weasel. They were but four in all, but to the panic-stricken weasels the hall seemed full of monstrous animals, gray, black, brown, and yellow, whooping and flourishing enormous cudgels; and they broke and fled with squeals of terror and dismay, this way and that, through the windows, up the chimney, anywhere to get out of reach of those terrible sticks.

The affair was soon over. Up and down, the whole length of the hall, strode the four friends, whacking with their sticks at every head that showed itself; and in five minutes the room was cleared. Through the broken windows the shrieks of terrified weasels escaping across the lawn were borne faintly to their ears; on the floor lay prostrate some dozen or so of the enemy, on whom the Mole was busily engaged in fitting handcuffs. The Badger, resting from his labors, leaned on his stick and wiped his honest brow.

"Mole," he said, "you're the best of fellows! Just cut along outside and look after those stoat-sentries of yours, and see what they're doing. I've an idea that, thanks to you, we shan't have much trouble from *them* tonight!"

The Mole vanished promptly through a window; and the Badger bade the other two set a table on its

legs again, pick up knives and forks and plates and glasses from the *débris* on the floor, and see if they could find material for a supper. "I want some grub, I do," he said, in that rather common way he had of speaking. "Stir your stumps, Toad, and look lively! We've got your house back for you, and you don't offer us so much as a sandwich."

Toad felt rather hurt that the Badger didn't say pleasant things to him, as he had to the Mole, and tell him what a fine fellow he was, and how splendidly he had fought; for he was rather particularly pleased with himself and the way he gone for the Chief Weasel and sent him flying across the table with one blow of his stick. But he bustled about,

and so did the Rat, and soon they found some guava jelly in a glass dish, and a cold chicken, a tongue that had hardly been touched, some trifle, and quite a lot of lobster salad; and in the pantry they came upon a basketful of French rolls and any quantity of cheese, butter, and celery. They were just about to sit down when the Mole clambered in through the window, chuckling, with an armful of rifles.

"It's all over," he reported. "From what I can make out, as soon as the stoats, who were very nervous and jumpy already, heard the shrieks and the yells and the uproar inside the hall, some of them threw down their rifles and fled. The others stood fast for a bit, but when the weasels came rushing out upon them they thought they were betrayed; and the stoats grappled with the weasels, and the weasels fought to get away, and they wrestled and wriggled and punched each other, and rolled over and over, till most of 'em rolled into the river! They've all disappeared by now, one way or another; and I've got their rifles. So *that's* all right!"

"Excellent and deserving animal!" said the Badger, his mouth full of chicken and trifle. "Now, there's just one more thing I want you to do, Mole, before you sit down to your supper along of us; and I wouldn't trouble you only I know I can trust you to see a thing done, and I wish I could say the same of everyone I know. I'd send the Rat, if he wasn't a poet. I want you to take those fellows on the floor there upstairs with you, and have some bedrooms cleaned out and tidied up and made really comfortable. See that they sweep *under* the beds, and put clean sheets and pillowcases on, and turn down one corner of the bedclothes, just as you know it ought to be done; and have a can of hot water, and clean towels, and fresh cakes of soap put in each room. And then you can give them a licking apiece, if it's any satisfaction to you, and put them out by the back door, and we shan't see any more of *them,* I fancy. And then come along and have some of this cold tongue. It's first rate. I'm very pleased with you, Mole!"

The good-natured Mole picked up a stick,

formed his prisoners up in a line on the floor, gave
them the order "Quick march!" and led his squad
off to the upper floor. After a time, he appeared
again, smiling, and said that every room was ready,
and as clean as a new pin. "And I didn't have to
lick them, either," he added. "I thought, on the
whole, they had licking enough for one night, and
the weasels, when I put the point to them, quite
agreed with me, and said they wouldn't think of
troubling me. They were very penitent, and said
they were extremely sorry for what they had done,
but it was all the fault of the Chief Weasel and the
stoats, and if ever they could do anything for us at
any time to make up, we had only got to mention
it. So I gave them a roll apiece, and let them out
at the back, and off they ran, as hard as they
could!"

Then the Mole pulled his chair up to the table,
and pitched into the cold tongue; and Toad, like
the gentleman he was, put all his jealousy from him,
and said heartily, "Thank you kindly, dear Mole,
for all your pains and trouble tonight, and especially for your cleverness this morning!" The
Badger was pleased at that, and said, "There spoke
my brave Toad!" So they finished their supper in
great joy and contentment, and presently retired to
rest between clean sheets, safe in Toad's ancestral
home, won back by matchless valor, consummate
strategy, and a proper handling of sticks.

The following morning, Toad, who had overslept
himself as usual, came down to breakfast disgrace-

fully late, and found on the table a certain quantity of eggshells, some fragments of cold and leathery toast, a coffeepot three-fourths empty, and really very little else; which did not tend to improve his temper, considering that, after all, it was his own house. Through the French windows of the breakfast room he could see the Mole and the Water Rat sitting in wicker chairs out on the lawn, evidently telling each other stories; roaring with laughter and kicking their short legs up in the air. The Badger, who was in an armchair and deep in the morning paper, merely looked up and nodded when Toad entered the room. But Toad knew his man, so he sat down and made the best breakfast he could, merely observing to himself that he would get square with the others sooner or later. When he had nearly finished, the Badger looked up and remarked rather shortly, "I'm sorry, Toad, but I'm afraid there's a heavy morning's work in front of you. You see, we really ought to have a Banquet at once, to celebrate this affair. It's expected of you —in fact, it's the rule."

"Oh, all right!" said the Toad readily. "Anything to oblige. Though why on earth you should want to have a Banquet in the morning I cannot understand. But you know I do not live to please myself, but merely to find out what my friends want, and then try and arrange it for 'em, you dear old Badger!"

"Don't pretend to be stupider than you really are," replied the Badger crossly; "and don't chuckle and splutter in your coffee while you're talking; it's not manners. What I mean is, the Banquet will be at night, of course, but the invitations will have to be written and got off at once, and you've got to write 'em. Now, sit down at the table—there's stacks of letter paper on it, with 'Toad Hall' at the top in blue and gold—and write invitations to all our friends, and if you stick to it we shall get them out before luncheon. And *I'll* bear a hand, too, and take my share of the burden. *I'll* order the Banquet."

"What!" cried the Toad, dismayed. "Me stop indoors and write a lot of rotten letters on a jolly morning like this, when I want to go around my property, and set everything and everybody to rights, and swagger about and enjoy myself! Certainly not! I'll be—I'll see you—Stop a minute, though! Why, of course, dear Badger! What is my pleasure or convenience compared with that of others! You wish it done, and it shall be done. Go, Badger, order the Banquet, order what you like; then join our young friends outside in their innocent mirth, oblivious of me and my care and toils. I sacrifice this fair morning on the altar of duty and friendship!"

The Badger looked at him very suspiciously, but Toad's frank, open countenance made it difficult to suggest any unworthy motive in this change of attitude. He quitted the room, accordingly, in the direction of the kitchen, and as soon as the door had closed behind him, Toad hurried to the writing table. He *would* write the invitations; and he would take care to mention the leading part he had taken in the fight, and how he had laid the Chief Weasel flat; and he would hint at his adventures, and what a career of triumph he had to tell about; and on the flyleaf he would give a sort of program of entertainment for the evening—something like this, as he sketched it out in his head:—

SPEECH   BY TOAD.
(There will be other speeches by TOAD
            during the evening.)
ADDRESS   BY TOAD.
    SYNOPSIS—Our Prison System—The
    Waterways of Old England—Horse
    dealing, and how to deal—Property,
    its rights and its duties—Back to the
    Land—A Typical English Squire.
SONG   BY TOAD.
        (Composed by himself.)
OTHER COMPOSITIONS   BY TOAD.
    will be sung in the course of the
    evening by the . . . COMPOSER.

The idea pleased him mightily, and he worked very hard and got all the letters finished by noon, at which hour it was reported to him that there was a small and rather bedraggled weasel at the door, inquiring timidly whether he could be of any service to the gentlemen. Toad swaggered out and found out it was one of the prisoners of the previous evening, very respectful and anxious to please. He patted him on the head, shoved the bundle of invitations into his paw, and told him to cut along quick and deliver them as fast as he could, and if he liked to come back again in the evening perhaps there might be a shilling for him, or, again, perhaps there mightn't; and the poor weasel seemed really quite grateful, and hurried off eagerly to do his mission.

When the other animals came back to luncheon, very boisterous and breezy after a morning on the river, the Mole, whose conscience had been pricking him, looked doubtfully at Toad, expecting to find him sulky or depressed. Instead, he was so uppish and inflated that the Mole began to suspect something; while the Rat and the Badger exchanged significant glances.

As soon as the meal was over, Toad thrust his paws deep into his trouser pockets, remarked casually, "Well, look after yourselves, you fellows! Ask for anything you want!" and was swaggering off in the direction of the garden, where he wanted to think out an idea or two for his coming speeches, when the Rat caught him by the arm.

Toad rather suspected what he was after, and did his best to get away; but when the Badger took him firmly by the other arm he began to see that the game was up. The two animals conducted him between them into the small smoking room that opened out of the entrance hall, shut the door, and put him into a chair. Then they both stood in front of him, while Toad sat silent and regarded them with much suspicion and ill-humor.

"Now, look here. Toad," said the Rat. "It's about this Banquet, and very sorry I am to have to speak to you like this. But we want you to understand clearly, once and for all, that there are going to be no speeches and no songs. Try and grasp the fact that on this occasion we're not arguing with you; we're just telling you."

Toad saw that he was trapped. They understood him, they saw through him, they had got ahead of him. His pleasant dream was shattered.

"Mayn't I sing them just one *little* song?" he pleaded piteously.

"No, not *one* little song," replied the Rat firmly, though his heart bled as he noticed the trembling lip of the poor disappointed Toad. "It's no good, Toady; you know well that your songs are all conceit and boasting and vanity; and your speeches are all self-praise and—and—well, and gross exaggeration and—and—"

"And gas," put in the Badger, in his common way.

"It's for your own good, Toady," went on the Rat. "You know you *must* turn over a new leaf sooner or later, and now seems a splendid time to begin; a sort of turning point in your career. Please don't think that saying all this doesn't hurt me more than it hurts you."

Toad remained a long while plunged in thought. At last he raised his head, and the traces of strong emotion were visible on his features. "You have conquered, my friends," he said in broken accents. "It was, to be sure, but a small thing that I asked—merely leave to blossom and expand for yet one more evening, to let myself go and hear the tumultuous applause that always seems to me—somehow —to bring out my best qualities. However, you are right, I know, and I am wrong. Henceforth I will be a very different Toad. My friends, you shall never have occasion to blush for me again. But, oh dear, oh dear, this is a hard world!"

And, pressing his handkerchief to his face, he left the room with faltering footsteps.

"Badger," said the Rat, "*I* feel like a brute; I wonder what *you* feel like?"

"Oh, I know, I know," said the Badger gloomily. "But the thing had to be done. This good fellow has got to live here, and hold his own, and be respected. Would you have him a common laughingstock, mocked and jeered at by stoats and weasels?"

"Of course not," said the Rat. "And, talking of weasels, it's lucky we came upon that little weasel, just as he was setting out with Toad's invitations. I suspected something from what you told me, and had a look at one or two; they were simply disgraceful. I confiscated the lot, and the good Mole is now sitting in the blue *boudoir,* filling up plain, simple invitation cards."

*   *   *   *   *

At last the hour for the Banquet began to draw near, and Toad, who on leaving the others had retired to his bedroom, was still sitting there, melancholy and thoughtful. His brow resting on his paw, he pondered long and deeply. Gradually his countenance cleared, and he began to smile long, slow smiles. Then he took to giggling in a shy, self-conscious manner. At last he got up, locked the door, drew the curtains across the windows, collected all the chairs in the room and arranged them in a semicircle, and took up his position in front of them, swelling visibly. Then he bowed, coughed twice, and letting himself go, with uplifted voice he sang to the enraptured audience that his imagination so clearly saw.

TOAD'S LAST LITTLE SONG!

The Toad—came—home!
There was panic in the parlor and howling in the
    hall,
There was crying in the cowshed and shrieking in
    the stall,
When the Toad—came—home!

When the Toad—came—home!
There was smashing in of window and crashing in
    of door,
There was chivying of weasels that fainted on the
    floor,
When the Toad—came—home!

Bang! go the drums!
The trumpeters are tooting and the soldiers are
    saluting,

And the cannon they are shooting and the motor-
    cars are hooting,
As the—Hero—comes!

Shout—Hooray!
And let each one of the crowd try and shout it very
    loud,
In honor of an animal of whom you're justly proud,
For it's Toad's—great—day!

He sang this very loud, with great unction and
expression; and when he had done, he sang it all
over again.

Then he heaved a deep sigh; a long, long, long
sigh.

Then he dipped his hairbrush in the water jug,
parted his hair in the middle, and plastered it down
very straight and sleek on each side of his face;
and, unlocking the door, went quietly down the
stairs to greet his guests, who he knew must be
assembling in the drawing room.

All the animals cheered when he entered, and
crowded round to congratulate him and say nice
things about his courage, and his cleverness, and
his fighting qualities; but Toad only smiled faintly
and murmured, "Not at all!" Or, sometimes, for a
change, "On the contrary!" Otter, who was standing at the hearthrug, describing to an admiring
circle of friends exactly how he would have managed things had he been there, came forward with
a shout, threw his arm round Toad's neck, and

tried to take him round the room in triumphal progress; but Toad, in a mild way, was rather snubby to him, remarking gently, as he disengaged himself, "Badger's was the mastermind; the Mole and the Water Rat bore the brunt of the fighting; I merely served in the ranks and did little or nothing." The animals were evidently puzzled and taken aback by this unexpected attitude of his; and Toad felt, as he moved from one guest to the other, making his modest responses, that he was an object of absorbing interest to everyone.

The Badger had ordered everything of the best, and the Banquet was a great success. There was much talking and laughter and chaff among the animals, but through it all Toad, who of course was in the chair, looked down his nose and murmured pleasant nothings to the animals on either side of him. At intervals he stole a glance at the Badger and the Rat, and always when he looked they were staring at each other with their mouths open; and this gave him the greatest satisfaction. Some of the younger and livelier animals, as the evening wore on, got whispering to each other that things were not so amusing as they used to be in the good old days; and there were some knockings on the table and cries of "Toad! Speech! Speech from Toad! Song! Mr. Toad's Song!" But Toad only shook his head gently, raised one paw in mild protest, and, by pressing delicacies on his guests, by topical small talk, and by earnest inquiries after members of their families not yet old enough to appear at social functions, managed to convey to them that this dinner was being run on strictly conventional lines.

He was indeed an altered Toad!

*   *   *   *   *

After this climax, the four animals continued to lead their lives, so rudely broken in upon by civil war, in great joy and contentment, undisturbed by further risings or invasions. Toad, after due consultation with his friends, selected a handsome gold chain and locket set with pearls, which he dispatched to the jailer's daughter with a letter that even the Badger admitted to be modest, grateful, and appreciative; and the engine driver, in his turn, was properly thanked and compensated for all his pains and trouble. Under severe compulsion from the Badger, even the bargewoman was, with some trouble, sought out and the value of her horse discreetly made good to her; though Toad kicked terribly at this, holding himself to be an instrument of Fate, sent to punish fat women with mottled arms who couldn't tell a real gentleman when they saw one. The amount involved, it was true, was not very burdensome, the gypsy's valuation being admitted by local assessors to be approximately correct.

Sometimes, in the course of long summer evenings, the friends would take a stroll together in the Wild Wood, now successfully tamed so far as they were concerned; and it was pleasing to see how respectfully they were greeted by the inhabitants, and how the mother weasels would bring their young ones to the mouths of their holes, and say, pointing, "Look, baby! There goes the great Mr. Toad! And that's the gallant Water Rat, a terrible fighter, walking along o' him! And yonder comes the famous Mr. Mole, of whom you so often have heard your father tell!" But when the infants were fractious and quite beyond control, they would quiet them by telling how, if they didn't hush them and not fret them, the terrible gray Badger would up and get them. This was a base libel on Badger, who, though he cared little about Society, was rather fond of children; but it never failed to have its full effect.

NATHANIEL HAWTHORNE

Tanglewood Tales

Illustrations by SHEILAH BECKETT

COMPANION LIBRARY

GROSSET & DUNLAP

Publishers   New York

Contents

The Wayside: Introductory   1
1 · The Minotaur · 11
2 · The Pygmies · 50
3 · The Dragon's Teeth · 77
4 · Circe's Palace · 116
5 · The Pomegranate Seeds · 157
6 · The Golden Fleece · 199

Tanglewood
Tales

The Wayside

INTRODUCTORY

A SHORT time ago, I was favored with a flying visit from my young friend Eustace Bright, whom I had not before met with since quitting the breezy mountains of Berkshire. It being the winter vacation at his college, Eustace was allowing himself a little relaxation, in the hope, he told me, of repairing the inroads which severe application to study had made upon his health; and I was happy to conclude, from the excellent physical condition in which I saw him, that the remedy had already been attended with very desirable success. He had now run up from Boston by the noon train, partly impelled by the friendly regard with which he is pleased to honor me, and partly, as I soon found, on a matter of literary business.

It delighted me to receive Mr. Bright, for the first time, under a roof, though a very humble one, which

I could really call my own. Nor did I fail (as is the custom of landed proprietors all about the world) to parade the poor fellow up and down over my half a dozen acres; secretly rejoicing, nevertheless, that the disarray of the inclement season, and particularly the six inches of snow then upon the ground, prevented him from observing the ragged neglect of soil and shrubbery into which the place has lapsed. It was idle, however, to imagine that an airy guest from Monument Mountain, Bald-Summit, and old Graylock, shaggy with primeval forests, could see anything to admire in my poor little hillside, with its growth of frail and insect-eaten locust trees. Eustace very frankly called the view from my hilltop tame; and so, no doubt, it was, after rough, broken, rugged, headlong Berkshire, and especially the northern parts of the county, with which his college residence had made him familiar. But to me there is a peculiar, quiet charm in these broad meadows and gentle eminences. They are better than mountains, because they do not stamp and stereotype themselves into the brain, and thus grow wearisome with the same strong impression, repeated day after day. A few summer weeks among mountains, a lifetime among green meadows and placid slopes, with outlines forever new, because continually fading out of the memory—such would be my sober choice.

I doubt whether Eustace did not internally pronounce the whole thing a bore, until I led him to my predecessor's little ruined, rustic summerhouse, midway on the hillside. It is a mere skeleton of slender,

decaying tree trunks, with neither walls nor a roof;
nothing but a tracery of branches and twigs, which
the next wintry blast will be very likely to scatter in
fragments along the terrace. It looks, and is, as eva-
nescent as a dream; and yet, in its rustic network of
boughs, it has somehow enclosed a hint of spiritual
beauty, and has become a true emblem of the subtile
and ethereal mind that planned it. I made Eustace
Bright sit down on a snowbank, which had heaped itself over the mossy seat, and gazing through the
arched window opposite, he acknowledged that the
scene at once grew picturesque.

"Simple as it looks," said he, "this little edifice
seems to be the work of magic. It is full of sugges-
tiveness, and, in its way, is as good as a cathedral.
Ah, it would be just the spot for one to sit in, of a
summer afternoon, and tell the children some more
of those wild stories from the classic myths!"

"It would, indeed," answered I. "The summerhouse itself, so airy and so broken, is like one of those
old tales, imperfectly remembered; and these living
branches of the Baldwin apple tree, thrusting themselves so rudely in, are like your unwarrantable inter-
polations. But, by the by, have you added any more
legends to the series, since the publication of the
Wonder Book?"

"Many more," said Eustace. "Primrose, Periwinkle, and the rest of them allow me no comfort of
my life, unless I tell them a story every day or two. I
have run away from home partly to escape the impor-
tunity of those little wretches! But I have written out

six of the new stories, and have brought them for you to look over."

"Are they as good as the first?" I inquired.

"Better chosen, and better handled," replied Eustace Bright. "You will say so when you read them."

"Possibly not," I remarked. "I know, from my own experience, that an author's last work is always his best one, in his own estimate, until it quite loses the red heat of composition. After that, it falls into its true place, quietly enough. But let us adjourn to my study and examine these new stories. It would hardly be doing yourself justice, were you to bring me acquainted with them, sitting here on this snowbank!"

So we descended the hill to my small, old cottage, and shut ourselves up in the southeastern room, where the sunshine comes in, warmly and brightly, through the better half of a winter's day. Eustace put his bundle of manuscript into my hands; and I skimmed through it pretty rapidly, trying to find out its merits and demerits by the touch of my fingers, as a veteran storyteller ought to know how to do.

It will be remembered that Mr. Bright condescended to avail himself of my literary experience by constituting me editor of the *Wonder Book*. As he had no reason to complain of the reception of that erudite work by the public, he was now disposed to retain me in a similar position, with respect to the present volume, which he entitled *Tanglewood Tales*. Not, as Eustace hinted, that there was any real necessity for my services as introductor, inasmuch as his own name had become established, in

some good degree of favor, with the literary world. But the connection with myself, he was kind enough to say, had been highly agreeable; nor was he by any means desirous, as most people are, of kicking away the ladder that had perhaps helped him to reach his present elevation. My young friend was willing, in short, that the fresh verdure of his growing reputation should spread over my straggling and half-naked boughs; even as I have sometimes thought of training a vine, with its broad leafiness, and purple fruitage, over the worm-eaten posts and rafters of the rustic summerhouse. I was not insensible to the advantages of his proposal, and gladly assured him of my acceptance.

Merely from the titles of the stories, I saw at once that the subjects were not less rich than those of the former volume; nor did I at all doubt that Mr. Bright's audacity (so far as that endowment might avail) had enabled him to take full advantage of whatever capabilities they offered. Yet, in spite of my experience of his free way of handling them, I did not quite see, I confess, how he could have obviated all the difficulties in the way of rendering them presentable to children. These old legends, so brimming over with everything that is most abhorrent to our Christianized moral sense—some of them so hideous, others so melancholy and miserable, amid which the Greek tragedians sought their themes, and molded them into the sternest forms of grief that ever the world saw; was such material the stuff that children's playthings should be made of! How were

they to be purified? How was the blessed sunshine to be thrown into them?

But Eustace told me that these myths were the most singular things in the world, and that he was invariably astonished, whenever he began to relate one, by the readiness with which it adapted itself to the childish purity of his auditors. The objectionable characteristics seem to be a parasitical growth, having no essential connection with the original fable. They fall away, and are thought of no more, the instant he puts his imagination in sympathy with the innocent little circle, whose wide-open eyes are fixed so eagerly upon him. Thus the stories (not by any strained effort of the narrator's, but in harmony with their inherent germ) transform themselves, and reassume the shapes which they might be supposed to possess in the pure childhood of the world. When the first poet or romancer told these marvelous legends (such is Eustace Bright's opinion), it was still the Golden Age. Evil had never yet existed; and sorrow, misfortune, crime, were mere shadows which the mind fancifully created for itself, as a shelter against too sunny realities; or, at most, but prophetic dreams, to which the dreamer himself did not yield a waking credence. Children are now the only representatives of the men and women of that happy era; and therefore it is that we must raise the intellect and fancy to the level of childhood, in order to re-create the original myths.

I let the youthful author talk as much and as extravagantly as he pleased, and was glad to see him commencing life with such confidence in himself and

his performances. A few years will do all that is necessary towards showing him the truth in both respects. Meanwhile, it is but right to say, he does really appear to have overcome the moral objections against these fables, although at the expense of such liberties with their structure as must be left to plead their own excuse, without any help from me. Indeed, except that there was a necessity for it—and that the inner life of the legends cannot be come at save by making them entirely one's own property—there is no defense to be made.

Eustace informed me that he had told his stories to the children in various situations—in the woods, on the shore of the lake, in the dell of Shadow Brook, in the playroom, at Tanglewood fireside, and in a magnificent palace of snow, with ice windows, which he helped his little friends to build. His auditors were even more delighted with the contents of the present volume than with the specimens which have already been given to the world. The classically learned Mr. Pringle, too, had listened to two or three of the tales, and censured them even more bitterly than he did "The Three Golden Apples"; so that, what with praise, and what with criticism, Eustace Bright thinks that there is good hope of at least as much success with the public as in the case of the *Wonder Book*.

I made all sorts of inquiries about the children, not doubting that there would be great eagerness to hear of their welfare among some good little folks who have written to me, to ask for another volume of myths. They are all, I am happy to say (unless we except

Clover), in excellent health and spirits. Primrose is now almost a young lady and, Eustace tells me, is just as saucy as ever. She pretends to consider herself quite beyond the age to be interested by such idle stories as these; but, for all that, whenever a story is to be told, Primrose never fails to be one of the listeners, and to make fun of it when finished. Periwinkle is very much grown, and is expected to shut up her baby-house and throw away her doll in a month or two more. Sweet Fern has learned to read and write, and has put on a jacket and pair of pantaloons—all of which improvements I am sorry for. Squash-Blossom, Blue Eye, Plantain, and Buttercup have had the scarlet fever, but came easily through it. Huckleberry, Milkweed, and Dandelion were attacked with the whooping cough, but bore it bravely, and kept out of doors whenever the sun shone. Cowslip, during the autumn, had either the measles, or some eruption that looked very much like it, but was hardly sick a day. Poor Clover has been a good deal troubled with her second teeth, which have made her meager in aspect and rather fractious in temper; nor, even when she smiles, is the matter much mended, since it discloses a gap just within her lips, almost as wide as the barn door. But all this will pass over, and it is predicted that she will turn out a very pretty girl.

As for Mr. Bright himself, he is now in his Senior year at Williams College, and has a prospect of graduating with some degree of honorable distinction at the next Commencement. In his oration for the bachelor's degree, he gives me to understand, he will treat

of the classical myths, viewed in the aspect of baby stories, and has a great mind to discuss the expediency of using up the whole of ancient history for the same purpose. I do not know what he means to do with himself after leaving college, but trust that, by dabbling so early with the dangerous and seductive business of authorship, he will not be tempted to become an author by profession. If so, I shall be very sorry for the little that I have had to do with the matter, in encouraging these first beginnings.

I wish there were any likelihood of my soon seeing Primrose, Periwinkle, Dandelion, Sweet Fern, Clover, Plantain, Huckleberry, Milkweed, Cowslip, Buttercup, Blue Eye, and Squash-Blossom again. But as I do not know when I shall revisit Tanglewood, and as Eustace Bright probably will not ask me to edit a third *Wonder Book,* the public of little folks must not expect to hear any more about those dear children from me. Heaven bless them, and everybody else, whether grown people or children!

THE WAYSIDE, CONCORD, MASS.
March 13, 1853.

The Minotaur

IN THE old city of Trœzene, at the foot of a lofty mountain, there lived, a very long time ago, a little boy named Theseus. His grandfather, King Pittheus, was the sovereign of that country, and was reckoned a very wise man; so that Theseus, being brought up in the royal palace, and being naturally a bright lad, could hardly fail of profiting by the old king's instructions. His mother's name was Æthra. As for his father, the boy had never seen him. But, from his earliest remembrance, Æthra used to go with little Theseus into a wood, and sit down upon a moss-grown rock, which was deeply sunken into the earth. Here she often talked with her son about his father, and said that he was called Ægeus, and that he was a great king, and ruled over Attica, and dwelled at Athens, which was as famous a city as any in the

world. Theseus was very fond of hearing about King Ægeus, and often asked his good mother Æthra why he did not come and live with them at Trœzene.

"Ah, my dear son," answered Æthra, with a sigh, "a monarch has his people to take care of. The men and women over whom he rules are in the place of children to him; and he can seldom spare time to love his own children as other parents do. Your father will never be able to leave his kingdom for the sake of seeing his little boy."

"Well, but dear mother," asked the boy, "why cannot I go to this famous city of Athens, and tell King Ægeus that I am his son?"

"That may happen by and by," said Æthra. "Be patient, and we shall see. You are not yet big and strong enough to set out on such an errand."

"And how soon shall I be strong enough?" Theseus persisted in inquiring.

"You are but a tiny boy as yet," replied his mother. "See if you can lift this rock on which we are sitting."

The little fellow had a great opinion of his own strength. So, grasping the rough protuberances of the rock, he tugged and toiled amain, and got himself quite out of breath, without being able to stir the heavy stone. It seemed to be rooted into the ground. No wonder he could not move it; for it would have taken all the force of a very strong man to lift it out of its earthy bed.

His mother stood looking on, with a sad kind of a smile on her lips and in her eyes, to see the zealous

and yet puny efforts of her little boy. She could not help being sorrowful at finding him already so impatient to begin his adventures in the world.

"You see how it is, my dear Theseus," said she. "You must possess far more strength than now before I can trust you to go to Athens and tell King Ægeus that you are his son. But when you can lift this rock, and show me what is hidden beneath it, I promise you my permission to depart."

Often and often, after this, did Theseus ask his mother whether it was yet time for him to go to Athens; and still his mother pointed to the rock, and told him that, for years to come, he could not be strong enough to move it. And again and again the rosy-cheeked and curly-headed boy would tug and strain at the huge mass of stone, striving, child as he was, to do what a giant could hardly have done without taking both of his great hands to the task. Meanwhile the rock seemed to be sinking farther and farther into the ground. The moss grew over it thicker and thicker, until at last it looked almost like a soft green seat, with only a few gray knobs of granite peeping out. The overhanging trees, also, shed their brown leaves upon it, as often as the autumn came; and at its base grew ferns and wild flowers, some of which crept quite over its surface. To all appearance, the rock was as firmly fastened as any other portion of the earth's substance.

But, difficult as the matter looked, Theseus was now growing up to be such a vigorous youth, that, in his own opinion, the time would quickly come when he

might hope to get the upper hand of this ponderous lump of stone.

"Mother, I do believe it has started!" cried he, after one of his attempts. "The earth around it is certainly a little cracked!"

"No, no, child!" his mother hastily answered. "It is not possible you can have moved it, such a boy as you still are!"

Nor would she be convinced, although Theseus showed her the place where he fancied that the stem of a flower had been partly uprooted by the movement of the rock. But Æthra sighed and looked disquieted; for, no doubt, she began to be conscious that her son was no longer a child, and that, in a little while hence, she must send him forth among the perils and troubles of the world.

It was not more than a year afterwards when they were again sitting on the moss-covered stone. Æthra had once more told him the oft-repeated story of his father, and how gladly he would receive Theseus at his stately palace, and how he would present him to his courtiers and the people, and tell them that here was the heir of his dominions. The eyes of Theseus glowed with enthusiasm, and he would hardly sit still to hear his mother speak.

"Dear mother Æthra," he exclaimed, "I never felt half so strong as now! I am no longer a child, nor a boy, nor a mere youth! I feel myself a man! It is now time to make one earnest trial to remove the stone."

"Ah, my dearest Theseus," replied his mother, "not yet! Not yet!"

"Yes, mother," said he resolutely, "the time has come."

Then Theseus bent himself in good earnest to the task, and strained every sinew, with manly strength and resolution. He put his whole brave heart into the effort. He wrestled with the big and sluggish stone, as if it had been a living enemy. He heaved, he lifted, he resolved now to succeed, or else to perish there, and let the rock be his monument forever! Æthra stood gazing at him, and clasped her hands, partly with a mother's pride, and partly with a mother's sorrow. The great rock stirred! Yes, it was raised slowly from the bedded moss and earth, uprooting the shrubs and flowers along with it, and was turned upon its side. Theseus had conquered!

While taking breath, he looked joyfully at his mother, and she smiled upon him through her tears.

"Yes, Theseus," she said, "the time has come, and you must stay no longer at my side! See what King Ægeus, your royal father, left for you beneath the stone, when he lifted it in his mighty arms and laid it on the spot whence you have now removed it."

Theseus looked, and saw that the rock had been placed over another slab of stone, containing a cavity within it; so that it somewhat resembled a roughly made chest or coffer, of which the upper mass had served as the lid. Within the cavity lay a sword with a golden hilt, and a pair of sandals.

"That was your father's sword," said Æthra, "and those were his sandals. When he went to be king of Athens, he bade me treat you as a child until you

should prove yourself a man by lifting this heavy stone. That task being accomplished, you are to put on his sandals, in order to follow in your father's footsteps, and to gird on his sword, so that you may fight giants and dragons, as King Ægeus did in his youth."

"I will set out for Athens this very day!" cried Theseus.

But his mother persuaded him to stay a day or two longer, while she got ready some necessary articles for his journey. When his grandfather, the wise King Pittheus, heard that Theseus intended to present himself at his father's palace, he earnestly advised him to get on board a vessel, and go by sea; because he might thus arrive within fifteen miles of Athens, without either fatigue or danger.

"The roads are very bad by land," quoth the venerable king; "and they are terribly infested with robbers and monsters. A mere lad like Theseus is not fit to be trusted on such a perilous journey, all by himself. No, no; let him go by sea!"

But when Theseus heard of robbers and monsters, he pricked up his ears, and was so much the more eager to take the road along which they were to be met with. On the third day, therefore, he bade a respectful farewell to his grandfather, thanking him for all his kindness, and, after affectionately embracing his mother, he set forth, with a good many of her tears glistening on his cheeks, and some, if the truth must be told, that had gushed out of his own eyes. But he let the sun and wind dry them, and walked stoutly on, playing with the golden hilt of his sword

and taking very manly strides in his father's sandals.

I cannot stop to tell you hardly any of the adventures that befell Theseus on the road to Athens. It is enough to say that he quite cleared that part of the country of the robbers, about whom King Pittheus had been so much alarmed. One of these bad people was named Procrustes; and he was indeed a terrible fellow, and had an ugly way of making fun of the poor travelers who happened to fall into his clutches. In his cavern he had a bed, on which, with great pretence of hospitality, he invited his guests to lie down; but if they happened to be shorter than the bed, this wicked villain stretched them out by main force; or, if they were too long, he lopped off their heads or feet, and laughed at what he had done, as an excellent joke. Thus, however weary a man might be, he never liked to lie in the bed of Procrustes. Another of these robbers, named Scinis, must likewise have been a very great scoundrel. He was in the habit of flinging his victims off a high cliff into the sea; and, in order to give him exactly his deserts, Theseus tossed him off the very same place. But if you will believe me, the sea would not pollute itself by receiving such a bad person into its bosom, neither would the earth, having once got rid of him, consent to take him back; so that, between the cliff and the sea, Scinis stuck fast in the air, which was forced to bear the burden of his naughtiness.

After these memorable deeds, Theseus heard of an enormous sow, which ran wild and was the terror of all the farmers round about; and, as he did not con-

sider himself above doing any good thing that came
in his way, he killed this monstrous creature, and gave
the carcass to the poor people for bacon. The great
sow had been an awful beast, while ramping about
the woods and fields, but was a pleasant object
enough when cut up into joints, and smoking on I
know not how many dinner tables.

Thus, by the time he reached his journey's end,
Theseus had done many valiant feats with his father's
golden-hilted sword, and had gained the renown of
being one of the bravest young men of the day. His
fame traveled faster than he did, and reached Athens
before him. As he entered the city, he heard the inhabitants talking at the street corners, and saying that
Hercules was brave, and Jason too, and Castor and
Pollux likewise, but that Theseus, the son of their
own king, would turn out as great a hero as the best
of them. Theseus took longer strides on hearing this,
and fancied himself sure of a magnificent reception
at his father's court, since he came thither with Fame
to blow her trumpet before him, and cry to King
Ægeus, "Behold your son!"

He little suspected, innocent youth that he was, that
here, in this very Athens, where his father reigned, a
greater danger awaited him than any which he had
encountered on the road. Yet this was the truth. You
must understand that the father of Theseus, though
not very old in years, was almost worn out with the
cares of government, and had thus grown aged before
his time. His nephews, not expecting him to live a
very great while, intended to get all the power of the

kingdom into their own hands. But when they heard that Theseus had arrived in Athens, and learned what a gallant young man he was, they saw that he would not be at all the kind of person to let them steal away his father's crown and scepter, which ought to be his own by right of inheritance. Thus these bad-hearted nephews of King Ægeus, who were the own cousins of Theseus, at once became his enemies. A still more dangerous enemy was Medea, the wicked enchantress; for she was now the king's wife, and wanted to give the kingdom to her son Medus, instead of letting it be given to the son of Æthra, whom she hated.

It so happened that the king's nephews met Theseus, and found out who he was, just as he reached the entrance of the royal palace. With all their evil designs against him, they pretended to be their cousin's best friends, and expressed great joy at making his acquaintance. They proposed to him that he should come into the king's presence as a stranger, in order to try whether Ægeus would discover in the young man's features any likeness either to himself or his mother Æthra, and thus recognize him for a son. Theseus consented; for he fancied that his father would know him in a moment, by the love that was in his heart. But, while he waited at the door, the nephews ran and told King Ægeus that a young man had arrived in Athens, who, to their certain knowledge, intended to put him to death, and get possession of his royal crown.

"And he is now waiting for admission to your Majesty's presence," added they.

"Aha!" cried the old king, on hearing this. "Why, he must be a very wicked young fellow indeed! Pray, what would you advise me to do with him?"

In reply to this question, the wicked Medea put in her word. As I have already told you, she was a famous enchantress. According to some stories, she was in the habit of boiling old people in a large caldron, under pretence of making them young again; but King Ægeus, I suppose, did not fancy such an uncomfortable way of growing young, or perhaps was contented to be old, and therefore would never let himself be popped into the caldron. If there were time to spare from more important matters, I should be glad to tell you of Medea's fiery chariot, drawn by winged dragons, in which the enchantress used often to take an airing among the clouds. This chariot, in fact, was the vehicle that first brought her to Athens, where she had done nothing but mischief ever since her arrival. But these and many other wonders must be left untold; and it is enough to say that Medea, amongst a thousand other bad things, knew how to prepare a poison that was instantly fatal to whomsoever might so much as touch it with his lips.

So, when the king asked what he should do with Theseus, this naughty woman had an answer ready at her tongue's end.

"Leave that to me, please your Majesty," she replied. "Only admit this evil-minded young man to your presence, treat him civilly, and invite him to drink a goblet of wine. Your Majesty is well aware that I sometimes amuse myself with distilling very

powerful medicines. Here is one of them in this small phial. As to what it is made of, that is one of my secrets of state. Do but let me put a single drop into the goblet, and let the young man taste it; and I will answer for it, he shall quite lay aside the bad designs with which he comes hither."

As she said this, Medea smiled; but, for all her smiling face, she meant nothing less than to poison the poor innocent Theseus, before his father's eyes. And King Ægeus, like most other kings, thought any punishment mild enough for a person who was accused of plotting against his life. He therefore made little or no objection to Medea's scheme, and as soon as the poisonous wine was ready, gave orders that the young stranger should be admitted into his presence. The goblet was set on a table beside the king's throne; and a fly, meaning just to sip a little from the brim, immediately tumbled into it, dead. Observing this, Medea looked round at the nephews, and smiled again.

When Theseus was ushered into the royal apartment, the only object that he seemed to behold was the white-bearded old king. There he sat on his magnificent throne, a dazzling crown on his head, and a scepter in his hand. His aspect was stately and majestic, although his years and infirmities weighed heavily upon him, as if each year were a lump of lead, and each infirmity a ponderous stone, and all were bundled up together, and laid upon his weary shoulders. The tears both of joy and sorrow sprang into the young man's eyes; for he thought how sad it was

to see his dear father so infirm, and how sweet it would be to support him with his own youthful strength, and to cheer him up with the alacrity of his living spirit. When a son takes his father into his warm heart, it renews the old man's youth in a better way than by the heat of Medea's magic caldron. And this was what Theseus resolved to do. He could scarcely wait to see whether King Ægeus would recognize him, so eager was he to throw himself into his arms.

Advancing to the foot of the throne, he attempted to make a little speech, which he had been thinking about, as he came up the stairs. But he was almost choked by a great many tender feelings that gushed out of his heart and swelled into his throat, all struggling to find utterance together. And therefore, unless he could have laid his full, over-brimming heart into the king's hand, poor Theseus knew not what to do or say. The cunning Medea observed what was passing in the young man's mind. She was more wicked at that moment than ever she had been before; for (and it makes me tremble to tell you of it) she did her worst to turn all this unspeakable love with which Theseus was agitated, to his own ruin and destruction.

"Does your Majesty see his confusion?" she whispered in the king's ear. "He is so conscious of guilt that he trembles and cannot speak. The wretch lives too long! Quick! Offer him the wine!"

Now King Ægeus had been gazing earnestly at the

young stranger, as he drew near the throne. There was something, he knew not what, either in his white brow, or in the fine expression of his mouth, or in his beautiful and tender eyes, that made him indistinctly feel as if he had seen this youth before; as if, indeed, he had trotted him on his knee when a baby, and had beheld him growing to be a stalwart man, while he himself grew old. But Medea guessed how the king felt, and would not suffer him to yield to these natural sensibilities; although they were the voice of his deepest heart, telling him, as plainly as it could speak, that here was his dear son, and Æthra's son, coming to claim him for a father. The enchantress again whispered in the king's ear, and compelled him, by her witchcraft, to see everything under a false aspect.

He made up his mind, therefore, to let Theseus drink off the poisoned wine.

"Young man," said he, "you are welcome! I am proud to show hospitality to so heroic a youth. Do me the favor to drink the contents of this goblet. It is brimming over, as you see, with delicious wine, such as I bestow only on those who are worthy of it! None is more worthy to quaff it than yourself!"

So saying, King Ægeus took the golden goblet from the table, and was about to offer it to Theseus. But, partly through his infirmities, and partly because it seemed so sad a thing to take away this young man's life, however wicked he might be, and partly, no doubt, because his heart was wiser than his head, and quaked within him at the thought of what he

was going to do—for all these reasons, the king's hand trembled so much that a great deal of the wine slopped over. In order to strengthen his purpose, and fearing lest the whole of the precious poison should be wasted, one of his nephews now whispered to him:

"Has your Majesty any doubt of this stranger's guilt? There is the very sword with which he meant to slay you. How sharp and bright and terrible it is! Quick! Let him taste the wine, or perhaps he may do the deed even yet."

At these words, Ægeus drove every thought and feeling out of his breast, except the one idea of how justly the young man deserved to be put to death. He sat erect on his throne, and held out the goblet of wine with a steady hand, and bent on Theseus a frown of kingly severity; for, after all, he had too noble a spirit to murder even a treacherous enemy with a deceitful smile upon his face.

"Drink!" said he, in the stern tone with which he was wont to condemn a criminal to be beheaded. "You have well deserved of me such wine as this!"

Theseus held out his hand to take the wine. But, before he touched it, King Ægeus trembled again. His eyes had fallen on the gold-hilted sword that hung at the young man's side. He drew back the goblet.

"That sword!" he cried. "How came you by it?"

"It was my father's sword," replied Theseus, with a tremulous voice. "These were his sandals. My dear mother (her name is Æthra) told me his story while I was yet a little child. But it is only a month since

I grew strong enough to lift the heavy stone, and take the sword and sandals from beneath it, and come to Athens to seek my father."

"My son! my son!" cried King Ægeus, flinging away the fatal goblet, and tottering down from the throne to fall into the arms of Theseus. "Yes, these are Æthra's eyes. It is my son."

I have quite forgotten what became of the king's nephews. But when the wicked Medea saw this new turn of affairs, she hurried out of the room, and going to her private chamber, lost no time in setting her enchantments at work. In a few moments, she heard a great noise of hissing snakes outside of the chamber window; and, behold! there was her fiery chariot, and four huge winged serpents, wriggling and twisting in the air, flourishing their tails higher than the top of the palace, and all ready to set off on an aerial journey. Medea stayed only long enough to take her son with her, and to steal the crown jewels, together with the king's best robes, and whatever other valuable things she could lay hands on; and getting into the chariot, she whipped up the snakes, and ascended high over the city.

The king, hearing the hiss of the serpents, scrambled as fast as he could to the window, and bawled out to the abominable enchantress never to come back. The whole people of Athens, too, who had run out of doors to see this wonderful spectacle, set up a shout of joy at the prospect of getting rid of her. Medea, almost bursting with rage, uttered precisely such a hiss as one of her own snakes, only ten times

more venomous and spiteful; and glaring fiercely out of the blaze of the chariot, she shook her hands over the multitude below, as if she were scattering a million of curses among them. In so doing, however, she unintentionally let fall about five hundred diamonds of the first water, together with a thousand great pearls, and two thousand emeralds, rubies, sapphires, opals, and topazes, to which she had helped herself out of the king's strongbox. All these came pelting down, like a shower of many-colored hailstones, upon the heads of grown people and children, who forthwith gathered them up and carried them back to the palace. But King Ægeus told them that they were welcome to the whole, and to twice as many more, if he had them, for the sake of his delight at finding his son, and losing the wicked Medea. And, indeed, if you had seen how hateful was her last look, as the flaming chariot flew upward, you would not have wondered that both king and people should think her departure a good riddance.

And now Prince Theseus was taken into great favor by his royal father. The old king was never weary of having him sit beside him on his throne (which was quite wide enough for two), and of hearing him tell about his dear mother, and his childhood, and his many boyish efforts to lift the ponderous stone. Theseus, however, was much too brave and active a young man to be willing to spend all his time in relating things which had already happened. His ambition was to perform other and more heroic deeds, which should be better worth telling in prose

and verse. Nor had he been long in Athens before he caught and chained a terrible mad bull, and made a public show of him, greatly to the wonder and admiration of good King Ægeus and his subjects. But pretty soon, he undertook an affair that made all his foregone adventures seem like mere boy's play. The occasion of it was as follows:

One morning, when Prince Theseus awoke, he fancied that he must have had a very sorrowful dream, and that it was still running in his mind, even now that his eyes were open. For it appeared as if the air was full of a melancholy wail; and when he listened more attentively, he could hear sobs and groans, and screams of woe, mingled with deep, quiet sighs, which came from the king's palace, and from the streets, and from the temples, and from every habitation in the city. And all these mournful noises, issuing out of thousands of separate hearts, united themselves into the one great sound of affliction, which had startled Theseus from slumber. He put on his clothes as quickly as he could (not forgetting his sandals and gold-hilted sword), and hastening to the king, inquired what it all meant.

"Alas, my son," quoth King Ægeus, heaving a long sigh, "here is a very lamentable matter in hand! This is the wofullest anniversary in the whole year. It is the day when we annually draw lots to see which of the youths and maidens of Athens shall go to be devoured by the horrible Minotaur!"

"The Minotaur!" exclaimed Prince Theseus; and, like a brave young prince as he was, he put his hand

to the hilt of his sword. "What kind of a monster may that be? Is it not possible, at the risk of one's life, to slay him?"

But King Ægeus shook his venerable head, and to convince Theseus that it was quite a hopeless case, he gave him an explanation of the whole affair. It seems that in the island of Crete there lived a certain dreadful monster, called a Minotaur, which was shaped partly like a man and partly like a bull, and was altogether such a hideous sort of a creature that it is really disagreeable to think of him. If he were suffered to exist at all, it should have been on some desert island, or in the duskiness of some deep cavern, where nobody would ever be tormented by his abominable aspect. But King Minos, who reigned over Crete, laid out a vast deal of money in building a habitation for the Minotaur, and took great care of his health and comfort, merely for mischief's sake. A few years before this time, there had been a war between the city of Athens and the island of Crete, in which the Athenians were beaten, and compelled to beg for peace. No peace could they obtain, however, except on condition that they should send seven young men and seven maidens, every year, to be devoured by the pet monster of the cruel King Minos. For three years past, this grievous calamity had been borne. And the sobs and groans and shrieks with which the city was now filled, were caused by the people's woe, because the fatal day had come again, when the fourteen victims were to be chosen by lot; and the old people feared lest their sons or daughters

might be taken, and the youths and damsels dreaded
lest they themselves might be destined to glut the
ravenous maw of that detestable man-brute.

But when Theseus heard the story, he straightened
himself up, so that he seemed taller than ever before;
and as for his face, it was indignant, despiteful, bold,
tender, and compassionate, all in one look.

"Let the people of Athens, this year, draw lots for
only six young men, instead of seven," said he. "I
will myself be the seventh; and let the Minotaur devour me, if he can!"

"Oh, my dear son," cried King Ægeus, "why
should you expose yourself to this horrible fate? You
are a royal prince, and have a right to hold yourself
above the destinies of common men."

"It is because I am a prince, your son, and the
rightful heir of your kingdom, that I freely take upon
me the calamity of your subjects," answered Theseus.
"And you, my father, being king over this people, and
answerable to Heaven for their welfare, are bound to
sacrifice what is dearest to you, rather than that the
son or daughter of the poorest citizen should come
to any harm."

The old king shed tears, and besought Theseus not
to leave him desolate in his old age, more especially
as he had but just begun to know the happiness of
possessing a good and valiant son. Theseus, however,
felt that he was in the right, and therefore would not
give up his resolution. But he assured his father that
he did not intend to be eaten up, unresistingly, like a
sheep, and that, if the Minotaur devoured him, it

should not be without a battle for his dinner. And finally, since he could not help it, King Ægeus consented to let him go. So a vessel was got ready, and rigged with black sails; and Theseus, with six other young men, and seven tender and beautiful damsels, came down to the harbor to embark. A sorrowful multitude accompanied them to the shore. There was the poor old king, too, leaning on his son's arm, and looking as if his single heart held all the grief of Athens.

Just as Prince Theseus was going on board, his father bethought himself of one last word to say.

"My beloved son," said he, grasping the prince's hand, "you observe that the sails of this vessel are black; as indeed they ought to be, since it goes upon a voyage of sorrow and despair. Now, being weighed down with infirmities, I know not whether I can survive till the vessel shall return. But, as long as I do live, I shall creep daily to the top of yonder cliff, to watch if there be a sail upon the sea. And, dearest Theseus, if by some happy chance you should escape the jaws of the Minotaur, then tear down those dismal sails, and hoist others that shall be bright as the sunshine. Beholding them on the horizon, myself and all the people will know that you are coming back victorious, and will welcome you with such a festal uproar as Athens never heard before."

Theseus promised that he would do so. Then, going on board, the mariners trimmed the vessel's black sails to the wind, which blew faintly off the shore, being pretty much made up of the sighs that everybody

kept pouring forth on this melancholy occasion. But by and by, when they had got fairly out to sea, there came a stiff breeze from the northwest, and drove them along as merrily over the white-capped waves as if they had been going on the most delightful errand imaginable. And though it was a sad business enough, I rather question whether fourteen young people, without any old persons to keep them in order, could continue to spend the whole time of the voyage in being miserable. There had been some few dances upon the undulating deck, I suspect, and some hearty bursts of laughter, and other such unseasonable merriment among the victims, before the high, blue mountains of Crete began to show themselves among the far-off clouds. That sight, to be sure, made them all very grave again.

Theseus stood among the sailors, gazing eagerly towards the land; although, as yet, it seemed hardly more substantial than the clouds, amidst which the mountains were looming up. Once or twice, he fancied that he saw a glare of some bright object, a long way off, flinging a gleam across the waves.

"Did you see that flash of light?" he inquired of the master of the vessel.

"No, prince; but I have seen it before," answered the master. "It came from Talus, I suppose."

As the breeze came fresher just then, the master was busy with trimming his sails and had no more time to answer questions. But while the vessel flew faster and faster towards Crete, Theseus was astonished to behold a human figure, gigantic in size,

which appeared to be striding with a measured movement, along the margin of the island. It stepped from cliff to cliff, and sometimes from one headland to another, while the sea foamed and thundered on the shore beneath, and dashed its jets of spray over the giant's feet. What was still more remarkable, whenever the sun shone on this huge figure, it flickered and glimmered. Its vast countenance, too, had a metallic luster, and threw great flashes of splendor through the air. The folds of its garments, moreover, instead of waving in the wind, fell heavily over its limbs, as if woven of some kind of metal.

The nigher the vessel came, the more Theseus wondered what this immense giant could be, and whether it actually had life or no. For though it walked, and made other lifelike motions, there yet was a kind of jerk in its gait, which, together with its brazen aspect, caused the young prince to suspect that it was no true giant, but only a wonderful piece of machinery. The figure looked all the more terrible because it carried an enormous brass club on its shoulder.

"What is this wonder?" Theseus asked of the master of the vessel, who was now at leisure to answer him.

"It is Talus, the Man of Brass," said the master.

"And is he a live giant, or a brazen image?" asked Theseus.

"That, truly," replied the master, "is the point which has always perplexed me. Some say, indeed, that this Talus was hammered out for King Minos by Vulcan himself, the skillfullest of all workers in

metal. But who ever saw a brazen image that had sensc enough to walk round an island three times a day, as this giant walks round the island of Crete, challenging every vessel that comes nigh the shore? And, on the other hand, what living thing, unless his sinews were made of brass, would not be weary of marching eighteen hundred miles in the twenty-four hours, as Talus does, without ever sitting down to rest? He is a puzzler, take him how you will."

Still the vessel went bounding onward; and now Theseus could hear the brazen clangor of the giant's footsteps, as he trod heavily upon the sea-beaten rocks, some of which were seen to crack and crumble into the foamy waves beneath his weight. As they approached the entrance of the port, the giant straddled clear across it, with a foot firmly planted on each headland, and uplifting his club to such a height that its butt end was hidden in a cloud, he stood in that formidable posture, with the sun gleaming all over his metallic surface. There seemed nothing else to be expected but that, the next moment, he would fetch his great club down, slam bang, and smash the vessel into a thousand pieces, without heeding how many innocent people he might destroy; for there is seldom any mercy in a giant, you know, and quite as little in a piece of brass clockwork. But just when Theseus and his companions thought the blow was coming, the brazen lips unclosed themselves, and the figure spoke.

"Whence come you, strangers?"

And when the ringing voice ceased, there was just

such a reverberation as you may have heard within a great church bell, for a moment or two after the stroke of the hammer.

"From Athens!" shouted the master in reply.

"On what errand?" thundered the Man of Brass.

And he whirled his club aloft more threateningly than ever, as if he were about to smite them with a thunder-stroke right amidships, because Athens, so little while ago, had been at war with Crete.

"We bring the seven youths and the seven maidens," answered the master, "to be devoured by the Minotaur!"

"Pass!" cried the brazen giant.

That one loud word rolled all about the sky, while again there was a booming reverberation within the figure's breast. The vessel glided between the headlands of the port, and the giant resumed his march. In a few moments, this wondrous sentinel was far away, flashing in the distant sunshine, and revolving with immense strides around the island of Crete, as it was his never-ceasing task to do.

No sooner had they entered the harbor than a party of the guards of King Minos came down to the waterside, and took charge of the fourteen young men and damsels. Surrounded by these armed warriors, Prince Theseus and his companions were led to the king's palace, and ushered into his presence. Now, Minos was a stern and pitiless king. If the figure that guarded Crete was made of brass, then the monarch who ruled over it might be thought to have a still harder metal in his breast, and might have been

called a man of iron. He bent his shaggy brows upon the poor Athenian victims. Any other mortal, beholding their fresh and tender beauty, and their innocent looks, would have felt himself sitting on thorns until he had made every soul of them happy, by bidding them go free as the summer wind. But this immitigable Minos cared only to examine whether they were plump enough to satisfy the Minotaur's appetite. For my part, I wish he himself had been the only victim; and the monster would have found him a pretty tough one.

One after another, King Minos called these pale, frightened youths and sobbing maidens to his footstool, gave them each a poke in the ribs with his scepter (to try whether they were in good flesh or no), and dismissed them with a nod to his guards. But when his eyes rested on Theseus, the king looked at him more attentively, because his face was calm and brave.

"Young man," asked he, with his stern voice, "are you not appalled at the certainty of being devoured by this terrible Minotaur?"

"I have offered my life in a good cause," answered Theseus, "and therefore I give it freely and gladly. But thou, King Minos, art thou not thyself appalled, who, year after year, hast perpetrated this dreadful wrong, by giving seven innocent youths and as many maidens to be devoured by a monster? Dost thou not tremble, wicked king, to turn thine eyes inward on thine own heart? Sitting there on thy golden throne, and in thy robes of majesty, I tell thee to thy face,

King Minos, thou art a more hideous monster than the Minotaur himself!"

"Aha! do you think me so?" cried the king, laughing in his cruel way. "Tomorrow, at breakfast time, you shall have an opportunity of judging which is the greater monster, the Minotaur or the king! Take them away, guards; and let this free-spoken youth be the Minotaur's first morsel!"

Near the king's throne (though I had no time to tell you so before) stood his daughter Ariadne. She was a beautiful and tenderhearted maiden, and looked at these poor doomed captives with very different feelings from those of the iron-breasted King Minos. She really wept, indeed, at the idea of how much human happiness would be needlessly thrown away, by giving so many young people, in the first bloom and rose blossom of their lives, to be eaten up by a creature who, no doubt, would have preferred a fat ox, or even a large pig, to the plumpest of them. And when she beheld the brave, spirited figure of Prince Theseus bearing himself so calmly in his terrible peril, she grew a hundred times more pitiful than before. As the guards were taking him away, she flung herself at the king's feet, and besought him to set all the captives free, and especially this one young man.

"Peace, foolish girl!" answered King Minos. "What hast thou to do with an affair like this? It is a matter of state policy, and therefore quite beyond thy weak comprehension. Go water thy flowers, and think no more of these Athenian caitiffs, whom the

Minotaur shall as certainly eat up for breakfast as I
will eat a partridge for my supper."

So saying, the king looked cruel enough to devour
Theseus and all the rest of the captives himself, had
there been no Minotaur to save him the trouble. As
he would hear not another word in their favor, the
prisoners were now led away, and clapped into a
dungeon, where the jailer advised them to go to sleep
as soon as possible, because the Minotaur was in the
habit of calling for breakfast early. The seven maidens and six of the young men soon sobbed themselves to slumber! But Theseus was not like them. He
felt conscious that he was wiser and braver and stronger than his companions, and that therefore he had
the responsibility of all their lives upon him, and
must consider whether there was no way to save
them, even in this last extremity. So he kept himself
awake, and paced to and fro across the gloomy dungeon in which they were shut up.

Just before midnight, the door was softly unbarred,
and the gentle Ariadne showed herself, with a torch
in her hand.

"Are you awake, Prince Theseus?" she whispered.

"Yes," answered Theseus. "With so little time
to live, I do not choose to waste any of it in sleep."

"Then follow me," said Ariadne, "and tread
softly."

What had become of the jailer and the guards,
Theseus never knew. But however that might be,
Ariadne opened all the doors, and led him forth from
the darksome prison into the pleasant moonlight.

"Theseus," said the maiden, "you can now get on board your vessel, and sail away for Athens."

"No," answered the young man, "I will never leave Crete unless I can first slay the Minotaur, and save my poor companions, and deliver Athens from this cruel tribute."

"I knew that this would be your resolution," said Ariadne. "Come, then, with me, brave Theseus. Here is your own sword, which the guards deprived you of. You will need it; and pray Heaven you may use it well."

Then she led Theseus along by the hand until they came to a dark, shadowy grove, where the moonlight wasted itself on the tops of the trees, without shedding hardly so much as a glimmering beam upon their pathway. After going a good way through this obscurity, they reached a high, marble wall, which was overgrown with creeping plants that made it shaggy with their verdure. The wall seemed to have no door, nor any windows, but rose up, lofty, and massive, and mysterious, and was neither to be clambered over, nor, so far as Theseus could perceive, to be passed through. Nevertheless, Ariadne did but press one of her soft little fingers against a particular block of marble, and, though it looked as solid as any other part of the wall, it yielded to her touch, disclosing an entrance just wide enough to admit them. They crept through, and the marble stone swung back into its place.

"We are now," said Ariadne, "in the famous labyrinth which Dædalus built before he made himself a

pair of wings, and flew away from our island like a bird. That Dædalus was a very cunning workman; but of all his artful contrivances, this labyrinth is the most wondrous. Were we to take but a few steps from the doorway, we might wander about all our lifetime, and never find it again. Yet in the very center of this labyrinth is the Minotaur; and, Theseus, you must go thither to seek him."

"But how shall I ever find him," asked Theseus, "if the labyrinth so bewilders me as you say it will?"

Just as he spoke they heard a rough and very disagreeable roar, which greatly resembled the lowing of a fierce bull, but yet had some sort of sound like the human voice. Theseus even fancied a rude articulation in it, as if the creature that uttered it were trying to shape his hoarse breath into words. It was at some distance, however, and he really could not tell whether it sounded most like a bull's roar or a man's harsh voice.

"That is the Minotaur's noise," whispered Ariadne, closely grasping the hand of Theseus, and pressing one of her own hands to her heart, which was all in a tremble. "You must follow that sound through the windings of the labyrinth, and, by and by, you will find him. Stay! take the end of this silken string; I will hold the other end; and then, if you win the victory, it will lead you again to this spot. Farewell, brave Theseus."

So the young man took the end of the silken string in his left hand, and his gold-hilted sword, ready drawn from its scabbard, in the other, and trod

boldly into the inscrutable labyrinth. How this labyrinth was built is more than I can tell you. But so
cunningly contrived a mizmaze was never seen in the
world, before nor since. There can be nothing else so
intricate, unless it were the brain of a man like Dædalus, who planned it, or the heart of any ordinary man;
which last, to be sure, is ten times as great a mystery
as the labyrinth of Crete. Theseus had not taken five
steps before he lost sight of Ariadne; and in five more
his head was growing dizzy. But still he went on,
now creeping through a low arch, now ascending a
flight of steps, now in one crooked passage and now
in another, with here a door opening before him, and
there one banging behind, until it really seemed as if
the walls spun round, and whirled him round along
with them. And all the while, through these hollow
avenues, now nearer, now farther off again, resounded the cry of the Minotaur; and the sound was
so fierce, so cruel, so ugly, so like a bull's roar, and
withal so like a human voice, and yet like neither of
them, that the brave heart of Theseus grew sterner
and angrier at every step; for he felt it an insult to the
moon and sky, and to our affectionate and simple
Mother Earth, that such a monster should have the
audacity to exist.

As he passed onward, the clouds gathered over the
moon, and the labyrinth grew so dusky that Theseus
could no longer discern the bewilderment through
which he was passing. He would have felt quite lost,
and utterly hopeless of ever again walking in a
straight path, if, every little while, he had not been

conscious of a gentle twitch at the silken cord. Then
he knew that the tenderhearted Ariadne was still
holding the other end, and that she was fearing for
him, and hoping for him, and giving him just as
much of her sympathy as if she were close by his side.
Oh, indeed, I can assure you, there was a vast deal of
of human sympathy running along that slender
thread of silk. But still he followed the dreadful roar
of the Minotaur, which now grew louder and louder,
and finally so very loud that Theseus fully expected
to come close upon him, at every new zigzag and
wriggle of the path. And at last, in an open space, at
the very center of the labyrinth, he did discern the
hideous creature.

Sure enough, what an ugly monster it was! Only
his horned head belonged to a bull; and yet, somehow or other, he looked like a bull all over, prepos-
terously waddling on his hind legs; or, if you happened to view him in another way, he seemed wholly
a man, and all the more monstrous for being so. And
there he was, the wretched thing, with no society, no
companion, no kind of a mate, living only to do mischief, and incapable of knowing what affection
means. Theseus hated him, and shuddered at him,
and yet could not but be sensible of some sort of
pity; and all the more, the uglier and more detestable
the creature was. For he kept striding to and fro in a
solitary frenzy of rage, continually emitting a hoarse
roar, which was oddly mixed up with half-shaped
words; and, after listening awhile, Theseus understood that the Minotaur was saying to himself how

miserable he was, and how hungry, and how he hated everybody, and how he longed to eat up the human race alive.

Ah, the bull-headed villain! And oh, my good little people, you will perhaps see, one of these days, as I do now, that every human being who suffers anything evil to get into his nature, or to remain there, is a kind of Minotaur, an enemy of his fellow creatures, and separated from all good companionship, as this poor monster was.

Was Theseus afraid? By no means, my dear auditors. What! A hero like Theseus afraid! Not had the Minotaur had twenty bull heads instead of one. Bold as he was, however, I rather fancy that it strengthened his valiant heart, just at this crisis, to feel a tremulous twitch at the silken cord, which he was still holding in his left hand. It was as if Ariadne were giving him all her might and courage; and, much as he already had, and little as she had to give, it made his own seem twice as much. And to confess the honest truth, he needed the whole; for now the Minotaur, turning suddenly about, caught sight of Theseus, and instantly lowered his horribly sharp horns, exactly as a mad bull does when he means to rush against an enemy. At the same time, he belched forth a tremendous roar, in which there was something like the words of human language, but all disjointed and shaken to pieces by passing through the gullet of a miserably enraged brute.

Theseus could only guess what the creature intended to say, and that rather by his gestures than his

words; for the Minotaur's horns were sharper than his wits, and of a great deal more service to him than his tongue. But probably this was the sense of what he uttered:

"Ah, wretch of a human being! I'll stick my horns through you, and toss you fifty feet high, and eat you up the moment you come down."

"Come on then, and try it!" was all that Theseus deigned to reply; for he was far too magnanimous to assault his enemy with insolent language.

Without more words on either side, there ensued the most awful fight between Theseus and the Minotaur that ever happened beneath the sun or moon. I really know not how it might have turned out, if the monster, in his first headlong rush against Theseus, had not missed him, by a hair's-breadth, and broken one of his horns short off against the stone wall. On this mishap, he bellowed so intolerably that a part of the labyrinth tumbled down, and all the inhabitants of Crete mistook the noise for an uncommonly heavy thunderstorm. Smarting with the pain, he galloped around the open space in so ridiculous a way that Theseus laughed at it, long afterwards, though not precisely at the moment. After this, the two antagonists stood valiantly up to one another, and fought sword to horn, for a long while. At last, the Minotaur made a run at Theseus, grazed his left side with his horn, and flung him down; and thinking that he had stabbed him to the heart, he cut a great caper in the air, opened his bull mouth from ear to ear, and prepared to snap his head off. But Theseus by this

The Minotaur made a run at Theseus and flung him down

time had leaped up, and caught the monster off his guard. Fetching a sword stroke at him with all his force, he hit him fair upon the neck, and made his bull head skip six yards from his human body, which fell down flat upon the ground.

So now the battle was ended. Immediately the moon shone out as brightly as if all the troubles of the world, and all the wickedness and the ugliness that infest human life, were past and gone forever. And Theseus, as he leaned on his sword, taking breath, felt another twitch of the silken cord; for all through the terrible encounter he had held it fast in his left hand. Eager to let Ariadne know of his success, he followed the guidance of the thread, and soon found himself at the entrance of the labyrinth.

"Thou hast slain the monster!" cried Ariadne, clasping her hands.

"Thanks to thee, dear Ariadne," answered Theseus. "I return victorious."

"Then," said Ariadne, "we must quickly summon thy friends, and get them and thyself on board the vessel before dawn. If morning finds thee here, my father will avenge the Minotaur."

To make my story short, the poor captives were awakened, and, hardly knowing whether it was not a joyful dream, were told of what Theseus had done, and that they must set sail for Athens before daybreak. Hastening down to the vessel, they all clambered on board, except Prince Theseus, who lingered behind them, on the strand, holding Ariadne's hand clasped in his own.

"Dear maiden," said he, "thou wilt surely go with us. Thou art too gentle and sweet a child for such an iron-hearted father as King Minos. He cares no more for thee than a granite rock cares for the little flower that grows in one of its crevices. But my father, King Ægeus, and my dear mother, Æthra, and all the fathers and mothers in Athens, and all the sons and daughters too, will love and honor thee as their benefactress. Come with us, then; for King Minos will be very angry when he knows what thou hast done."

Now, some low-minded people, who pretend to tell the story of Theseus and Ariadne, have the face to say that this royal and honorable maiden did really flee away, under cover of the night, with the young stranger whose life she had preserved. They say, too, that Prince Theseus (who would have died sooner than wrong the meanest creature in the world) ungratefully deserted Ariadne, on a solitary island, where the vessel touched on its voyage to Athens. But, had the noble Theseus heard these falsehoods, he would have served their slanderous authors as he served the Minotaur! Here is what Ariadne answered, when the brave Prince of Athens besought her to accompany him:

"No, Theseus," the maiden said, pressing his hand, and then drawing back a step or two, "I cannot go with you. My father is old, and has nobody but myself to love him. Hard as you think his heart is, it would break to lose me. At first King Minos will be angry; but he will soon forgive his only child; and,

by and by, he will rejoice, I know, that no more youths and maidens must come from Athens to be devoured by the Minotaur. I have saved you, Theseus, as much for my father's sake as for your own. Farewell! Heaven bless you!"

All this was so true, and so maiden-like, and was spoken with so sweet a dignity, that Theseus would have blushed to urge her any longer. Nothing remained for him, therefore, but to bid Ariadne an affectionate farewell, and go on board the vessel, and set sail.

In a few moments the white foam was boiling up before their prow, as Prince Theseus and his companions sailed out of the harbor with a whistling breeze behind them. Talus, the brazen giant, on his never-ceasing sentinel's march, happened to be approaching that part of the coast; and they saw him, by the glimmering of the moonbeams on his polished surface, while he was yet a great way off. As the figure moved like clockwork, however, and could neither hasten his enormous strides nor retard them, he arrived at the port when they were just beyond the reach of his club. Nevertheless, straddling from headland to headland, as his custom was, Talus attempted to strike a blow at the vessel, and, overreaching himself, tumbled at full length into the sea, which splashed high over his gigantic shape, as when an iceberg turns a somerset. There he lies yet; and whoever desires to enrich himself by means of brass had better go thither with a diving bell, and fish up Talus.

On the homeward voyage, the fourteen youths and

damsels were in excellent spirits, as you will easily suppose. They spent most of their time in dancing, unless when the sidelong breeze made the deck slope too much. In due season, they came within sight of the coast of Attica, which was their native country. But here, I am grieved to tell you, happened a sad misfortune.

You will remember (what Theseus unfortunately forgot) that his father, King Ægeus, had enjoined it upon him to hoist sunshine sails, instead of black ones, in case he should overcome the Minotaur, and return victorious. In the joy of their success, however, and amidst the sports, dancing, and other merriment, with which these young folks wore away the time, they never once thought whether their sails were black, white, or rainbow colored, and, indeed, left it entirely to the mariners whether they had any sails at all. Thus the vessel returned, like a raven, with the same sable wings that had wafted her away. But poor King Ægeus, day after day, infirm as he was, had clambered to the summit of a cliff that overhung the sea, and there sat watching for Prince Theseus, homeward bound; and no sooner did he behold the fatal blackness of the sails, than he concluded that his dear son, whom he loved so much, and felt so proud of, had been eaten by the Minotaur. He could not bear the thought of living any longer; so, first flinging his crown and scepter into the sea, (useless baubles that they were to him now!) King Ægeus merely stooped forward, and fell headlong over the cliff, and

was drowned, poor soul, in the waves that foamed at its base!

This was melancholy news for Prince Theseus, who, when he stepped ashore, found himself king of all the country, whether he would or no; and such a turn of fortune was enough to make any young man feel very much out of spirits. However, he sent for his dear mother to Athens, and, by taking her advice in matters of state, became a very excellent monarch, and was greatly beloved by his people.

The Pygmies

A GREAT while ago, when the world was full of wonders, there lived an earth-born Giant named Antæus,
and a million or more of curious little earth-born people, who were called Pygmies. This Giant and these
Pygmies being children of the same mother (that is to
say, our good old Grandmother Earth), were all brethren and dwelled together in a very friendly and affectionate manner, far, far off, in the middle of hot Africa.
The Pygmies were so small, and there were so many
sandy deserts and such high mountains between them
and the rest of mankind, that nobody could get a peep
at them oftener than once in a hundred years. As for
the Giant, being of a very lofty stature, it was easy
enough to see him, but safest to keep out of his sight.

Among the Pygmies, I suppose, if one of them grew
to the height of six or eight inches, he was reckoned a

prodigiously tall man. It must have been very pretty to behold their little cities, with streets two or three feet wide, paved with the smallest pebbles, and bordered by habitations about as big as a squirrel's cage. The king's palace attained to the stupendous magnitude of Periwinkle's baby-house, and stood in the center of a spacious square, which could hardly have been covered by our hearthrug. Their principal temple, or cathedral, was as lofty as yonder bureau, and was looked upon as a wonderfully sublime and magnificent edifice. All these structures were built neither of stone nor wood. They were neatly plastered together by the Pygmy workmen, pretty much like birds' nests, out of straw, feathers, eggshells, and other small bits of stuff, with stiff clay instead of mortar; and when the hot sun had dried them, they were just as snug and comfortable as a Pygmy could desire.

The country round about was conveniently laid out in fields, the largest of which was nearly of the same extent as one of Sweet Fern's flowerbeds. Here the Pygmies used to plant wheat and other kinds of grain, which, when it grew up and ripened, overshadowed these tiny people, as the pines, and the oaks, and the walnut and chestnut trees overshadow you and me, when we walk in our own tracts of woodland. At harvest time, they were forced to go with their little axes and cut down the grain, exactly as a woodcutter makes a clearing in the forest; and when a stalk of wheat, with its overburdened top, chanced to come crashing down upon an unfortunate Pygmy, it was apt to be a very sad affair. If it did not smash him all to

pieces, at least, I am sure, it must have made the poor little fellow's head ache. And oh, my stars! if the fathers and mothers were so small, what must the children and babies have been? A whole family of them might have been put to bed in a shoe, or have crept into an old glove, and played at hide-and-seek in its thumb and fingers. You might have hidden a year-old baby under a thimble.

Now these funny Pygmies, as I told you before, had a Giant for their neighbor and brother, who was bigger, if possible, than they were little. He was so very tall that he carried a pine tree, which was eight feet through the butt, for a walking stick. It took a far-sighted Pygmy, I can assure you, to discern his summit without the help of a telescope; and sometimes, in misty weather, they could not see his upper half, but only his long legs, which seemed to be striding about by themselves. But at noonday, in a clear atmosphere, when the sun shone brightly over him, the Giant Antæus presented a very grand spectacle. There he used to stand, a perfect mountain of a man, with his great countenance smiling down upon his little brothers, and his one vast eye (which was as big as a cartwheel, and placed right in the center of his forehead) giving a friendly wink to the whole nation at once.

The Pygmies loved to talk with Antæus; and fifty times a day, one or another of them would turn up his head, and shout through the hollow of his fists, "Halloo, brother Antæus! How are you, my good fellow?"

and when the small, distant squeak of their voices reached his ear, the Giant would make answer, "Pretty well, brother Pygmy, I thank you," in a thunderous roar that would have shaken down the walls of their strongest temple, only that it came from so far aloft.

It was a happy circumstance that Antæus was the Pygmy people's friend; for there was more strength in his little finger than in ten million of such bodies as theirs. If he had been as ill-natured to them as he was to everybody else, he might have beaten down their biggest city at one kick, and hardly have known that he did it. With the tornado of his breath, he could have stripped the roofs from a hundred dwellings, and sent thousands of the inhabitants whirling through the air. He might have set his immense foot upon a multitude; and when he took it up again, there would have been a pitiful sight, to be sure. But, being the son of Mother Earth, as they likewise were, the Giant gave them his brotherly kindness, and loved them with as big a love as it was possible to feel for creatures so very small. And, on their parts, the Pygmies loved Antæus with as much affection as their tiny hearts could hold. He was always ready to do them any good offices that lay in his power; as, for example, when they wanted a breeze to turn their windmills, the Giant would set all the sails a-going with the mere natural respiration of his lungs. When the sun was too hot, he often sat himself down, and let his shadow fall over the kingdom, from one frontier to the other; and as for matters in general, he was wise enough to let them alone, and leave the

Pygmies to manage their own affairs—which, after all, is about the best thing that great people can do for little ones.

In short, as I said before, Antæus loved the Pygmies, and the Pygmies loved Antæus. The Giant's life being as long as his body was large, while the lifetime of a Pygmy was but a span, this friendly intercourse had been going on for innumerable generations and ages. It was written about in the Pygmy histories, and talked about in their ancient traditions. The most venerable and white-bearded Pygmy had never heard of a time, even in his greatest of grandfathers' days, when the Giant was not their enormous friend. Once, to be sure (as was recorded on an obelisk, three feet high, erected on the place of the catastrophe), Antæus sat down upon about five thousand Pygmies, who were assembled at a military review. But this was one of those unlucky accidents for which nobody is to blame; so that the small folks never took it to heart, and only requested the Giant to be careful forever afterwards to examine the acre of ground where he intended to squat himself.

It is a very pleasant picture to imagine Antæus standing among the Pygmies, like the spire of the tallest cathedral that ever was built, while they ran about like pismires at his feet; and to think that, in spite of their difference in size, there were affection and sympathy between them and him! Indeed, it has always seemed to me that the Giant needed the little people more than the Pygmies needed the Giant. For, unless they had been his neighbors and well-wishers, and, as

we may say, his playfellows, Antæus would not have had a single friend in the world. No other being like himself had ever been created. No creature of his own size had ever talked with him, in thunder-like accents, face to face. When he stood with his head among the clouds, he was quite alone, and had been so for hundreds of years, and would be so forever. Even if he had met another Giant, Antæus would have fancied the world not big enough for two such vast personages, and, instead of being friends with him, would have fought him till one of the two was killed. But with the Pygmies he was the most sportive, and humorous, and merry-hearted, and sweet-tempered old Giant that ever washed his face in a wet cloud.

His little friends, like all other small people, had a great opinion of their own importance, and used to assume quite a patronizing air towards the Giant.

"Poor creature!" they said one to another. "He has a very dull time of it, all by himself; and we ought not to grudge wasting a little of our precious time to amuse him. He is not half so bright as we are, to be sure; and, for that reason, he needs us to look after his comfort and happiness. Let us be kind to the old fellow. Why, if Mother Earth had not been very kind to ourselves, we might all have been Giants too."

On all their holidays, the Pygmies had excellent sport with Antæus. He often stretched himself out at full length on the ground, where he looked like the long ridge of a hill; and it was a good hour's walk, no doubt, for a short-legged Pygmy to journey from head to foot of the Giant. He would lay down his great hand

flat on the grass, and challenge the tallest of them to clamber upon it, and straddle from finger to finger. So fearless were they, that they made nothing of creeping in among the folds of his garments. When his head lay sidewise on the earth, they would march boldly up, and peep into the great cavern of his mouth, and take it all as a joke (as indeed it was meant) when Antæus gave a sudden snap with his jaws, as if he were going to swallow fifty of them at once. You would have laughed to see the children dodging in and out among his hair, or swinging from his beard. It is impossible to tell half of the funny tricks that they played with their huge comrade; but I do not know that anything was more curious than when a party of boys were seen running races on his forehead, to try which of them could get first round the circle of his one great eye. It was another favorite feat with them to march along the bridge of his nose, and jump down upon his upper lip.

If the truth must be told, they were sometimes as troublesome to the Giant as a swarm of ants or mosquitoes, especially as they had a fondness for mischief, and liked to prick his skin with their little swords and lances, to see how thick and tough it was. But Antæus took it all kindly enough; although, once in a while, when he happened to be sleepy, he would grumble out a peevish word or two, like the muttering of a tempest, and ask them to have done with their nonsense. A great deal oftener, however, he watched their merriment and gambols until his huge, heavy, clumsy wits were completely stirred up by them; and then would he roar out such a tremendous volume of immeasurable

laughter that the whole nation of Pygmies had to put their hands to their ears, else it would certainly have deafened them.

"Ho! ho! ho!" quoth the Giant, shaking his mountainous sides. "What a funny thing it is to be little! If I were not Antæus, I should like to be a Pygmy, just for the joke's sake."

The Pygmies had but one thing to trouble them in the world. They were constantly at war with the cranes, and had always been so, ever since the long-lived Giant could remember. From time to time very terrible battles had been fought, in which sometimes the little men won the victory, and sometimes the cranes. According to some historians, the Pygmies used to go to the battle, mounted on the backs of goats and rams; but such animals as these must have been far too big for Pygmies to ride upon; so that, I rather suppose, they rode on squirrel-back, or rabbit-back, or rat-back, or perhaps got upon hedgehogs, whose prickly quills would be very terrible to the enemy. However this might be, and whatever creatures the Pygmies rode upon, I do not doubt that they made a formidable appearance, armed with sword and spear, and bow and arrow, blowing their tiny trumpets, and shouting their little war cry. They never failed to exhort one another to fight bravely, and recollect that the world had its eyes upon them; although, in simple truth, the only spectator was the Giant Antæus, with his one great stupid eye in the middle of his forehead.

When the two armies joined battle, the cranes would rush forward, flapping their wings and stretching out

their necks, and would perhaps snatch up some of the Pygmies crosswise in their beaks. Whenever this happened, it was truly an awful spectacle to see those little men of might kicking and sprawling in the air, and at last disappearing down the crane's long, crooked throat, swallowed up alive. A hero, you know, must hold himself in readiness for any kind of fate; and doubtless the glory of the thing was a consolation to him, even in the crane's gizzard. If Antæus observed that the battle was going hard against his little allies, he generally stopped laughing, and ran with mile-long strides to their assistance, flourishing his club aloft and shouting at the cranes, who quacked and croaked, and retreated as fast as they could. Then the Pygmy army would march homeward in triumph, attributing the victory entirely to their own valor, and to the warlike skill and strategy of whomsoever happened to be captain general; and for a tedious while afterwards, nothing would be heard of but grand processions, and public banquets, and brilliant illuminations, and shows of waxwork, with likenesses of the distinguished officers as small as life.

In the above-described warfare, if a Pygmy chanced to pluck out a crane's tail-feather, it proved a very great feather in his cap. Once or twice, if you will believe me, a little man was made chief ruler of the nation for no other merit in the world than bringing home such a feather.

But I have now said enough to let you see what a gallant little people these were, and how happily they and their forefathers, for nobody knows how many

generations, had lived with the immeasurable Giant
Antæus. In the remaining part of the story, I shall tell
you of a far more astonishing battle than any that was
fought between the Pygmies and the cranes.

One day the mighty Antæus was lolling at full
length among his little friends. His pine-tree walking
stick lay on the ground close by his side. His head was
in one part of the kingdom, and his feet extended
across the boundaries of another part; and he was
taking whatever comfort he could get, while the Pygmies scrambled over him, and peeped into his cavernous mouth, and played among his hair. Sometimes, for
a minute or two, the Giant dropped asleep, and
snored like the rush of a whirlwind. During one of
these little bits of slumber, a Pygmy chanced to climb
upon his shoulder, and took a view around the horizon, as from the summit of a hill; and he beheld something, a long way off, which made him rub the bright
specks of his eyes, and look sharper than before. At
first he mistook it for a mountain, and wondered how
it had grown up so suddenly out of the earth. But soon
he saw the mountain move. As it came nearer and
nearer, what should it turn out to be but a human
shape, not so big as Antæus, it is true, although a very
enormous figure, in comparison with Pygmies, and a
vast deal bigger than the men whom we see nowadays.

When the Pygmy was quite satisfied that his eyes
had not deceived him, he scampered, as fast as his legs
would carry him, to the Giant's ear, and stooping over
its cavity, shouted lustily into it:

"Halloo, brother Antæus! Get up this minute and

take your pine-tree walking stick in your hand. Here comes another Giant to have a tussle with you."

"Poh, poh!" grumbled Antæus, only half awake. "None of your nonsense, my little fellow! Don't you see I'm sleepy? There is not a Giant on earth for whom I would take the trouble to get up."

But the Pygmy looked again, and now perceived that the stranger was coming directly towards the prostrate form of Antæus. With every step he looked less like a blue mountain, and more like an immensely large man. He was soon so nigh that there could be no possible mistake about the matter. There he was, with the sun flaming on his golden helmet and flashing from his polished breastplate; he had a sword by his side, and a lion's skin over his back, and on his right shoulder he carried a club, which looked bulkier and heavier than the pine-tree walking stick of Antæus.

By this time, the whole nation of Pygmies had seen the new wonder, and a million of them set up a shout, all together; so that it really made quite an audible squeak.

"Get up, Antæus! Bestir yourself, you lazy old Giant! Here comes another Giant, as strong as you are, to fight with you."

"Nonsense, nonsense!" growled the sleepy Giant. "I'll have my nap out, come who may."

Still the stranger drew nearer; and now the Pygmies could plainly discern that, if his stature were less lofty than the Giant's, yet his shoulders were even broader. And, in truth, what a pair of shoulders they must have been! As I told you, a long while ago, they once upheld

the sky. The Pygmies, being ten times as vivacious as their great numskull of a brother, could not abide the Giant's slow movements, and were determined to have him on his feet. So they kept shouting to him, and even went so far as to prick him with their swords.

"Get up, get up, get up!" they cried. "Up with you, lazy bones! The strange Giant's club is bigger than your own, his shoulders are the broadest, and we think him the stronger of the two."

Antæus could not endure to have it said that any mortal was half so mighty as himself. This latter remark of the Pygmies pricked him deeper than their swords; and, sitting up, in rather a sulky humor, he gave a gape of several yards wide, rubbed his eye, and finally turned his stupid head in the direction whither his little friends were eagerly pointing.

No sooner did he set eye on the stranger than, leaping on his feet, and seizing his walking stick, he strode a mile or two to meet him; all the while brandishing the sturdy pine tree, so that it whistled through the air.

"Who are you?" thundered the Giant. "And what do you want in my dominions?"

There was one strange thing about Antæus, of which I have not yet told you, lest, hearing of so many wonders all in a lump, you might not believe much more than half of them. You are to know, then, that whenever this redoubtable Giant touched the ground, either with his hand, his foot, or any other part of his body, he grew stronger than ever he had been before. The Earth, you remember, was his mother, and was very fond of him, as being almost the biggest of her

children; and so she took this method of keeping him always in full vigor. Some persons affirm that he grew ten times stronger at every touch; others say that it was only twice as strong. But only think of it! Whenever Antæus took a walk, supposing it were but ten miles, and that he stepped a hundred yards at a stride, you may try to cipher out how much mightier he was, on sitting down again, than when he first started. And whenever he flung himself on the earth to take a little repose, even if he got up the very next instant, he would be as strong as exactly ten just such giants as his former self. It was well for the world that Antæus happened to be of a sluggish disposition, and liked ease better than exercise; for, if he had frisked about like the Pygmies, and touched the earth as often as they did, he would long ago have been strong enough to pull down the sky about people's ears. But these great lubberly fellows resemble mountains, not only in bulk, but in their disinclination to move.

Any other mortal man, except the very one whom Antæus had now encountered, would have been half frightened to death by the Giant's ferocious aspect and terrible voice. But the stranger did not seem at all disturbed. He carelessly lifted his club, and balanced it in his hand, measuring Antæus with his eye from head to foot, not as if wonder-smitten at his stature, but as if he had seen a great many Giants before, and this was by no means the biggest of them. In fact, if the Giant had been no bigger than the Pygmies (who stood pricking up their ears, and looking and listening to what was going forward), the stranger could not have been less afraid of him.

"Who are you, I say?" roared Antæus again. "What's your name? Why do you come hither? Speak, you vagabond, or I'll try the thickness of your skull with my walking stick."

"You are a very discourteous Giant," answered the stranger quietly, "and I shall probably have to teach you a little civility, before we part. As for my name, it is Hercules. I have come hither because this is my most convenient road to the garden of the Hesperides, whither I am going to get three of the golden apples for King Eurystheus."

"Caitiff, you shall go no farther!" bellowed Antæus, putting on a grimmer look than before; for he had heard of the mighty Hercules, and hated him because he was said to be so strong. "Neither shall you go back whence you came!"

"How will you prevent me," asked Hercules, "from going whither I please?"

"By hitting you a rap with this pine tree here," shouted Antæus, scowling so that he made himself the ugliest monster in Africa. "I am fifty times stronger than you; and, now that I stamp my foot upon the ground, I am five hundred times stronger! I am ashamed to kill such a puny little dwarf as you seem to be. I will make a slave of you, and you shall likewise be the slave of my brethren, here, the Pygmies. So throw down your club and your other weapons; and as for that lion's skin, I intend to have a pair of gloves made of it."

"Come and take it off my shoulders, then," answered Hercules, lifting his club.

Then the Giant, grinning with rage, strode towerlike

towards the stranger (ten times strengthened at every step), and fetched a monstrous blow at him with his pinc trec, which Hercules caught upon his club; and being more skillful than Antæus, he paid him back such a rap upon the sconce, that down tumbled the great lumbering man-mountain, flat upon the ground. The poor little Pygmies (who really never dreamed that anybody in the world was half so strong as their brother Antæus) were a good deal dismayed at this. But no sooner was the Giant down, than up he bounced again, with tenfold might, and such a furious visage as was horrible to behold. He aimed another blow at Hercules, but struck awry, being blinded with wrath, and only hit his poor, innocent Mother Earth, who groaned and trembled at the stroke. His pine tree went so deep into the ground, and stuck there so fast, that before Antæus could get it out, Hercules brought down his club across his shoulders with a mighty thwack, which made the Giant roar as if all sorts of intolerable noises had come screeching and rumbling out of his immeasurable lungs in that one cry. Away it went, over mountains and valleys, and, for aught I know, was heard on the other side of the African deserts.

As for the Pygmies, their capital city was laid in ruins by the concussion and vibration of the air; and, though there was uproar enough without their help, they all set up a shriek out of three millions of little throats, fancying, no doubt, that they swelled the Giant's bellow by at least ten times as much. Meanwhile, Antæus had scrambled upon his feet again, and

pulled his pine tree out of the earth; and, all aflame with fury, and more outrageously strong than ever, he ran at Hercules, and brought down another blow.

"This time, rascal," shouted he, "you shall not escape me."

But once more Hercules warded off the stroke with his club, and the Giant's pine tree was shattered into a thousand splinters, most of which flew among the Pygmies, and did them more mischief than I like to think about. Before Antæus could get out of the way, Hercules let drive again, and gave him another knockdown blow, which sent him heels over head, but served only to increase his already enormous and insufferable strength. As for his rage, there is no telling what a fiery furnace it had now got to be. His one eye was nothing but a circle of red flame. Having now no weapons but his fists, he doubled them up (each bigger than a hogshead), smote one against the other, and danced up and down with absolute frenzy, flourishing his immense arms about, as if he meant not merely to kill Hercules, but to smash the whole world to pieces.

"Come on!" roared this thundering Giant. "Let me hit you but one box on the ear, and you'll never have the headache again."

Now Hercules (though strong enough, as you already know, to hold the sky up) began to be sensible that he should never win the victory, if he kept on knocking Antæus down; for, by and by, if he hit him such hard blows, the Giant would inevitably, by the help of his Mother Earth, become stronger than the mighty Hercules himself. So, throwing down his club,

with which he had fought so many dreadful battles, the hero stood ready to receive his antagonist with naked arms.

"Step forward," cried he. "Since I've broken your pine tree, we'll try which is the better man at a wrestling match."

"Aha! Then I'll soon satisfy you," shouted the Giant; for, if there was one thing on which he prided himself more than another, it was his skill in wrestling. "Villain, I'll fling you where you can never pick yourself up again."

On came Antæus, hopping and capering with the scorching heat of his rage, and getting new vigor wherewith to wreak his passion, every time he hopped. But Hercules, you must understand, was wiser than this numskull of a Giant, and had thought of a way to fight him—huge, earth-born monster that he was—and to conquer him too, in spite of all that his Mother Earth could do for him. Watching his opportunity, as the mad Giant made a rush at him, Hercules caught him round the middle with both hands, lifted him high into the air, and held him aloft overhead.

Just imagine it, my dear little friends! What a spectacle it must have been, to see this monstrous fellow sprawling in the air, face downward, kicking out his long legs and wriggling his whole vast body, like a baby when its father holds it at arm's-length towards the ceiling.

But the most wonderful thing was that, as soon as Antæus was fairly off the earth, he began to lose the vigor which he had gained by touching it. Hercules

Hercules lifted him high into the air and held him aloft

very soon perceived that his troublesome enemy was growing weaker, both because he struggled and kicked with less violence, and because the thunder of his big voice subsided into a grumble. The truth was, that, unless the Giant touched Mother Earth as often as once in five minutes, not only his overgrown strength, but the very breath of his life would depart from him. Hercules had guessed this secret; and it may be well for us all to remember it, in case we should ever have to fight a battle with a fellow like Antæus. For these earth-born creatures are only difficult to conquer on their own ground, but may easily be managed if we can contrive to lift them into a loftier and purer region. So it proved with the poor Giant, whom I am really a little sorry for, notwithstanding his uncivil way of treating strangers who came to visit him.

When his strength and breath were quite gone Hercules gave his huge body a toss, and flung it about a mile off, where it fell heavily, and lay with no more motion than a sand hill. It was too late for the Giant's Mother Earth to help him now; and I should not wonder if his ponderous bones were lying on the same spot to this very day, and were mistaken for those of an uncommonly large elephant.

But, alas me! What a wailing did the poor little Pygmies set up when they saw their enormous brother treated in this terrible manner! If Hercules heard their shrieks, however, he took no notice, and perhaps fancied them only the shrill, plaintive twittering of small birds that had been frightened from their nests by the uproar of the battle between himself and Antæus. In-

deed, his thoughts had been so much taken up with the Giant that he had never once looked at the Pygmies, nor even knew that there was such a funny little nation in the world. And now, as he had traveled a good way, and was also rather weary with his exertions in the fight, he spread out his lion's skin on the ground, and reclining himself upon it, fell fast asleep.

As soon as the Pygmies saw Hercules preparing for a nap, they nodded their little heads at one another, and winked with their little eyes. And when his deep, regular breathing gave them notice that he was asleep, they assembled together in an immense crowd, spreading over a space of about twenty-seven feet square. One of their most eloquent orators (and a valiant warrior enough, besides, though hardly so good at any other weapon as he was with his tongue) climbed upon a toadstool, and, from that elevated position, addressed the multitude. His sentiments were pretty much as follows; or, at all events, something like this was probably the upshot of his speech:

"Tall Pygmies and mighty little men! You and all of us have seen what a public calamity has been brought to pass, and what an insult has here been offered to the majesty of our nation. Yonder lies Antæus, our great friend and brother, slain, within our territory, by a miscreant who took him at disadvantage, and fought him (if fighting it can be called) in a way that neither man, nor Giant, nor Pygmy ever dreamed of fighting until this hour. And, adding a grievous contumely to the wrong already done us, the miscreant has now fallen asleep as quietly as if nothing were to be

dreaded from our wrath! It behooves you, fellow countrymen, to consider in what aspect we shall stand before the world, and what will be the verdict of impar-
tial history, should we suffer these accumulated
outrages to go unavenged.

"Antæus was our brother, born of that same beloved
parent to whom we owe the thews and sinews, as well
as the courageous hearts, which made him proud of our
relationship. He was our faithful ally, and fell fighting
as much for our national rights and immunities as
for his own personal ones. We and our forefathers
have dwelled in friendship with him, and held affectionate intercourse, as man to man, through immemorial
generations. You remember how often our entire
people have reposed in his great shadow, and how
our little ones have played at hide-and-seek in the
tangles of his hair, and how his mighty footsteps have
familiarly gone to and fro among us, and never trodden upon any of our toes. And there lies this dear
brother—this sweet and amiable friend—this brave
and faithful ally—this virtuous Giant—this blameless
and excellent Antæus—dead! Dead! Silent! Powerless!
A mere mountain of clay! Forgive my tears! Nay, I
behold your own! Were we to drown the world with
them, could the world blame us?

"But to resume: Shall we, my countrymen, suffer
this wicked stranger to depart unharmed, and triumph
in his treacherous victory, among distant communities
of the earth? Shall we not rather compel him to leave
his bones here on our soil, by the side of our slain
brother's bones, so that, while one skeleton shall re-

main as the everlasting monument of our sorrow, the other shall endure as long, exhibiting to the whole human race a terrible example of Pygmy vengeance? Such is the question. I put it to you in full confidence of a response that shall be worthy of our national character, and calculated to increase, rather than diminish, the glory which our ancestors have transmitted to us, and which we ourselves have proudly vindicated in our warfare with the cranes."

The orator was here interrupted by a burst of irrepressible enthusiasm; every individual Pygmy crying out that the national honor must be preserved at all hazards. He bowed, and making a gesture for silence, wound up his harangue in the following admirable manner:

"It only remains for us, then, to decide whether we shall carry on the war in our national capacity—one united people against a common enemy—or whether some champion, famous in former fights, shall be selected to defy the slayer of our brother Antæus to single combat. In the latter case, though not unconscious that there may be taller men among you, I hereby offer myself for that enviable duty. And, believe me, dear countrymen, whether I live or die, the honor of this great country, and the fame bequeathed us by our heroic progenitors, shall suffer no diminution in my hands. Never, while I can wield this sword, of which I now fling away the scabbard—never, never, never, even if the crimson hand that slew the great Antæus shall lay me prostrate, like him, on the soil which I give my life to defend."

So saying, this valiant Pygmy drew out his weapon (which was terrible to behold, being as long as the blade of a penknife), and sent the scabbard whirling over the heads of the multitude. His speech was followed by an uproar of applause, as its patriotism and self-devotion unquestionably deserved; and the shouts and clapping of hands would have been greatly prolonged had they not been rendered quite inaudible by a deep respiration, vulgarly called a snore, from the sleeping Hercules.

It was finally decided that the whole nation of Pygmies should set to work to destroy Hercules; not, be it understood, from any doubt that a single champion would be capable of putting him to the sword, but because he was a public enemy, and all were desirous of sharing in the glory of his defeat. There was a debate whether the national honor did not demand that a herald should be sent with a trumpet, to stand over the ear of Hercules, and, after blowing a blast right into it, to defy him to the combat by formal proclamation. But two or three venerable and sagacious Pygmies, well versed in state affairs, gave it as their opinion that war already existed, and that it was their rightful privilege to take the enemy by surprise. Moreover, if awakened, and allowed to get upon his feet, Hercules might happen to do them a mischief before he could be beaten down again. For, as these sage counselors remarked, the stranger's club was really very big, and had rattled like a thunderbolt against the skull of Antæus. So the Pygmies resolved to

set aside all foolish punctilios, and assail their antagonist at once.

Accordingly, all the fighting men of the nation took their weapons, and went boldly up to Hercules, who still lay fast asleep, little dreaming of the harm which the Pygmies meant to do him. A body of twenty thousand archers marched in front, with their little bows all ready, and the arrows on the string. The same number were ordered to clamber upon Hercules, some with spades to dig his eyes out, and others with bundles of hay, and all manner of rubbish, with which they intended to plug up his mouth and nostrils, so that he might perish for lack of breath. These last, however, could by no means perform their appointed duty; inasmuch as the enemy's breath rushed out of his nose in an obstreperous hurricane and whirlwind, which blew the Pygmies away as fast as they came nigh. It was found necessary, therefore, to hit upon some other method of carrying on the war.

After holding a council, the captains ordered their troops to collect sticks, straws, dry weeds, and whatever combustible stuff they could find, and make a pile of it, heaping it high around the head of Hercules. As a great many thousand Pygmies were employed in this task, they soon brought together several bushels of inflammatory matter, and raised so tall a heap, that, mounting on its summit, they were quite upon a level with the sleeper's face. The archers, meanwhile, were stationed within bow-shot, with orders to let fly at Hercules the instant that he stirred. Everything being

in readiness, a torch was applied to the pile, which immediately burst into flames, and soon waxed hot enough to roast the enemy, had he but chosen to lie still. A Pygmy, you know, though so very small, might set the world on fire, just as easily as a Giant could; so that this was certainly the very best way of dealing with their foe, provided they could have kept him quiet while the conflagration was going forward.

But no sooner did Hercules begin to be scorched, than up he started, with his hair in a red blaze.

"What's all this?" he cried, bewildered with sleep, and staring about him as if he expected to see another Giant.

At that moment the twenty thousand archers twanged their bowstrings, and the arrows came whizzing, like so many winged mosquitoes, right into the face of Hercules. But I doubt whether more than half a dozen of them punctured the skin, which was remarkably tough, as you know the skin of a hero has good need to be.

"Villain!" shouted all the Pygmies at once. "You have killed the Giant Antæus, our great brother, and the ally of our nation. We declare bloody war against you and will slay you on the spot."

Surprised at the shrill piping of so many little voices, Hercules, after putting out the conflagration of his hair, gazed all round about, but could see nothing. At last, however, looking narrowly on the ground, he espied the innumerable assemblage of Pygmies at his feet. He stooped down, and taking up the nearest one between his thumb and finger, set him on the palm of

his left hand, and held him at a proper distance for examination. It chanced to be the very identical Pygmy who had spoken from the top of the toadstool and had offered himself as a champion to meet Hercules in single combat.

"What in the world, my little fellow," ejaculated Hercules, "may you be?"

"I am your enemy," answered the valiant Pygmy in his mightiest squeak. "You have slain the enormous Antæus, our brother by the mother's side, and for ages the faithful ally of our illustrious nation. We are determined to put you to death; and for my own part, I challenge you to instant battle, on equal ground."

Hercules was so tickled with the Pygmy's big words and warlike gestures that he burst into a great explosion of laughter, and almost dropped the poor little mite of a creature off the palm of his hand, through the ecstasy and convulsion of his merriment.

"Upon my word," cried he, "I thought I had seen wonders before today—hydras with nine heads, stags with golden horns, six-legged men, three-headed dogs, giants with furnaces in their stomachs, and nobody knows what besides. But here, on the palm of my hand, stands a wonder that outdoes them all! Your body, my little friend, is about the size of an ordinary man's finger. Pray, how big may your soul be?"

"As big as your own!" said the Pygmy.

Hercules was touched with the little man's dauntless courage, and could not help acknowledging such a brotherhood with him as one hero feels for another.

"My good little people," said he, making a low

obeisance to the grand nation, "not for all the world would I do an intentional injury to such brave fellows as you! Your hearts seem to me so exceedingly great, that, upon my honor, I marvel how your small bodies can contain them. I sue for peace, and, as a condition of it, will take five strides, and be out of your kingdom at the sixth. Good-by. I shall pick my steps carefully, for fear of treading upon some fifty of you, without knowing it. Ha, ha, ha! Ho, ho, ho! For once, Hercules acknowledges himself vanquished."

Some writers say that Hercules gathered up the whole race of Pygmies in his lion's skin, and carried them home to Greece, for the children of King Eurystheus to play with. But this is a mistake. He left them, one and all, within their own territory, where, for aught I can tell, their descendants are alive to the present day, building their little houses, cultivating their little fields, spanking their little children, waging their little warfare with the cranes, doing their little business, whatever it may be, and reading their little histories of ancient times. In those histories, perhaps, it stands recorded that, a great many centuries ago, the valiant Pygmies avenged the death of the Giant Antæus by scaring away the mighty Hercules.

The Dragon's Teeth

CADMUS, PHŒNIX, and Cilix, the three sons of King
Agenor, and their little sister Europa (who was a very
beautiful child) were at play together, near the seashore, in their father's kingdom of Phœnicia. They had
rambled to some distance from the palace where their
parents dwelled, and were now in a verdant meadow,
on one side of which lay the sea, all sparkling and dim-
pling in the sunshine, and murmuring gently against
the beach. The three boys were very happy, gathering
flowers, and twining them into garlands, with which
they adorned the little Europa. Seated on the grass, the
child was almost hidden under an abundance of buds
and blossoms, whence her rosy face peeped merrily
out, and, as Cadmus said, was the prettiest of all the
flowers.

Just then, there came a splendid butterfly, fluttering

along the meadow; and Cadmus, Phœnix, and Cilix set off in pursuit of it, crying out that it was a flower with wings. Europa, who was a little wearied with playing all day long, did not chase the butterfly with her brothers, but sat still where they had left her, and closed her eyes. For a while, she listened to the pleasant murmur of the sea, which was like a voice saying, "Hush!" and bidding her go to sleep. But the pretty child, if she slept at all, could not have slept more than a moment, when she heard something trample on the grass, not far from her, and peeping out from the heap of flowers, beheld a snow-white bull.

And whence could this bull have come? Europa and her brothers had been a long time playing in the meadow, and had seen no cattle, nor other living thing, either there or on the neighboring hills.

"Brother Cadmus!" cried Europa, starting up out of the midst of the roses and lilies. "Phœnix! Cilix! Where are you all? Help! Help! Come and drive away this bull!"

But her brothers were too far off to hear; especially as the fright took away Europa's voice, and hindered her from calling very loudly. So there she stood, with her pretty mouth wide open, as pale as the white lilies that were twisted among the other flowers in her garlands.

Nevertheless, it was the suddenness with which she had perceived the bull, rather than anything frightful in his appearance, that caused Europa so much alarm. On looking at him more attentively, she began to see that he was a beautiful animal, and even fancied a

particularly amiable expression in his face. As for his
breath—the breath of cattle, you know, is always
sweet—it was as fragrant as if he had been grazing on
no other food than rosebuds, or, at least, the most
delicate of clover blossoms. Never before did a bull
have such bright and tender eyes, and such smooth
horns of ivory, as this one. And the bull ran little races,
and capered sportively around the child; so that she
quite forgot how big and strong he was, and, from the
gentleness and playfulness of his actions, soon came to
consider him as innocent a creature as a pet lamb.

Thus, frightened as she at first was, you might by
and by have seen Europa stroking the bull's forehead
with her small white hand, and taking the garlands off
her own head to hang them on his neck and ivory
horns. Then she pulled up some blades of grass, and he
ate them out of her hand, not as if he were hungry, but
because he wanted to be friends with the child, and
took pleasure in eating what she had touched. Well,
my stars! Was there ever such a gentle, sweet, pretty,
and amiable creature as this bull, and ever such a nice
playmate for a little girl?

When the animal saw (for the bull had so much
intelligence that it is really wonderful to think of),
when he saw that Europa was no longer afraid of him,
he grew overjoyed, and could hardly contain himself
for delight. He frisked about the meadow, now here,
now there, making sprightly leaps, with as little effort
as a bird expends in hopping from twig to twig. Indeed, his motion was as light as if he were flying
through the air, and his hoofs seemed hardly to leave

their print in the grassy soil over which he trod. With his spotless hue, he resembled a snowdrift, wafted along by the wind. Once he galloped so far away that Europa feared lest she might never see him again; so, setting up her childish voice, she called him back.

"Come back, pretty creature!" she cried. "Here is a nice clover blossom."

And then it was delightful to witness the gratitude of his amiable bull, and how he was so full of joy and thankfulness that he capered higher than ever. He came running, and bowed his head before Europa, as if he knew her to be a king's daughter, or else recognized the important truth that a little girl is everybody's queen. And not only did the bull bend his neck, he absolutely knelt down at her feet, and made such intelligent nods and other inviting gestures that Europa understood what he meant just as well as if he had put it in so many words.

"Come, dear child," was what he wanted to say, "let me give you a ride on my back."

At the first thought of such a thing, Europa drew back. But then she considered in her wise little head that there could be no possible harm in taking just one gallop on the back of this docile and friendly animal, who would certainly set her down the very instant she desired it. And how it would surprise her brothers to see her riding across the green meadow! And what merry times they might have, either taking turns for a gallop, or clambering on the gentle creature, all four children together, and careering round the field with shouts of laughter that would be heard as far off as King Agenor's palace!

"I think I will do it," said the child to herself.

And, indeed, why not? She cast a glance around, and caught a glimpse of Cadmus, Phœnix, and Cilix, who were still in pursuit of the butterfly, almost at the other end of the meadow. It would be the quickest way of rejoining them, to get upon the white bull's back. She came a step nearer to him, therefore; and— sociable creature that he was—he showed so much joy at this mark of her confidence, that the child could not find it in her heart to hesitate any longer. Making one bound (for this little princess was as active as a squirrel), there sat Europa on the beautiful bull, holding an ivory horn in each hand, lest she should fall off.

"Softly, pretty bull, softly!" she said, rather frightened at what she had done. "Do not gallop too fast."

Having got the child on his back, the animal gave a leap into the air, and came down so like a feather that Europa did not know when his hoofs touched the ground. He then began a race to that part of the flowery plain where her three brothers were, and where they had just caught their splendid butterfly. Europa screamed with delight; and Phœnix, Cilix, and Cadmus stood gaping at the spectacle of their sister mounted on a white bull, not knowing whether to be frightened or to wish the same good luck for themselves. The gentle and innocent creature (for who could possibly doubt that he was so?) pranced round among the children as sportively as a kitten. Europa all the while looked down upon her brothers, nodding and laughing, but yet with a sort of stateliness in her rosy little face. As the bull wheeled about to take another gallop across the meadow, the child waved her

hand, and said, "Good-by," playfully pretending that she was now bound on a distant journey, and might not see her brothers again for nobody could tell how long.

"Good-by," shouted Cadmus, Phœnix, and Cilix, all in one breath.

But, together with her enjoyment of the sport, there was still a little remnant of fear in the child's heart; so that her last look at the three boys was a troubled one, and made them feel as if their dear sister were really leaving them forever. And what do you think the snowy bull did next? Why, he set off, as swift as the wind, straight down to the seashore, scampered across the sand, took an airy leap, and plunged right in among the foaming billows. The white spray rose in a shower over him and little Europa, and fell spattering down upon the water.

Then what a scream of terror did the poor child send forth! The three brothers screamed manfully, likewise, and ran to the shore as fast as their legs would carry them, with Cadmus at their head. But it was too late. When they reached the margin of the sand, the treacherous animal was already far away in the wide blue sea, with only his snowy head and tail emerging, and poor little Europa between them, stretching out one hand towards her dear brothers, while she grasped the bull's ivory horn with the other. And there stood Cadmus, Phœnix, and Cilix, gazing at this sad spectacle, through their tears, until they could no longer distinguish the bull's snowy head from the white-capped billows that seemed to boil up out of the sea's depths around him. Nothing more was ever seen

*The white spray rose in a shower over him and little
Europa*

of the white bull—nothing more of the beautiful child.

This was a mournful story, as you may well think, for the three boys to carry home to their parents. King Agenor, their father, was the ruler of the whole country; but he loved his little daughter Europa better than his kingdom, or than all his other children, or than anything else in the world. Therefore, when Cadmus and his two brothers came crying home, and told him how that a white bull had carried off their sister, and swam with her over the sea, the king was quite beside himself with grief and rage. Although it was now twilight, and fast growing dark, he bade them set out instantly in search of her.

"Never shall you see my face again," he cried, "unless you bring me back my little Europa, to gladden me with her smiles and her pretty ways. Begone, and enter my presence no more, till you come leading her by the hand."

As King Agenor said this, his eyes flashed fire (for he was a very passionate king), and he looked so terribly angry that the poor boys did not even venture to ask for their suppers, but slunk away out of the palace, and only paused on the steps a moment to consult whither they should go first. While they were standing there, all in dismay, their mother, Queen Telephassa (who happened not to be by when they told the story to the king), came hurrying after them, and said that she too would go in quest of her daughter.

"Oh no, mother!" cried the boys. "The night is dark, and there is no knowing what troubles and perils we may meet with."

"Alas! my dear children," answered poor Queen Telephassa, weeping bitterly, "that is only another reason why I should go with you. If I should lose you, too, as well as my little Europa, what would become of me?"

"And let me go likewise!" said their playfellow Thasus, who came running to join them.

Thasus was the son of a seafaring person in the neighborhood; he had been brought up with the young princes, and was their intimate friend, and loved Europa very much; so they consented that he should accompany them. The whole party, therefore, set forth together; Cadmus, Phœnix, Cilix, and Thasus clustered round Queen Telephassa, grasping her skirts, and begging her to lean upon their shoulders whenever she felt weary. In this manner they went down the palace steps, and began a journey which turned out to be a great deal longer than they dreamed of. The last that they saw of King Agenor, he came to the door, with a servant holding a torch beside him, and called after them into the gathering darkness:

"Remember! Never ascend these steps again without the child!"

"Never!" sobbed Queen Telephassa; and the three brothers and Thasus answered, "Never! Never! Never! Never!"

And they kept their word. Year after year King Agenor sat in the solitude of his beautiful palace, listening in vain for their returning footsteps, hoping to hear the familiar voice of the queen, and the cheerful talk of his sons and their playfellow Thasus, entering

the door together, and the sweet, childish accents of little Europa in the midst of them. But so long a time went by that, at last, if they had really come, the king would not have known that this was the voice of Telephassa, and these the younger voices that used to make such joyful echoes when the children were playing about the palace. We must now leave King Agenor to sit on his throne, and must go along with Queen Telephassa and her four youthful companions.

They went on and on, and traveled a long way, and passed over mountains and rivers, and sailed over seas. Here and there and everywhere, they made continual inquiry if any person could tell them what had become of Europa. The rustic people, of whom they asked this question, paused a little while from their labors in the field, and looked very much surprised. They thought it strange to behold a woman in the garb of a queen (for Telephassa, in her haste, had forgotten to take off her crown and her royal robes), roaming about the country, with four lads around her, on such an errand as this seemed to be. But nobody could give them any tidings of Europa; nobody had seen a little girl dressed like a princess, and mounted on a snow-white bull, which galloped as swiftly as the wind.

I cannot tell you how long Queen Telephassa, and Cadmus, Phœnix, and Cilix, her three sons, and Thasus, their playfellow, went wandering along the highways and bypaths, or through the pathless wildernesses of the earth, in this manner. But certain it is, that, before they reached any place of rest, their splendid garments were quite worn out. They all looked very

much travel-stained, and would have had the dust of many countries on their shoes, if the streams, through which they waded, had not washed it all away. When they had been gone a year, Telephassa threw away her crown, because it chafed her forehead.

"It has given me many a headache," said the poor queen, "and it cannot cure my heartache."

As fast as their princely robes got torn and tattered, they exchanged them for such mean attire as ordinary people wore. By and by they came to have a wild and homeless aspect; so that you would much sooner have taken them for a gypsy family than a queen and three princes, and a young nobleman, who had once a palace for their home, and a train of servants to do their bidding. The four boys grew up to be tall young men, with sunburned faces. Each of them girded on a sword, to defend themselves against the perils of the way. When the husbandmen, at whose farmhouses they sought hospitality, needed their assistance in the harvest field, they gave it willingly; and Queen Telephassa (who had done no work in her palace, save to braid silk threads with golden ones) came behind them to bind the sheaves. If payment was offered, they shook their heads, and only asked for tidings of Europa.

"There are bulls enough in my pasture," the old farmers would reply, "but I never heard of one like this you tell me of. A snow-white bull with a little princess on his back! Ho! ho! I ask your pardon, good folks; but there never was such a sight seen hereabouts."

At last, when his upper lip began to have the down on it, Phœnix grew weary of rambling hither and

thither to no purpose. So, one day, when they happened to be passing through a pleasant and solitary tract of country, he sat himself down on a heap of moss.

"I can go no farther," said Phœnix. "It is a mere foolish waste of life, to spend it, as we do, in always wandering up and down, and never coming to any home at nightfall. Our sister is lost, and never will be found. She probably perished in the sea; or, to whatever shore the white bull may have carried her, it is now so many years ago, that there would be neither love nor acquaintance between us should we meet again. My father has forbidden us to return to his palace; so I shall build me a hut of branches and dwell here."

"Well, son Phœnix," said Telephassa sorrowfully, "you have grown to be a man, and must do as you judge best. But, for my part, I will still go in quest of my poor child."

"And we three will go along with you!" cried Cadmus and Cilix, and their faithful friend Thasus.

But, before setting out, they all helped Phœnix to build a habitation. When completed, it was a sweet rural bower, roofed overhead with an arch of living boughs. Inside there were two pleasant rooms, one of which had a soft heap of moss for a bed, while the other was furnished with a rustic seat or two, curiously fashioned out of the crooked roots of trees. So comfortable and homelike did it seem that Telephassa and her three companions could not help sighing, to think that they must still roam about the world, instead of

spending the remainder of their lives in some such cheerful abode as they had here built for Phœnix. But, when they bade him farewell, Phœnix shed tears, and probably regretted that he was no longer to keep them company.

However, he had fixed upon an admirable place to dwell in. And by and by there came other people, who chanced to have no homes; and, seeing how pleasant a spot it was, they built themselves huts in the neighborhood of Phœnix's habitation. Thus, before many years went by, a city had grown up there, in the center of which was seen a stately palace of marble, wherein dwelled Phœnix, clothed in a purple robe, and wearing a golden crown upon his head. For the inhabitants of the new city, finding that he had royal blood in his veins, had chosen him to be their king. The very first decree of state which King Phœnix issued was, that if a maiden happened to arrive in the kingdom, mounted on a snow-white bull, and calling herself Europa, his subjects should treat her with the greatest kindness and respect, and immediately bring her to the palace. You may see, by this, that Phœnix's conscience never quite ceased to trouble him, for giving up the quest of his dear sister, and sitting himself down to be comfortable, while his mother and her companions went onward.

But often and often, at the close of a weary day's journey, did Telephassa and Cadmus, Cilix and Thasus, remember the pleasant spot in which they had left Phœnix. It was a sorrowful prospect for these wanderers, that on the morrow they must again set forth, and that, after many nightfalls, they would perhaps be no

nearer the close of their toilsome pilgrimage than now. These thoughts made them all melancholy at times, but appeared to torment Cilix more than the rest of the party. At length, one morning, when they were taking their staffs in hand to set out, he thus addressed them:

"My dear mother, and you, good brother Cadmus, and my friend Thasus, methinks we are like people in a dream. There is no substance in the life which we are leading. It is such a dreary length of time since the white bull carried off my sister Europa, that I have quite forgotten how she looked, and the tones of her voice, and, indeed, almost doubt whether such a little girl ever lived in the world. And whether she once lived or no, I am convinced that she no longer survives, and that therefore it is the merest folly to waste our own lives and happiness in seeking her. Were we to find her, she would now be a woman grown, and would look upon us all as strangers. So, to tell you the truth, I have resolved to take up my abode here; and I entreat you, mother, brother, and friend, to follow my example."

"Not I, for one," said Telephassa; although the poor queen, firmly as she spoke, was so travel-worn that she could hardly put her foot to the ground—"not I, for one! In the depths of my heart, little Europa is still the rosy child who ran to gather flowers so many years ago. She has not grown to womanhood, nor forgotten me. At noon, at night, journeying onward, sitting down to rest, her childish voice is always in my ears, calling, 'Mother! Mother!' Stop here who may, there is no repose for me."

"Nor for me," said Cadmus, "while my dear mother pleases to go onward."

And the faithful Thasus, too, was resolved to bear them company. They remained with Cilix a few days, however, and helped him to build a rustic bower, resembling the one which they had formerly built for Phœnix.

When they were bidding him farewell, Cilix burst into tears, and told his mother that it seemed just as melancholy a dream to stay there, in solitude, as to go onward. If she really believed that they would ever find Europa, he was willing to continue the search with them, even now. But Telephassa bade him remain there, and be happy, if his own heart would let him. So the pilgrims took their leave of him, and departed, and were hardly out of sight before some other wandering people came along that way, and saw Cilix's habitation, and were greatly delighted with the appearance of the place. There being abundance of unoccupied ground in the neighborhood, these strangers built huts for themselves, and were soon joined by a multitude of new settlers, who quickly formed a city. In the middle of it was seen a magnificent palace of colored marble, on the balcony of which, every noontide, appeared Cilix, in a long purple robe, and with a jeweled crown upon his head; for the inhabitants, when they found out that he was a king's son, had considered him the fittest of all men to be a king himself.

One of the first acts of King Cilix's government was to send out an expedition, consisting of a grave ambassador and an escort of bold and hardy young men,

with orders to visit the principal kingdoms of the earth, and inquire whether a young maiden had passed through those regions, galloping swiftly on a white bull. It is, therefore, plain to my mind, that Cilix secretly blamed himself for giving up the search for Europa, as long as he was able to put one foot before the other.

As for Telephassa, and Cadmus, and the good Thasus, it grieves me to think of them, still keeping up that weary pilgrimage. The two young men did their best for the poor queen, helping her over the rough places, often carrying her across rivulets in their faithful arms, and seeking to shelter her at nightfall, even when they themselves lay on the ground. Sad, sad it was to hear them asking of every passer-by if he had seen Europa, so long after the white bull had carried her away. But, though the gray years thrust themselves between, and made the child's figure dim in their remembrance, neither of these true-hearted three ever dreamed of giving up the search.

One morning, however, poor Thasus found that he had sprained his ankle, and could not possibly go a step farther.

"After a few days, to be sure," said he mournfully, "I might make shift to hobble along with a stick. But that would only delay you, and perhaps hinder you from finding dear little Europa, after all your pains and trouble. Do you go forward, therefore, my beloved companions, and leave me to follow as I may."

"Thou hast been a true friend, dear Thasus," said Queen Telephassa, kissing his forehead. "Being neither my son, nor the brother of our lost Europa, thou

hast shown thyself truer to me and her than Phœnix and Cilix did, whom we have left behind us. Without thy loving help, and that of my son Cadmus, my limbs could not have borne me half so far as this. Now, take thy rest, and be at peace. For—and it is the first time I have owned it to myself—I begin to question whether we shall ever find my beloved daughter in this world."

Saying this, the poor queen shed tears, because it was a grievous trial to the mother's heart to confess that her hopes were growing faint. From that day forward, Cadmus noticed that she never traveled with the same alacrity of spirit that had heretofore supported her. Her weight was heavier upon his arm.

Before setting out, Cadmus helped Thasus build a bower; while Telephassa, being too infirm to give any great assistance, advised them how to fit it up and furnish it, so that it might be as comfortable as a hut of branches could. Thasus, however, did not spend all his days in this green bower. For it happened to him, as to Phœnix and Cilix, that other homeless people visited the spot and liked it, and built themselves habitations in the neighborhood. So here, in the course of a few years, was another thriving city with a red freestone palace in the center of it, where Thasus sat upon a throne, doing justice to the people, with a purple robe over his shoulders, a scepter in his hand, and a crown upon his head. The inhabitants had made him king, not for the sake of any royal blood (for none was in his veins), but because Thasus was an upright, true-hearted, and courageous man, and therefore fit to rule.

But, when the affairs of his kingdom were all set-

tled, King Thasus laid aside his purple robe, and crown, and scepter, and bade his worthiest subject distribute justice to the people in his stead. Then, grasping the pilgrim's staff that had supported him so long, he set forth again, hoping still to discover some hoofmark of the snow-white bull, some trace of the vanished child. He returned, after a lengthened absence, and sat down wearily upon his throne. To his latest hour, nevertheless, King Thasus showed his true-hearted remembrance of Europa, by ordering that a fire should always be kept burning in his palace, and a bath steaming hot, and food ready to be served up, and a bed with snow-white sheets, in case the maiden should arrive, and require immediate refreshment. And though Europa never came, the good Thasus had the blessings of many a poor traveler, who profited by the food and lodging which were meant for the little playmate of the king's boyhood.

Telephassa and Cadmus were now pursuing their weary way, with no companion but each other. The queen leaned heavily upon her son's arm, and could walk only a few miles a day. But for all her weakness and weariness, she would not be persuaded to give up the search. It was enough to bring tears into the eyes of bearded men to hear the melancholy tone with which she inquired of every stranger whether he could tell her any news of the lost child.

"Have you seen a little girl—no, no, I mean a young maiden of full growth—passing by this way, mounted on a snow-white bull, which gallops as swiftly as the wind?"

"We have seen no such wondrous sight," the people would reply. And very often, taking Cadmus aside, they whispered to him, "Is this stately and sad-looking woman your mother? Surely she is not in her right mind; and you ought to take her home, and make her comfortable, and do your best to get this dream out of her fancy."

"It is no dream," said Cadmus. "Everything else is a dream, save that."

But, one day, Telephassa seemed feebler than usual and leaned almost her whole weight on the arm of Cadmus, and walked more slowly than ever before. At last they reached a solitary spot, where she told her son that she must needs lie down, and take a good, long rest.

"A good, long rest!" she repeated, looking Cadmus tenderly in the face—"a good, long rest, thou dearest one!"

"As long as you please, dear mother," answered Cadmus.

Telephassa bade him sit down on the turf beside her, and then she took his hand.

"My son," said she, fixing her dim eyes most lovingly upon him, "this rest that I speak of will be very long indeed! You must not wait till it is finished. Dear Cadmus, you do not comprehend me. You must make a grave here, and lay your mother's weary frame into it. My pilgrimage is over."

Cadmus burst into tears, and, for a long time, refused to believe that his dear mother was now to be taken from him. But Telephassa reasoned with him,

and kissed him, and at length made him discern that it was better for her spirit to pass away out of the toil, the weariness, the grief, and disappointment which had burdened her on earth, ever since the child was lost. He therefore repressed his sorrow, and listened to her last words.

"Dearest Cadmus," said she, "thou hast been the truest son that ever mother had, and faithful to the very last. Who else would have borne with my infirmities as thou hast! It is owing to thy care, thou tenderest child, that my grave was not dug long years ago, in some valley, or on some hillside, that lies far, far behind us. It is enough. Thou shalt wander no more on this hopeless search. But when thou hast laid thy mother in the earth, then go, my son, to Delphi, and inquire of the oracle what thou shalt do next."

"Oh, mother, mother," cried Cadmus, "couldst thou but have seen my sister before this hour!"

"It matters little now," answered Telephassa, and there was a smile upon her face. "I go now to the better world, and, sooner or later, shall find my daughter there."

I will not sadden you, my little hearers, with telling how Telephassa died and was buried, but will only say, that her dying smile grew brighter, instead of vanishing from her dead face; so that Cadmus felt convinced that, at her very first step into the better world, she had caught Europa in her arms. He planted some flowers on his mother's grave, and left them to grow there, and make the place beautiful, when he should be far away.

After performing this last sorrowful duty, he set forth alone, and took the road towards the famous

oracle of Delphi, as Telephassa had advised him. On his way thither, he still inquired of most people whom he met whether they had seen Europa; for, to say the truth, Cadmus had grown so accustomed to ask the question that it came to his lips as readily as a remark about the weather. He received various answers. Some told him one thing, and some another. Among the rest, a mariner affirmed that, many years before, in a distant country, he had heard a rumor about a white bull, which came swimming across the sea with a child on his back, dressed up in flowers that were blighted by the sea water. He did not know what had become of the child or the bull; and Cadmus suspected, indeed, by a queer twinkle in the mariner's eyes, that he was putting a joke upon him, and had never really heard anything about the matter.

Poor Cadmus found it more wearisome to travel alone than to bear all his dear mother's weight while she had kept him company. His heart, you will understand, was now so heavy that it seemed impossible, sometimes, to carry it any farther. But his limbs were strong and active, and well accustomed to exercise. He walked swiftly along, thinking of King Agenor and Queen Telephassa, and his brothers, and the friendly Thasus, all of whom he had left behind him, at one point of his pilgrimage or another, and never expected to see them any more. Full of these remembrances, he came within sight of a lofty mountain, which the people thereabouts told him was called Parnassus. On the slope of Mount Parnassus was the famous Delphi, whither Cadmus was going.

This Delphi was supposed to be the very midmost

spot of the whole world. The place of the oracle was a certain cavity in the mountainside, over which, when Cadmus came thither, he found a rude bower of branches. It reminded him of those which he had helped to build for Phœnix and Cilix, and afterwards for Thasus. In later times, when multitudes of people came from great distances to put questions to the oracle, a spacious temple of marble was erected over the spot. But in the days of Cadmus, as I have told you, there was only this rustic bower, with its abundance of green foliage, and a tuft of shrubbery, that ran wild over the mysterious hole in the hillside.

When Cadmus had thrust a passage through the tangled boughs, and made his way into the bower, he did not at first discern the half-hidden cavity. But soon he felt a cold stream of air rushing out of it, with so much force that it shook the ringlets on his cheek. Pulling away the shrubbery which clustered over the hole, he bent forward, and spoke in a distinct but reverential tone, as if addressing some unseen personage inside of the mountain.

"Sacred oracle of Delphi," said he, "whither shall I go next in quest of my dear sister Europa?"

There was at first a deep silence, and then a rushing sound, or a noise like a long sigh, proceeding out of the interior of the earth. This cavity, you must know, was looked upon as a sort of fountain of truth, which sometimes gushed out in audible words; although, for the most part, these words were such a riddle that they might just as well have stayed at the bottom of the hole. But Cadmus was more fortunate than many oth-

ers who went to Delphi in search of truth. By and by, the rushing noise began to sound like articulate language. It repeated, over and over again, the following sentence, which, after all, was so like the vague whistle of a blast of air that Cadmus really did not quite know whether it meant anything or not:

"Seek her no more! Seek her no more! Seek her no more!"

"What, then, shall I do?" asked Cadmus.

For, ever since he was a child, you know, it had been the great object of his life to find his sister. From the very hour that he left following the butterfly in the meadow, near his father's palace, he had done his best to follow Europa, over land and sea. And now, if he must give up the search, he seemed to have no more business in the world.

But again the sighing gust of air grew into something like a hoarse voice.

"Follow the cow!" it said. "Follow the cow! Follow the cow!"

And when these words had been repeated until Cadmus was tired of hearing them (especially as he could not imagine what cow it was, or why he was to follow her), the gusty hole gave vent to another sentence.

"Where the stray cow lies down, there is your home."

These words were pronounced but a single time, and died away into a whisper before Cadmus was fully satisfied that he had caught the meaning. He put other questions, but received no answer; only the gust of wind sighed continually out of the cavity, and blew the

withered leaves rustling along the ground before it.

"Did there really come any words out of the hole?" thought Cadmus, "or have I been dreaming all this while?"

He turned away from the oracle, and thought himself no wiser than when he came thither. Caring little what might happen to him, he took the first path that offered itself, and went along at a sluggish pace; for, having no object in view, nor any reason to go one way more than another, it would certainly have been foolish to make haste. Whenever he met anybody, the old question was at his tongue's end:

"Have you seen a beautiful maiden, dressed like a king's daughter, and mounted on a snow-white bull, that gallops as swiftly as the wind?"

But, remembering what the oracle had said, he only half uttered the words, and then mumbled the rest indistinctly; and from his confusion, people must have imagined that this handsome young man had lost his wits.

I know not how far Cadmus had gone, nor could he himself have told you, when, at no great distance before him, he beheld a brindled cow. She was lying down by the wayside, and quietly chewing her cud; nor did she take any notice of the young man until he had approached pretty nigh. Then, getting leisurely upon her feet, and giving her head a gentle toss, she began to move along at a moderate pace, often pausing just long enough to crop a mouthful of grass. Cadmus loitered behind, whistling idly to himself, and scarcely noticing the cow; until the thought occurred to him,

whether this could possibly be the animal which, according to the oracle's response, was to serve him for a guide. But he smiled at himself for fancying such a thing. He could not seriously think that this was the cow, because she went along so quietly, behaving just like any other cow. Evidently she neither knew nor cared so much as a wisp of hay about Cadmus, and was only thinking how to get her living along the wayside, where the herbage was green and fresh. Perhaps she was going home to be milked.

"Cow, cow, cow!" cried Cadmus. "Hey, Brindle, hey! Stop, my good cow."

He wanted to come up with the cow, so as to examine her, and see if she would appear to know him, or whether there were any peculiarities to distinguish her from a thousand other cows, whose only business is to fill the milk pail, and sometimes kick it over. But still the brindled cow trudged on, whisking her tail to keep the flies away, and taking as little notice of Cadmus as she well could. If he walked slowly, so did the cow, and seized the opportunity to graze. If he quickened his pace, the cow went just so much the faster; and once, when Cadmus tried to catch her by running, she threw out her heels, stuck her tail straight on end, and set off at a gallop, looking as queerly as cows generally do, while putting themselves to their speed.

When Cadmus saw that it was impossible to come up with her, he walked on moderately, as before. The cow, too, went leisurely on, without looking behind. Wherever the grass was greenest, there she nibbled a mouthful or two. Where a brook glistened brightly

across the path, there the cow drank, and breathed a comfortable sigh, and drank again, and trudged onward at the pace that best suited herself and Cadmus.

"I do believe," thought Cadmus, "that this may be the cow that was foretold me. It if be the one, I suppose she will lie down somewhere hereabouts."

Whether it were the oracular cow or some other one, it did not seem reasonable that she should travel a great way farther. So, whenever they reached a particularly pleasant spot on a breezy hillside, or in a sheltered vale, or flowery meadow, on the shore of a calm lake, or along the bank of a clear stream, Cadmus looked eagerly around to see if the situation would suit him for a home. But still, whether he liked the place or no, the brindled cow never offered to lie down. On she went at the quiet pace of a cow going homeward to the barnyard; and, every moment, Cadmus expected to see a milkmaid approaching with a pail, or a herdsman running to head the stray animal, and turn her back towards the pasture. But no milkmaid came; no herdsman drove her back; and Cadmus followed the stray Brindle till he was almost ready to drop down with fatigue.

"Oh, brindled cow," cried he, in a tone of despair, "do you never mean to stop?"

He had now grown too intent on following her to think of lagging behind, however long the way, and whatever might be his fatigue. Indeed, it seemed as if there were something about the animal that bewitched people. Several persons who happened to see the brindled cow, and Cadmus following behind, began to

trudge after her, precisely as he did. Cadmus was glad of somebody to converse with, and therefore talked very freely to these good people. He told them all his adventures, and how he had left King Agenor in his palace, and Phœnix at one place, and Cilix at another, and Thasus at a third, and his dear mother, Queen Telephassa, under a flowery sod; so that now he was quite alone, both friendless and homeless. He mentioned, likewise, that the oracle had bidden him be guided by a cow, and inquired of the strangers whether they supposed that this brindled animal could be the one.

"Why, 'tis a very wonderful affair," answered one of his new companions. "I am pretty well acquainted with the ways of cattle, and I never knew a cow, of her own accord, to go so far without stopping. If my legs will let me, I'll never leave following the beast till she lies down."

"Nor I!" said a second.

"Nor I!" cried a third. "If she goes a hundred miles farther, I'm determined to see the end of it."

The secret of it was, you must know, that the cow was an enchanted cow, and that, without their being conscious if it, she threw some of her enchantment over everybody that took so much as half a dozen steps behind her. They could not possibly help following her, though, all the time, they fancied themselves doing it of their own accord. The cow was by no means very nice in choosing her path; so that sometimes they had to scramble over rocks, or wade through mud and mire, and were all in a terribly be-

draggled condition, and tired to death, and very hungry, into the bargain. What a weary business it was!

But still they kept trudging stoutly forward, and talking as they went. The strangers grew very fond of Cadmus, and resolved never to leave him, but to help him build a city wherever the cow might lie down. In the center of it there should be a noble palace, in which Cadmus might dwell, and be their king, with a throne, a crown and scepter, a purple robe, and everything else that a king ought to have; for in him there was the royal blood, and the royal heart, and the head that knew how to rule.

While they were talking of these schemes, and beguiling the tediousness of the way with laying out the plan of the new city, one of the company happened to look at the cow.

"Joy! Joy!" cried he, clapping his hands. "Brindle is going to lie down."

They all looked; and, sure enough, the cow had stopped, and was staring leisurely about her, as other cows do when on the point of lying down. And slowly, slowly did she recline herself on the soft grass, first bending her forelegs, and then crouching her hind ones. When Cadmus and his companions came up with her, there was the brindled cow taking her ease, chewing her cud, and looking them quietly in the face; as if this was just the spot she had been seeking for, and as if it were all a matter of course.

"This, then," said Cadmus, gazing around him, "this is to be my home."

It was a fertile and lovely plain, with great trees

flinging their sun-speckled shadows over it, and hills
fencing it in from the rough weather. At no great
distance, they beheld a river gleaming in the sunshine.
A home feeling stole into the heart of poor Cadmus.
He was very glad to know that here he might awake in
the morning, without the necessity of putting on his
dusty sandals to travel farther and farther. The days
and the years would pass over him, and find him still in
this pleasant spot. If he could have had his brothers
with him, and his friend Thasus, and could have seen
his dear mother under a roof of his own, he might here
have been happy, after all their disappointments.
Some day or other, too, his sister Europa might have
come quietly to the door of his home, and smiled
round upon the familiar faces. But, indeed, since there
was no hope of regaining the friends of his boyhood,
or ever seeing his dear sister again. Cadmus resolved to
make himself happy with these new companions, who
had grown so fond of him while following the cow.

"Yes, my friends," said he to them, "this is to be our
home. Here we will build our habitations. The brindled cow, which has led us hither, will supply us with
milk. We will cultivate the neighboring soil, and lead
an innocent and happy life."

His companions joyfully assented to this plan; and,
in the first place, being very hungry and thirsty, they
looked about them for the means of providing a comfortable meal. Not far off, they saw a tuft of trees,
which appeared as if there might be a spring of water
beneath them. They went thither to fetch come, leaving Cadmus stretched on the ground along with the

brindled cow; for, now that he had found a place of rest, it seemed as if all the weariness of his pilgrimage, ever since he left King Agenor's palace, had fallen upon him at once. But his new friends had not long been gone, when he was suddenly startled by cries, shouts, and screams, and the noise of a terrible struggle, and in the midst of it all, a most awful hissing, which went right through his ears like a rough saw.

Running towards the tuft of trees, he beheld the head and fiery eyes of an immense serpent or dragon, with the widest jaws that ever a dragon had, and a vast many rows of horribly sharp teeth. Before Cadmus could reach the spot, this pitiless reptile had killed his poor companions, and was busily devouring them, making but a mouthful of each man.

It appears that the fountain of water was enchanted, and that the dragon had been set to guard it, so that no mortal might ever quench his thirst there. As the neighboring inhabitants carefully avoided the spot, it was now a long time (not less than a hundred years, or thereabouts) since the monster had broken his fast; and, as was natural enough, his appetite had grown to be enormous, and was not half satisfied by the poor people whom he had just eaten up. When he caught sight of Cadmus, therefore, he set up another abominable hiss, and flung back his immense jaws, until his mouth looked like a great red cavern, at the farther end of which were seen the legs of his last victim, whom he had hardly had time to swallow.

But Cadmus was so enraged at the destruction of his friends that he cared neither for the size of the drag-

on's jaws nor for his hundreds of sharp teeth. Drawing his sword, he rushed at the monster, and flung himself right into his cavernous mouth. This bold method of attacking him took the dragon by surprise; for, in fact, Cadmus had leaped so far down into his throat, that the rows of terrible teeth could not close upon him, not do him the least harm in the world. Thus, though the struggle was a tremendous one, and though the dragon shattered the tuft of trees into small splinters by the lashing of his tail, yet, as Cadmus was all the while slashing and stabbling at his very vitals, it was not long before the scaly wretch bethought himself of slipping away. He had not gone his length, however, when the brave Cadmus gave him a sword thrust that finished the battle; and, creeping out of the gateway of the creature's jaws, there he beheld him still wriggling his vast bulk, although there was no longer life enough in him to harm a little child.

But do not you suppose that it made Cadmus sorrowful to think of the melancholy fate which had befallen those poor, friendly people, who had followed the cow along with him? It seemed as if he were doomed to lose everybody whom he loved, or to see them perish in one way or another. And here he was, after all his toils and troubles, in a solitary place, with not a single human being to help him build a hut.

"What shall I do?" cried he aloud. "It were better for me to have been devoured by the dragon, as my poor companions were."

"Cadmus," said a voice—but whether it came from above or below him, or whether it spoke within his

own breast, the young man could not tell—"Cadmus, pluck out the dragon's teeth, and plant them in the earth."

This was a strange thing to do; nor was it very easy, I should imagine, to dig out all those deep-rooted fangs from the dead dragon's jaws. But Cadmus toiled and tugged, and after pounding the monstrous head almost to pieces with a great stone, he at last collected as many teeth as might have filled a bushel or two. The next thing was to plant them. This likewise, was a tedious piece of work, especially as Cadmus was already exhausted with killing the dragon and knocking his head to pieces, and had nothing to dig the earth with, that I know of, unless it were his sword blade. Finally, however, a sufficiently large tract of ground was turned up, and sown with this new kind of seed; although half of the dragon's teeth still remained to be planted some other day.

Cadmus, quite out of breath, stood leaning upon his sword, and wondering what was to happen next. He had waited but a few moments, when he began to see a sight, which was as great a marvel as the most marvelous thing I ever told you about.

The sun was shining slantwise over the field, and showed all the moist, dark soil just like any other newly planted piece of ground. All at once, Cadmus fancied he saw something glisten very brightly, first at one spot, then at another, and than at a hundred and a thousand spots together. Soon he perceived them to be the steel heads of spears, sprouting up everywhere like so many stalks of grain, and continually growing taller

and taller. Next appeared a vast number of bright sword blades, thrusting themselves up in the same way. A moment afterwards, the whole surface of the ground was broken up by a multitude of polished brass helmets, coming up like a crop of enormous beans. So rapidly did they grow that Cadmus now discerned the fierce countenance of a man beneath every one. In short, before he had time to think what a wonderful affair it was, he beheld an abundant harvest of what looked like human beings, armed with helmets and breastplates, shields, swords and spears; and before they were well out of the earth, they brandished their weapons, and clashed them one against another, seeming to think, little while as they had yet lived, that they had wasted too much of life without a battle. Every tooth of the dragon had produced one of these sons of deadly mischief.

Up sprouted, also, a great many trumpeters; and with the first breath that they drew, they put their brazen trumpets to their lips, and sounded a tremendous and ear-shattering blast; so that the whole space, just now so quiet and solitary, reverberated with the clash and clang of arms, the bray of warlike music, and the shouts of angry men. So enraged did they all look that Cadmus fully expected them to put the whole world to the sword. How fortunate would it be for a great conqueror, if he could get a bushel of the dragon's teeth to sow!

"Cadmus," said the same voice which he had before heard, "throw a stone into the midst of the armed men."

So Cadmus seized a large stone, and, flinging it into the middle of the earth army, saw it strike the breast-plate of a gigantic and fierce-looking warrior. Immediately on feeling the blow, he seemed to take it for granted that somebody had struck him; and, uplifting his weapon, he smote his next neighbor a blow that cleft his helmet asunder, and stretched him on the ground. In an instant, those nearest the fallen warrior began to strike at one another with their swords and stab with their spears. The confusion spread wider and wider. Each man smote down his brother, and was himself smitten down before he had time to exult in his victory. The trumpeters, all the while blew their blasts shriller and shriller; each soldier shouted a battle cry and often fell with it on his lips. It was the strangest spectacle of causeless wrath, and of mischief for no good end, that had ever been witnessed; but, after all, it was neither more foolish nor more wicked than a thousand battles that have since been fought, in which men have slain their brothers with just as little reason as these children of the dragon's teeth. It ought to be considered, too, that the dragon people were made for nothing else; whereas other mortals were born to love and help one another.

Well, this memorable battle continued to rage until the ground was strewn with helmeted heads that had been cut off. Of all the thousands that began the fight, there were only five left standing. These now rushed from different parts of the field, and, meeting in the middle of it, clashed their swords, and struck at each other's hearts as fiercely as ever.

"Cadmus," said the voice again, "bid those five war-

riors sheathe their swords. They will help you to build the city."

Without hesitating an instant, Cadmus stepped forward, with the aspect of a king and a leader, and extending his drawn sword among them, spoke to the warriors in a stern and commanding voice.

"Sheathe your weapons!" said he.

And forthwith, feeling themselves bound to obey him, the five remaining sons of the dragon's teeth made him a military salute with their swords, returned them to the scabbards, and stood before Cadmus in a rank, eyeing him as soldiers eye their captain, while awaiting the word of command.

These five men had probably sprung from the biggest of the dragon's teeth, and were the boldest and strongest of the whole army. They were almost giants, indeed, and had good need to be so, else they never could have lived through so terrible a fight. They still had a very furious look, and, if Cadmus happened to glance aside, would glare at one another, with fire flashing out of their eyes. It was strange, too, to observe how the earth, out of which they had so lately grown, was incrusted, here and there, on their bright breastplates, and even begrimed their faces, just as you may have seen it clinging to beets and carrots when pulled out of their native soil. Cadmus hardly knew whether to consider them as men, or some odd kind of vegetable; although, on the whole, he concluded that there was human nature in them, because they were so fond of trumpets and weapons, and so ready to shed blood.

They looked him earnestly in the face, waiting for

his next order, and evidently desiring no other employment than to follow him from one battlefield to another, all over the wide world. But Cadmus was wiser than these earth-born creatures, with the dragon's fierceness in them, and knew better how to use their strength and hardihood.

"Come!" said he. "You are sturdy fellows. Make yourselves useful! Quarry some stones with those great swords of yours, and help me to build a city."

The five soldiers grumbled a little, and muttered that it was their business to overthrow cities, not to build them up. But Cadmus looked at them with a stern eye, and spoke to them in a tone of authority, so that they knew him for their master, and never again thought of disobeying his commands. They set to work in good earnest, and toiled so diligently that, in a very short time, a city began to make its appearance. At first, to be sure, the workmen showed a quarrelsome disposition. Like savage beasts, they would doubtless have done one another a mischief, if Cadmus had not kept watch over them and quelled the fierce old serpent that lurked in their hearts, when he saw it gleaming out of their wild eyes. But, in course of time, they got accustomed to honest labor, and had sense enough to feel that there was more true enjoyment in living at peace, and doing good to one's neighbor, than in striking at him with a two-edged sword. It may not be too much to hope that the rest of mankind will by and by grow as wise and peaceable as these five earth-begrimed warriors, who sprang from the dragon's teeth.

And now the city was built, and there was a home in it for each of the workmen. But the palace of Cadmus was not yet erected, because they had left it till the last, meaning to introduce all the new improvements of architecture, and make it very commodious as well as stately and beautiful. After finishing the rest of their labors, they all went to bed betimes, in order to rise in the gray of the morning, and get at least the foundation of the edifice laid before nightfall. But, when Cadmus arose, and took his way towards the site where the palace was to be built, followed by his five sturdy workmen marching all in a row, what do you think he saw?

What should it be but the most magnificent palace that had ever been seen in the world? It was built of marble and other beautiful kinds of stone, and rose high into the air, with a splendid dome and a portico along the front, and carved pillars, and everything else that befitted the habitation of a mighty king. It had grown up out of the earth in almost as short a time as it had taken the armed host to spring from the dragon's teeth; and what made the matter more strange, no seed of this stately edifice had ever been planted.

When the five workmen beheld the dome, with the morning sunshine making it look golden and glorious, they gave a great shout.

"Long live King Cadmus," they cried, "in his beautiful palace."

And the new king, with his five faithful followers at his heels, shouldering their pickaxes and marching in a rank (for they still had a soldier-like sort of behavior,

as their nature was), ascended the palace steps. Halting at the entrance, they gazed through a long vista of lofty pillars that were ranged from end to end of a great hall. At the farther extremity of this hall, approaching slowly towards him, Cadmus beheld a female figure, wonderfully beautiful, and adorned with a royal robe, and a crown of diamonds over her golden ringlets, and the richest necklace that ever a queen wore. His heart thrilled with delight. He fancied it his long-lost sister Europa, now grown to womanhood, coming to make him happy, and to repay him, with her sweet sisterly affection, for all those weary wanderings in quest of her since he left King Agenor's palace—for the tears that he had shed, on parting with Phœnix, and Cilix, and Thasus—for the heartbreakings that had made the whole world seem dismal to him over his dear mother's grave.

But as Cadmus advanced to meet the beautiful stranger, he saw that her features were unknown to him, although, in the little time that it required to tread along the hall, he had already felt a sympathy betwixt himself and her.

"No, Cadmus," said the same voice that had spoken to him in the field of the armed men, "this is not that dear sister Europa whom you have sought so faithfully all over the wide world. This is Harmonia, a daughter of the sky, who is given you instead of sister, and brothers, and friend, and mother. You will find all those dear ones in her alone."

So King Cadmus dwelled in the palace with his new friend Harmonia, and found a great deal of comfort in

his magnificent abode, but would doubtless have found as much, if not more, in the humblest cottage by the wayside. Before many years went by, there was a group of rosy little children (but how they came thither has always been a mystery to me) sporting in the great hall, and on the marble steps of the palace, and running joyfully to meet King Cadmus when affairs of state left him at leisure to play with them. They called him father, and Queen Harmonia mother. The five old soldiers of the dragon's teeth grew very fond of these small urchins, and were never weary of showing them how to shoulder sticks, flourish wooden swords and march in military order, blowing a penny trumpet or beating an abominable rub-a-dub upon a little drum.

But King Cadmus, lest there should be too much of the dragon's tooth in his children's disposition, used to find time from his kingly duties to teach them their A B C—which he invented for their benefit, and for which many little people, I am afraid, are not half so grateful to him as they ought to be.

Circe's Palace

SOME OF you have heard, no doubt, of the wise King Ulysses, and how he went to the siege of Troy, and how, after that famous city was taken and burned, he spent ten long years in trying to get back again to his own little kingdom of Ithaca. At one time in the course of this weary voyage, he arrived at an island that looked very green and pleasant, but the name of which was unknown to him. For, only a little while before he came thither, he had met with a terrible hurricane, or rather a great many hurricanes at once, which drove his fleet of vessels into a strange part of the sea, where neither himself nor any of his mariners had ever sailed. This misfortune was entirely owing to the foolish curiosity of his shipmates, who, while Ulysses lay asleep, had untied some very bulky leathern bags, in which they supposed a valuable treasure to be con-

cealed. But in each of these stout bags, King Æolus, the ruler of the winds, had tied up a tempest, and had given it to Ulysses to keep, in order that he might be sure of a favorable passage homeward to Ithaca; and when the strings were loosened, forth rushed the whistling blasts, like air out of a blown bladder, whitening the sea with foam, and scattering the vessels nobody could tell whither.

Immediately after escaping from this peril, a still greater one had befallen him. Scudding before the hurricane, he reached a place, which, as he afterwards found, was called Læstrygonia, where some monstrous giants had eaten up many of his companions, and had sunk every one of his vessels, except that in which he himself sailed, by flinging great masses of rock at them, from the cliffs along the shore. After going through such troubles as these, you cannot wonder that King Ulysses was glad to moor his tempest-beaten bark in a quiet cove of the green island, which I began with telling you about. But he had encountered so many dangers from giants, and one-eyed Cyclopes, and monsters of the sea and land, that he could not help dreading some mischief, even in this pleasant and seemingly solitary spot. For two days, therefore, the poor weather-worn voyagers kept quiet, and either stayed on board their vessel, or merely crept along under cliffs that bordered the shore; and to keep themselves alive, they dug shellfish out of the sand, and sought for any little rill of fresh water that might be running towards the sea.

Before the two days were spent, they grew very

weary of this kind of life; for the followers of King Ulysses, as you will find it important to remember, were terrible gormandizers, and pretty sure to grumble if they missed their regular meals, and their irregular ones besides. Their stock of provisions was quite exhausted, and even the shellfish began to get scarce, so that they had now to choose between starving to death or venturing into the interior of the island, where, perhaps, some huge three-headed dragon, or other horrible monster, had his den. Such misshapen creatures were very numerous in those days; and nobody ever expected to make a voyage, or take a journey, without running more or less risk of being devoured by them.

But King Ulysses was a bold man as well as a prudent one; and on the third morning he determined to discover what sort of a place the island was, and whether it were possible to obtain a supply of food for the hungry mouths of his companions. So, taking a spear in his hand, he clambered to the summit of a cliff, and gazed round about him. At a distance, towards the center of the island, he beheld the stately towers of what seemed to be a palace, built of snow-white marble, and rising in the midst of a grove of lofty trees. The thick branches of these trees stretched across the front of the edifice, and more than half concealed it, although, from the portion which he saw, Ulysses judged it to be spacious and exceedingly beautiful, and probably the residence of some great nobleman or prince. A blue smoke went curling up from the chimney, and was almost the pleasantest part of the

spectacle to Ulysses. For, from the abundance of this smoke, it was reasonable to conclude that there was a good fire in the kitchen, and that, at dinnertime, a plentiful banquet would be served up to the inhabitants of the palace, and to whatever guests might happen to drop in.

With so agreeable a prospect before him, Ulysses fancied that he could not do better than to go straight to the palace gate, and tell the master of it that there was a crew of poor shipwrecked mariners, not far off, who had eaten nothing for a day or two save a few clams and oysters, and would therefore be thankful for a little food. And the prince or nobleman must be a very stingy curmudgeon, to be sure, if, at least, when his own dinner was over, he would not bid them welcome to the broken victuals from the table.

Pleasing himself with this idea, King Ulysses had made a few steps in the direction of the palace, when there was a great twittering and chirping from the branch of a neighboring tree. A moment afterwards, a bird came flying towards him, and hovered in the air, so as almost to brush his face with its wings. It was a very pretty little bird, with purple wings and body, and yellow legs, and in a circle of golden feathers round its neck, and on its head a golden tuft, which looked like a king's crown in miniature. Ulysses tried to catch the bird. But it fluttered nimbly out of his reach, still chirping in a piteous tone, as if it could have told a lamentable story, had it only been gifted with human language. And when he attempted to drive it away, the bird flew no farther than the bough of the next tree,

and again came fluttering about his head, with its doleful chirp as soon as he showed a purpose of going forward.

"Have you anything to tell me, little bird?" asked Ulysses.

And he was ready to listen attentively to whatever the bird might communicate; for at the siege of Troy, and elsewhere, he had known such odd things to happen that he would not have considered it much out of the common run had this little feathered creature talked as plainly as himself.

"Peep!" said the bird, "peep, peep, pe—weep!" And nothing else would it say, but only, "Peep, peep, pe—weep!" in a melancholy cadence, and over and over and over again. As often as Ulysses moved forward, however, the bird showed the greatest alarm, and did its best to drive him back, with the anxious flutter of its purple wings. Its unaccountable behavior made him conclude, at last, that the bird knew of some danger that awaited him, and which must needs be very terrible, beyond all question, since it moved even a little fowl to feel compassion for a human being. So he resolved, for the present, to return to the vessel, and tell his companions what he had seen.

This appeared to satisfy the bird. As soon as Ulysses turned back, it ran up the trunk of a tree and began to pick insects out of the bark with its long, sharp bill; for it was a kind of woodpecker, you must know, and had to get its living in the same manner as other birds of that species. But every little while, as it pecked at the bark of the tree, the purple bird bethought itself of

some secret sorrow, and repeated its plaintive note of "Peep, peep, pe—weep!"

On his way to the shore, Ulysses had the good luck to kill a large stag by thrusting his spear into its back. Taking it on his shoulders (for he was a remarkably strong man), he lugged it along with him, and flung it down before his hungry companions. I have already hinted to you what gormandizers some of the comrades of King Ulysses were. From what is related of them, I reckon that their favorite diet was pork, and that they had lived upon it until a good part of their physical substance was swine's flesh, and their tempers and dispositions were very much akin to the hog. A dish of venison, however, was no unacceptable meal to them, especially after feeding so long on oysters and clams. So, beholding the dead stag, they felt of its ribs in a knowing way, and lost no time in kindling a fire, of driftwood, to cook it. The rest of the day was spent in feasting; and it these enormous eaters got up from table at sunset, it was only because they could not scrape another morsel off the poor animal's bones.

The next morning their appetites were as sharp as ever. They looked at Ulysses, as if they expected him to clamber up the cliff again and come back with another fat deer upon his shoulders. Instead of setting out, however, he summoned the whole crew together, and told them it was in vain to hope that he could kill a stag every day for their dinner, and therefore it was advisable to think of some other mode of satisfying their hunger.

"Now," said he, "when I was on the cliff yesterday, I

discovered that this island is inhabited. At a considerable distance from the shore stood a marble palace, which appeared to be very spacious, and had a great deal of smoke curling out of one of its chimneys."

"Aha!" muttered some of his companions, smacking their lips. "That smoke must have come from the kitchen fire. There was a good dinner on the spit; and no doubt there will be as good a one today."

"But," continued the wise Ulysses, "you must remember, my good friends, our misadventure in the cavern of one-eyed Polyphemus, the Cyclops! Instead of his ordinary milk diet, did he not eat up two of our comrades for his supper, and a couple more for breakfast, and two at his supper again? Methinks I see him yet, the hideous monster, scanning us with that great red eye, in the middle of his forehead, to single out the fattest. And then again only a few days ago, did we not fall into the hands of the king of the Læstrygons, and those other horrible giants, his subjects, who devoured a great many more of us than are now left? To tell you the truth, if we go to yonder palace, there can be no question that we shall make our appearance at the dinner table; but whether seated as guests, or served up as food, is a point to be seriously considered."

"Either way," murmured some of the hungriest of the crew, "it will be better than starvation; particularly if one could be sure of being well fattened beforehand, and daintily cooked afterwards."

"That is a matter of taste," said King Ulysses, "and, for my own part, neither the most careful fattening nor

the daintiest of cookery would reconcile me to being dished at last. My proposal is, therefore, that we divide ourselves into two equal parties, and ascertain, by drawing lots, which of the two shall go to the palace, and beg for food and assistance. If these can be obtained, all is well. If not, and if the inhabitants prove as inhospitable as Polyphemus, or the Læstrygons, then there will but half of us perish, and the remainder may set sail and escape."

As nobody objected to this scheme, Ulysses proceeded to count the whole band, and found that there were forty-six men including himself. He then numbered off twenty-two of them, and put Eurylochus (who was one of his chief officers, and second only to himself in sagacity) at their head. Ulysses took command of the remaining twenty-two men, in person. Then, taking off his helmet, he put two shells into it, on one of which was written, "Go," and on the other "Stay." Another person now held the helmet, while Ulysses and Eurylochus drew out each a shell; and the word "Go" was found written on that which Eurylochus had drawn. In this manner, it was decided that Ulysses and his twenty-two men were to remain at the seaside until the other party should have found out what sort of treatment they might expect at the mysterious palace. As there was no help for it, Eurylochus immediately set forth at the head of his twenty-two followers, who went off in a very melancholy state of mind, leaving their friends in hardly better spirits than themselves.

No sooner had they clambered up the cliff, than

they discerned the tall marble towers of the palace, ascending, as white as snow, out of the lovely green shadow of the trees which surrounded it. A gush of smoke came from a chimney in the rear of the edifice. This vapor rose high in the air, and, meeting with a breeze, was wafted seaward and made to pass over the heads of the hungry mariners. When people's appetites are keen, they have a very quick scent for anything savory in the wind.

"That smoke comes from the kitchen!" cried one of them, turning up his nose as high as he could, and snuffing eagerly. "And, as sure as I'm a half-starved vagabond, I smell roast meat in it."

"Pig, roast pig!" said another. "Ah, the dainty little porker! My mouth waters for him."

"Let us make haste," cried the others, "or we shall be too late for the good cheer!"

But scarcely had they made half a dozen steps from the edge of the cliff, when a bird came fluttering to meet them. It was the same pretty little bird, with the purple wings and body, the yellow legs, the golden collar round its neck, and the crown-like tuft upon its head, whose behavior had so much surprised Ulysses. It hovered about Eurylochus, and almost brushed his face with its wings.

"Peep, peep, pe—weep!" chirped the bird.

So plaintively intelligent was the sound that it seemed as if the little creature were going to break its heart with some mighty secret that it had to tell, and only this one poor note to tell it with.

"My pretty bird," said Eurylochus—for he was a

wary person, and let no token of harm escape his notice—"my pretty bird, who sent you hither? And what is the message which you bring?"

"Peep, peep, pe—weep!" replied the bird very sorrowfully.

Then it flew towards the edge of the cliff, and looked round at them, as if exceedingly anxious that they should return whence they came. Eurylochus and a few of the others were inclined to turn back. They could not help suspecting that the purple bird must be aware of something mischievous that would befall them at the palace, and the knowledge of which affected its airy spirit with a human sympathy and sorrow. But the rest of the voyagers, snuffing up the smoke from the palace kitchen, ridiculed the idea of returning to the vessel. One of them (more brutal than his fellows, and the most notorious gormandizer in the whole crew) said such a cruel and wicked thing that I wonder the mere thought did not turn him into a wild beast in shape, as he already was in his nature.

"This troublesome and impertinent little fowl," said he, "would make a delicate titbit to begin dinner with. Just one plump morsel, melting away between the teeth. If he comes within my reach, I'll catch him, and give him to the palace cook to be roasted on a skewer."

The words were hardly out of his mouth, before the purple bird flew away, crying "Peep, peep, pe—weep," more dolorously than ever.

"That bird," remarked Eurylochus, "knows more than we do about what awaits us at the palace."

"Come on, then," cried his comrades, "and we'll soon know as much as he does."

The party, accordingly, went onward through the green and pleasant wood. Every little while they caught new glimpses of the marble palace, which looked more and more beautiful the nearer they approached it. They soon entered a broad pathway, which seemed to be very neatly kept, and which went winding along with streaks of sunshine falling across it, and specks of light quivering among the deepest shadows that fell from the lofty trees. It was bordered, too, with a great many sweet-smelling flowers, such as the mariners had never seen before. So rich and beautiful they were that, if the shrubs grew wild here, and were native in the soil, then this island was surely the flower garden of the whole earth; or, if transplanted from some other clime, it must have been from the Happy Islands that lay towards the golden sunset.

"There has been a great deal of pains foolishly wasted on these flowers," observed one of the company; and I tell you what he said, that you may keep in mind what gormandizers they were. "For my part, if I were the owner of the palace, I would bid my gardener cultivate nothing but savory potherbs to make a stuffing for roast meat, or to flavor a stew with."

"Well said!" cried the others. "But I'll warrant you there's a kitchen garden in the rear of the palace."

At one place they came to a crystal spring, and paused to drink at it for want of liquor which they liked better. Looking into its bosom, they beheld their own faces dimly reflected, but so extravagantly dis-

torted by the gush and motion of the water, that each one of them appeared to be laughing at himself and all his companions. So ridiculous were these images of themselves, indeed, that they did really laugh aloud, and could hardly be grave again as soon as they wished. And after they had drunk, they grew still merrier than before.

"It has a twang of the wine cask in it," said one, smacking his lips.

"Make haste!" cried his fellows. "We'll find the wine cask itself at the palace; and that will be better than a hundred crystal fountains."

Then they quickened their pace, and capered for joy at the thought of the savory banquet at which they hoped to be guests. But Eurylochus told them that he felt as if he were walking in a dream.

"If I am really awake," continued he, "then, in my opinion, we are on the point of meeting with some stranger adventure than any that befell us in the cave of Polyphemus, or among the gigantic man-eating Læstrygons, or in the windy palace of King Æolus, which stands on a brazen-walled island. This kind of dreamy feeling always comes over me before any wonderful occurrence. If you take my advice, you will turn back."

"No, no," answered his comrades, snuffing the air, in which the scent from the palace kitchen was now very perceptible. "We would not turn back, though we were certain that the king of the Læstrygons, as big as a mountain, would sit at the head of the table, and huge Polyphemus, the one-eyed Cyclops, at its foot."

At length they came within full sight of the palace, which proved to be very large and lofty, with a great number of airy pinnacles upon its roof. Though it was now midday, and the sun shone brightly over the marble front, yet its snowy whiteness and its fantastic style of architecture made it look unreal, like the frostwork on a windowpane, or like the shapes of castles which one sees among the clouds by moonlight. But, just then, a puff of wind brought down the smoke of the kitchen chimney among them, and caused each man to smell the odor of the dish that he liked best; and, after scenting it, they thought everything else moonshine, and nothing real save this palace, and save the banquet that was evidently ready to be served up in it.

So they hastened their steps towards the portal, but had not got halfway across the wide lawn, when a pack of lions, tigers, and wolves came bounding to meet them. The terrified mariners started back, expecting no better fate than to be torn to pieces and devoured. To their surprise and joy, however, these wild beasts merely capered around them, wagging their tails, offering their heads to be stroked and patted, and behaving just like so many well-bred housedogs, when they wish to express their delight at meeting their master, or their master's friends. The biggest lion licked the feet of Eurylochus; and every other lion, and every wolf and tiger, singled out one of his two-and-twenty followers, whom the beast fondled as if he loved him better than a beef bone.

But, for all that, Eurylochus imagined that he saw something fierce and savage in their eyes; nor would he

have been surprised, at any moment, to feel the big lion's terrible claws, or to see each of the tigers make a deadly spring, or each wolf leap at the throat of the man whom he had fondled. Their mildness seemed unreal, and a mere freak; but their savage nature was as true as their teeth and claws.

Nevertheless, the men went safely across the lawn with the wild beasts frisking about them, and doing no manner of harm; although, as they mounted the steps of the palace, you might possibly have heard a low growl, particularly from the wolves; as if they thought it a pity, after all, to let the strangers pass without so much as tasting what they were made of.

Eurylochus and his followers now passed under a lofty portal, and looked through the open doorway into the interior of the palace. The first thing that they saw was a spacious hall, and a fountain in the middle of it, gushing up towards the ceiling out of a marble basin, and falling back into it with a continual plash. The water of this fountain, as it spouted upward, was constantly taking new shapes, not very distinctly, but plainly enough for a nimble fancy to recognize what they were. Now it was the shape of a man in a long robe, the fleecy whiteness of which was made out of the fountain's spray; now it was a lion, or a tiger, or a wolf, or an ass, or, as often as anything else, a hog, wallowing in the marble basin as if it were his sty. It was either magic or some very curious machinery that caused the gushing waterspout to assume all these forms. But, before the strangers had time to look closely at this wonderful sight, their attention was

drawn off by a very sweet and agreeable sound. A woman's voice was singing melodiously in another room of the palace, and with her voice was mingled the noise of a loom, at which she was probably seated, weaving a rich texture of cloth, and intertwining the high and low sweetness of her voice into a rich tissue of harmony.

By and by, the song came to an end; and then, all at once, there were several feminine voices, talking airily and cheerfully, with now and then a merry burst of laughter, such as you may always hear when three or four young women sit at work together.

"What a sweet song that was!" exclaimed one of the voyagers.

"Too sweet, indeed," answered Eurylochus, shaking his head. "Yet it was not so sweet as the song of the Sirens, those birdlike damsels who wanted to tempt us on the rocks, so that our vessel might be wrecked, and our bones left whitening along the shore."

"But just listen to the pleasant voices of those maidens, and that buzz of the loom, as the shuttle passes to and fro," said another comrade. "What a domestic, household, homelike sound it is! Ah, before that weary siege of Troy, I used to hear the buzzing loom and the women's voices under my own roof. Shall I never hear them again? nor taste those nice little savory dishes which my dearest wife knew how to serve up?"

"Tush! we shall fare better here," said another. "But how innocently those women are babbling together, without guessing that we overhear them! And mark that richest voice of all, so pleasant and familiar, but

which yet seems to have the authority of a mistress among them. Let us show ourselves at once. What harm can the lady of the palace and her maidens do to mariners and warriors like us?"

"Remember," said Eurylochus, "that it was a young maiden who beguiled three of our friends into the palace of the king of the Læstrygons, who ate up one of them in the twinkling of an eye."

No warning or persuasion, however, had any effect on his companions. They went up to a pair of folding doors at the farther end of the hall, and, throwing them wide open, passed into the next room. Eurylochus, meanwhile, had stepped behind a pillar. In the short moment while the folding doors opened and closed again, he caught a glimpse of a very beautiful woman rising from the loom, and coming to meet the poor weather-beaten wanderers, with a hospitable smile, and her hand stretched out in welcome. There were four other young women, who joined their hands and danced merrily forward, making gestures of obeisance to the strangers. They were only less beautiful than the lady who seemed to be their mistress. Yet Eurylochus fancied that one of them had sea-green hair, and that the close-fitting bodice of a second looked like the bark of a tree, and that both the others had something odd in their aspect, although he could not quite determine what it was, in the little while that he had to examine them.

The folding doors swung quickly back, and left him standing behind the pillar, in the solitude of the outer hall. There Eurylochus waited until he was quite

weary, and listened eagerly to every sound, but without hearing anything that could help him to guess what had become of his friends. Footsteps, it is true, seemed to be passing and repassing in other parts of the palace. Then there was a clatter of silver dishes, or golden ones, which made him imagine a rich feast in a splendid banqueting hall. But by and by he heard a tremendous grunting and squealing, and then a sudden scampering, like that of small, hard hoofs over a marble floor, while the voices of the mistress and her four handmaidens were screaming all together, in tones of anger and derision. Eurylochus could not conceive what had happened, unless a drove of swine had broken into the palace, attracted by the smell of the feast. Chancing to cast his eyes at the fountain, he saw that it did not shift its shape, as formerly, nor looked either like a long-robed man, or a lion, a tiger, a wolf, or an ass. It looked like nothing but a hog, which lay wallowing in the marble basin, and filled it from brim to brim.

But we must leave the prudent Eurylochus waiting in the outer hall, and follow his friends into the inner secrecy of the palace. As soon as the beautiful woman saw them, she arose from the loom, as I have told you, and came forward, smiling, and stretching out her hand. She took the hand of the foremost among them, and bade him and the whole party welcome.

"You have been long expected, my good friends," said she. "I and my maidens are well acquainted with you, although you do not appear to recognize us. Look at this piece of tapestry, and judge if your faces must not have been familiar to us."

So the voyagers examined the web of cloth which the beautiful woman had been weaving in her loom; and, to their vast astonishment they saw their own figures perfectly represented in different colored threads. It was a lifelike picture of their recent adventures, showing them in the cave of Polyphemus, and how they had put out his one great moony eye; while in another part of the tapestry they were untying the leathern bags, puffed out with contrary winds; and farther on, they beheld themselves scampering away from the gigantic king of the Læstrygons, who had caught one of them by the leg. Lastly, there they were, sitting on the desolate shore of this very island, hungry and downcast, and looking ruefully at the bare bones of the stag which they devoured yesterday. This was as far as the work had yet proceeded; but when the beautiful woman should again sit down at her loom, she would probably make a picture of what had since happened to the strangers, and of what was now going to happen.

"You see," she said, "that I know all about your troubles; and you cannot doubt that I desire to make you happy for as long a time as you may remain with me. For this purpose, my honored guests, I have ordered a banquet to be prepared. Fish, fowl, and flesh, roasted, and in luscious stews, and seasoned, I trust, to all your tastes, are ready to be served up. If your appetites tell you it is dinnertime, then come with me to the festal saloon."

At this kind invitation, the hungry mariners were quite overjoyed; and one of them, taking upon himself to be spokesman, assured their hospitable hostess that

any hour of the day was dinnertime with them, whenever they could get flesh to put in the pot, and fire to boil it with. So the beautiful woman led the way; and the four maidens (one of them had sea-green hair, another a bodice of oak bark, a third sprinkled a shower of water drops from her fingers' ends, and the fourth had some other oddity, which I have forgotten), all these followed behind, and hurried the guests along, until they entered a magnificent saloon. It was built in a perfect oval, and lighted from a crystal dome above. Around the walls were ranged two-and-twenty thrones, overhung by canopies of crimson and gold, and provided with the softest of cushions, which were tasseled and fringed with gold cord. Each of the strangers was invited to sit down; and there they were, two-and-twenty storm-beaten mariners, in worn and tattered garb, sitting on two-and-twenty cushioned and canopied thrones, so rich and gorgeous that the proudest monarch had nothing more splendid in his stateliest hall.

Then you might have seen the guests nodding, winking with one eye, and leaning from one throne to another, to communicate their satisfaction in hoarse whispers. "Our good hostess has made kings of us all," said one. "Ha! Do you smell the feast? I'll engage it will be fit to set before two-and-twenty kings."

"I hope," said another, "it will be, mainly, good substantial joints, sirloins, spareribs, and hinder quarters, without too many kickshaws. If I thought the good lady would not take it amiss, I should call for a fat slice of fried bacon to begin with."

Ah, the gluttons and gormandizers! You see how it was with them. In the loftiest seats of dignity, on royal thrones, they could think of nothing but their greedy appetite, which was the portion of their nature that they shared with wolves and swine; so that they resembled those vilest of animals far more than they did kings—if, indeed, kings were what they ought to be.

But the beautiful woman now clapped her hands; and immediately there entered a train of two-and-twenty serving men, bringing dishes of the richest food, all hot from the kitchen fire, and sending up such a steam that it hung like a cloud below the crystal dome of the saloon. An equal number of attendants brought great flagons of wine, of various kinds, some of which sparkled as it was poured out, and went bubbling down the throat; while, of other sorts, the purple liquor was so clear that you could see the wrought figures at the bottom of the goblet. While the servants supplied the two-and-twenty guests with food and drink, the hostess and her four maidens went from one throne to another, exhorting them to eat their fill, and to quaff wine abundantly, and thus to recompense themselves, at this one banquet, for the many days when they had gone without a dinner. But, whenever the mariners were not looking at them (which was pretty often, as they looked chiefly into the basins and platters), the beautiful woman and her damsels turned aside and laughed. Even the servants, as they knelt down to present the dishes, might be seen to grin and sneer, while the guests were helping themselves to the offered dainties.

The hostess and her four maidens went from one throne to another, exhorting them to eat their fill

And, once in a while, the strangers seemed to taste something that they did not like.

"Here is an odd kind of a spice in this dish," said one. "I can't say it quite suits my palate. Down it goes, however."

"Send a good draft of wine down your throat," said his comrade on the next throne. "That is the stuff to make this sort of cookery relish well. Though I must needs say, the wine has a queer taste too. But the more I drink of it the better I like the flavor."

Whatever little fault they might find with the dishes, they sat at dinner a prodigiously long while; and it would really have made you ashamed to see how they swilled down the liquor and gobbled up the food. They sat on golden thrones, to be sure; but they behaved like pigs in a sty; and, if they had had their wits about them, they might have guessed that this was the opinion of their beautiful hostess and her maidens. It brings a blush into my face to reckon up, in my own mind, what mountains of meat and pudding, and what gallons of wine, these two-and-twenty guzzlers and gormandizers ate and drank. They forgot all about their homes, and their wives and children, and all about Ulysses, and everything else, except this banquet, at which they wanted to keep feasting forever. But at length they began to give over, from mere incapacity to hold any more.

"That last bit of fat is too much for me," said one.

"And I have not room for another morsel," said his next neighbor, heaving a sigh. "What a pity! My appetite is as sharp as ever."

In short, they all left off eating, and leaned back on their thrones, with such a stupid and helpless aspect as made them ridiculous to behold. When their hostess saw this, she laughed aloud; so did her four damsels; so did the two-and-twenty serving men that bore the dishes, and their two-and-twenty fellows that poured out the wine. And the louder they all laughed, the more stupid and helpless did the two-and-twenty gormandizers look. Then the beautiful woman took her stand in the middle of the saloon, and stretching out a slender rod (it had been all the while in her hand, although they never noticed it till this moment), she turned it from one guest to another, until each had felt it pointed at himself. Beautiful as her face was, and though there was a smile on it, it looked just as wicked and mischievous as the ugliest serpent that ever was seen; and fat-witted as the voyagers had made themselves, they began to suspect that they had fallen into the power of an evil-minded enchantress.

"Wretches," cried she, "you have abused a lady's hospitality; and in this princely saloon your behavior has been suited to a hogpen. You are already swine in everything but the human form, which you disgrace, and which I myself should be ashamed to keep a moment longer, were you to share it with me. But it will require only the slightest exercise of magic to make the exterior conform to the hoggish disposition. Assume your proper shapes, gormandizers, and begone to the sty!"

Uttering these last words, she waved her wand; and stamping her foot imperiously, each of the guests was

struck aghast at beholding, instead of his comrades in human shape, one-and-twenty hogs sitting on the same number of golden thrones. Each man (as he still supposed himself to be) essayed to give a cry of surprise, but found that he could merely grunt, and that, in a word, he was just such another beast as his companions. It looked so intolerably absurd to see hogs on cushioned thrones, that they made haste to wallow down upon all fours, like other swine. They tried to groan and beg for mercy, but forthwith emitted the most awful grunting and squealing that ever came out of swinish throats. They would have wrung their hands in despair, but, attempting to do so, grew all the more desperate for seeing themselves squatted on their hams, and pawing the air with their fore trotters. Dear me! What pendulous ears they had! What little red eyes, half buried in fat! And what long snouts, instead of Grecian noses!

But brutes as they certainly were, they yet had enough of human nature in them to be shocked at their own hideousness; and, still intending to groan, they uttered a viler grunt and squeal than before. So harsh and ear-piercing it was, that you would have fancied a butcher was sticking his knife into each of their throats, or, at the very least, that somebody was pulling every hog by his funny little twist of a tail.

"Begone to your sty!" cried the enchantress, giving them some smart strokes with her wand; and then she turned to the serving men, "Drive out these swine, and throw down some acorns for them to eat."

The door of the saloon being flung open, the drove

of hogs ran in all directions save the right one, in accordance with their hoggish perversity, but were finally driven into the backyard of the palace. It was a sight to bring tears into one's eyes (and I hope none of you will be cruel enough to laugh at it), to see the poor creatures go snuffing along, picking up here a cabbage leaf and there a turnip top, and rooting their noses in the earth for whatever they could find. In their sty, moreover, they behaved more piggishly than the pigs that had been born so; for they bit and snorted at one another, put their feet in the trough, and gobbled up their victuals in a ridiculous hurry; and when there was nothing more to be had, they made a great pile of themselves among some unclean straw, and fell fast asleep. If they had any human reason left, it was just enough to keep them wondering when they should be slaughtered, and what quality of bacon they should make.

Meantime, as I told you before, Eurylochus had waited and waited and waited, in the entrance hall of the palace, without being able to comprehend what had befallen his friends. At last, when the swinish uproar resounded through the palace, and when he saw the image of a hog in the marble basin, he thought it best to hasten back to the vessel, and inform the wise Ulysses of these marvelous occurrences. So he ran as fast as he could down the steps, and never stopped to draw breath till he reached the shore.

"Why do you come alone?" asked King Ulysses, as soon as he saw him. "Where are your two-and-twenty comrades?"

At these questions, Eurylochus burst into tears.

"Alas!" cried he, "I greatly fear that we shall never see one of their faces again."

Then he told Ulysses all that had happened, as far as he knew it, and added that he suspected the beautiful woman to be a vile enchantress, and the marble palace, magnificent as it looked, to be only a dismal cavern in reality. As for his companions, he could not imagine what had become of them, unless they had been given to the swine to be devoured alive. At this intelligence all the voyagers were greatly affrighted. But Ulysses lost no time in girding on his sword, and hanging his bow and quiver over his shoulders, and taking a spear in his right hand. When his followers saw their wise leader making these preparations, they inquired whither he was going and earnestly besought him not to leave them.

"You are our king," cried they, "and what is more, you are the wisest man in the whole world, and nothing but your wisdom and courage can get us out of this danger. If you desert us, and go to the enchanted palace, you will suffer the same fate as our poor companions, and not a soul of us will ever see our dear Ithaca again."

"As I am your king," answered Ulysses, "and wiser than any of you, it is therefore the more my duty to see what has befallen our comrades, and whether anything can yet be done to rescue them. Wait for me here until tomorrow. If I do not then return, you must hoist sail, and endeavor to find your way to our native land. For my part, I am answerable for the fate of these poor

mariners, who have stood by my side in battle, and been so often drenched to the skin, along with me, by the same tempestuous surges. I will either bring them back with me or perish."

Had his followers dared, they would have detained him by force. But King Ulysses frowned sternly on them, and shook his spear, and bade them stop him at their peril. Seeing him so determined, they let him go, and sat down on the sand, as disconsolate a set of people as could be, waiting and praying for his return.

It happened to Ulysses, just as before, that, when he had gone a few steps from the edge of the cliff, the purple bird came fluttering towards him, crying, "Peep, peep, pe—weep!" and using all the art it could to persuade him to go no farther.

"What mean you, little bird?" cried Ulysses. "You are arrayed like a king in purple and gold, and wear a golden crown upon your head. Is it because I too am a king that you desire so earnestly to speak with me? If you can talk in human language, say what you would have me do."

"Peep!" answered the purple bird very dolorously. "Peep, peep, pe—we—ep!"

Certainly there lay some heavy anguish at the little bird's heart; and it was a sorrowful predicament that he could not, at least, have the consolation of telling what it was. But Ulysses had no time to waste in trying to get at the mystery. He therefore quickened his pace, and had gone a good way along the pleasant wood-path, when there met him a young man of very brisk and intelligent aspect, and clad in a rather singular

garb. He wore a short cloak, and a sort of cap that seemed to be furnished with a pair of wings; and from the lightness of his step, you would have supposed that there might likewise be wings on his feet. To enable him to walk still better (for he was always on one journey or another), he carried a winged staff, around which two serpents were wriggling and twisting. In short, I have said enough to make you guess that it was Quicksilver; and Ulysses (who knew him of old, and had learned a great deal of his wisdom from him) recognized him in a moment.

"Whither are you going in such a hurry, wise Ulysses?" asked Quicksilver. "Do you not know that this island is enchanted? The wicked enchantress (whose name is Circe, the sister of King Æetes) dwells in the marble palace which you see yonder among the trees. By her magic arts, she changes every human being into the brute, beast, or fowl whom he happens most to resemble."

"That little bird which met me at the edge of the cliff," exclaimed Ulysses, "was he a human being once?"

"Yes," answered Quicksilver. "He was once a king, named Picus, and a pretty good sort of a king too, only rather too proud of his purple robe, and his crown, and the golden chain about his neck; so he was forced to take the shape of a gaudy-feathered bird. The lions and wolves and tigers who will come running to meet you, in front of the palace, were formerly fierce and cruel men, resembling in their dispositions the wild beasts whose forms they now rightfully wear."

"And my poor companions," said Ulysses. "Have they undergone a similar change, through the arts of this wicked Circe?"

"You well know what gormandizers they were," replied Quicksilver; and, rogue that he was, he could not help laughing at the joke. "So you will not be surprised to hear that they have all taken the shape of swine! If Circe had never done anything worse, I really should not think her so very much to blame."

"But can I do nothing to help them?" inquired Ulysses.

"It will require all your wisdom," said Quicksilver, "and a little of my own into the bargain, to keep your royal and sagacious self from being transformed into a fox. But do as I bid you; and the matter may end better than it has begun."

While he was speaking, Quicksilver seemed to be in search of something; he went stooping along the ground, and soon laid his hand on a little plant with a snow-white flower, which he plucked and smelled of. Ulysses had been looking at that very spot only just before; and it appeared to him that the plant had burst into full flower the instant when Quicksilver touched it with his fingers.

"Take this flower, King Ulysses," said he. "Guard it as you do your eyesight; for I can assure you it is exceedingly rare and precious, and you might seek the whole earth over without ever finding another like it. Keep it in your hand, and smell of it frequently after you enter the palace, and while you are talking with the enchantress. Especially when she offers you food,

or a draft of wine out of her goblet, be careful to fill your nostrils with the flower's fragrance. Follow these directions, and you may defy her magic arts to change you into a fox."

Quicksilver then gave him some further advice how to behave, and, bidding him be bold and prudent, again assured him that, powerful as Circe was, he would have a fair prospect of coming safely out of her enchanted palace. After listening attentively, Ulysses thanked his good friend, and resumed his way. But he had taken only a few steps, when, recollecting some other questions which he wished to ask, he turned round again, and beheld nobody on the spot where Quicksilver had stood; for that winged cap of his, and those winged shoes, with the help of the winged staff, had carried him quickly out of sight.

When Ulysses reached the lawn, in front of the palace, the lions and other savage animals came bounding to meet him, and would have fawned upon him and licked his feet. But the wise king struck at them with his long spear, and sternly bade them begone out of his path; for he knew that they had once been bloodthirsty men, and would now tear him limb from limb, instead of fawning upon him, could they do the mischief that was in their hearts. The wild beasts yelped and glared at him, and stood at a distance while he ascended the palace steps.

On entering the hall, Ulysses saw the magic fountain in the center of it. The up-gushing water had now again taken the shape of a man in a long, white, fleecy robe, who appeared to be making gestures of welcome.

The king likewise heard the noise of the shuttle in the loom, and the sweet melody of the beautiful woman's song, and then the pleasant voices of herself and the four maidens talking together, with peals of merry laughter intermixed. But Ulysses did not waste much time in listening to the laughter or the song. He leaned his spear against one of the pillars of the hall, and then, after loosening his sword in the scabbard, stepped boldly forward, and threw the folding doors wide open. The moment she beheld his stately figure standing in the doorway, the beautiful woman rose from the loom, and ran to meet him with a glad smile throwing its sunshine over her face, and both her hands extended.

"Welcome, brave stranger!" cried she. "We were expecting you."

And the nymph with the sea-green hair made a curtsy down to the ground, and likewise bade him welcome; so did her sister with the bodice of oaken bark, and she that sprinkled dewdrops from her fingers' ends, and the fourth one with some oddity which I cannot remember. And Circe, as the beautiful enchantress was called (who had deluded so many persons that she did not doubt of being able to delude Ulysses, not imagining how wise he was), again addressed him.

"Your companions," said she, "have already been received into my palace, and have enjoyed the hospitable treatment to which the propriety of their behavior so well entitles them. If such be your pleasure, you shall first take some refreshment, and then join them in

the elegant apartment which they now occupy. See, I and my maidens have been weaving their figures into this piece of tapestry."

She pointed to the web of beautifully woven cloth in the loom. Circe and the four numphs must have been very diligently at work since the arrival of the mariners; for a great many yards of tapestry had now been wrought, in addition to what I before described. In this new part, Ulysses saw his two-and-twenty friends represented as sitting on cushioned and canopied thrones, greedily devouring dainties and quaffing deep drafts of wine. The work had not yet gone any further. Oh no, indeed. The enchantress was far too cunning to let Ulysses see the mischief which her magic arts had since brought upon the gormandizers.

"As for yourself, valiant sir," said Circe, "judging by the dignity of your aspect, I take you to be nothing less than a king. Deign to follow me, and you shall be treated as befits your rank."

So Ulysses followed her into the oval saloon, where his two-and-twenty comrades had devoured the banquet, which ended so disastrously for themselves. But, all this while, he had held the snow-white flower in his hand, and had constantly smelled of it while Circe was speaking; and as he crossed the threshold of the saloon, he took good care to inhale several long and deep snuffs of its fragrance. Instead of two-and-twenty thrones, which had before been ranged around the wall, there was now only a single throne, in the center of the apartment. But this was surely the most magnificent seat that ever a king or an emperor reposed him-

self upon, all made of chased gold, studded with precious stones, with a cushion that looked like a soft heap of living roses, and overhung by a canopy of sunlight which Circe knew how to weave into drapery. The enchantress took Ulysses by the hand, and made him sit down upon this dazzling throne. Then, clapping her hands, she summoned the chief butler.

"Bring hither," said she, "the goblet that is set apart for kings to drink out of. And fill it with the same delicious wine which my royal brother, King Æetes, praised so highly, when he last visited me with my fair daughter Medea. That good and amiable child! Were she now here, it would delight her to see me offering this wine to my honored guest."

But Ulysses, while the butler was gone for the wine, held the snow-white flower to his nose.

"Is it a wholesome wine?" he asked.

At this the four maidens tittered; whereupon the enchantress looked round at them, with an aspect of severity.

"It is the wholesomest juice that ever was squeezed out of the grape," said she. "For, instead of disguising a man, as other liquor is apt to do, it brings him to his true self, and shows him as he ought to be."

The chief butler liked nothing better than to see people turned into swine, or making any kind of a beast of themselves; so he made haste to bring the royal goblet, filled with a liquid as bright as gold, and which kept sparkling upward, and throwing a sunny spray over the brim. But, delightfully as the wine looked, it was mingled with the most potent enchant-

ments that Circe knew how to concoct. For every drop of the pure grape juice there were two drops of the pure mischief; and the danger of the thing was, that the mischief made it taste all the better. The mere smell of the bubbles, which effervesced at the brim, was enough to turn a man's beard into pig's bristles, or make a lion's claws grow out of his fingers, or a fox's brush behind him.

"Drink, my noble guest," said Circe, smiling as she presented him with the goblet. "You will find in this draft a solace for all your troubles."

King Ulysses took the goblet with his right hand, while with his left he held the snow-white flower to his nostrils, and drew in so long a breath that his lungs were quite filled with its pure and simple fragrance. Then, drinking off all the wine, he looked the enchantress calmly in the face.

"Wretch," cried Circe, giving him a smart stroke with her wand, "how dare you keep your human shape a moment longer? Take the form of the brute whom you most resemble. If a hog, go join your fellow swine in the sty; if a lion, a wolf, a tiger, go howl with the wild beasts on the lawn: if a fox, go exercise your craft in stealing poultry. Thou hast quaffed off my wine, and canst be man no longer."

But, such was the virtue of the snow-white flower, instead of wallowing down from his throne in swinish shape, or taking any other brutal form, Ulysses looked even more manly and kinglike than before. He gave the magic goblet a toss, and sent it clashing over the marble floor, to the farthest end of the saloon. Then,

drawing his sword, he seized the enchantress by her beautiful ringlets, and made a gesture as if he meant to strike off her head at one blow.

"Wicked Circe," cried he in a terrible voice, "this sword shall put an end to thy enchantments. Thou shalt die, vile wretch, and do no more mischief in the world, by tempting human beings into the vices which make beasts of them."

The tone and countenance of Ulysses were so awful, and his sword gleamed so brightly, and seemed to have so intolerably keen an edge, that Circe was almost killed by the mere fright, without waiting for a blow. The chief butler scrambled out of the saloon, picking up the golden goblet as he went; and the enchantress and the four maidens fell on their knees, wringing their hands and screaming for mercy.

"Spare me!" cried Circe—"spare me, royal and wise Ulysses. For now I know that thou art he of whom Quicksilver forewarned me, the most prudent of mortals, against whom no enchantments can prevail. Thou only couldst have conquered Circe. Spare me, wisest of men. I will show thee true hospitality, and even give myself to be thy slave, and this magnificent palace to be henceforth thy home."

The four nymphs, meanwhile, were making a most piteous ado; and especially the ocean nymph, with the sea-green hair, wept a great deal of salt water, and the fountain nymph, besides scattering dewdrops from her finger's ends, nearly melted away into tears. But Ulysses would not be pacified until Circe had taken a solemn oath to change back his companions, and as

"Spare me!" cried Circe. "Spare me, royal and wise Ulysses!"

many others as he should direct, from their present forms of beast or bird into their former shapes of men.

"On these conditions," said he, "I consent to spare your life. Otherwise you must die upon the spot."

With a sword drawn hanging over her, the enchantress would readily have consented to do as much good as she had hitherto done mischief, however little she might like such employment. She therefore led Ulysses out of the back entrance of the palace, and showed him the swine in their sty. There were about fifty of these unclean beasts in the whole herd; and though the greater part were hogs by birth and education, there was wonderfully little difference to be seen betwixt them and their new brethren who had so recently worn the human shape. To speak critically, indeed, the latter rather carried the thing to excess, and seemed to make it a point to wallow in the miriest part of the sty, and otherwise to outdo the original swine in their own natural vocation. When men once turn to brutes, the trifle of man's wit that remains in them adds tenfold to their brutality.

The comrades of Ulysses, however, had not quite lost the remembrance of having formerly stood erect. When he approached the sty, two-and-twenty enormous swine separated themselves from the herd, and scampered towards him, with such a chorus of horrible squealing as made him clap both hands to his ears. And yet they did not seem to know what they wanted, nor whether they were merely hungry, or miserable from some other cause. It was curious, in the midst of their distress, to observe them thrusting their noses

into the mire, in quest of something to eat. The nymph with the bodice of oaken bark (she was the hamadryad of an oak) threw a handful of acorns among them; and the two-and-twenty hogs scrambled and fought for the prize, as if they had tasted not so much as a noggin of sour milk for a twelvemonth.

"These must certainly be my comrades," said Ulysses. "I recognize their dispositions. They are hardly worth the trouble of changing them into the human form again. Nevertheless, we will have it done, lest their bad example should corrupt the other hogs. Let them take their original shapes, therefore, Dame Circe, if your skill is equal to the task. It will require greater magic, I trow, than it did to make swine of them."

So Circe waved her wand again, and repeated a few magic words, at the sound of which the two-and-twenty hogs pricked up their pendulous ears. It was a wonder to behold how their snouts grew shorter and shorter, and their mouths (which they seemed to be sorry for, because they could not gobble so expeditiously) smaller and smaller, and how one and another began to stand upon his hind legs, and scratch his nose with his fore trotters. At first the spectators hardly knew whether to call them hogs or men, but by and by came to the conclusion that they rather resembled the latter. Finally, there stood the twenty-two comrades of Ulysses, looking pretty much the same as when they left the vessel.

You must not imagine, however, that the swinish quality had entirely gone out of them. When once it fastens itself into a person's character, it is very diffi-

cult getting rid of it. This was proved by the hama-dryad, who, being exceedingly fond of mischief, threw another handful of acorns before the twenty-two newly restored people; whereupon down they wallowed, in a moment, and gobbled them up in a very shameful way. Then, recollecting themselves, they scrambled to their feet, and looked more than commonly foolish.

"Thanks, noble Ulysses!" they cried. "From brute beasts you have restored us to the condition of men again."

"Do not put yourselves to the trouble of thanking me," said the wise king. "I fear I have done but little for you."

To say the truth, there was a suspicious kind of a grunt in their voices, and for a long time afterwards they spoke gruffly, and were apt to set up a squeal.

"It must depend on your own future behavior," added Ulysses, "whether you do not find your way back to the sty."

At this moment, the note of a bird sounded from the branch of a neighboring tree.

"Peep, peep, pe—wee—ep!"

It was the purple bird, who, all this while, had been sitting over their heads, watching what was going forward, and hoping that Ulysses would remember how he had done his utmost to keep him and his followers out of harm's way. Ulysses ordered Circe instantly to make a king of this good little fowl, and leave him exactly as she found him. Hardly were the words spoken, and before the bird had time to utter another "Pe—weep," King Picus leaped down from the bough

of the tree, as majestic a sovereign as any in the world, dressed in a long purple robe and gorgeous yellow stockings, with a splendidly wrought collar about his neck, and a golden crown upon his head. He and King Ulysses exchanged with one another the courtesies which belong to their elevated rank. But from that time forth, King Picus was no longer proud of his crown and his trappings of royalty, nor of the fact of his being a king; he felt himself merely the upper servant of his people, and that it must be his lifelong labor to make them better and happier.

As for the lions, tigers, and wolves (though Circe would have restored them to their former shapes at his slightest word), Ulysses thought it advisable that they should remain as they now were, and thus give warning of their cruel dispositions, instead of going about under the guise of men, and pretending to human sympathies, while their hearts had the bloodthirstiness of wild beasts. So he let them howl as much as they liked, but never troubled his head about them. And, when everything was settled according to his pleasure, he sent to summon the remainder of his comrades, whom he had left at the seashore. These being arrived, with the prudent Eurylochus at their head, they all made themselves comfortable in Circe's enchanted palace, until quite rested and refreshed from the toils and hardships of their voyage.

"Oh no, dear Proserpina," cried the sea nymphs, "we dare not go with you upon the dry land."

The Pomegranate Seeds

MOTHER CERES was exceedingly fond of her daughter
Proserpina, and seldom let her go alone into the fields.
But, just at the time when my story begins, the good
lady was very busy, because she had the care of the
wheat, and the Indian corn, and the rye and barley,
and, in short, of the crops of every kind, all over the
earth. And as the season had thus far been uncommonly backward, it was necessary to make the harvest
ripen more speedily than usual. So she put on her
turban, made of poppies (a kind of flower which she
was always noted for wearing), and got into her car
drawn by a pair of winged dragons, and was just ready
to set off.

"Dear mother," said Proserpina, "I shall be very
lonely while you are away. May I not run down to the
shore, and ask some of the sea nymphs to come up out
of the waves and play with me?"

"Yes, child," answered Mother Ceres. "The sea nymphs are good creatures, and will never lead you into any harm. But you must take care not to stray away from them, nor go wandering about the fields by yourself. Young girls, without their mothers to take care of them, are very apt to get into mischief."

The child promised to be as prudent as if she were a grown-up woman, and, by the time the winged dragons had whirled the car out of sight, she was already on the shore, calling to the sea nymphs to come and play with her. They knew Proserpina's voice, and were not long in showing their glistening faces and sea-green hair above the water, at the bottom of which was their home. They brought along with them a great many beautiful shells; and, sitting down on the moist sand, where the surf wave broke over them, they busied themselves in making a necklace, which they hung round Proserpina's neck. By way of showing her gratitude, the child besought them to go with her a little way into the fields, so that they might gather abundance of flowers, with which she would make each of her kind playmates a wreath.

"Oh no, dear Proserpina," cried the sea nymphs; "we dare not go with you upon the dry land. We are apt to grow faint, unless at every breath we can snuff up the salt breeze of the ocean. And don't you see how careful we are to let the surf wave break over us every moment or two, so as to keep ourselves comfortably moist? If it were not for that, we should soon look like bunches of uprooted seaweed dried in the sun."

"It is a great pity," said Proserpina. "But do you wait for me here, and I will run and gather my apron

full of flowers, and be back again before the surf wave has broken ten times over you. I long to make you some wreaths that shall be as lovely as this necklace of many-colored shells."

"We will wait, then," answered the sea nymphs. "But while you are gone, we may as well lie down on a bank of soft sponge, under the water. The air today is a little too dry for our comfort. But we will pop up our heads every few minutes to see if you are coming."

The young Proserpina ran quickly to a spot where, only the day before, she had seen a great many flowers. These, however, were now a little past their bloom; and wishing to give her friends the freshest and loveliest blossoms, she strayed farther into the fields, and found some that made her scream with delight. Never had she met with such exquisite flowers before— violets, so large and fragrant—roses with so rich and delicate a blush—such superb hyacinths and such aromatic pinks—and many others, some of which seemed to be of new shapes and colors. Two or three times, moreover, she could not help thinking that a tuft of most splendid flowers had suddenly sprouted out of the earth before her very eyes, as if on purpose to tempt her a few steps farther. Proserpina's apron was soon filled and brimming over with delightful blossoms. She was on the point of turning back in order to rejoin the sea nymphs, and sit with them on the moist sands, all twining wreaths together. But, a little farther on, what should she behold? It was a large shrub, completely covered with the most magnificent flowers in the world.

"The darlings!" cried Proserpina; and then she

thought to herself, "I was looking at that spot only a moment ago. How strange it is that I did not see the flowers!"

The nearer she approached the shrub, the more attractive it looked, until she came quite close to it; and then, although its beauty was richer than words can tell, she hardly knew whether to like it or not. It bore above a hundred flowers of the most brilliant hues, and each different from the others, but all having a kind of resemblance among themselves, which showed them to be sister blossoms. But there was a deep, glossy luster on the leaves of the shrub, and on the petals of the flowers, that made Proserpina doubt whether they might not be poisonous. To tell you the truth, foolish as it may seem, she was half inclined to turn around and run away.

"What a silly child I am!" thought she, taking courage. "It is really the most beautiful shrub that ever sprang out of the earth. I will pull it up by the roots, and carry it home, and plant it in my mother's garden."

Holding up her apron full of flowers with her left hand, Proserpina seized the large shrub with the other, and pulled and pulled, but was hardly able to loosen the soil about its roots. What a deep-rooted plant it was! Again the girl pulled with all her might, and observed that the earth began to stir and crack to some distance around the stem. She gave another pull, but relaxed her hold, fancying that there was a rumbling sound right beneath her feet. Did the roots extend down into some enchanted cavern? Then, laughing at herself for so childish a notion, she made another ef-

fort; up came the shrub, and Proserpina staggered back, holding the stem triumphantly in her hand, and gazing at the deep hole which its roots had left in the soil.

Much to her astonishment, this hole kept spreading wider and wider, and growing deeper and deeper, until it really seemed to have no bottom; and all the while, there came a rumbling noise out of its depths, louder and louder, and nearer and nearer, and sounding like the tramp of horses' hoofs and the rattling of wheels. Too much frightened to run away, she stood straining her eyes into this wonderful cavity, and soon saw a team of four sable horses, snorting smoke out of their nostrils, and tearing their way out of the earth with a splendid golden chariot whirling at their heels. They leaped out of the bottomless hole, chariot and all; and there they were, tossing their black manes, flourishing their black tails, and curvetting with every one of their hoofs off the ground at once, close by the spot where Proserpina stood. In the chariot sat the figure of a man, richly dressed, with a crown on his head, all flaming with diamonds. He was of a noble aspect, and rather handsome, but looked sullen and discontented; and he kept rubbing his eyes and shading them with his hand, as if he did not live enough in the sunshine to be very fond of its light.

As soon as this personage saw the affrighted Proserpina, he beckoned her to come a little nearer.

"Do not be afraid," said he, with as cheerful a smile as he knew how to put on. "Come! Will not you like to ride a little way with me, in my beautiful chariot?"

But Proserpina was so alarmed that she wished for

nothing but to get out of his reach. And no wonder. The stranger did not look remarkably good-natured, in spite of his smile; and as for his voice, its tones were deep and stern, and sounded as much like the rumbling of an earthquake underground as anything else. As is always the case with children in trouble, Proserpina's first thought was to call for her mother.

"Mother, Mother Ceres!" cried she, all in a tremble. "Come quickly and save me."

But her voice was too faint for her mother to hear. Indeed, it is most probable that Ceres was then a thousand miles off, making the corn grow in some far-distant country. Nor could it have availed her poor daughter, even had she been within hearing; for no sooner did Proserpina begin to cry out, than the stranger leaped to the ground, caught the child in his arms, and again mounting the chariot, shook the reins, and shouted to the four black horses to set off. They immediately broke into so swift a gallop that it seemed rather like flying through the air than running along the earth. In a moment, Proserpina lost sight of the pleasant vale of Enna, in which she had always dwelled. Another instant, and even the summit of Mount Ætna had become so blue in the distance that she could scarcely distinguish it from the smoke that gushed out of its crater. But still the poor child screamed, and scattered her apron full of flowers along the way, and left a long cry trailing behind the chariot; and many mothers, to whose ears it came, ran quickly to see if any mischief had befallen their children. But Mother Ceres was a great way off, and could not hear the cry.

As they rode on, the stranger did his best to soothe her.

"Why should you be so frightened, my pretty child?" said he, trying to soften his rough voice. "I promise not to do you any harm. What! You have been gathering flowers? Wait till we come to my palace, and I will give you a garden full of prettier flowers than those, all made of pearls, and diamonds, and rubies. Can you guess who I am? They call my name Pluto, and I am the king of diamonds and all other precious stones. Every atom of the gold and silver that lies under the earth belongs to me, to say nothing of the copper and iron, and of the coal mines, which supply me with abundance of fuel. Do you see this splendid crown upon my head? You may have it for a plaything. Oh, we shall be very good friends, and you will find me more agreeable than you expect, when once we get out of this troublesome sunshine."

"Let me go home!" cried Proserpina. "Let me go home!"

"My home is better than your mother's," answered King Pluto. "It is a palace, all made of gold, with crystal windows; and because there is little or no sunshine thereabouts, the apartments are illuminated with diamond lamps. You never saw anything half so magnificent as my throne. If you like, you may sit down on it, and be my little queen, and I will sit on the footstool."

"I don't care for golden palaces and thrones," sobbed Proserpina. "Oh, my mother, my mother! Carry me back to my mother!"

But King Pluto, as he called himself, only shouted to his steeds to go faster.

"Pray do not be foolish, Proserpina," said he, in rather a sullen tone. "I offer you my palace and my crown, and all the riches that are under the earth; and you treat me as if I were doing you an injury. The one thing which my palace needs is a merry little maid to run upstairs and down, and cheer up the rooms with her smile. And this is what you must do for King Pluto."

"Never!" answered Proserpina, looking as miserable as she could. "I shall never smile again till you set me down at my mother's door."

But she might just as well have talked to the wind that whistled past them; for Pluto urged on his horses, and went faster than ever. Proserpina continued to cry out, and screamed so long and so loudly that her poor little voice was almost screamed away; and when it was nothing but a whisper, she happened to cast her eyes over a great, broad field of waving grain—and whom do you think she saw? Who, but Mother Ceres, making the corn grow, and too busy to notice the golden chariot as it went rattling along. The child mustered all her strength, and gave one more scream, but was out of sight before Ceres had time to turn her head.

King Pluto had taken a road which now began to grow excessively gloomy. It was bordered on each side with rocks and precipices, between which the rumbling of the chariot wheels was reverberated with a noise like rolling thunder. The trees and bushes that grew in the

crevices of the rocks had very dismal foliage; and by and by, although it was hardly noon, the air became obscured with a gray twilight. The black horses had rushed along so swiftly that they were already beyond the limits of the sunshine. But the duskier it grew, the more did Pluto's visage assume an air of satisfaction. After all, he was not an ill-looking person, especially when he left off twisting his features into a smile that did not belong to them. Proserpina peeped at his face through the gathering dusk, and hoped that he might not be so very wicked as she at first thought him.

"Ah, this twilight is truly refreshing," said King Pluto, "after being so tormented with that ugly and impertinent glare of the sun. How much more agreeable is lamplight or torchlight, more particularly when reflected from diamonds! It will be a magnificent sight when we get to my palace."

"Is it much farther?" asked Proserpina. "And will you carry me back when I have seen it?"

"We will talk of that by and by," answered Pluto. "We are just entering my dominions. Do you see that tall gateway before us? When we pass those gates, we are at home. And there lies my faithful mastiff at the threshold. Cerberus! Cerberus! Come hither, my good dog!"

So saying, Pluto pulled at the reins, and stopped the chariot right between the tall, massive pillars of the gateway. The mastiff of which he had spoken got up from the threshold, and stood on his hinder legs, so as to put his forepaws on the chariot wheel. But, my stars, what a strange dog it was! Why, he was a big, rough,

ugly-looking monster, with three separate heads, and each of them fiercer than the two others; but, fierce as they were, King Pluto patted them all. He seemed as fond of his three-headed dog as if it had been a sweet little spaniel, with silken ears and curly hair. Cerberus, on the other hand, was evidently rejoiced to see his master, and expressed his attachment, as other dogs do, by wagging his tail at a great rate. Proserpina's eyes being drawn to it by its brisk motion, she saw that this tail was neither more nor less than a live dragon, with fiery eyes, and fangs that had a very poisonous aspect. And while the three-headed Cerberus was fawning so lovingly on King Pluto, there was the dragon tail wagging against its will, and looking as cross and ill-natured as you can imagine, on its own separate account.

"Will the dog bite me?" asked Proserpina, shrinking closer to Pluto. "What an ugly creature he is!"

"Oh, never fear," answered her companion. "He never harms people, unless they try to enter my dominions without being sent for, or to get away when I wish to keep them here. Down, Cerberus! Now, my pretty Proserpina, we will drive on."

On went the chariot, and King Pluto seemed greatly pleased to find himself once more in his own kingdom. He drew Proserpina's attention to the rich veins of gold that were to be seen among the rocks, and pointed to several places where one stroke of a pickaxe would loosen a bushel of diamonds. All along the road, indeed, there were sparkling gems, which would have been of inestimable value above ground, but which

were here reckoned of the meaner sort, and hardly worth a beggar's stooping for.

Not far from the gateway, they came to a bridge, which seemed to be built of iron. Pluto stopped the chariot, and bade Proserpina look at the stream which was gliding so lazily beneath it. Never in her life had she beheld so torpid, so black, so muddy-looking a stream. Its waters reflected no images of anything that was on the banks, and it moved as sluggishly as if it had quite forgotten which way it ought to flow, and had rather stagnate than flow either one way or the other.

"This is the river Lethe," observed King Pluto. "Is it not a very pleasant stream?"

"I think it a very dismal one," said Proserpina.

"It suits my taste, however," answered Pluto, who was apt to be sullen when anybody disagreed with him. "At all events, its water has one very excellent quality; for a single draft of it makes people forget every care and sorrow that has hitherto tormented them. Only sip a little of it, my dear Proserpina, and you will instantly cease to grieve for your mother, and will have nothing in your memory that can prevent your being perfectly happy in my palace. I will send for some, in a golden goblet, the moment we arrive."

"Oh no, no, no!" cried Proserpina, weeping afresh. "I had a thousand times rather be miserable with remembering my mother, than be happy in forgetting her. That dear, dear mother! I never, never will forget her."

"We shall see," said King Pluto. "You do not know

what fine times we will have in my palace. Here we are just at the portal. These pillars are solid gold, I assure you."

He alighted from the chariot, and taking Proserpina in his arms, carried her up a lofty flight of steps into the great hall of the palace. It was splendidly illuminated by means of large precious stones, of various hues, which seemed to burn like so many lamps, and glowed with a hundred-fold radiance all through the vast apartment. And yet there was a kind of gloom in the midst of this enchanted light; nor was there a single object in the hall that was really agreeable to behold, except the little Proserpina herself, a lovely child, with one earthly flower which she had not let fall from her hand. It is my opinion that even King Pluto had never been happy in his palace, and that this was the true reason why he had stolen away Proserpina, in order that he might have something to love, instead of cheating his heart any longer with this tiresome magnificence. And, though he pretended to dislike the sunshine of the upper world, yet the effect of the child's presence, bedimmed as she was by her tears, was as if a faint and watery sunbeam had somehow or other found its way into the enchanted hall.

Pluto now summoned his domestics, and bade them lose no time in preparing a most sumptuous banquet, and above all things, not to fail of setting a golden beaker of the water of Lethe by Proserpina's plate.

"I will neither drink that nor anything else," said Proserpina. "Nor will I taste a morsel of food, even if you keep me forever in your palace."

Taking Proserpina in his arms, Pluto carried her up a lofty flight of steps

"I should be sorry for that," replied King Pluto, patting her cheek; for he really wished to be kind, if he had only known how. "You are a spoiled child, I perceive, my little Proserpina; but when you see the nice things which my cook will make for you, your appetite will quickly come again."

Then, sending for the head cook, he gave strict orders that all sorts of delicacies, such as young people are usually fond of, should be set before Proserpina. He had a secret motive in this; for, you are to understand, it is a fixed law that, when persons are carried off to the land of magic, if they once taste any food there, they can never get back to their friends. Now, if King Pluto had been cunning enough to offer Proserpina some fruit, or bread and milk (which was the simple fare to which the child had always been accustomed), it is very probable that she would soon have been tempted to eat it. But he left the matter entirely to his cook, who, like all other cooks, considered nothing fit to eat unless it were rich pastry, or highly seasoned meat, or spiced sweet cakes—things which Proserpina's mother had never given her, and the smell of which quite took away her appetite, instead of sharpening it.

But my story must now clamber out of King Pluto's dominions, and see what Mother Ceres has been about, since she was bereft of her daughter. We had a glimpse of her, as you remember, half hidden among the waving grain, while the four black steeds were swiftly whirling along the chariot in which her beloved Proserpina was so unwillingly borne away. You recol-

lect, too, the loud scream which Proserpina gave, just when the chariot was out of sight.

Of all the child's outcries, this last shriek was the only one that reached the ears of Mother Ceres. She had mistaken the rumbling of the chariot wheels for a peal of thunder, and imagined that a shower was coming up, and that it would assist her in making the corn grow. But, at the sound of Proserpina's shriek, she started, and looked about in every direction, not knowing whence it came, but feeling almost certain that it was her daughter's voice. It seemed so unaccountable, however, that the girl should have strayed over so many lands and seas (which she herself could not have traversed without the aid of her winged dragons), that the good Ceres tried to believe that it must be the child of some other parent, and not her own darling Proserpina, who had uttered this lamentable cry. Nevertheless, it troubled her with a vast many tender fears, such as are ready to bestir themselves in every mother's heart, when she finds it necessary to go away from her dear children without leaving them under the care of some maiden aunt, or other such faithful guardian. So she quickly left the field in which she had been so busy; and, as her work was not half done, the grain looked, next day, as if it needed both sun and rain, and as if it were blighted in the ear, and had something the matter with its roots.

The pair of dragons must have had very nimble wings; for, in less than an hour, Mother Ceres had alighted at the door of her home, and found it empty. Knowing, however, that the child was fond of sporting

on the seashore, she hastened thither as fast as she could, and there beheld the wet faces of the poor sea nymphs peeping over a wave. All this while, the good creatures had been waiting on the bank of sponge, and, once every half-minute or so, had popped up their four heads above water, to see if their play-mate were yet coming back. When they saw Mother Ceres, they sat down on the crest of the surf wave, and let it toss them ashore at her feet.

"Where is Proserpina?" cried Ceres. "Where is my child? Tell me, you naughty sea nymphs, have you enticed her under the sea?"

"Oh no, good Mother Ceres," said the innocent sea nymphs, tossing back their green ringlets, and looking her in the face. "We never should dream of such a thing. Proserpina has been at play with us, it is true; but she left us a long while ago, meaning only to run a little way upon the dry land, and gather some flowers for a wreath. This was early in the day, and we have seen nothing of her since."

Ceres scarcely waited to hear what the nymphs had to say, before she hurried off to make inquiries all through the neighborhood. But nobody told her anything that could enable the poor mother to guess what had become of Proserpina. A fisherman, it is true, had noticed her little footprints in the sand, as he went homeward along the beach with a basket of fish; a rustic had seen the child stooping to gather flowers; several persons had heard either the rattling of chariot wheels, or the rumbling of distant thunder; and one old woman, while plucking vervain and catnip, had

heard a scream, but supposed it to be some childish nonsense, and therefore did not take the trouble to look up. The stupid people! It took them such a tedious while to tell the nothing that they knew, that it was dark night before Mother Ceres found out that she must seek her daughter elsewhere. So she lighted a torch, and set forth, resolving never to come back until Proserpina was discovered.

In her haste and trouble of mind, she quite forgot her car and the winged dragons; or, it may be, she thought that she could follow up the search more thoroughly on foot. At all events, this was the way in which she began her sorrowful journey, holding her torch before her, and looking carefully at every object along the path. And as it happened, she had not gone far before she found one of the magnificent flowers which grew on the shrub that Proserpina had pulled up.

"Ha!" thought Mother Ceres, examining it by torchlight. "Here is mischief in this flower! The earth did not produce it by any help of mine, nor of its own accord. It is the work of enchantment, and is therefore poisonous; and perhaps it has poisoned my poor child."

But she put the poisonous flower in her bosom, not knowing whether she might ever find any other memorial of Proserpina.

All night long, at the door of every cottage and farmhouse, Ceres knocked, and called up the weary laborers to inquire if they had seen her child; and they stood, gaping and half asleep, at the threshold, and answered her pityingly, and besought her to come in

and rest. At the portal of every palace, too, she made so loud a summons that the menials hurried to throw open the gate, thinking that it must be some great king or queen, who would demand a banquet for supper and a stately chamber to repose in. And when they saw only a sad and anxious woman, with a torch in her hand and a wreath of withered poppies on her head, they spoke rudely, and sometimes threatened to set the dogs upon her. But nobody had seen Proserpina, nor could give Mother Ceres the least hint which way to seek her. Thus passed the night; and still she continued her search without sitting down to rest, or stopping to take food, or even remembering to put out the torch; although first the rosy dawn and then the glad light of the morning sun made its red flame look thin and pale. But I wonder what sort of stuff this torch was made of; for it burned dimly through the day and, at night, was as bright as ever, and never was extinguished by the rain or wind, in all the weary days and nights while Ceres was seeking for Proserpina.

It was not merely of human beings that she asked tidings of her daughter. In the woods and by the streams, she met creatures of another nature, who used, in those old times, to haunt the pleasant and solitary places, and were very sociable with persons who understood their language and customs, as Mother Ceres did. Sometimes, for instance, she tapped with her finger against the knotted trunk of a majestic oak; and immediately its rude bark would cleave asunder, and forth would step a beautiful maiden, who was the hamadryad of the oak, dwelling inside of it, and

sharing its long life, and rejoicing when its green leaves
sported with the breeze. But not one of these leafy
damsels had seen Proserpina. Then, going a little farther, Ceres would, perhaps, come to a fountain, gushing out of a pebbly hollow in the earth, and would
dabble with her hand in the water. Behold, up through
its sandy and pebbly bed, along with the fountain's
gush, a young woman with dripping hair would arise,
and stand gazing at Mother Ceres, half out of the
water, and undulating up and down with its ever-
restless motion. But when the mother asked whether
her poor lost child had stopped to drink out of the
fountain, the naiad, with weeping eyes (for these water
nymphs had tears to spare for everybody's grief),
would answer, "No!" in a murmuring voice, which was
just like the murmur of the stream.

Often, likewise, she encountered fauns, who looked
like sunburned country people, except that they had
hairy ears, and little horns upon their foreheads, and
the hinder legs of goats, on which they gamboled merrily about the woods and fields. They were a frolic-
some kind of creature, but grew as sad as their cheerful
dispositions would allow when Ceres inquired for her
daughter, and they had no good news to tell. But
sometimes she came suddenly upon a rude gang of
satyrs, who had faces like monkeys and horses' tails
behind them, and who were generally dancing in a
very boisterous manner, with shouts of noisy laughter.
When she stopped to question them, they would only
laugh the louder, and make new merriment out of the
lone woman's distress. How unkind of those ugly sat-

yrs! And once, while crossing a solitary sheep pasture, she saw a personage named Pan, seated at the foot of a tall rock, and making music on a shepherd's flute. He, too, had horns and hairy ears and goat's feet; but, being acquainted with Mother Ceres, he answered her question as civilly as he knew how, and invited her to taste some milk and honey out of a wooden bowl. But neither could Pan tell her what had become of Proserpina, any better than the rest of these wild people.

And thus Mother Ceres went wandering about for nine long days and nights, finding no trace of Proserpina, unless it were now and then a withered flower; and these she picked up and put in her bosom, because she fancied that they might have fallen from her poor child's hand. All day she traveled onward through the hot sun; and at night, again, the flame of the torch would redden and gleam along the pathway, and she continued her search by its light, without ever sitting down to rest.

On the tenth day, she chanced to espy the mouth of a cavern, within which (though it was bright noon everywhere else) there would have been only a dusky twilight; but it so happened that a torch was burning there. It flickered, and struggled with the duskiness, but could not half light up the gloomy cavern with all its melancholy glimmer. Ceres was resolved to leave no spot without a search; so she peeped into the entrance of the cave, and lighted it up a little more, by holding her own torch before her. In so doing, she caught a glimpse of what seemed to be a woman, sitting on the brown leaves of the last autumn, a great heap of which

had been swept into the cave by the wind. This woman (if woman it were) was by no means so beautiful as many of her sex; for her head, they tell me, was shaped very much like a dog's, and, by way of ornament, she wore a wreath of snakes around it. But Mother Ceres, the moment she saw her, knew that this was an odd kind of a person, who put all her enjoyment in being miserable, and never would have a word to say to other people, unless they were as melancholy and wretched as she herself delighted to be.

"I am wretched enough now," thought poor Ceres, "to talk with this melancholy Hecate, were she ten times sadder than ever she was yet."

So she stepped into the cave, and sat down on the withered leaves by the dog-headed woman's side. In all the world, since her daughter's loss, she had found no other companion.

"Oh, Hecate," said she, "if ever you lose a daughter, you will know what sorrow is. Tell me, for pity's sake, have you seen my poor child Proserpina pass by the mouth of your cavern?"

"No," answered Hecate, in a cracked voice, and sighing betwixt every word or two—"no, Mother Ceres, I have seen nothing of your daughter. But my ears, you must know, are made in such a way that all cries of distress and affright, all over the world are pretty sure to find their way to them; and nine days ago, as I sat in my cave, making myself very miserable, I heard the voice of a young girl, shrieking as if in great distress. Something terrible has happened to the child, you may rest assured. As well as I could judge, a

dragon, or some other cruel monster, was carrying her away."

"You kill me by saying so," cried Ceres, almost ready to faint. "Where was the sound, and which way did it seem to go?"

"It passed very swiftly along," said Hecate, "and, at the same time, there was a heavy rumbling of wheels towards the eastward. I can tell you nothing more, except that, in my honest opinion, you will never see your daughter again. The best advice I can give you is, to take up your abode in this cavern, where we will be the two most wretched women in the world."

"Not yet, dark Hecate," replied Ceres. "But do you first come with your torch, and help me to seek for my lost child. And when there shall be no more hope of finding her (if that black day is ordained to come), then, if you will give me room to fling myself down, either on these withered leaves or on the naked rock, I will show you what it is to be miserable. But until I know that she has perished from the face of the earth, I will not allow myself space even to grieve."

The dismal Hecate did not much like the idea of going abroad into the sunny world. But then she reflected that the sorrow of the disconsolate Ceres would be like a gloomy twilight round about them both, let the sun shine ever so brightly, and that therefore she might enjoy her bad spirits quite as well as if she were to stay in the cave. So she finally consented to go, and they set out together, both carrying torches, although it was broad daylight and clear sunshine. The torchlight seemed to make a gloom; so that the people whom

they met along the road could not very distinctly see their figures; and, indeed, if they once caught a glimpse of Hecate, with the wreath of snakes round her forehead, they generally thought it prudent to run away, without waiting for a second glance.

As the pair traveled along in this woebegone manner, a thought struck Ceres.

"There is one person," she exclaimed, "who must have seen my poor child, and can doubtless tell what has become of her. Why did not I think of him before? It is Phœbus."

"What," said Hecate, "the young man that always sits in the sunshine? Oh, pray do not think of going near him. He is a gay, light, frivolous young fellow, and will only smile in your face. And besides, there is such a glare of the sun about him that he will quite blind my poor eyes, which I have almost wept away already."

"You have promised to be my companion," answered Ceres. "Come, let us make haste, or the sunshine will be gone, and Phœbus along with it."

Accordingly, they went along in quest of Phœbus, both of them sighing grievously, and Hecate, to say the truth, making a great deal worse lamentation than Ceres; for all the pleasure she had, you know, lay in being miserable, and therefore she made the most of it. By and by, after a pretty long journey, they arrived at the sunniest spot in the whole world. There they beheld a beautiful young man, with long, curling ringlets which seemed to be made of golden sunbeams; his garments were like light summer clouds; and the

expression of his face was so exceedingly vivid that
Hecate held her hands before her eyes, muttering that
he ought to wear a black veil. Phœbus (for this was the
very person whom they were seeking) had a lyre in his
hands, and was making its chords tremble with sweet
music; at the same time singing a most exquisite song,
which he had recently composed. For, besides a great
many other accomplishments, this young man was renowned for his admirable poetry.

As Ceres and her dismal companion approached
him, Phœbus smiled on them so cheerfully that Hecate's wreath of snakes gave a spiteful hiss, and Hecate
heartily wished herself back in her cave. But as for
Ceres, she was too earnest in her grief either to know
or care whether Phœbus smiled or frowned.

"Phœbus!" exclaimed she, "I am in great trouble,
and have come to you for assistance. Can you tell me
what has become of my dear child Proserpina?"

"Proserpina! Proserpina, did you call her name?"
answered Phœbus, endeavoring to recollect; for there
was such a continual flow of pleasant ideas in his mind
that he was apt to forget what had happened no longer
ago than yesterday. "Ah, yes, I remember her now. A
very lovely child, indeed. I am happy to tell you, my
dear madam, that I did see the little Proserpina not
many days ago. You may make yourself perfectly easy
about her. She is safe and in excellent hands."

"Oh, where is my dear child?" cried Ceres, clasping
her hands and flinging herself at his feet.

"Why," said Phœbus—and as he spoke, he kept
touching his lyre so as to make a thread of music run

in and out among his words—"as the little damsel was gathering flowers (and she has really a very exquisite taste for flowers) she was suddenly snatched up by King Pluto, and carried off to his dominions. I have never been in that part of the universe; but the royal palace, I am told, is built in a very noble style of architecture, and of the most splendid and costly materials. Gold, diamonds, pearls, and all manner of precious stones will be your daughter's ordinary playthings. I recommend to you, my dear lady, to give yourself no uneasiness. Proserpina's sense of beauty will be duly gratified, and, even in spite of the lack of sunshine, she will lead a very enviable life."

"Hush! Say not such a word!" answered Ceres indignantly. "What is there to gratify her heart? What are all the splendors you speak of, without affection? I must have her back again. Will you go with me, Phœbus, to demand my daughter of this wicked Pluto?"

"Pray excuse me," replied Phœbus, with an elegant obeisance. "I certainly wish you success, and regret that my own affairs are so immediately pressing that I cannot have the pleasure of attending you. Besides, I am not upon the best of terms with King Pluto. To tell you the truth, his three-headed mastiff would never let me pass the gateway; for I should be compelled to take a sheaf of sunbeams along with me, and those, you know, are forbidden things in Pluto's kingdom."

"Ah, Phœbus," said Ceres, with bitter meaning in her words, "you have a harp instead of a heart. Farewell."

"Will not you stay a moment," asked Phœbus, "and hear me turn the pretty and touching story of Proserpina into extemporary verses?"

But Ceres shook her head, and hastened away, along with Hecate. Phœbus (who, as I have told you, was an exquisite poet) forthwith began to make an ode about the poor mother's grief; and, if we were to judge of his sensibility by this beautiful production, he must have been endowed with a very tender heart. But when a poet gets into the habit of using his heartstrings to make chords for his lyre, he may thrum upon them as much as he will, without any great pain to himself. Accordingly, though Phœbus sang a very sad song, he was as merry all the while as were the sunbeams amid which he dwelled.

Poor Mother Ceres had now found out what had become of her daughter, but was not a whit happier than before. Her case, on the contrary, looked more desperate than ever. As long as Proserpina was above ground there might have been hopes of regaining her. But now that the poor child was shut up within the iron gates of the king of the mines, at the threshold of which lay the three-headed Cerberus, there seemed no possibility of her ever making her escape. The dismal Hecate, who loved to take the darkest view of things, told Ceres that she had better come with her to the cavern, and spend the rest of her life in being miserable. Ceres answered that Hecate was welcome to go back thither herself, but that, for her part, she would wander about the earth in quest of the entrance to

King Pluto's dominions. And Hecate took her at her word, and hurried back to her beloved cave, frightening a great many little children with a glimpse of her dog's face, as she went.

Poor Mother Ceres! It is melancholy to think of her, pursuing her toilsome way all alone, and holding up that never-dying torch, the flame of which seemed an emblem of the grief and hope that burned together in her heart. So much did she suffer that, though her aspect had been quite youthful when her troubles began, she grew to look like an elderly person in a very brief time. She cared not how she was dressed, nor had she ever thought of flinging away the wreath of withered poppies, which she put on the very morning of Proserpina's disappearance. She roamed about in so wild a way, and with her hair so disheveled that people took her for some distracted creature, and never dreamed that this was Mother Ceres, who had the oversight of every seed which the husbandman planted. Nowadays, however, she gave herself no trouble about seedtime nor harvest, but left the farmers to take care of their own affairs, and the crops to fade or flourish, as the case might be. There was nothing, now, in which Ceres seemed to feel an interest, unless when she saw children at play, or gathering flowers along the wayside. Then, indeed, she would stand and gaze at them with tears in her eyes. The children, too, appeared to have a sympathy with her grief, and would cluster themselves in a little group about her knees, and look up wistfully in her face; and Ceres, after

giving them a kiss all round, would lead them to their homes, and advise their mothers never to let them stray out of sight.

"For if they do," said she, "it may happen to you, as it has to me, that the iron-hearted King Pluto will take a liking to your darlings, and snatch them up in his chariot, and carry them away."

One day, during her pilgrimage in quest of the entrance to Pluto's kingdom, she came to the palace of King Celeus, who reigned at Eleusis. Ascending a lofty flight of steps, she entered the portal, and found the royal household in very great alarm about the queen's baby. The infant, it seems, was sickly (being troubled with its teeth, I suppose), and would take no food, and was all the time moaning with pain. The queen—her name was Metanira—was desirous of finding a nurse; and when she beheld a woman of matronly aspect coming up the palace steps, she thought, in her own mind, that here was the very person whom she needed. So Queen Metanira ran to the door, with the poor wailing baby in her arms, and besought Ceres to take charge of it, or, at least, to tell her what would do it good.

"Will you trust the child entirely to me?" asked Ceres.

"Yes, and gladly too," answered the queen, "if you will devote all your time to him. For I can see that you have been a mother."

"You are right," said Ceres. "I once had a child of my own. Well; I will be the nurse of this poor, sickly boy. But beware, I warn you, that you do not interfere

with any kind of treatment which I may judge proper for him. If you do so, the poor infant must suffer for his mother's folly."

Then she kissed the child, and it seemed to do him good; for he smiled and nestled closely into her bosom.

So Mother Ceres set her torch in a corner (where it kept burning all the while), and took up her abode in the palace of King Celeus, as nurse to the little Prince Demophoön. She treated him as if he were her own child, and allowed neither the king nor the queen to say whether he should be bathed in warm or cold water, or what he should eat, or how often he should take the air, or when he should be put to bed. You would hardly believe me, if I were to tell how quickly the baby prince got rid of his ailments, and grew fat and rosy and strong and how he had two rows of ivory teeth in less time than any other little fellow, before or since. Instead of the palest, and wretchedest, and puniest imp in the world (as his own mother confessed him to be when Ceres first took him in charge), he was now a strapping baby, crowing, laughing, kicking up his heels, and rolling from one end of the room to the other. All the good women of the neighborhood crowded to the palace, and held up their hands, in unutterable amazement, at the beauty and wholesomeness of this darling little prince. Their wonder was the greater, because he was never seen to taste any food; not even so much as a cup of milk.

"Pray, nurse," the queen kept saying, "how is it that you make the child thrive so?"

"I was a mother once," Ceres always replied, "and

having nursed my own child, I know what other children need."

But Queen Metanira, as was very natural, had a great curiosity to know precisely what the nurse did to her child. One night, therefore, she hid herself in the chamber where Ceres and the little prince were accustomed to sleep. There was a fire in the chimney, and it had now crumbled into great coals and embers, which lay glowing on the hearth, with a blaze flickering up now and then, and flinging a warm and ruddy light upon the walls. Ceres sat before the hearth with the child in her lap, and the firelight making her shadow dance upon the ceiling overhead. She undressed the little prince, and bathed him all over with some fragrant liquid out of a vase. The next thing she did was to rake back the red embers, and make a hollow place among them, just where the backlog had been. At last, while the baby was crowing and clapping its fat little hands and laughing in the nurse's face (just as you may have seen your little brother or sister do before going into its warm bath), Ceres suddenly laid him, all naked as he was, in the hollow among the red-hot embers. She then raked the ashes over him, and turned quietly away.

You may imagine, if you can, how Queen Metanira shrieked, thinking nothing less than that her dear child would be burned to a cinder. She burst forth from her hiding place, and running to the hearth, raked open the fire, and snatched up poor little Prince Demophoön out of his bed of live coals, one of which he was gripping in each of his fists. He immediately set up a

grievous cry, as babies are apt to do when rudely startled out of a sound sleep. To the queen's astonishment and joy, she could perceive no token of the child's being injured by the hot fire in which he had lain. She now turned to Mother Ceres and asked her to explain the mystery.

"Foolish woman," answered Ceres, "did you not promise to intrust this poor infant entirely to me? You little know the mischief you have done him. Had you left him to my care, he would have grown up like a child of celestial birth, endowed with superhuman strength and intelligence, and would have lived forever. Do you imagine that earthly children are to become immortal without being tempered to it in the fiercest heat of the fire? But you have ruined your own son. For though he will be a strong man and a hero in his day, yet, on account of your folly, he will grow old and finally die, like the sons of other women. The weak tenderness of his mother has cost the poor boy an immortality. Farewell."

Saying these words, she kissed the little prince Demophoön, and sighed to think what he had lost, and took her departure without heeding Queen Metanira, who entreated her to remain, and cover up the child among the hot embers as often as she pleased. Poor baby! He never slept so warmly again.

While she dwelled in the king's palace, Mother Ceres had been so continually occupied with taking care of the young prince that her heart was a little lightened of its grief for Proserpina. But now, having nothing else to busy herself about, she became just as wretched as

before. At length, in her despair, she came to the dreadful resolution that not a stalk of grain, nor a blade of grass, not a potato, nor a turnip, nor any other vegetable that was good for man or beast to eat, should be suffered to grow until her daughter were restored. She even forbade the flowers to bloom, lest sombody's heart should be cheered by their beauty.

Now, as not so much as a head of asparagus ever presumed to poke itself out of the ground, without the especial permission of Ceres, you may conceive what a terrible calamity had here fallen upon the earth. The husbandmen plowed and planted as usual; but there lay the rich black furrows, all as barren as a desert of sand. The pastures looked as brown in the sweet month of June as ever they did in chill November. The rich man's broad acres and the cottager's small garden patch were equally blighted. Every little girl's flowerbed showed nothing but dry stalks. The old people shook their white heads, and said that the earth had grown aged like themselves, and was no longer capable of wearing the warm smile of summer on its face. It was really piteous to see the poor, starving cattle and sheep, how they followed behind Ceres, lowing and bleating, as if their instinct taught them to expect help from her; and everybody that was acquainted with her power besought her to have mercy on the human race, and, at all events, to let the grass grow. But Mother Ceres, though naturally of an affectionate disposition, was now inexorable.

"Never," said she. "If the earth is ever again to see

any verdure, it must first grow along the path which my daughter will tread in coming back to me."

Finally, as there seemed to be no other remedy, our old friend Quicksilver was sent post haste to King Pluto, in hopes that he might be persuaded to undo the mischief he had done, and to set everything right again, by giving up Proserpina. Quicksilver accordingly made the best of his way to the great gate, took a flying leap right over the three-headed mastiff, and stood at the door of the palace in an inconceivably short time. The servants knew him both by his face and garb; for his short cloak, and his winged cap and shoes, and his snaky staff had often been seen thereabouts in times gone by. He requested to be shown immediately into the king's presence; and Pluto, who heard his voice from the top of the stairs, and who loved to recreate himself with Quicksilves's merry talk, called out to him to come up. And while they settle their business together, we must inquire what Proserpina has been doing ever since we saw her last.

The child had declared, as you may remember, that she would not taste a mouthful of food as long as she should be compelled to remain in King Pluto's palace. How she contrived to maintain her resolution, and at the same time to keep herself tolerably plump and rosy, is more than I can explain; but some young ladies, I am given to understand, possess the faculty of living on air, and Proserpina seems to have possessed it too. At any rate, it was now six months since she left the outside of the earth; and not a morsel, so far as the

attendants were able to testify, had yet passed between her teeth. This was the more creditable to Proserpina, inasmuch as King Pluto had caused her to be tempted day after day, with all manner of sweetmeats, and richly preserved fruits, and delicacies of every sort, such as young people are generally most fond of. But her good mother had often told her of the hurtfulness of these things; and for that reason alone, if there had been no other, she would have resolutely refused to taste them.

All this time, being of a cheerful and active disposition, the little damsel was not quite so unhappy as you may have supposed. The immense palace had a thousand rooms, and was full of beautiful and wonderful objects. There was a never-ceasing gloom, it is true, which half hid itself among the innumerable pillars, gliding before the child as she wandered among them, and treading stealthily behind her in the echo of her footsteps. Neither was all the dazzle of the precious stones, which flamed with their own light, worth one gleam of natural sunshine; nor could the most brilliant of the many-colored gems, which Proserpina had for playthings, vie with the simple beauty of the flowers she used to gather. But still, wherever the girl went, among those gilded halls and chambers, it seemed as if she carried nature and sunshine along with her, and as if she scattered dewy blossoms on her right hand and on her left. After Proserpina came, the palace was no longer the same abode of stately artifice and dismal magnificence that it had before been. The inhabitants all felt this, and King Pluto more than any of them.

"My own little Proserpina," he used to say, "I wish you could like me a little better. We gloomy and cloudy-natured persons have often as warm hearts at bottom, as those of a more cheerful character. If you would only stay with me of your own accord, it would make me happier than the possession of a hundred such palaces as this."

"Ah," said Proserpina, "you should have tried to make me like you before carrying me off. And the best thing you can do now is to let me go again. Then I might remember you sometimes, and think that you were as kind as you knew how to be. Perhaps, too, one day or other, I might come back and pay you a visit."

"No, no," answered Pluto, with his gloomy smile, "I will not trust you for that. You are too fond of living in the broad daylight, and gathering flowers. What an idle and childish taste that is! Are not these gems, which I have ordered to be dug for you, and which are richer than any in my crown—are they not prettier than a violet?"

"Not half so pretty," said Proserpina, snatching the gems from Pluto's hand, and flinging them to the other end of the hall. "Oh, my sweet violets, shall I never see you again?"

And then she burst into tears. But young people's tears have very little saltness or acidity in them, and do not inflame the eyes so much as those of grown persons; so that it is not to be wondered at if, a few moments afterwards, Proserpina was sporting through the hall almost as merrily as she and the four sea nymphs had sported along the edge of the surf wave.

King Pluto gazed after her, and wished that he, too, was a child. And little Proserpina, when she turned about and beheld this great king standing in his splendid hall, and looking so grand, and so melancholy, and so lonesome, was smitten with a kind of pity. She ran back to him, and, for the first time in all her life, put her small, soft hand in his.

"I love you a little," whispered she, looking up in his face.

"Do you, indeed, my dear child?" cried Pluto, bending his dark face down to kiss her. But Proserpina shrank away from the kiss, for though his features were noble, they were very dusky and grim. "Well, I have not deserved it of you, after keeping you a prisoner for so many months, and starving you, besides. Are you not terribly hungry? Is there nothing which I can get you to eat?"

In asking this question, the king of the mines had a very cunning purpose; for, you will recollect, if Proserpina tasted a morsel of food in his dominions, she would never afterwards be at liberty to quit them.

"No, indeed," said Proserpina. "Your head cook is always baking, and stewing, and roasting, and rolling out paste, and contriving one dish or another, which he imagines may be to my liking. But he might just as well save himself the trouble, poor, fat little man that he is. I have no appetite for anything in the world, unless it were a slice of bread of my mother's own baking, or a little fruit out of her garden."

When Pluto heard this, he began to see that he had mistaken the best method of tempting Proserpina to

eat. The cook's made dishes and artificial dainties were not half so delicious, in the good child's opinion, as the simple fare to which Mother Ceres had accustomed her. Wondering that he had never thought of it before, the king now sent one of his trusty attendants, with a large basket, to get some of the finest and juiciest pears, peaches, and plums which could anywhere be found in the upper world. Unfortunately, however, this was during the time when Ceres had forbidden any fruits or vegetables to grow; and, after seeking all over the earth, King Pluto's servant found only a single pomegranate, and that so dried up as to be not worth eating. Nevertheless, since there was no better to be had, he brought this dry, old, withered pomegranate home to the palace, put it on a magnificent golden salver, and carried it up to Proserpina. Now it happened, curiously enough, that, just as the servant was bringing the pomegranate into the back door of the palace, our friend Quicksilver had gone up the front steps, on his errand to get Proserpina away from King Pluto.

As soon as Proserpina saw the pomegranate on the golden salver, she told the servant he had better take it away again.

"I shall not touch it, I assure you," said she. "If I were ever so hungry, I should never think of eating such a miserable, dry pomegranate as that."

"It is the only one in the world," said the servant.

He set down the golden salver, with the wizened pomegranate upon it, and left the room. When he was gone, Proserpina could not help coming close to the

table, and looking at this poor specimen of dried fruit with a great deal of eagerness; for, to say the truth, on seeing something that suited her taste, she felt all the six months' appetite taking possession of her at once. To be sure, it was a very wretched-looking pomegranate, and seemed to have no more juice in it than an oyster shell. But there was no choice of such things in King Pluto's palace. This was the first fruit she had seen there, and the last she was ever likely to see. And unless she ate it up immediately, it would grow drier than it already was, and be wholly unfit to eat.

"At least, I may smell it," thought Proserpina.

So she took up the pomegranate, and applied it to her nose; and, somehow or other, being in such close neighborhood to her mouth, the fruit found its way into that little red cave. Dear me! What an everlasting pity! Before Proserpina knew what she was about, her teeth had actually bitten it, of their own accord. Just as this fatal deed was done, the door of the apartment opened, and in came King Pluto, followed by Quicksilver, who had been urging him to let his little prisoner go. At the first noise of their entrance, Proserpina withdrew the pomegranate from her mouth. But Quicksilver (whose eyes were very keen, and his wits the sharpest that ever anybody had) perceived that the child was a little confused; and seeing the empty salver, he suspected that she had been taking a sly nibble of something or other. As for honest Pluto, he never guessed at the secret.

"My little Proserpina," said the king, sitting down, and affectionately drawing her between his knees.

"Here is Quicksilver, who tells me that a great many misfortunes have befallen innocent people on account of my detaining you in my dominions. To confess the truth, I myself had already reflected that it was an unjustifiable act to take you away from your good mother. But, then, you must consider, my dear child, that this vast palace is apt to be gloomy (although the precious stones certainly shine very bright), and that I am not of the most cheerful disposition, and that therefore it was a natural thing enough to seek for the society of some merrier creature than myself. I hoped you would take my crown for a plaything, and me—ah, you laugh, naughty Proserpina—me, grim as I am, for a playmate. It was a silly expectation."

"Not so extremely silly," whispered Proserpina. "You have really amused me very much, sometimes."

"Thank you," said King Pluto, rather dryly. "But I can see, plainly enough, that you think my palace a dusky prison, and me the iron-hearted keeper of it. And an iron heart I should surely have, if I could detain you here any longer, my poor child, when it is now six months since you tasted food. I give you your liberty. Go with Quicksilver. Hasten home to your dear mother."

Now, although you may not have supposed it, Proserpina found it impossible to take leave of poor King Pluto without some regrets, and a good deal of compunction for not telling him about the pomegranate. She even shed a tear or two, thinking how lonely and cheerless the great palace would seem to him, with all its ugly glare of artificial light, after she herself—his

one little ray of natural sunshine, whom he had stolen, to be sure, but only because he valued her so much—after she should have departed. I know not how many kind things she might have said to the disconsolate king of the mines, had not Quicksilver hurried her away.

"Come along quickly," whispered he in her ear, "or his Majesty may change his royal mind. And take care, above all things, that you say nothing of what was brought you on the golden salver."

In a very short time, they had passed the great gateway (leaving the three-headed Cerberus barking and yelping and growling, with threefold din, behind them), and emerged upon the surface of the earth. It was delightful to behold, as Proserpina hastened along, how the path grew verdant behind and on either side of her. Wherever she set her blessed foot, there was at once a dewy flower. The violets gushed up along the wayside. The grass and the grain began to sprout with tenfold vigor and luxuriance, to make up for the dreary months that had been wasted in barrenness. The starved cattle immediately set to work grazing, after their long fast, and ate enormously all day, and got up at midnight to eat more. But I can assure you it was a busy time of year with the farmers, when they found the summer coming upon them with such a rush. Nor must I forget to say that all the birds in the whole world hopped about upon the newly blossoming trees, and sang together in a prodigious ecstasy of joy.

Mother Ceres had returned to her deserted home, and was sitting disconsolately on the doorstep, with

her torch burning in her hand. She had been idly watching the flame for some moments past, when, all at once, it flickered and went out.

"What does this mean?" thought she. "It was an enchanted torch, and should have kept burning till my child came back."

Lifting her eyes, she was surprised to see a sudden verdure flashing over the brown and barren fields, exactly as you may have observed a golden hue gleaming far and wide across the landscape, from the just risen sun.

"Does the earth disobey me?" exclaimed Mother Ceres indignantly. "Does it presume to be green, when I have bidden it be barren until my daughter shall be restored to my arms?"

"Then open your arms, dear mother," cried a well-known voice, "and take your little daughter into them."

And Proserpina came running, and flung herself upon her mother's bosom. Their mutual transport is not to be described. The grief of their separation had caused both of them to shed a great many tears; and now they shed a great many more, because their joy could not so well express itself in any other way.

When their hearts had grown a little more quiet, Mother Ceres looked anxiously at Proserpina.

"My child," said she, "did you taste any food while you were in King Pluto's palace?"

"Dearest mother," answered Proserpina, "I will tell you the whole truth. Until this very morning, not a morsel of food had passed my lips. But today, they

brought me a pomegranate (a very dry one it was, and all shriveled up, till there was little left of it but seeds and skin), and having seen no fruit for so long a time, and being faint with hunger, I was tempted just to bite it. The instant I tasted it, King Pluto and Quicksilver came into the room. I had not swallowed a morsel; but—dear mother, I hope it was no harm—but six of the pomegranate seeds, I am afraid, remained in my mouth."

"Ah, unfortunate child, and miserable me!" exclaimed Ceres. "For each of those six pomegranate seeds you must spend one month of every year in King Pluto's palace. You are but half restored to your mother. Only six months with me, and six with that good-for-nothing King of Darkness!"

"Do not speak so harshly of poor King Pluto," said Proserpina, kissing her mother. "He has some very good qualities, and I really think I can bear to spend six months in his palace, if he will only let me spend the other six with you. He certainly did very wrong to carry me off. But then, as he says, it was but a dismal sort of life for him, to live in that great gloomy place, all alone; and it has made a wonderful change in his spirits to have a little girl to run upstairs and down. There is some comfort in making him so happy; and so, upon the whole, dearest mother, let us be thankful that he is not to keep me the whole year round."

The Golden Fleece

WHEN JASON, the son of the dethroned King of Iolchos, was a little boy, he was sent away from his
parents, and placed under the queerest schoolmaster
that ever you heard of. This learned person was one of
the people, or quadrupeds, called Centaurs. He lived
in a cavern, and had the body and legs of a white
horse, with the head and shoulders of a man. His name
was Chiron. And, in spite of his odd appearance, he
was a very excellent teacher, and had several scholars
who afterwards did him credit by making a great figure
in the world. The famous Hercules was one, and so
was Achilles, and Philoctetes, likewise, and
Æsculapius, who acquired immense repute as a doctor.
The good Chiron taught his pupils how to play upon
the harp, and how to cure diseases, and how to use the
sword and shield, together with various other branches

of education, in which the lads of those days used to be instructed, instead of writing and arithmetic.

I have sometimes suspected that Master Chiron was not really very different from other people, but that, being a kind-hearted and merry old fellow, he was in the habit of making believe that he was a horse, and scrambling about the schoolroom on all fours, and letting the little boys ride upon his back. And so, when his scholars had grown up, and grown old, and were trotting their grandchildren on their knees, they told them about the sports of their schooldays; and these young folks took the idea that their grandfathers had been taught their letters by a Centaur, half man and half horse. Little children, not quite understanding what is said to them, often get such absurd notions into their heads, you know.

Be that as it may, it has always been told for a fact (and always will be told, as long as the world lasts), that Chiron, with the head of a schoolmaster, had the body and legs of a horse. Just imagine the grave old gentleman clattering and stamping into the school-room on his four hoofs, perhaps treading on some little fellow's toes, flourishing his switch tail instead of a rod, and, now and then, trotting out of doors to eat a mouthful of grass! I wonder what the blacksmith charged him for a set of iron shoes.

So Jason dwelled in the cave, with this four-footed Chiron, from the time that he was an infant, only a few months old, until he had grown to the full height of a man. He became a very good harper, I suppose, and

skillful in the use of weapons, and tolerably acquainted with herbs and other doctor's stuff, and, above all, an admirable horseman; for, in teaching young people to ride, the good Chiron must have been without a rival among schoolmasters. At length, being now a tall and athletic youth, Jason resolved to seek his fortune in the world, without asking Chiron's advice, or telling him anything about the matter. This was very unwise, to be sure; and I hope none of you, my little hearers, will ever follow Jason's example. But, you are to understand, he had heard how that he himself was a prince royal, and how his father, King Æson, had been deprived of the kingdom of Iolchos by a certain Pelias, who would also have killed Jason, had he not been hidden in the Centaur's cave. And, being come to the strength of a man, Jason determined to set all this business to rights, and to punish the wicked Pelias for wronging his dear father, and to cast him down from the throne, and seat himself there instead.

With this intention, he took a spear in each hand, and threw a leopard's skin over his shoulders, to keep off the rain, and set forth on his travels, with his long yellow ringlets waving in the wind. The part of his dress on which he most prided himself was a pair of sandals, that had been his father's. They were handsomely embroidered, and were tied upon his feet with strings of gold. But his whole attire was such as people did not very often see; and as he passed along, the women and children ran to the doors and windows, wondering whither this beautiful youth was journey-

ing, with his leopard's skin and his golden-tied sandals, and what heroic deeds he meant to perform, with a spear in his right hand and another in his left.

I know not how far Jason had traveled, when he came to a turbulent river, which rushed right across his pathway, with specks of white foam among its black eddies, hurrying tumultuously onward, and roaring angrily as it went. Though not a very broad river in the dry seasons of the year, it was now swollen by heavy rains and by the melting of the snow on the sides of Mount Olympus. And it thundered so loudly, and looked so wild and dangerous that Jason, bold as he was, thought it prudent to pause upon the brink. The bed of the stream seemed to be strewn with sharp and rugged rocks, some of which thrust themselves above the water. By and by, an uprooted tree, with shattered branches, came drifting along the current, and got entangled among the rocks. Now and then, a drowned sheep, and once the carcass of a cow, floated past.

In short, the swollen river had already done a great deal of mischief. It was evidently too deep for Jason to wade, and too boisterous for him to swim; he could see no bridge; and as for a boat, had there been any, the rocks would have broken it to pieces in an instant.

"See the poor lad," said a cracked voice close to his side. "He must have had but a poor education, since he does not know how to cross a little stream like this. Or is he afraid of wetting his fine golden-stringed sandals? It is a pity his four-footed schoolmaster is not here to carry him safely across on his back!"

Jason looked round greatly surprised, for he did not know that anybody was near. But beside him stood an old woman, with a ragged mantle over her head, leaning on a staff, the top of which was carved into the shape of a cuckoo. She looked very aged and wrinkled and infirm; and yet her eyes, which were as brown as those of an ox, were so extremely large and beautiful, that, when they were fixed on Jason's eyes, he could see nothing else but them. The old woman had a pomegranate in her hand, although the fruit was then quite out of season.

"Whither are you going, Jason?" she now asked.

She seemed to know his name, you will observe; and, indeed, those great brown eyes looked as if they had a knowledge of everything, whether past or to come. While Jason was gazing at her, a peacock strutted forward and took his stand at the old woman's side.

"I am going to Iolchos," answered the young man, "to bid the wicked King Pelias come down from my father's throne, and let me reign in his stead."

"Ah, well, then," said the old woman, still with the same cracked voice, "if that is all your business, you need not be in a very great hurry. Just take me on your back, there's a good youth, and carry me across the river. I and my peacock have something to do on the other side, as well as yourself."

"Good mother," replied Jason, "your business can hardly be so important as the pulling down a king from his throne. Besides, as you may see for yourself, the river is very boisterous; and if I should chance to stumble, it would sweep both of us away more easily

than it has carried off yonder uprooted tree. I would gladly help you if I could; but I doubt whether I am strong enough to carry you across."

"Then," said she very scornfully, "neither are you strong enough to pull King Pelias off his throne. And, Jason, unless you will help an old woman at her need, you ought not to be a king. What are kings made for, save to succor the feeble and distressed? But do as you please. Either take me on your back, or with my poor old limbs I shall try my best to struggle across the stream."

Saying this, the old woman poked with her staff in the river, as if to find the safest place in its rocky bed where she might make the first step. But Jason, by this time, had grown ashamed of his reluctance to help her. He felt that he could never forgive himself if this poor feeble creature should come to any harm in attempting to wrestle against the headlong current. The good Chiron, whether half horse or no, had taught him that the noblest use of his strength was to assist the weak; and also that he must treat every young woman as if she were his sister, and every old one like a mother. Remembering these maxims, the vigorous and beautiful young man knelt down, and requested the good dame to mount upon his back.

"The passage seems to me not very safe," he remarked. "But as your business is so urgent, I will try to carry you across. If the river sweeps you away, it shall take me too."

"That, no doubt, will be a great comfort to both of

us," quoth the old woman. "But never fear. We shall get safely across."

So she threw her arms around Jason's neck; and lifting her from the ground, he stepped boldly into the raging and foamy current, and began to stagger away from the shore. As for the peacock, it alighted on the old dame's shoulder. Jason's two spears, one in each hand, kept him from stumbling, and enabled him to feel his way among the hidden rocks; although, every instant, he expected that his companion and himself would go down the stream, together with the driftwood of shattered trees, and the carcasses of the sheep and cow. Down came the cold, snowy torrent from the steep side of Olympus, raging and thundering as if it had a real spite against Jason, or, at all events, were determined to snatch off his living burden from his shoulders. When he was halfway across, the uprooted tree (which I have already told you about) broke loose from among the rocks, and bore down upon him, with all its splintered branches sticking out like the hundred arms of the giant Briareus. It rushed past, however, without touching him. But the next moment, his foot was caught in a crevice between two rocks, and stuck there so fast that, in the effort to get free, he lost one of his golden-stringed sandals.

At this accident Jason could not help uttering a cry of vexation.

"What is the matter, Jason?" asked the old woman.

"Matter enough," said the young man. "I have lost a sandal here among the rocks. And what sort of a figure

shall I cut at the court of King Pelias, with a golden-stringed sandal on one foot, and the other foot bare!"

"Do not take it to heart," answered his companion cheerily. "You never met with better fortune than in losing that sandal. It satisfies me that you are the very person whom the Speaking Oak has been talking about."

There was no time, just then, to inquire what the Speaking Oak had said. But the briskness of her tone encouraged the young man; and besides, he had never in his life felt so vigorous and mighty as since taking this old woman on his back. Instead of being exhausted, he gathered strength as he went on; and, struggling up against the torrent, he at last gained the opposite shore, clambered up the bank, and set down the old dame and her peacock safely on the grass. As soon as this was done, however, he could not help looking rather despondently at his bare foot, with only a remnant of the golden string of the sandal clinging round his ankle.

"You will get a handsomer pair of sandals by and by," said the old woman, with a kindly look out of her beautiful brown eyes. "Only let King Pelias get a glimpse of that bare foot, and you shall see him turn as pale as ashes, I promise you. There is your path. Go along, my good Jason, and my blessing go with you. And when you sit on your throne, remember the old woman whom you helped over the river."

With these words, she hobbled away, giving him a smile over her shoulder as she departed. Whether the light of her beautiful brown eyes threw a glory round

about her, or whatever the cause might be, Jason fancied that there was something very noble and majestic in her figure, after all, and that, though her gait seemed to be a rheumatic hobble, yet she moved with as much grace and dignity as any queen on earth. Her peacock, which had now fluttered down from her shoulder, strutted behind her in prodigious pomp, and spread out its magnificent tail on purpose for Jason to admire it.

When the old dame and her peacock were out of sight, Jason set forward on his journey. After traveling a pretty long distance, he came to a town situated at the foot of a mountain, and not a great way from the shore of the sea. On the outside of the town there was an immense crowd of people, not only men and women, but children, too, all in their best clothes, and evidently enjoying a holiday. The crowd was thickest towards the seashore; and in that direction, over the people's heads, Jason saw a wreath of smoke curling upward to the blue sky. He inquired of one of the multitude what town it was, near by, and why so many persons were here assembled together.

"This is the kingdom of Iolchos," answered the man, "and we are the subjects of King Pelias. Our monarch has summoned us together, that we may see him sacrifice a black bull to Neptune, who, they say, is his Majesty's father. Yonder is the king, where you see the smoke going up from the altar."

While the man spoke he eyed Jason with great curiosity; for his garb was quite unlike that of the Iolchians, and it looked very odd to see a youth with a

leopard's skin over his shoulders, and each hand grasping a spear. Jason perceived, too, that the man stared particularly at his feet, one of which, you remember, was bare, while the other was decorated with his father's golden-stringed sandal.

"Look at him! Only look at him!" said the man to his next neighbor. "Do you see? He wears but one sandal!"

Upon this, first one person and then another began to stare at Jason, and everybody seemed to be greatly struck with something in his aspect; though they turned their eyes much oftener towards his feet than to any other part of his figure. Besides, he could hear them whispering to one another.

"One sandal! One sandal!" they kept saying. "The man with one sandal! Here he is at last! Whence has he come? What does he mean to do? What will the king say to the one-sandaled man?"

Poor Jason was greatly abashed, and made up his mind that the people of Iolchos were exceedingly ill bred, to take such public notice of an accidental deficiency in his dress. Meanwhile, whether it were that they hustled him forward, or that Jason, of his own accord, thrust a passage through the crowd, it so happened that he soon found himself close to the smoking altar, where King Pelias was sacrificing the black bull. The murmur and hum of the multitude, in their surprise at the spectacle of Jason with his one bare foot, grew so loud that it disturbed the ceremonies; and the king, holding the great knife with which he was just going to cut the bull's throat, turned angrily about, and

fixed his eyes on Jason. The people had now with-
drawn from around him, so that the youth stood in an
open space near the smoking altar, front to front with
the angry King Pelias.

"Who are you?" cried the king, with a terrible
frown. "And how dare you make this disturbance,
while I am sacrificing a black bull to my father Neptune?"

"It is no fault of mine," answered Jason. "Your
Majesty must blame the rudeness of your subjects, who
have raised all this tumult because one of my feet
happens to be bare."

When Jason said this, the king gave a quick, startled
glance down at his feet.

"Ha!" muttered he, "here is the one-sandaled fellow,
sure enough! What can I do with him?"

And he clutched more closely the great knife in his
hand, as if he were half a mind to slay Jason instead of
the black bull. The people round about caught up the
king's words indistinctly as they were uttered; and first
there was a murmur among them and then a loud
shout.

"The one-sandaled man has come! The prophecy
must be fulfilled!"

For you are to know that, many years before, King
Pelias had been told by the Speaking Oak of Dodona
that a man with one sandal should cast him down from
his throne. On this account, he had given strict orders
that nobody should ever come into his presence, unless
both sandals were securely tied upon his feet; and he
kept an officer in his palace, whose sole business it was

to examine people's sandals, and to supply them with a new pair, at the expense of the royal treasury, as soon as the old ones began to wear out. In the whole course of the king's reign, he had never been thrown into such a fright and agitation as by the spectacle of poor Jason's bare foot. But, as he was naturally a bold and hard-hearted man, he soon took courage, and began to consider in what way he might rid himself of this terrible one-sandaled stranger.

"My good young man," said King Pelias, taking the softest tone imaginable, in order to throw Jason off his guard, "you are excessively welcome to my kingdom. Judging by your dress, you must have traveled a long distance; for it is not the fashion to wear leopard skins in this part of the world. Pray what may I call your name? And where did you receive your education?"

"My name is Jason," answered the young stranger. "Ever since my infancy, I have dwelled in the cave of Chiron the Centaur. He was my instructor, and taught me music, and horsemanship, and how to cure wounds, and likewise how to inflict wounds with my weapons!"

"I have heard of Chiron the schoolmaster," replied King Pelias, "and how that there is an immense deal of learning and wisdom in his head, although it happens to be set on a horse's body. It gives me great delight to see one of his scholars at my court. But, to test how much you have profited under so excellent a teacher, will you allow me to ask you a single question?"

"I do not pretend to be very wise," said Jason. "But

ask me what you please, and I will answer to the best of my ability."

Now King Pelias meant cunningly to entrap the young man, and to make him say something that should be the cause of mischief and destruction to himself. So with a crafty and evil smile upon his face, he spoke as follows:

"What would you do, brave Jason," asked he, "if there were a man in the world, by whom, as you had reason to believe, you were doomed to be ruined and slain—what would you do, I say, if that man stood before you, and in your power?"

When Jason saw the malice and wickedness which King Pelias could not prevent from gleaming out of his eyes, he probably guessed that the king had discovered what he came for, and that he intended to turn his own words against himself. Still he scorned to tell a falsehood. Like an upright and honorable prince, as he was, he determined to speak out the real truth. Since the king had chosen to ask him the question, and since Jason had promised him an answer, there was no right way, save to tell him precisely what would be the most prudent thing to do, if he had his worst enemy in his power.

Therefore, after a moment's consideration, he spoke up with a firm and manly voice.

"I would send such a man," said he, "in quest of the Golden Fleece!"

This enterprise, you will understand, was, of all others, the most difficult and dangerous in the world.

In the first place, it would be necessary to make a long voyage through unknown seas. There was hardly a hope, or a possibility, that any young man who should undertake this voyage would either succeed in obtaining the Golden Fleece, or would survive to return home, and tell of the perils he had run. The eyes of King Pelias sparkled with joy, therefore, when he heard Jason's reply.

"Well said, wise man with the one sandal!" cried he. "Go, then, and, at the peril of your life, bring me back the Golden Fleece."

"I go," answered Jason composedly. "If I fail, you need not fear that I will ever come back to trouble you again. But if I return to Iolchos with the prize, then, King Pelias, you must hasten down from your lofty throne, and give me your crown and scepter."

"That I will," said the king, with a sneer. "Meantime, I will keep them very safely for you."

The first thing that Jason thought of doing, after he left the king's presence, was to go to Dodona, and inquire of the Talking Oak what course it was best to pursue. This wonderful tree stood in the center of an ancient wood. Its stately trunk rose up a hundred feet into the air, and threw a broad and dense shadow over more than an acre of ground. Standing beneath it, Jason looked up among the knotted branches and green leaves, and into the mysterious heart of the old tree, and spoke aloud, as if he were addressing some person who was hidden in the depths of the foliage.

"What shall I do," said he, "in order to win the Golden Fleece?"

At first there was a deep silence, not only within the shadow of the Talking Oak, but all through the solitary wood. In a moment or two, however, the leaves of the oak began to stir and rustle, as if a gentle breeze were wandering amongst them, although the other trees of the wood were perfectly still. The sound grew louder, and became like the roar of a high wind. By and by, Jason imagined that he could distinguish words, but very confusedly, because each separate leaf of the tree seemed to be a tongue, and the whole myriad of tongues were babbling at once. But the noise waxed broader and deeper, until it resembled a tornado sweeping through the oak, and making one great utterance out of the thousand and thousand of little murmurs which each leafy tongue had caused by its rustling. And now, though it still had the tone of mighty wind roaring among the branches, it was also like a deep bass voice, speaking, as distinctly as a tree could be expected to speak, the following words:

"Go to Argus, the shipbuilder, and bid him build a galley with fifty oars."

Then the voice melted again into the indistinct murmur of the rustling leaves, and died gradually away. When it was quite gone, Jason felt inclined to doubt whether he had actually heard the words, or whether his fancy had not shaped them out of the ordinary sound made by a breeze, while passing through the thick foliage of the tree.

But on inquiry among the people of Iolchos, he found that there was really a man in the city, by the name of Argus, who was a very skillful builder of

vessels. This showed some intelligence in the oak; else how should it have known that any such person existed? At Jason's request, Argus readily consented to build him a galley so big that it should require fifty strong men to row it; although no vessel of such a size and burden had heretofore been seen in the world. So the head carpenter and all his journeymen and apprentices began their work; and for a good while afterwards, there they were, busily employed, hewing out the timbers, and making a great clatter with their hammers; until the new ship, which was called the *Argo*, seemed to be quite ready for sea. And, as the Talking Oak had already given him such good advice, Jason thought that it would not be amiss to ask for a little more. He visited it again, therefore, and standing beside its huge, rough trunk, inquired what he should do next.

This time, there was no such universal quivering of the leaves throughout the whole tree as there had been before. But after a while, Jason observed that the foliage of a great branch which stretched above his head had begun to rustle, as if the wind were stirring that one bough, while all the other boughs of the oak were at rest.

"Cut me off!" said the branch, as soon as it could speak distinctly. "Cut me off! Cut me off! And carve me into a figurehead for your galley."

Accordingly, Jason took the branch at its word, and lopped it off the tree. A carver in the neighborhood engaged to make the figurehead. He was a tolerably good workman, and had already carved several figure-

heads, in what he intended for feminine shapes, and looking pretty much like those which we see nowadays stuck up under a vessel's bowsprit, with great staring eyes, that never wink at the bash of the spray. But (what was very strange) the carver found that his hand was guided by some unseen power, and by a skill beyond his own, and that his tools shaped out an image which he had never dreamed of. When the work was finished, it turned out to be the figure of a beautiful woman with a helmet on her head, from beneath which the long ringlets fell down upon her shoulders. On the left arm was a shield, and in its center appeared a lifelike representation of the head of Medusa with the snaky locks. The right arm was extended, as if pointing onward. The face of this wonderful statue, though not angry or forbidding, was so grave and majestic that perhaps you might call it severe; and as for the mouth, it seemed just ready to unclose its lips, and utter words of the deepest wisdom.

Jason was delighted with the oaken image, and gave the carver no rest until it was completed, and set up where a figurehead has always stood, from that time to this, in the vessel's prow.

"And now," cried he, as he stood gazing at the calm, majestic face of the statue, "I must go to the Talking Oak, and inquire what next to do."

"There is no need of that, Jason," said a voice which, though it was far lower, reminded him of the mighty tones of the great oak. "When you desire good advice, you can seek it of me."

Jason had been looking straight into the face of the

image when these words were spoken. But he could hardly believe either his ears or his eyes. The truth was, however, that the oaken lips had moved, and, to all appearance, the voice had proceeded from the statue's mouth. Recovering a little from his surprise, Jason bethought himself that the image had been carved out of the wood of the Talking Oak, and that, therefore, it was really no great wonder, but on the contrary, the most natural thing in the world, that it should possess the faculty of speech. It would have been very odd, indeed, if it had not. But certainly it was a great piece of good fortune that he should be able to carry so wise a block of wood along with him in his perilous voyage.

"Tell me, wondrous image," exclaimed Jason, "since you inherit the wisdom of the Speaking Oak of Dodona, whose daughter you are—tell me, where shall I find fifty bold youths, who will take each of them an oar of my galley? They must have sturdy arms to row, and brave hearts to encounter perils, or we shall never win the Golden Fleece."

"Go," replied the oaken image, "go, summon all the heroes of Greece."

And, in fact, considering what a great deed was to be done, could any advice be wiser than this which Jason received from the figurehead of his vessel? He lost no time in sending messengers to all the cities and making known to the whole people of Greece, that Prince Jason, the son of King Æson, was going in quest of the Fleece of Gold, and that he desired the help of forty-nine of the bravest and strongest young

men alive, to row his vessel and share his dangers. And Jason himself would be the fiftieth.

At this news, the adventurous youths all over the country began to bestir themselves. Some of them had already fought with giants, and slain dragons; and the younger ones, who had not yet met with such good fortune, thought it a shame to have lived so long without getting astride of a flying serpent, or sticking their spears into a Chimæra, or, at least, thrusting their right arms down a monstrous lion's throat. There was a fair prospect that they would meet with plenty of such adventures before finding the Golden Fleece. As soon as they could furbish up their helmets and shields, therefore, and gird on their trusty swords, they came thronging to Iolchos, and clambered on board the new galley. Shaking hands with Jason, they assured him that they did not care a pin for their lives, but would help row the vessel to the remotest edge of the world, and as much farther as he might think it best to go.

Many of these brave fellows had been educated by Chiron, the four-footed pedagogue, and were therefore old schoolmates of Jason, and knew him to be a lad of spirit. The mighty Hercules, whose shoulders afterwards held up the sky, was one of them. And there were Castor and Pollux, the twin brothers, who were never accused of being chicken-hearted, although they had been hatched out of an egg; and Theseus, who was so renowned for killing the Minotaur; and Lynceus, with his wonderfully sharp eyes, which could see through a millstone, or look right down into the depths of the earth, and discover the treasures that were there;

and Orpheus, the very best of harpers, who sang and played upon his lyre so sweetly that the brute beasts stood upon their hind legs and capered merrily to the music. Yes, and at some of his more moving tunes, the rocks bestirred their moss-grown bulk out of the ground, and a grove of forest trees uprooted themselves and, nodding their tops to one another, performed a country dance.

One of the rowers was a beautiful young woman, named Atalanta, who had been nursed among the mountains by a bear. So light of foot was this fair damsel that she could step from one foamy crest of a wave to the foamy crest of another, without wetting more than the sole of her sandal. She had grown up in a very wild way, and talked much about the rights of women, and loved hunting and war far better than her needle. But, in my opinion, the most remarkable of this famous company were two sons of the North Wind (airy youngsters, and of rather a blustering disposition), who had wings on their shoulders, and, in case of a calm, could puff out their cheeks, and blow almost as fresh a breeze as their father. I ought not to forget the prophets and conjurers of whom there were several in the crew, and who could foretell what would happen tomorrow, or the next day, or a hundred years hence, but were generally quite unconscious of what was passing at the moment.

Jason appointed Tiphys to be helmsman, because he was a stargazer, and knew the points of the compass. Lynceus, on account of his sharp sight, was stationed as a lookout in the prow, where he saw a whole day's

sail ahead, but was rather apt to overlook things that lay directly under his nose. If the sea only happened to be deep enough, however, Lynceus could tell you exactly what kind of rocks or sands were at the bottom of it; and he often cried out to his companions that they were sailing over heaps of sunken treasure, which yet he was none the richer for beholding. To confess the truth, few people believed him when he said it.

Well! But when the Argonauts, as these fifty brave adventurers were called, had prepared everything for the voyage, an unforeseen difficulty threatened to end it before it was begun. The vessel, you must understand, was so long and broad and ponderous that the united force of all the fifty was insufficient to shove her into the water. Hercules, I suppose, had not grown to his full strength, else he might have set her afloat as easily as a little boy launches his boat upon a puddle. But here were these fifty heroes pushing and straining and growing red in the face, without making the *Argo* start an inch. At last, quite wearied out, they sat themselves down on the shore, exceedingly disconsolate, and thinking that the vessel must be left to rot and fall in pieces, and that they must either swim across the sea or lose the Golden Fleece.

All at once, Jason bethought himself of the galley's miraculous figurehead.

"O daughter of the Talking Oak," cried he, "how shall we set to work to get our vessel into the water?"

"Seat yourselves," answered the image (for it had known what ought to be done from the very first, and was only waiting for the question to be put)—"seat

yourselves, and handle your oars, and let Orpheus play upon his harp."

Immediately the fifty heroes got on board, and seizing their oars, held them perpendicularly in the air, while Orpheus (who liked such a task far better than rowing) swept his fingers across the harp. At the first ringing note of the music, they felt the vessel stir. Orpheus thrummed away briskly, and the galley slid at once into the sea, dipping her prow so deeply that the figurehead drank the wave with its marvelous lips, and rose again as buoyant as a swan. The rowers plied their fifty oars; the white foam boiled up before the prow; the water gurgled and bubbled in their wake; while Orpheus continued to play so lively a strain of music that the vessel seemed to dance over the billows by way of keeping time to it. Thus triumphantly did the *Argo* sail out of the harbor, amidst the huzzas and good wishes of everybody except the wicked old Pelias, who stood on a promontory, scowling at her, and wishing that he could blow out of his lungs the tempest of wrath that was in his heart, and so sink the galley with all on board. When they had sailed about fifty miles over the sea, Lynceus happened to cast his sharp eyes behind, and said that there was this bad-hearted king, still perched upon the promontory, and scowling so gloomily that it looked like a black thundercloud in that quarter of the horizon.

In order to make the time pass away more pleasantly during the voyage, the heroes talked about the Golden Fleece. It originally belonged, it appears, to a Bœotian ram, who had taken on his back two children,

when in danger of their lives, and fled with them over land and sea, as far as Colchis. One of the children, whose name was Helle, fell into the sea and was drowned. But the other (a little boy, named Phrixus) was brought safe ashore by the faithful ram, who, however, was so exhausted that he immediately lay down and died. In memory of this good deed, and as a token of his true heart, the fleece of the poor dead ram was miraculously changed to gold, and became one of the most beautiful objects ever seen on earth. It was hung upon a tree in a sacred grove, where it had now been kept I know not how many years, and was the envy of mighty kings, who had nothing so magnificent in any of their palaces.

If I were to tell you all the adventures of the Argonauts, it would take me till nightfall, and perhaps a great deal longer. There was no lack of wonderful events, as you may judge from what you may have already heard. At a certain island they were hospitably received by King Cyzicus, its sovereign, who made a feast for them, and treated them like brothers. But the Argonauts saw that this good king looked downcast and very much troubled, and they therefore inquired of him what was the matter. King Cyzicus hereupon informed them that he and his subjects were greatly abused and incommoded by the inhabitants of a neighboring mountain, who made war upon them, and killed many people, and ravaged the country. And while they were talking about it, Cyzicus pointed to the mountain and asked Jason and his companions what they saw there.

"I see some very tall objects," answered Jason, "but they are at such a distance that I cannot distinctly make out what they are. To tell your Majesty the truth, they look so very strangely that I am inclined to think them clouds, which have chanced to take something like human shapes."

"I see them very plainly," remarked Lynceus, whose eyes, you know, were as farsighted as a telescope. "They are a band of enormous giants, all of whom have six arms apiece, and a club, a sword, or some other weapon in each of their hands."

"You have excellent eyes," said King Cyzicus. "Yes, they are six-armed giants, as you say, and these are the enemies whom I and my subjects have to contend with."

The next day, when the Argonauts were about setting sail, down came these terrible giants, stepping a hundred yards at a stride, brandishing their six arms apiece, and looking very formidable, so far aloft in the air. Each of these monsters was able to carry on a whole war by himself, for with one of his arms he could fling immense stones, and wield a club with another, and a sword with a third, while the fourth was poking a long spear at the enemy, and the fifth and sixth were shooting him with a bow and arrow. But, luckily, though the giants were so huge, and had so many arms they had each but one heart, and that no bigger nor braver than the heart of an ordinary man. Besides, if they had been like the hundred-armed Briareus, the brave Argonauts would have given them their hands full of fight. Jason and his friends went boldly to meet

them, slew a great many, and made the rest take to their heels, so that, if the giants had had six legs apiece instead of six arms, it would have served them better to run away with.

Another strange adventure happened when the voyagers came to Thrace, where they found a poor blind king, named Phineus, deserted by his subjects, and living in a very sorrowful way, all by himself. On Jason's inquiring whether they could do him any service, the king answered that he was terribly tormented by the three great winged creatures called Harpies, which had the faces of women, and the wings, bodies, and claws of vultures. These ugly wretches were in the habit of snatching away his dinner, and allowed him no peace of his life. Upon hearing this, the Argonauts spread a plentiful feast on the seashore, well knowing, from what the blind king said of their greediness, that the Harpies would snuff up the scent of the victuals, and quickly come to steal them away. And so it turned out; for, hardly was the table set, before the three hideous vulture women came flapping their wings, seized the food in their talons, and flew off as fast as they could. But the two sons of the North Wind drew their swords, spread their pinions, and set off through the air in pursuit of the thieves, whom they at last overtook among some islands, after a chase of hundreds of miles. The two winged youths blustered terribly at the Harpies (for they had the rough temper of their father), and so frightened them with their drawn swords that they solemnly promised never to trouble King Phineus again.

Then the Argonauts sailed onward, and met with many other marvelous incidents any one of which would make a story by itself. At one time, they landed on an island, and were reposing on the grass, when they suddenly found themselves assailed by what seemed a shower of steel-headed arrows. Some of them stuck in the ground, while others hit against their shields, and several penetrated their flesh. The fifty heroes started up, and looked about them for the hidden enemy, but could find none, nor see any spot, on the whole island, where even a single archer could lie concealed. Still, however, the steel-headed arrows came whizzing among them; and, at last, happening to look upward, they beheld a large flock of birds, hovering and wheeling aloft, and shooting their feathers down upon the Argonauts. These feathers were the steel-headed arrows that had so tormented them. There was no possibility of making any resistance; and the fifty heroic Argonauts might all have been killed or wounded by a flock of troublesome birds, without ever setting eyes on the Golden Fleece, if Jason had not thought of asking the advice of the oaken image.

So he ran to the galley as fast as his legs would carry him.

"O daughter of the Speaking Oak," cried he, all out of breath, "we need your wisdom more than ever before! We are in great peril from a flock of birds, who are shooting us with their steel-pointed feathers. What can we do to drive them away?"

"Make a clatter on your shields," said the image.

On receiving this excellent counsel, Jason hurried

"O daughter of the Talking Oak," cried Jason, "we need your wisdom more than ever before!"

back to his companions (who were far more dismayed than when they fought with the six-armed giants), and bade them strike with their swords upon their brazen shields. Forthwith the fifty heroes set heartily to work, banging with might and main, and raised such a terrible clatter that the birds made what haste they could to get away; and though they had shot half the feathers out of their wings, they were soon seen skimming among the clouds, a long distance off, and looking like a flock of wild geese. Orpheus celebrated this victory by playing a triumphant anthem on his harp, and sang so melodiously that Jason begged him to desist, lest, as the steel-feathered birds had been driven away by an ugly sound, they might be enticed back again by a sweet one.

While the Argonauts remained on this island, they saw a small vessel approaching the shore, in which were two young men of princely demeanor, and exceedingly handsome, as young princes generally were in those days. Now, who do you imagine these two voyagers turned out to be? Why, if you will believe me, they were the sons of that very Phrixus, who, in his childhood, had been carried to Colchis on the back of the golden-fleeced ram. Since that time, Phrixus had married the king's daughter; and the two young princes had been born and brought up at Colchis, and had spent their play days in the outskirts of the grove, in the center of which the Golden Fleece was hanging upon a tree. They were now on their way to Greece, in hopes of getting back a kingdom that had been wrongfully taken from their father.

When the princes understood whither the Argonauts were going, they offered to turn back and guide them to Colchis. At the same time, however, they spoke as if it were very doubtful whether Jason would succeed in getting the Golden Fleece. According to their account, the tree on which it hung was guarded by a terrible dragon, who never failed to devour, at one mouthful, every person who might venture within his reach.

"There are other difficulties in the way," continued the young princes. "But is not this enough? Ah, brave Jason, turn back before it is too late. It would grieve us to the heart, if you and your nine-and-forty brave companions should be eaten up, at fifty mouthfuls, by this execrable dragon."

"My young friends," quietly replied Jason, "I do not wonder that you think the dragon very terrible. You have grown up from infancy in the fear of this monster, and therefore still regard him with the awe that children feel for the bugbears and hobgoblins which their nurses have talked to them about. But, in my view of the matter, the dragon is merely a pretty large serpent, who is not half so likely to snap me up at one mouthful as I am to cut off his ugly head, and strip the skin from his body. At all events, turn back who may, I will never see Greece again unless I carry with me the Golden Fleece."

"We will none of us turn back!" cried his nine-and-forty brave comrades. "Let us get on board the galley this instant; and if the dragon is to make a breakfast of us, much good may it do him."

And Orpheus (whose custom it was to set every-

thing to music) began to harp and sing most gloriously, and made every mother's son of them feel as if nothing in this world were so delectable as to fight dragons, and nothing so truly honorable as to be eaten up at one mouthful, in case of the worst.

After this (being now under the guidance of the two princes, who were well acquainted with the way), they quickly sailed to Colchis. When the king of the country, whose name was Æetes, heard of their arrival, he instantly summoned Jason to court. The king was a stern and cruel-looking potentate; and though he put on as polite and hospitable an expression as he could, Jason did not like his face a whit better than that of the wicked King Pelias, who dethroned his father.

"You are welcome, brave Jason," said King Æetes. "Pray, are you on a pleasure voyage? Or do you meditate the discovery of unknown islands? Or what other cause has procured me the happiness of seeing you at my court?"

"Great sir," replied Jason, with an obeisance—for Chiron had taught him how to behave with propriety, whether to kings or beggars—"I have come hither with a purpose which I now beg your Majesty's permission to execute. King Pelias, who sits on my father's throne (to which he has no more right than to the one on which your excellent Majesty is now seated), has engaged to come down from it, and to give me his crown and scepter, provided I bring him the Golden Fleece. This, as your Majesty is aware, is now hanging on a tree here at Colchis; and I humbly solicit your gracious leave to take it away."

In spite of himself, the king's face twisted itself into an angry frown; for, above all things else in the world, he prized the Golden Fleece, and was even suspected of having done a very wicked act, in order to get it into his own possession. It put him into the worst possible humor, therefore, to hear that the gallant Prince Jason, and forty-nine of the bravest young warriors of Greece, had come to Colchis with the sole purpose of taking away his chief treasure.

"Do you know," asked King Æetes, eying Jason very sternly, "what are the conditions which you must fulfill before getting possession of the Golden Fleece?"

"I have heard," rejoined the youth, "that a dragon lies beneath the tree on which the prize hangs, and that whoever approaches him runs the risk of being devoured at a mouthful."

"True," said the king, with a smile that did not look particularly good-natured. "Very true, young man. But there are other things as hard, or perhaps a little harder, to be done, before you can even have the privilege of being devoured by the dragon. For example, you must first tame my two brazen-footed and brazen-lunged bulls, which Vulcan, the wonderful blacksmith, made for me. There is a furnace in each of their stomachs; and they breathe such hot fire out of their mouths and nostrils, that nobody has hitherto gone nigh them without being instantly burned to a small, black cinder. What do you think of this, my brave Jason?"

"I must encounter the peril," answered Jason composedly, "since it stands in the way of my purpose."

"After taming the fiery bulls," continued King Æetes, who was determined to scare Jason if possible, "you must yoke them to a plow, and must plow the sacred earth in the grove of Mars, and sow some of the same dragon's teeth from which Cadmus raised a crop of armed men. They are an unruly set of reprobates, those sons of the dragon's teeth; and unless you treat them suitably, they will fall upon you sword in hand. You and your nine-and-forty Argonauts, my bold Jason, are hardly numerous or strong enough to fight with such a host as will spring up."

"My master Chiron," replied Jason, "taught me, long ago, the story of Cadmus. Perhaps I can manage the quarrelsome sons of the dragon's teeth as well as Cadmus did."

"I wish the dragon had him," muttered King Æetes to himself, "and the four-footed pedant, his schoolmaster, into the bargain. Why, what a foolhardy, self-conceited coxcomb he is! We'll see what my fire-breathing bulls will do for him. Well, Prince Jason," he continued, aloud, and as complaisantly as he could, "make yourself comfortable for today, and tomorrow morning, since you insist upon it, you shall try your skill at the plow."

While the king talked with Jason, a beautiful young woman was standing behind the throne. She fixed her eyes earnestly upon the youthful stranger, and listened attentively to every word that was spoken; and when Jason withdrew from the king's presence, this young woman followed him out of the room.

"I am the king's daughter," she said to him, "and

my name is Medea. I know a great deal of which other young princesses are ignorant, and can do many things which they would be afraid so much as to dream of. If you will trust to me, I can instruct you how to tame the fiery bulls, and sow the dragon's teeth, and get the Golden Fleece."

"Indeed, beautiful princess," answered Jason, "if you will do me this service, I promise to be grateful to you my whole life long."

Gazing at Medea, he beheld a wonderful intelligence in her face. She was one of those persons whose eyes are full of mystery; so that, while looking into them, you seem to see a very great way, as into a deep well, yet can never be certain whether you see into the farthest depths, or whether there be not something else hidden at the bottom. If Jason had been capable of fearing anything, he would have been afraid of making this young princess his enemy; for, beautiful as she now looked, she might, the very next instant, become as terrible as the dragon that kept watch over the Golden Fleece.

"Princess," he exclaimed, "you seem indeed very wise and very powerful. But how can you help me to do the things of which you speak? Are you an enchantress?"

"Yes, Prince Jason," answered Medea, with a smile, "you have hit upon the truth. I am an enchantress. Circe, my father's sister, taught me to be one, and I could tell you, if I pleased, who was the old woman with the peacock, the pomegranate, and the cuckoo staff, whom you carried over the river; and, likewise,

who it is that speaks through the lips of the oaken image that stands in the prow of your galley. I am acquainted with some of your secrets, you perceive. It is well for you that I am favorably inclined; for, otherwise, you would hardly escape being snapped up by the dragon."

"I should not so much care for the dragon," replied Jason, "if I only knew how to manage the brazen-footed and fiery-lunged bulls."

"If you are as brave as I think you, and as you have need to be," said Medea, "your own bold heart will teach you that there is but one way of dealing with a mad bull. What it is I leave you to find out in the moment of peril. As for the fiery breath of these animals, I have a charmed ointment here, which will prevent you from being burned up, and cure you if you chance to be a little scorched."

So she put a golden box into his hand, and directed him how to apply the perfumed unguent which it contained, and where to meet her at midnight.

"Only be brave," added she, "and before daybreak the brazen bulls shall be tamed."

The young man assured her that his heart would not fail him. He then rejoined his comrades, and told them what had passed between the princess and himself, and warned them to be in readiness in case there might be need of their help.

At the appointed hour he met the beautiful Medea on the marble steps of the king's palace. She gave him a basket, in which were the dragon's teeth, just as they had been pulled out of the monster's jaws by Cadmus,

long ago. Medea then led Jason down the palace steps, and through the silent streets of the city, and into the royal pasture ground, where the two brazen-footed bulls were kept. It was a starry night, with a bright gleam along the eastern edge of the sky, where the moon was soon going to show herself. After entering the pasture, the princess paused and looked around.

"There they are," said she, "reposing themselves and chewing their fiery cuds in that farthest corner of the field. It will be excellent sport, I assure you, when they catch a glimpse of your figure. My father and all his court delight in nothing so much as to see a stranger trying to yoke them, in order to come at the Golden Fleece. It makes a holiday in Colchis whenever such a thing happens. For my part, I enjoy it immensely. You cannot imagine in what a mere twinkling of an eye their hot breath shrivels a young man into a black cinder."

"Are you sure, beautiful Medea," asked Jason, "quite sure that the unguent in the gold box will prove a remedy against those terrible burns?"

"If you doubt, if you are in the least afraid," said the princess, looking him in the face by the dim starlight, "you had better never have been born than go a step nigher to the bulls."

But Jason had set his heart steadfastly on getting the Golden Fleece; and I positively doubt whether he would have gone back without it, even had he been certain of finding himself turned into a red-hot cinder, or a handful of white ashes, the instant he made a step farther. He therefore let go Medea's hand, and walked

boldly forward in the direction whither she had pointed. At some distance before him he perceived four streams of fiery vapor, regularly appearing, and again vanishing, after dimly lighting up the surrounding obscurity. These, you will understand, were caused by the breath of the brazen bulls, which was quietly stealing out of their four nostrils, as they lay chewing their cuds.

At the first two or three steps which Jason made, the four fiery streams appeared to gush out somewhat more plentifully; for the two brazen bulls had heard his foot-tramp, and were lifting up their hot noses to snuff the air. He went a little farther, and by the way in which the red vapor now spouted forth, he judged that the creatures had got upon their feet. Now he could see glowing sparks and vivid jets of flame. At the next step, each of the bulls made the pasture echo with a terrible roar, while the burning breath, which they thus belched forth, lit up the whole field with a momentary flash. One other stride did bold Jason make. And, suddenly, as a streak of lightning, on came these fiery animals, roaring like thunder, and sending out sheets of white flame, which so kindled up the scene that the young man could discern every object more distinctly than by daylight. Most distinctly of all he saw the two horrible creatures galloping right down upon him, their brazen hoofs rattling and ringing over the ground, and their tails sticking up stiffly into the air, as has always been the fashion with angry bulls. Their breath scorched the herbage before them. So intensely hot it was, indeed, that it caught a dry tree, under

which Jason was now standing, and set it all in a light blaze. But as for Jason himself (thanks to Medea's enchanted ointment), the white flame curled around his body, without injuring him a jot more than if he had been made of asbestos.

Greatly encouraged at finding himself not yet turned into a cinder, the young man awaited the attack of the bulls. Just as the brazen brutes fancied themselves sure of tossing him into the air, he caught one of them by the horn, and the other by his screwed-up tail, and held them in a grip like that of an iron vice, one with his right hand, the other with his left. Well, he must have been wonderfully strong in his arms, to be sure. But the secret of the matter was, that the brazen bulls were enchanted creatures, and that Jason had broken the spell of their fiery fierceness by his bold way of handling them. And, ever since that time, it has been the favorite method of brave men, when danger assails them, to do what they call "taking the bull by the horns"; and to grip him by the tail is pretty much the same thing—that is, to throw aside fear, and overcome the peril by despising it.

It was now easy to yoke the bulls, and to harness them to the plow, which had lain rusting on the ground for a great many years gone by; so long was it before anybody could be found capable of plowing that piece of land. Jason, I suppose, had been taught how to draw a furrow by the good old Chiron, who perhaps, used to allow himself to be harnessed to the plow. At any rate, our hero succeeded perfectly well in breaking up the greensward; and, by the time that the moon was

a quarter of her journey up the sky, the plowed field lay before him, a large tract of black earth, ready to be sown with the dragon's teeth. So Jason scattered them broadcast, and harrowed them into the soil with a brush-harrow, and took his stand on the edge of the field, anxious to see what would happen next.

"Must we wait long for harvest time?" he inquired of Medea, who was now standing by his side.

"Whether sooner or later, it will be sure to come," answered the princess. "A crop of armed men never fails to spring up, when the dragon's teeth have been sown."

The moon was now high aloft in the heavens, and threw its bright beams over the plowed field, where as yet there was nothing to be seen. Any farmer, on viewing it, would have said that Jason must wait weeks before the green blades would peep from among the clods, and whole months before the yellow grain would be ripened for the sickle. But by and by, all over the field, there was something that glistened in the moonbeams, like sparkling drops of dew. These bright objects sprouted higher, and proved to be the steel heads of spears. Then there was a dazzling gleam from a vast number of polished brass helmets, beneath which, as they grew farther out of the soil, appeared the dark and bearded visages of warriors, struggling to free themselves from the imprisoning earth. The first look that they gave at the upper world was a glare of wrath and defiance. Next were seen their bright breast-plates. In every right hand there was a sword or a spear, and on each left arm a shield. And when this

strange crop of warriors had but half grown out of the earth, they struggled—such was their impatience of restraint—and, as it were, tore themselves up by the roots. Wherever a dragon's tooth had fallen, there stood a man armed for battle. They made a clangor with their swords against their shields, and eyed one another fiercely; for they had come into this beautiful world, and into the peaceful moonlight, full of rage and stormy passions, and ready to take the life of every human brother, in recompense of the boon of their own existence.

There have been many other armies in the world that seemed to possess the same fierce nature with the one which had now sprouted from the dragon's teeth, but these, in the moonlit field, were the more excusable, because they never had women for their mothers. And how it would have rejoiced any great captain who was bent on conquering the world, like Alexander or Napoleon, to raise a crop of armed soldiers as easily as Jason did!

For a while, the warriors stood flourishing their weapons, clashing their swords against their shields, and boiling over with the red-hot thirst for battle. Then they began to shout, "Show us the enemy! Lead us to the charge! Death or victory! Come on, brave comrades! Conquer or die!" and a hundred other outcries, such as men always bellow forth on a battlefield, and which these dragon people seemed to have at their tongues' ends. At last, the front rank caught sight of Jason, who, beholding the flash of so many weapons in the moonlight, had thought it best to draw his sword.

In a moment all the sons of the dragon's teeth appeared to take Jason for an emeny; and crying with one voice, "Guard the Golden Fleece!" they ran at him with uplifted swords and protruded spears. Jason knew that it would be impossible to withstand this bloodthirsty battalion with his single arm, but determined, since there was nothing better to be done, to die as valiantly as if he himself had sprung from a dragon's tooth.

Medea, however, bade him snatch up a stone from the ground.

"Throw it among them quickly!" cried she. "It is the only way to save yourself."

The armed men were now so nigh that Jason could discern the fire flashing out of their enraged eyes, when he let fly the stone, and saw it strike the helmet of a tall warrior, who was rushing upon him with his blade aloft. The stone glanced from this man's helmet to the shield of his nearest comrade, and thence flew right into the angry face of another, hitting him smartly between the eyes. Each of the three who had been struck by the stone took it for granted that his next neighbor had given him a blow; and instead of running any farther towards Jason, they began a fight among themselves. The confusion spread through the host, so that it seemed scarcely a moment before they were all hacking, hewing, and stabbing at one another, lopping off arms, heads, and legs, and doing such memorable deeds that Jason was filled with immense admiration; although, at the same time, he could not help laughing to behold these mighty men punishing each other for an offence which he himself had committed. In an

incredibly short space of time (almost as short, indeed, as it had taken them to grow up), all but one of the heroes of the dragon's teeth were stretched lifeless on the field. The last survivor, the bravest and strongest of the whole, had just force enough to wave his crimson sword over his head, and give a shout of exultation, crying, "Victory! Victory! Immortal fame!" when he himself fell down, and lay quietly among his slain brethren.

And there was the end of the army that had sprouted from the dragon's teeth. That fierce and feverish fight was the only enjoyment which they had tasted on this beautiful earth.

"Let them sleep in the bed of honor," said the Princess Medea, with a sly smile at Jason. "The world will always have simpletons enough, just like them, fighting and dying for they know not what, and fancying that posterity will take the trouble to put laurel wreaths on their rusty and battered helmets. Could you help smiling, Prince Jason, to see the self-conceit of that last fellow, just as he tumbled down?"

"It made me very sad," answered Jason gravely. "And, to tell you the truth, princess, the Golden Fleece does not appear so well worth the winning, after what I have here beheld."

"You will think differently in the morning," said Medea. "True, the Golden Fleece may not be so valuable as you have thought it; but then there is nothing better in the world; and one must needs have an object, you know. Come! Your night's work has been well performed; and tomorrow you can inform King

Æetes that the first part of your alloted task is fulfilled."

Agreeable to Medea's advice, Jason went betimes in the morning to the palace of King Æetes. Entering the presence chamber, he stood at the foot of the throne, and made a low obeisance.

"Your eyes look heavy, Prince Jason," observed the king. "You appear to have spent a sleepless night. I hope you have been considering the matter a little more wisely, and have concluded not to get yourself scorched to a cinder, in attempting to tame my brazen-lunged bulls."

"That is already accomplished, may it please your Majesty," replied Jason. "The bulls have been tamed and yoked; the field has been plowed; the dragon's teeth have been sown broadcast, and harrowed into the soil; the crop of armed warriors has sprung up, and they have slain one another, to the last man. And now I solicit your Majesty's permission to encounter the dragon, that I may take down the Golden Fleece from the tree, and depart with my nine-and-forty comrades."

King Æetes scowled, and looked very angry and excessively disturbed; for he knew that, in accordance with his kingly promise, he ought now to permit Jason to win the Fleece, if his courage and skill should enable him to do so. But, since the young man had met with such good luck in the matter of the brazen bulls and the dragon's teeth, the king feared that he would be equally successful in slaying the dragon. And therefore, though he would gladly have seen Jason snapped

up at a mouthful, he was resolved (and it was a very wrong thing of this wicked potentate) not to run any further risk of losing his beloved Fleece.

"You never would have succeeded in this business, young man," said he, "if my undutiful daughter Medea had not helped you with her enchantments. Had you acted fairly, you would have been, at this instant, a black cinder, or a handful of white ashes. I forbid you, on pain of death, to make any more attempts to get the Golden Fleece. To speak my mind plainly, you shall never set eyes on so much as one of its glistening locks."

Jason left the king's presence in great sorrow and anger. He could think of nothing better to be done than to summon together his forty-nine brave Argonauts, march at once to the grove of Mars, slay the dragon, take possession of the Golden Fleece, get on board the *Argo,* and spread all sail for Iolchos. The success of the scheme depended, it it true, on the doubtful point whether all the fifty heroes might not be snapped up, at so many mouthfuls, by the dragon. But, as Jason was hastening down the palace steps, the Princess Medea called after him, and beckoned him to return. Her black eyes shone upon him with such a keen intelligence that he felt as if there were a serpent peeping out of them; and although she had done him so much service only the night before, he was by no means very certain that she would not do him an equally great mischief before sunset. These enchantresses, you must know, are never to be depended upon.

"What says King Æetes, my royal and upright father?" inquired Medea, slightly smiling. "Will he give you the Golden Fleece, without any further risk or trouble?"

"On the contrary," answered Jason, "he is very angry with me for taming the brazen bulls and sowing the dragon's teeth. And he forbids me to make any more attempts, and positively refuses to give up the Golden Fleece, whether I slay the dragon or no."

"Yes, Jason," said the princess, "and I can tell you more. Unless you set sail from Colchis before tomorrow's sunrise, the king means to burn your fifty-oared galley, and put yourself and your forty-nine brave comrades to the sword. But be of good courage. The Golden Fleece you shall have, if it lies within the power of my enchantments to get it for you. Wait for me here an hour before midnight."

At the appointed hour, you might again have seen Prince Jason and the Princess Medea, side by side, stealing through the streets of Colchis, on their way to the sacred grove, in the center of which the Golden Fleece was suspended to a tree. While they were crossing the pastureground, the brazen bulls came towards Jason, lowing, nodding their head, and thrusting forth their snouts, which, as other cattle do, they loved to have rubbed and caressed by a friendly hand. Their fierce nature was thoroughly tamed; and, with their fierceness, the two furnaces in their stomachs had likewise been extinguished, insomuch that they probably enjoyed far more comfort in grazing and chewing their cuds than ever before. Indeed, it had heretofore been

a great inconvenience to these poor animals that, whenever they wished to eat a mouthful of grass, the fire out of their nostrils had shriveled it up, before they could manage to crop it. How they contrived to keep themselves alive is more than I can imagine. But now, instead of emitting jets of flame and streams of sulphurous vapor, they breathed the very sweetest of cow breath.

After kindly patting the bulls, Jason followed Medea's guidance into the grove of Mars, where the great oak trees, that had been growing for centuries, threw so thick a shade that the moonbeams struggled vainly to find their way through it. Only here and there a glimmer fell upon the leaf-strewn earth, or now and then a breeze stirred the boughs aside, and gave Jason a glimpse of the sky, lest, in that deep obscurity, he might forget that there was one overhead. At length, when they had gone farther and farther into the heart of the duskiness, Medea squeezed Jason's hand.

"Look yonder," she whispered. "Do you see it?"

Gleaming among the venerable oaks, there was a radiance, not like the moonbeams, but rather resembling the golden glory of the setting sun. It proceeded from an object which appeared to be suspended at about a man's height from the ground, a little farther within the wood.

"What is it?" asked Jason.

"Have you come so far to seek it," exclaimed Medea, "and do you not recognize the meed of all your toils and perils, when it glitters before your eyes? It is the Golden Fleece."

Jason went onward a few steps farther, and then stopped to gaze. Oh, how beautiful it looked, shining with a marvelous light of its own, that inestimable prize, which so many heroes had longed to behold, but had perished in the quest of it, either by the perils of their voyage, or by the fiery breath of the brazen-lunged bulls.

"How gloriously it shines!" cried Jason, in a rapture. "It has surely been dipped in the richest gold of sunset. Let me hasten onward, and take it to my bosom."

"Stay," said Medea, holding him back. "Have you forgotten what guards it?"

To say the truth, in the joy of beholding the object of his desires, the terrible dragon had quite slipped out of Jason's memory. Soon, however, something came to pass that reminded him what perils were still to be encountered. An antelope, that probably mistook the yellow radiance for sunrise, came bounding fleetly through the grove. He was rushing straight towards the Golden Fleece, when suddenly there was a frightful hiss, and the immense head and half the scaly body of the dragon was thrust forth (for he was twisted round the trunk of the tree on which the Fleece hung), and seizing the poor antelope, swallowed him with one snap of his jaws.

After this feat, the dragon seemed sensible that some other living creature was within reach on which he felt inclined to finish his meal. In various directions he kept poking his ugly snout among the trees, stretching out his neck a terrible long way, now here, now

there, and now close to the spot where Jason and the princess were hiding behind an oak. Upon my word, as the head came waving and undulating through the air, and reaching almost within arm's-length of Prince Jason, it was a very hideous and uncomfortable sight. The gape of his enormous jaws was nearly as wide as the gateway of the king's palace.

"Well, Jason," whispered Medea (for she was ill-natured, as all enchantresses are, and wanted to make the bold youth tremble), "what do you think now of your prospect of winning the Golden Fleece?"

Jason answered only by drawing his sword and making a step forward.

"Stay, foolish youth," said Medea, grasping his arm. "Do not you see you are lost, without me as your good angel? In this gold box I have a magic potion, which will do the dragon's business far more effectually than your sword."

The dragon had probably heard the voices; for, swift as lightning, his black head and forked tongue came hissing among the trees again, darting full forty feet at a stretch. As it approached, Medea tossed the contents of the gold box right down the monster's wide open throat. Immediately, with an outrageous hiss and a tremendous wriggle—flinging his tail up to the tiptop of the tallest tree, and shattering all its branches as it crashed heavily down again—the dragon fell at full length upon the ground and lay quite motionless.

"It is only a sleeping potion," said the enchantress to Prince Jason. "One always finds a use for these mischievous creatures, sooner or later; so I did not wish to

"Stay, foolish youth," said Medea, grasping Jason's arm

kill him outright. Quick! Snatch the prize, and let us begone. You have won the Golden Fleece."

Jason caught the fleece from the tree, and hurried through the grove, the deep shadows of which were illuminated as he passed, by the golden glory of the precious object that he bore along. A little way before him, he beheld the old woman whom he had helped over the stream, with her peacock beside her. She clapped her hands for joy, and beckoning him to make haste, disappeared among the duskiness of the trees. Espying the two winged sons of the North Wind (who were disporting themselves in the moonlight, a few hundred feet aloft), Jason bade them tell the rest of the Argonauts to embark as speedily as possible. But Lynceus, with his sharp eyes, had already caught a glimpse of him, bringing the Golden Fleece, although several stone walls, a hill, and the black shadows of the grove of Mars intervened between. By his advice, the heroes had seated themselves on the benches of the galley, with their oars held perpendicularly, ready to let fall into the water.

As Jason drew near, he heard the Talking Image calling to him with more than ordinary eagerness, in its grave, sweet voice:

"Make haste, Prince Jason! For your life, make haste!"

With one bound he leaped aboard. At sight of the glorious radiance of the Golden Fleece, the nine-and-forty heroes gave a mighty shout, and Orpheus, striking his harp, sang a song of triumph, to the cadence of which the galley flew over the water, homeward bound, as if careering along with wings!